Salim Must Die

An alumnus of La Martiniere College, Lucknow, the National Defence Academy, Pune and the Indian Military Academy, Dehradun, Mukul Deva was commissioned in December 1981 into the Sikh Light Infantry of the Indian Army. He took premature retirement after fifteen years of service, including a decade of active combat duty/ operations in India and overseas. He is now an entrepreneur settled in New Delhi, India. Other books written by him are:

Time After Time...It All Happened;
S.T.R.I.P.T.E.A.S.E: The Art of Corporate Warfare;
M.O.D.E.L.: The Return of the Employee; and
Lashkar.

'Uncannily prescient. Unputdownable. *Salim Must Die* enthrones Deva as the undisputed Master of Thrills'
– Sarthak Dasgupta, film-maker

Praise for *Lashkar*

'An edge-of-the-seat-thriller'
– *The Hindustan Times*

'Exciting... with some action, some introspection, some retrospection... A racy read'
– *The Times of India*

'For the first time, an Indian thriller set in contemporary times... a gripping tale'
– *The Pioneer*

'*Lashkar* tries to make sense of the terror that surrounds our lives'

– *The Hindu*

'Ludlumesque'

– *The Tribune*

'A glance is enough to discover... this is a Tom Clancy on the LOC'

– *Time Out*

'A real page-turner… a riveting read'

– *Business Standard*

'Written with style and panache'

– *Sahara Time*

'A real-life take on how the so-called jehadis are picked up from anonymous Indian streets… *Lashkar* tells many tales with great ease'

– *MetroPlus*

'Lashkar is gripping... racy and visually captivating'

– *Indo Asian News Service*

'Magnificently paced, rich and real in imagery… Deva is a visionary'

– Sarthak Dasgupta, film-maker

Salim Must Die

Mukul Deva

HarperCollins *Publishers* India

First published in India by
HarperCollins *Publishers* in 2009

Building 10, Tower A, 4th Floor, DLF Cyber City, Phase II,
Gurugram Haryana – 122002, India
www.harpercollins.co.in

4 6 8 10 9 7 5 3

P-ISBN: 978-81-7223-819-3
E-ISBN: 978-93-5029-458-1

This is a work of fiction and all characters and incidents described in this book are the product of the author's imagination. Any resemblance to actual persons, living or dead, is entirely coincidental.

Typeset in 10/14 Class Garamond BT
Jojy Philip New Delhi - 15

Printed and bound at
MicroPrints India, New Delhi

For Meher, my favourite younger daughter,
the best gift God could possibly have given us

and in fond memory of Homzi Vesuna,
dear friend and comrade-in-arms.
Rest in peace!

Author's Note

THIS BOOK IS A WORK OF FICTION ALTHOUGH SOME OF THE events mentioned here have actually taken place.

All the characters, countries, places and organizations described or mentioned in this book are fictitious or have been fictitiously used and any resemblance to any person, living or dead, is unintentional.

The technical details of the various weapon systems and chemical and biological agents, and the specifications and methodologies of bomb making and weaponry, as well as the tactics and security procedures employed by any police, military, airline, airport security and/or militant organization, as also criminal, forensic and investigative procedures, have been deliberately kept vague, inaccurate and/or incomplete to prevent any misuse, accidental or otherwise.

There is no slur or malice intended against any religion, race, caste, creed, nation, organization or people.

Preface

THEY SAY FACT IS OFTEN STRANGER THAN FICTION. THIS WOULD be quite obvious to anyone who has been watching the global turn of events even casually.

Despite all the apparent progress and advancements we may have made as a race, it is undeniable that the world we live in today is definitely a far more unsafe and unpleasant place than it ever was. We talk glibly about quality of life, work-life balance, increased life expectancy, freedom for the individual and human rights, but the facts speak for themselves. And the story they tell is far from pleasant.

Nuclear, chemical and biological weapons, terrorism (including the state-sponsored type), drugs, the easy access to weapons of all kinds, a huge spurt in crime, pollution, global warming, climate change are only some of the hard realities we live with today. And this is the world we are leaving behind for our children to suffer in.

The question is, why? Why did it happen?

Who made it happen?

Who allowed it to happen?

The truth is that no single person or nation can be held responsible. All of us are, albeit in differing degrees.

Likewise, there is no single incident or event that has led to this situation. Hundreds of apparently unrelated and seemingly trivial events have brought the human race to the brink of disaster.

In this novel, I have mentioned a few such events that also form an essential backdrop to the lives and deeds of my characters. On the face of it some of them may not appear relevant or especially calamitous, but they are all inevitable parts of the same gigantic jigsaw puzzle.

Other than that, this story is essentially and completely a work of fiction. And I fervently hope that it remains so.

*'Fighting terrorism is like being a goalkeeper.
You can make a hundred brilliant saves,
but the only shot people remember
is the one that gets past you.'*

Paul Wilkinson

Iqbal

0340 Hours. Sector 35, Line of Control (LOC). Kashmir, India

THAT NIGHT ALPHA COMPANY OF 18 GRENADIERS HAD BEEN tasked to keep an eye on the various infiltration routes in Sector 35. The entire company, minus the platoon manning Kaman Post, was deployed in section strength patrols along the LOC. Havaldar Ranbir Singh commanded the last section deployed on the northern flank of the sector.

Ranbir was a hard-bitten combat veteran with seven operational tenures under his belt. In fact, this was his second tenure in the Kashmir valley. Though not a very imaginative individual, his tactical knowledge and field craft were decidedly above par. So was his iron-fisted control over the section he commanded. All these factors enabled him to react hard and fast when another routine night on the LOC turned into an eventful one. Though, if you stop to think about it, no night on the Kashmir LOC can be routine. After all, there are more men and guns deployed along this line than there are on any other border in the world.

And the guns are always cocked and ready to fire. As are the men wielding them.

IT WAS NOT THE INDIAN SOLDIER MANNING THE BATTLEFIELD surveillance radar who spotted the movement down on the rugged, barely visible mountain trail. It was the machine gunner who first heard the sounds and alerted Ranbir.

The sounds were muted and sporadic, but there was absolutely no doubt that someone was coming across the LOC. It was also clear that whoever was moving down the trail was close, very close. A wave of tension surged through the section. At this place and at this time of night it could only be an infiltrator. Nerves that were already on the edge moved closer to the brink.

There's no time to alert either the platoon or the company commander. Not that they could do anything right now even if I did manage to get through to them. Ranbir rapidly took stock of the situation. He gave the required field signals and silently pointed out the positions. Immediately, the section changed its profile and moved into new positions. Barely eighty seconds later, all six rifles of the section were trained on the narrow winding mountain trail. So was the section's machine gun. The ambush was firmly in place.

'Nobody fires till I give the signal,' Ranbir whispered as he primed the pencil flare. A very slight murmur rustled through the section as they acknowledged his command. The attention of each man and his weapon was riveted on the barely audible, but now continuous sounds coming from the mountain trail that lay just below the ledge on which they were positioned. Heartbeats ramped up even higher and hands tightened on weapons as a silhouette suddenly appeared on the crest. The man was not making much noise but he was not taking any precautions either. In fact, he seemed to be moving like a sleepwalker.

'Stupid shit!' Ranbir hissed to the rifleman beside him. 'Must be one of those newly trained morons coming back to conquer the world.'

By now the intruder had descended almost twenty metres down the rocky slope. Another eighty metres and he would be at the base of the defile and within range of the waiting guns. *So will the rest of the infiltrating party that is sure to be behind him.* Ranbir swallowed hard. His throat was suddenly dry and his was not the only one. No matter how many times you go into combat, each time is like the first time. The fear is starkly virginal.

Fear coiled tautly at the pit of every stomach and adrenaline-hyped bodies tensed, as they got ready to receive the hail of bullets sure to be flying around soon. *One never knows which one of them is destined to seek you out….* Ranbir pushed away the thought and focused on the task at hand.

'Usually, there are nine or ten of them in each

infiltration part,' the battalion Intelligence Officer had told them during induction training.

Ranbir only started to worry when the intruder had descended another fifty metres. *How come none of the others is visible even now? You never leave such large gaps between people while moving in such rough terrain.* Ranbir was perplexed. *How can it just be one man trying to cross the LOC? What the hell am I missing here?*

By now the intruder had almost reached the centre of the killing ground.

In another few moments he will be out of it and lost behind the bend in the mountain trail. The dilemma racked Ranbir briefly. *Should I wait for the others? Are there any others? Or should I take this one out?* In the end it was a simple decision. *A bird in the hand is worth two in the bush.* Ranbir nodded to himself. *I guess taking one of them down is better than going back empty handed.* 'Get ready, guys,' he whispered softly. 'I am going to hail him... if he doesn't stop, blow him away.'

An equally soft murmur let him know the section had heard him. Guns steadied as he raised the small hailer to his mouth. Experience has shown that a sudden loud voice booming out of the darkness more often than not freezes the unsuspecting person for a few seconds. In such conditions those few seconds are more than critical. They are what make the difference between life and death.

'Stop! Stop right there and raise your hands in the

air.' Amplified by the hailer, Ranbir's metallic voice blasted out of the undergrowth.

Then came the harsher metallic thud as a pencil flare snaked up in the sky and bathed the mountain-side in white, blinding light.

The man stumbling down the mountain track stopped abruptly. He turned to face the voice that had thundered out of the darkness. In the sharp light of the flare, his face, lined with tiredness, was devoid of expression. He seemed totally oblivious to everything happening around him.

The section tensed, as it got ready for the reaction. *Did we act too soon? Where is the rest of the infiltration party?* Unanswered questions flitted through their minds as they strained to see beyond the discontinuous illumination of the rapidly fading flare. There was a harsh click as Ranbir unleashed another flare into the sky. It effortlessly took over the mantle of light from the first one, which fell spent into the undergrowth.

There was still no movement. The intruder stood listlessly waiting for something to happen next. The tableau remained frozen for what seemed an eternity. Finally Ranbir murmured a low command. The machine gunner and the rest of the rifle group maintained a careful vigil, ready to provide fire support, as Ranbir and two riflemen moved swiftly towards the intruder.

Four minutes later, the intruder had been thoroughly searched, disarmed and handcuffed. Other than the inevitable semi-automatic rifle, they also found a Thuraya satellite phone and a telephone diary on him. Ranbir took custody of these. The captured man made no attempt to resist or avoid any of the questions thrown at him.

Twenty minutes later, Ranbir's patrol started back towards base, the intruder safely ensconced in their midst. It took them almost two hours to reach Kaman Post and present themselves to their post commander, Captain Vinod Rai of 18 Grenadiers.

RANBIR HAD ALREADY RADIOED AHEAD TO INFORM CAPTAIN Vinod Rai about the capture of the infiltrator on the radio set. As soon as the patrol entered the post, Rai strode up to them with youthful impatience.

The captive was in his early twenties, tall and broad-shouldered. Despite the grime and filth he was covered in and the fact that he had obviously not shaved or bathed for a few days, there was something clean-cut about his bearing that made Rai pause momentarily. *He doesn't look like the typical, semi-literate terrorist who has been picked off the street, given some bullshit training and then sent out to kill... and die. And why do his eyes have such a strange spaced out look... is it just that he has been taken captive... or is it something else? Is he one of the big fish who have...*

Rai sized up the man before him, as he began to question him. Like Havaldar Ranbir, Captain Rai also found the man willing to talk.

The minute the prisoner began to speak, his public school education came through in his tone and choice of words. More than a little surprised, Rai took a closer look at him. *Damn! That, but for the grace of God, could be me... or any of the other officers in the paltan. This guy could easily have been whatever he chose to be, if he had not strayed... or been misguided.* Then the captive's words began to strike home and dragged Rai back to reality.

THE INTRUDER HAD AN INTERESTING TALE TO TELL. IN FACT, what started out as the routine interrogation of yet another intruder captured during infiltration left the young captain open-mouthed and wide-eyed. When the man finally finished, Rai ordered him to be placed under guard. Then he stepped across to the communications hut and called his battalion commander on the secure line.

'He says his name is Iqbal. Says he is an Indian, a resident of Lucknow, but was studying in Delhi when he was recruited by the Lashkar and sent across to Pakistan for training. What? Yes, sir, I have. The man is more than willing to talk and he seems to be telling the truth.' Rai gave him all the details of the man and the items that had been found on him.

'Why was he crossing the LOC again? And that Thuraya satellite phone? I am sure you know that only very senior terrorists are given satellite phones... or those who are on a highly critical mission. Get into more details, Rai. Something doesn't smell right.'

'That's what I was coming to, sir,' Rai replied. 'He says he was trained at Muzaffarabad by the same group that carried out the terror bombings in Delhi last month. Apparently his mother and sister were among those killed by the bomb that exploded at Sarojini Nagar market. He came to know about it when he got back to Lucknow after the training, so he killed the maulavi in Delhi who'd recruited him, and then returned to Muzaffarabd to avenge their deaths by killing those who'd trained him and planned the bombings. It was the Lashkar-e-Toiba lunatics, as we all suspected.'

Rai paused. 'Incidentally, sir, the man says that when his party was infiltrating into India on the thirtieth of last month, they were launched from Chakoti Post and were ambushed by one of our patrols just after crossing the LOC.'

'On the thirtieth of last month? That would have been the ambush by Delta Company.'

'That's right, sir.'

'I thought they got everybody in that ambush.'

'Well, apparently they didn't,' Rai replied. 'Iqbal and two others got away from the ambush and managed to reach their camp, although one of them was injured and died later. He says it was the Paki instructor who had trained them and was escorting them across.'

'Hmmm.... Does this guy know where the camp is?'

'Yes sir, he does. He was not able to point it out

on the map but he says he can take us there. From the way he described the camp, it seems to be in the mountains above Hari. In fact, he is quite eager to take us there.'

'He is, is he?' There was a long pause as the old man thought it over. Finally, he spoke. 'Okay, Vinod. Take a platoon and get him to show you where the camp is. Take the southern approach. Meanwhile, I'm going to have Bravo and Delta companies set up stops on the other approaches.'

'Roger that, sir. I'll move out immediately.'

'Do that.' Pause. 'And listen, be careful… it may well be a trap. Okay?'

'Don't worry, sir, I will.'

'I'm paid to worry, son.' The smile in the old man's voice was evident. So was the steel of command. 'And Vinod, don't go pulling any Rambo shit on us.'

'Not at all, sir.' Rai grinned. He was quite used to the constant leg-pulling that he was subjected to ever since he had tried for a berth in the Special Forces. Despite the fact that he had given up halfway and returned to his battalion, the Rambo tag had stuck.

'As soon as you're done with that, send the prisoner back to base. And also the diary and that satellite telephone. I'm sure the spooks would love to get their hands on them.'

'Roger, sir.' Before the old man could terminate the call, Rai spoke again. 'Sir, would it be okay with you if I called up Colonel Anbu and shared Iqbal's story with him?'

'Anbu? The Force 22 CO….' He broke off. 'Why? You feel he might be interested?'

'I'm not sure, sir, just a gut instinct. I think he may be….' Rai's voice tapered off tentatively.

'Sure, go ahead. We're batting for the same side after all. In any case, we wouldn't want to go against your guts… would we now?'

Both men laughed as they ended the call. Rai waited for the dial tone to return. Then, dialling another number from memory, he waited impatiently for the phone to be picked up at the other end.

Force 22

THE SHARP, FLAT BANG OF THE GRENADE AND THE SOUND OF the shots fired hard in its wake drowned out the ringing of the phone. All six shots had been fired so rapidly that the sound had cannonaded into one thunderous roar.

Ignoring the pounding in his chest and the roaring in his eardrums, the gunman raced forward. Swallowing hard to ease his dry throat, he kicked open the door and tossed the XM-84 grenade into the room.

The XM-84 is a non-fragmentation, non-lethal Flash-and-Bang stun grenade that produces a blinding one million Candela light and a deafening 175 decibels of sound. The sudden surge of light activates all the photosensitive cells in the retina, making it impossible for the eye to see anything till the retina returns to its normal, un-stimulated state. Simultaneously, the incredibly loud sound disturbs the balance of the fluid in the semi-circular canal of the ear, thus disrupting a person's sense of balance.

The combined effect is enough to degrade a person's combat effectiveness for as long as one minute. In battle, a minute is a *very* long time – long enough for many people to die many times.

Tossing the grenade inside, the man dressed in battle fatigues stepped back instinctively and took cover as he mentally counted down. *Four, three, two....*

He was ready for the unbearably harsh explosion of sound and light when it came. He raced into the darkened room. He knew the stun grenade would give him a safe window of opportunity before the men inside could ride down the effect and respond effectively.

There are three men guarding the hostage, the voice of the Intel Officer echoed in his head as he raced inside. *All three are armed with automatic weapons. They have already killed the bodyguards and shown they'll have no hesitation in killing.*

A kaleidoscope of sporadic lights and shouts assaulted his senses. The gunman's aural and visual senses were sharply heightened by the adrenaline powering through his body. Sifting through the confused medley of light and sound, his pistol extended in the classic shooter's stance, he homed in on his targets.

The one closest to him fell to a neat headshot, right in the middle of the forehead. Fortunately, the second target was almost directly behind the first so he didn't have to alter his line of fire too much. He fired again, twice in quick succession, this time aiming for the upper torso since the target was not clear enough for him to try a headshot. The gunman did not wait to see the effects of the two shots as he swivelled rapidly to seek out the third target.

His senses were ferreting out the darkness when the twinkling flashes told him he had been fired at. His brain was still registering the alarm when he felt the shots slam into his body. Despite the body armour, the impact was harsh and staggered him. Luckily, his trained fingers had responded to the muzzle flashes instinctively and fired twice in quick succession before the incoming bullets impacted his body. The gunman saw the target fall as he himself staggered back.

THE GUNMAN WAS RIGHTING HIMSELF WHEN THE LIGHTS came on and two men entered the cordite-laden room. Both were beaming.

'Not bad, sir.' Captain Vikram Tiwathia of the Indian Army, the first man who entered, surveyed the mock carnage carefully. In his late twenties, the whiplash thin Tiwathia, with a streak of premature white falling over his forehead, walked with a perennial spring in his step. The young captain was a die-hard optimist and never failed to see the bright side of any situation. 'Not at all bad for an old man.' There was a wicked grin on his face.

'Old man, my foot,' Colonel Rajan Anbu shot back. 'You youngsters need to be shown a trick or two. From now on we will have minimum four targets for this exercise.'

'Yeah right, sir! And maybe just two bullets,' Captain Mohammed Sami, the second man, added with a laugh. 'You should thank the dame at DuPont for that jacket.' Sami pointed to the coloured splashes of paint which had been made by the training bullets on Anbu's body armour. He was referring to Stephanie Kwolek, an American scientist who had been working for DuPont as a research chemist and had discovered poly-paraphenylene terephtalamide, better known as Kevlar, while searching for new synthetic fibres of commercial importance. 'If it hadn't been for that, you'd be dead twice over for sure.'

With his six-foot tall frame, Mohammed Sami could well have been Tiwathia's twin, but for the fact that he was darker and more heavily built. Despite that, Sami moved with cat-like agility and gave the impression that he was straining to be unleashed. His relative youth notwithstanding, Sami was the senior most officer in Force 22 and hence Anbu's second-in-command. All three men carried a hard no-nonsense air about them, which seems to be a distinguishing feature of Special Forces men the world over.

'Anyway, you'd better get that phone, sir,' Tiwathia intervened. 'It's been screaming for a long time. What happened? Did you forget the wife's birthday?'

'And how likely is that?' Anbu quipped back as he reached for the mobile phone clamouring in his pocket. The stocky forty-two year old Colonel, born and bred in the suburbs of Chennai, was breathing hard, but he was feeling good about acquitting himself honourably during this morning's training. It was good to know that he could shoot as well as the extraordinary men and women he commanded. And that was no mean achievement considering that his unit, Force 22, comprised the crème de la crème of the country.

Every officer in Force 22 was handpicked either from the intelligence services or from the Indian Army, Navy or Air Force. Each one of them was a commissioned officer not below the rank of captain and was in superb physical condition, a high achiever amongst his/her peers, trained to fight on land, sea and air, skilled in most known methods of killing, and motivated to the highest possible levels. In fact, if degrees were to be awarded for proficiency in the art of killing, all of them would easily acquire doctorates.

Born of the bloody crucible of the decade long low intensity conflict that had been thrust upon India by the Pakistani military and intelligence establishments, Force 22 was meant to provide a rapid, highly professional and covert response to certain situations that could not (or should not) be dealt with by more conventional forces in a more conventional manner. This decision had been proved right and the force had acquitted itself honourably when the Indian Prime Minister had tasked it to punish those guilty of the horrific terror bomb attacks in Delhi in October 2005. Living up to its motto of 'Stealth, Speed and Surprise', Force 22 commandos struck at the very heart of the Pakistani-run terror organizations. The daring raids deep in Pakistan had taken out several key players and shaken the terror factory to its core.[1]

Anbu was not only the first CO of Force 22, he was also a fine example of that peculiar streak of controlled aggression which makes the Special Forces man stand apart and ahead of the pack. As is typical of such forces, Anbu led from the front and never expected from his men anything that he was not willing to do himself.

BACKING AWAY A BIT FROM THE OTHERS, ANBU REACHED FOR the mobile phone that was still shrilling away. The call was from an unknown outstation number. He slid open the phone and took the call. 'Anbu.' His tone was crisp.

'Good morning, sir. It's me, Vinod... Vinod Rai.'

'Rai!' A smile lit up Anbu's face. 'What a pleasant surprise!' The Colonel was very fond of Rai and had tried hard to dissuade him when he'd chosen to opt out of Force 22 last year, but he had finally let him go when he understood Rai's reasons. 'Long time, Vinod. Where have you been?'

'I'm back with my unit, sir. We're in the Valley these days.'

'That must be exciting.' Both men laughed. 'Tell me, Vinod. What reminded you of us today? Planning to rejoin the force?'

'No way, sir! Not until you knock a few miles off

[1] This part of the story has been told in *Lashkar*

the morning run.' They laughed again. 'Actually I called to tell you about something I thought might be of interest to you.' Rai's tone had become serious.

'Go ahead, Vinod.' Anbu grew sombre as he listened to the story of the man named Iqbal who had been captured along the LOC that morning. There was a long pause when Rai finished. 'Thanks for the heads up, Vinod. You were right to call me. Please do keep me posted about this... in case there are any further developments.'

Anbu was deep in thought as he disconnected the call and walked back to the command post. He switched on his laptop and began to access the databases of the various intelligence agencies in the country. As the CO of Force 22, Anbu had nearly unrestricted access and the freedom to seek out whatever information he deemed relevant. An hour later he had the confirmation he sought.

Maulana Fazlur Rehman was the founder and head of the Lashkar-e-Toiba, the terrorist organization that carried out the Delhi bombings a fortnight ago.

The intelligence agencies were abuzz with the news of his death, especially the manner in which he had been terminated. There was huge speculation as to who had taken him out.

So that is how that joker Fazlur Rehman died! It might be interesting to have a chat with the captured man... what did Vinod say his name was? Iqbal? Yes, Iqbal. I wonder what is in the memory of that Thuraya phone and in the phone book that he was carrying. If it did belong to Fazlur Rehman it must be a real gold mine of information.

Anbu shot off an email to Captain Manoj Khare, the Force 22 Intel Officer. Then he got down to the sheaf of papers that threatened to drown his IN tray. *Damn paperwork! The way things are going, one doesn't have to bother about shooting the enemy... you could just put him on the mailing list, drown the poor slob with paperwork and bore him to death.*

Anbu was reaching for the file on top of the heap when the secure phone on his desk rang. It wasn't the loud trilling that shook him alert. It was the fact that this particular phone rang very seldom and when it did, it generally meant that something seriously important was emerging on the horizon. He reached for it with a sudden sense of urgency.

'Morning sir, it's me... Jaggi.' Lieutenant Commander Sunil Jaggi of the Indian Navy, currently seconded to Force 22, was a happy-go-lucky man. His bulky build belied the blinding speed he was capable of moving at. Like his comrades in Force 22 the man was a highly skilled killing machine, but unlike several of them he also had an infectious though slightly wacky sense of humour. Today, however, Jaggi's normally exuberant tone was overlaid with a distinct layer of stress.

'How is the stint with the Punjab Police going, Sunil?'

Jaggi was presently in the first week of his cross-training with the Punjab Police Anti-Terrorist Task

Force (ATTF). Anbu had begun short attachments of his officers with the police forces of various states, to enhance their understanding of police functioning and to enable them to impart some specialized warfare methodologies to those policing extra sensitive areas. Quite unexpectedly, Jaggi had found himself in the thick of an anti-terrorist operation that they had stumbled on purely by chance.

'It's going well, sir. I'm here with Mr Balwant Singh. You remember what I spoke to you about the day before? We've been through the whole thing and....'

'It has been confirmed, Colonel.' Balwant's voice echoed slightly as it came through the speakerphone that they were using at the other end. A veteran of those horrifying days when the ISI-sponsored Khalistani militancy had sapped the soul of the vibrant state of Punjab, Balwant Singh was one of the most experienced cops on the beat, which was why he was the top cop in Amritsar's ATTF. Like Jaggi's, his voice too betrayed tiredness. 'We have even found the spot from where they have been carrying out the reconnaissance and we are monitoring them continuously.'

'I hope the surveillance teams are keeping it very low key,' Anbu said softly.

'They are. I have my best people on it. We're handling the whole thing with kid gloves.'

'Who are these guys in touch with? Is it the usual ISI conduit?'

'It is an ISI conduit, but definitely not the usual one.'

'We're still checking things out, sir,' Jaggi said. 'But the indications are that this is a rogue ISI element out to derail the Indo-Pak peace process that saner heads in both countries are desperately trying to breathe some life into.'

'*Rogue element of the ISI*?' Anbu laughed. 'Are you trying to be funny, Jaggi? The whole damn ISI is a rogue element.' There was a long pause as Anbu thought it over. 'You want me to send some more people down?' he finally asked.

'No, Colonel. I really appreciate the support, but I think we can handle it on our own.'

'Fine, but don't hesitate to call me if there's anything I can do.' Anbu did not want to push things any further. He was aware that the states were still coming to terms with the new, enhanced role that the PM was pushing Force 22 into, and acceptance was slow in coming. *Better to let things ease into place.* 'Please keep me posted. You guys are doing a great job.' He added simply, 'Make sure they don't get to know that we're on to them and let's try to take them red-handed.'

'That's exactly what our Minister said.' Balwant laughed grimly. 'Don't worry, Colonel. We will try our best.'

And they did. They did manage to catch them red-handed.

Unfortunately or fortunately, depending on how you looked at it, Balwant's boys did not manage to take them alive.

Peace Goes to Pieces

AMRITSAR, INDIA

THE BRAND NEW VOLVO BUS HAD BEEN WASHED AND POLISHED till it gleamed. It was capable of carrying a maximum of forty-five passengers. That morning, however, there were only twenty-eight people on board when it pulled out of the newly designated International Bus Terminus at 0900 hours and headed towards Radcliffe Point, where it was supposed to cross the Indo-Pak border.

Sixteen of these twenty-eight comprised an official delegation that also included three State Ministers. The other twelve were ordinary passengers, mostly people who wanted to enter the annals of history by being a part of the first Amritsar-to-Lahore Peace Bus. Had they known about the tremendous explosive power and destructive capability of the rocket launchers that awaited them, they would have willingly given history a miss.

THE BUS WAS PULLING OUT OF THE TERMINAL WHEN TWO Maruti vans pulled up on either side of the tall white building overlooking the road to Radcliffe Point.

The van in front came to a halt and there was no further activity. None of the four hard looking men sitting inside with Jaggi moved. They just sat watching the front of the building with unblinking eyes. The van's darkened windows shielded the battle-clad men from the gaze of passers-by and the noisy street around the van smothered the cold metallic snicks of weapons being cocked. The stops were in place to prevent any one from escaping the ambush site from the rear of the building.

On the other side of the building, as soon as the van came to a halt, five men spilled out from it. Crossing the pavement, they opened the door and raced up the stairs on silent feet. A variety of guns were held steady in their hands as they ran. Bulky body armour concealed by the loose shirts they all wore protected them from the hot, lethal lead that was certain to be thrown at them very soon.

Right at the top of the staircase was a flimsy wooden door that led to the terrace. The door gave way with a loud crack as the first two men slammed into it, and then all five gunmen erupted onto the terrace.

Caught in a tight huddle in a corner of the terrace were four men. Two of them shouldered Russian RPG-7V rocket launchers while the other two were assisting them. The rockets were pointed at the road along which the Peace Bus would travel shortly. The men were absorbed in their task and only realized they had company when the door burst open.

All four terrorists turned at the sound. Three of them froze. The fourth reacted instinctively, the way most armed amateurs do when confronted with anything that threatens their existence. He pulled the trigger. Unfortunately, he happened to be holding a rocket launcher and not a handgun. The rocket sped out of the launcher with a roar and impacted onto the concrete floor three feet away. It blew him and his able assistant into tiny pieces.

The back blast of the rocket launcher engulfed the remaining two in an unforgiving ball of fire. One of them died instantly. Consumed in flames, the fourth terrorist backed away. He did not even realize when he went over the low parapet wall. He was screaming as he went. The shrill high-pitched scream ended in a dull thud as his burning remains smashed onto the concrete pavement three floors below.

At the head of the four-man squad that had stormed the rooftop, Balwant watched open-mouthed as the four men in front of him faded away into death. *Shit! The Minister wanted them alive.* He sighed as he imagined the haranguing that would follow. Had he known how much worse things were soon going to get, he would not have been even remotely worried about the death of the four terror merchants.

THE THIRD ROCKET LAUNCHER WAS NOT OF RUSSIAN MAKE. It was a Swedish 84 mm Carl Gustav that had been stolen from an Indian Army Ordnance depot a few weeks earlier. The Carl Gustav is a highly versatile and lethally accurate weapon that is capable of firing a High Explosive (HE) round, a High Explosive Anti-Tank (HEAT) round or a Para-illuminating round. This morning, wielded by a surly looking man in his mid-thirties, the rocket launcher in question was loaded with a HEAT round.

At the precise moment that the four men on the rooftop were attacked and put out of circulation, the man with the third launcher was sitting in the rear of a soft-top Maruti jeep parked by the side of the road leading to Radcliffe Point. Deep lines of stress creased his nondescript face. Large pools of sweat accumulating in his armpits accounted for the stuffy smell blanketing the enclosed vehicle. He heard the roar of the rocket firing in the distance and knew the first team was blown. *That's okay.* He shrugged. *It was anticipated.* In fact, that had been the plan. Of course, those four men had not known that they were simply sacrificial red herrings.

His breathing quickened as he watched the Peace Bus come up the street. It was about three hundred metres away from him when it turned the corner. The escort was a hundred metres ahead of the bus. At that range, with the weapon he was wielding, the bus was an easy target.

Like a diver about to plunge into water, he took a deep breath before throwing off the jeep's soft canopy in one swift motion. When the man rose he was settling the already loaded rocket launcher on his shoulder. In one rapid motion he aimed at the bus. He was steadying the weapon to fire when the escort spotted him. The launcher came alive with an ear-shattering, thunderous roar; its flaming back-blast charred the canopy of the Gypsy and then reached out to the car parked just behind him, shattering its windscreen with an explosive snort before reducing it to a smouldering heap.

Despite the suddenness of the attack, the escort personnel reacted creditably fast. Three of the escort cops fired at the same time at the man with the rocket launcher. Unfortunately, the rocket launcher was a much bigger weapon and in a gunfight it's generally the guy with the bigger weapon who wins.

The terrorist wielding the rocket launcher took two of the umpteen bullets fired at him smack in his face and chest. But only a second or so after the rocket had left the launcher.

Whipping out of the tubular barrel, the 84-millimetre HEAT round hurtled through the air towards its target. It slashed past the stunned escort, went unhesitatingly through the front of the bus, then through the partition separating the driver's cabin from the passenger area and, striking the seat occupied by one of the three ministers in the doomed delegation, it exploded with an ear-shattering roar. Instantaneously, it killed most of the thirteen people seated in the front of the bus.

The Peace Bus did not meet a very peaceful end.

The peace process it was meant to initiate between the perennially hostile neighbours did not either, especially when it came to light that all five of the perpetrators had been permanent residents of Faisalabad, Pakistan.

Postmortem

THERE WAS A STERN EXPRESSION ON THE INDIAN PRIME Minister Dr Singh's normally placid face as he looked at the men sitting before him. Also markedly absent was the sense of calm confidence that one normally associated with him. A renowned scholar and a statesman of stature, the usually even-keeled and soft-spoken Dr Singh was the best man to occupy this critical chair in the turbulent times that India faced.

'How is it that we never seem to have enough hard intelligence?' Dr Singh confronted the Home Minister who, despite being a hardened politician with decades of experience, squirmed uncomfortably.

'That's not normally the case,' he replied sheepishly, almost under his breath. 'We detected the attempt well in time....'

'No! We detected only the red herring that they wanted us to,' the PM cut in sharply, 'and that too was just sheer coincidence.' Pause. 'We all know the truth.' Another pause. 'We all also know that our intelligence set-up is just too fragmented to ever work effectively which is why I am unable to understand the childish attitude the states are showing when it comes to the proposal to set up a National Intelligence Command.' The PM was so unusually worked up that he actually stopped to calm himself. 'I am sorry, gentlemen, but this attack is definitely the last straw. I am not going to jeopardize any more lives just because the states are feeling insecure about central interference or because our intelligence agencies are so busy protecting their own little turfs that they don't have time to do their job effectively.'

'I am completely with you. We have already faced eight major attacks in the past one year and each time we were caught with our pants down,' the normally recalcitrant Defence Minister butted in. 'I suggest we go ahead with the NIC right away. We have spent more than enough time and effort going over this issue.'

'That's exactly what I am going to do. We're going to table this right away.'

'What would be the NIC's mandate?'

'As the primary federal organization it will ensure seamless integration of intelligence from all other agencies and sources, with a special focus on terrorism. This will ensure that terror activities meet with a strong, coordinated and focused effort. Nothing will fall through the cracks any more.' The PM saw the expressions on the faces of the others and added, 'Look, I don't want anyone to worry; the NIC will not infringe on the scope or resources of any state or agency except to prevent duplication and wastage of efforts.'

'Okay! Who do you have in mind to take charge of the NIC?' the Home Minister queried. One could see the politicking starting in his mind almost immediately. 'I think the best person would be....' No one would know who he was going to suggest because the PM did not allow him to complete the sentence.

'I was thinking of bringing in G.K. Rao and appointing him as the National Intelligence Advisor.'

Every single person in that room knew about Rao. After all, the man was a legend in intelligence circles. He was also known to be totally above politics of any kind.

'Well...' the Home Minister said reluctantly, almost grudgingly. 'Rao would be quite... umm... ideal for the job... undoubtedly.'

'True. He also gets along well with Narayan, the National Security Advisor.'

The instant nods of approval across the room confirmed that the PM had chosen wisely.

'Good! That's settled then. We shall invite Rao to come on board as the NIA effective immediately,' the PM said firmly. 'I am going to tell him to first give all of us a presentation on the prevalent global situation.'

'We are going to be taught international relations and geopolitics now?' the Home Minister murmured. There was a hint of sarcasm in his voice.

'No harm in that... is there?' the PM asked, conveniently ignoring the sarcasm.

On that note, the meeting broke up.

STRIDING OUT OF THE MEETING, THE PM HEADED STRAIGHT for his office. He was reaching for the phone even before he sat down. 'Dhawan,' he said into the phone when his Principal Secretary answered. 'I want you to get hold of Colonel Anbu for me.'

Precisely seven minutes later, the PM's phone rang and Anbu's courteous voice greeted him at the other end.

'Good afternoon, Colonel,' the PM responded warmly. 'How are we doing today?' He seemed genuinely glad to be talking to him. It was no secret that after the successful retaliatory strike carried out by Force 22 inside Pakistan in the wake of the Delhi bomb blasts of October 2005, the PM had taken an inordinate liking for the perpetually cool, no-nonsense Colonel and respected his judgment.

'Very well, thank you, sir.'

'Excellent!' The PM got straight to the point. 'Have you been through the White Paper that was circulated by the RAW chief last month?'

'Yes sir, I have.'

'And? What do you think of it?'

'I think there is substantial merit in what has been pointed out,' Anbu replied. 'Despite everything that has been done over the past few years, our intelligence services are still very badly fragmented and disorganized. Too much intelligence is just slipping through the cracks.' As usual Anbu's tone was soft, but totally confident. 'That is why we have been let down at crucial junctures so often.'

'I agree with you,' the PM said. 'That's why I have decided to go ahead and order the National Intelligence Command to be set up.'

'That's an excellent decision, sir,' Anbu exclaimed. 'But you're going to have a hard time selling it to the states.'

'As usual you get straight to the point.' The PM laughed. 'No, you can bet the states are not going to like it.' He paused introspectively. 'But I don't think we have too many options available... not if we want our intelligence up to speed and able to deal with the huge threats to national security that are emerging daily... especially of the terrorist kind.'

'Very true sir, otherwise the day is not too far when India will suffer a 9/11 of her own.'

'Precisely! That is why I have decided to go ahead with the NIC and I am bringing in G.K. Rao as the National Intelligence Advisor to head it up.'

'That's an excellent choice, sir. There are few people better suited for the job. Mr Rao has the temperament and he certainly has the experience.'

'I am glad to hear that, Colonel.' The PM smiled, a trifle wickedly for a change. 'Because this is where you come in. I want you to depute two of your best officers to work with him for a few months.'

'My officers, sir?' Anbu had clearly not seen this coming. 'What pos....'

'Colonel, Rao will need some trusted hands to overcome the initial teething problems. In any case, you had wanted to depute a few of your people to RAW for a few weeks of familiarization. This is going to be even better, because your officers will get some rigorous hands-on training and also an excellent overview of our national intelligence set-up.'

'I see what you mean, sir,' Anbu concurred. 'It will be done. I have just the right officers to help Mr Rao get started.'

'I am sure you do, Colonel,' the PM replied. 'And finally, one other thing. The NIC will make its first presentation next fortnight. I want you here for it.'

'That's kind of you, sir. I am sure it will be most educative.'

'I am sure it will, Colonel.' There was a smile on the PM's face as he ended the call and asked his assistant to get Rao on the line for him.

At the other end, Anbu did not bother to put down the phone. He waited for the dial tone to return before he punched in the numbers he wanted.

'MS,' he said when it was picked up at the other end by Captain Mohammed Sami. 'Call from the Headman. We've got another assignment... a domestic one this time. Come on over so that I can brief you. And yes, get Khare and Bhatnagar along. They're going to be in the hot seat this time.'

'Right, sir, I will. Khare is here but Bhatnagar is

still at the firing range. I'll call her back and we will be with you in about forty-five minutes.'

'I'll be waiting, MS.'

Finally putting down the phone, Anbu leaned back in his black leather chair. The room around him gradually receded into darkness and his chair began to swivel gently as his mind wandered away slowly, back along the long, winding road that the calm man now known to the world as Colonel Rajan Anbu had travelled.

Becoming Anbu

THE UBIQUITOUS YELLOW COLOURED TWO-BEDROOM apartment was situated on the third floor of the building, between Chennai's famous Velankani church and the sea. Lost as it was in the midst of similar looking apartments, this one had two distinguishing features: it was the corner most house in the colony and, being on the top floor, it had a unique view of the sea. The fact that the tiny sliver of sea visible did not make for much of a view did nothing to alter the sea-facing tag, which came with the apartment. Perhaps this was why the family that stayed there always attracted special attention.

Not that there was anything unusual about them. It was your average middle-class Tamil family, deeply traditional, as such families tend to be. On opening the door, you would be greeted by a pantheon of gods. A deep-seated aroma of incense held sway over the air.

However, there was something distinct about the young lad who opened the door and raced down the steps towards a group of youngsters waiting impatiently at the foot of the building. The not-so-tall boy had the darkish complexion so typical of Tamil Nadu, but that was about where the stereotype ran out. Even at that early age, his body language bespoke a leader and his face radiated a particular calm that drew your attention to him like a magnet. When you looked at him you got the unmistakable feeling that you were looking at a winner.

'You're late, Anbu,' one of the kids clustered at the foot of the stairs complained. 'We have been waiting for hours.'

'What to do, man? Amma would not let me budge till I had finished my homework.'

'Why are you always fretting about homework? I thought you're planning to join the army… you don't need to study for that.'

'Right! Tell that to Amma.' They all laughed as they raced off towards the nearby park.

'Why do you want to join the army?' another voice piped up. 'Wouldn't you rather be an engineer like your dad?'

'No!'

'My mother says wars are bad. She says it's wrong to kill.'

'So does mine,' the boy named Anbu replied. 'She also says that India will only be as peaceful and prosperous as the strength of the army defending her.'

Then the innocent excitement of childhood

reclaimed their attention and they ran off to the waiting basketball game.

RAJAN ANBU HAD ALWAYS WANTED TO JOIN THE ARMY. HE had known this ever since he first set eyes on an army man. The olive-green uniform drew him like a magnet. His fascination did not wane with the passage of years. So it surprised no one when his name appeared right on top of the merit list for the entrance examination to the National Defence Academy and, three tumultuous and eventful years later, at the top of the Academy's merit list.

Then came the final year at the Indian Military Academy. This was when the young man really came into his own; unleashed by the rigorous military training, his innate leadership skills threw off the yoke of conditioning that burdens lesser men.

Whether it was during the years of initial training or the years that followed, the one thing that made Anbu stand ahead and apart from the pack was the sheer calm and confidence that he radiated. It surrounded him like a perennial halo that did not even desert him on the icy, head-spinning heights of the Siachen Glacier and Kargil, during the gut-wrenching close combat in the jungles of Sri Lanka or on the bullet-ridden roads of the Kashmir valley.

No one can ever say for sure why Anbu was one of the few who found himself moving from the turmoil of one battlefield to another in quick, nerve-wracking succession. Perhaps it was just bad karma in some past life or simply the fact that the gods had in mind for him a higher destiny, one that needed him to be better prepared than most. And, as those who have felt the heart-stopping rush of a bullet whistling past will tell you, there is no better conditioning than the battlefield....

It was this Buddha-like calm that helped him withstand the relentless roar of the Pakistani artillery guns that pounded his position on the Siachen Glacier. It did not desert him when he was confronted by the bodies of friends and foes, dismembered and disfigured by the savagery of artillery shells. It stood by him when he collected pieces of his comrades torn to bits by the LTTE landmines in the steaming jungles of Sri Lanka. It held him together safely and then delivered him to the Kashmir valley, once a vision of ethereal beauty, now a land torn apart by the conflict between India and Pakistan.

The memories that hurtled him back down those dark, narrow lanes, which he seldom allowed himself to consciously traverse, were neither calm nor forgiving.

DELHI WAS AGAIN REELING UNDER A MASSIVE, RELENTLESS power-cut, which made the already intolerable heat maddening. In fact, life seemed to be a perpetual power-cut these days. Anbu was struggling to go through the motions of another high-stress day, when the call came. It was Sanjeev Kanal. Anbu and Kanal went back a long way, to their Defence Academy days. There were two things they had always had in common – both loved reading and basketball. The minute Anbu heard the tone of Kanal's voice he knew that something was seriously wrong.

'Anbu, have you heard?'

'Heard what?' A sudden sense of foreboding flailed Anbu.

'Arjun is... is....' Kanal's voice faltered. 'He's no more.'

'*Arjun*? *No*!' Numbness overcame Anbu. 'What happened?' he said, struggling to stay calm. 'How?' As Kanal told him, the scene played out in Anbu's mind like some horrifying movie.

Arjun's battalion had been ordered to clear a mosque which had been taken over by the so-called freedom fighters, the mujahidin. Young kids, barely out of their teens, who didn't even realize that they were mere pawns in the unholy hands of some devilish general who, for his petty political ambitions, wanted to divert the attention of his countrymen from the problems their country was plagued with.

Arjun was leading the assault company, from the front, the way he'd been taught. The way the Indian Army always goes into battle.

They cleared the mosque in a few hours and then began combing the area around for militants who'd escaped in the fog of battle. It was the second-last house in the village. Arjun entered right after the point man. There were just two girls in the house, mere youngsters, barely ten years old.

'Did anyone come in here?' the point man asked.

Both girls shook their heads.

'Okay.' Arjun motioned to the point man. 'Let's go.' He turned to follow him as he exited.

Arjun was almost through the door when the little girl huddled in the extreme corner shot him.

'I don't think Arjun would have even felt the bullet.'

It must have been a fluke shot, because it couldn't have been done better, even if an expert marksman had aimed it. It went clean through the back of Arjun's head and disintegrated his face.

Both the kids went down in a blaze of gunfire as the point man retaliated, his fear ensuring that the magazine was empty before he even thought of releasing the trigger.

'Hey, are you there?' Kanal's voice broke into Anbu's numbed reverie.

'Yes,' Anbu replied when the question finally registered. 'I'm right here.'

'The body is being flown in... it should be here in a couple of hours. The funeral is in the... at... yes, I know... I'm so sorry....'

'I'll be there, Sanjeev. Of course I'll be there. Thanks for calling me,' Anbu replied, his mind still numb as he mechanically replaced the receiver.

How can Arjun be dead? It seems like only yesterday that we first met.

Anbu, being the senior subaltern, had come to meet him at the railway station when Arjun had first reported to the battalion after his familiarization training at the regimental centre.

It seemed like only yesterday that they had done the weapons course together. It seemed like only yesterday that they had scaled the icy mountain peaks of Kargil to throw the marauding Pakistanis off Indian soil. It seemed like only yesterday that Anbu had come across Arjun wiping his tears near the bodies of his men.

'Why?' Arjun's voice was anguished as he pointed at one of the mangled bodies lying in a neat row before them; the neatness with which they were laid out only served to highlight the horrific shape they were in. 'He'd just returned from leave after getting married. Why him?'

'Is there ever any reason? Can there ever be any justification for all this?' Anbu sighed, waving an arm at the battlefield around them. 'Come on, Arjun. They've done their duty, now it's time for us to do ours.' He touched his shoulder briefly, compassionately.

The gesture broke through to Arjun more than the words, pulling him back from that abysmal brink which is often called battlefield trauma and which afflicts even the bravest of soldiers.

'You're right,' Arjun whispered, more to himself than to be heard, 'I am a soldier and an officer... I cannot lose control.'

'That's right, Arjun. It is our karma to lead men into battle... with no second thoughts.' The two comrades had walked away, both the stronger for it all.

It seemed like only yesterday that they had met at the Defence Service Officers Institute and shared a couple of beers. Arjun had been on his way home, for the delivery of his second child.

He had called Anbu when the baby arrived. 'This one is a daughter… thank god… yeah, yeah, she's fine too… and sends all of you her love. Thanks a lot.' Even now the excitement and happiness in Arjun's voice reverberated in Anbu's memory.

The memories continued to crowd in, and Anbu could feel the tears accumulating, as his mind struggled to come to terms with the reality that Arjun was no more.

He shook his head to clear the fog. He could not cry now. He still had an example to set, a duty to fulfil. *That is what Arjun would have wanted me to do.*

Anbu still remembered that last day, not so long ago, when he had been posted out of the battalion. Arjun had come to the station to see him off. They were standing on the railway platform when the train hooted impatiently and made ready to pull out. Arjun embraced him as Anbu got ready to board the train.

'Take care, my friend. Don't let life bring you down. Never let faith in god or the confidence in yourself flag. Stand tall and make us all proud. No matter where you go, no matter what you do, let there be honour in your thoughts and your deeds.

Remember, although we may not be together, we're all going to be watching over you – just as you will, over the paltan... over all of us.'

'I'll call you when I reach, Arjun.' Anbu had hugged him hard and then broken free and run to the now moving train.

Anbu picked up the phone and dialled the number he remembered so well... that he had dialled so often. She was crying when she answered. *Maybe the Army HQ people got through to her first, maybe the media. God alone knows.*

'Tiny... don't cry... you've got to be strong, baby... the kids need you to be strong... Arjun would've wanted you to be strong... just remember that he was a soldier... soldiers die....' He could feel his voice begin to break and controlled it with a huge effort. 'It is their karma to stand in harm's way... it is ours to remember them with pride.'

For a very long time they just held the phone and cried together, brother and sister, he silently, she uncontrollably, her sobs tearing him apart. Then she finally said, 'Please come over. I need you.'

'I'm on my way.' Anbu put down the phone, trying to shut out the sound of the children crying in the background.

Later, as he was driving down, he remembered what he'd said to her on the phone and the thought struck home. *Why do people forget that soldiers have families too? Families who care for them, need them, love them, long for them and wait for them to come home, with fear and hope in their hearts... and so very often in vain.*

Unwittingly, Anbu slowed down as the car came up to the turning from where Arjun's house was visible. He dreaded having to face Tiny.

They all called her Tiny. Not just because she was a little pint-sized runt when she was born, but also because she'd been the youngest one in the family – and a very late arrival at that. To Anbu she wasn't just a kid sister. She was more like a daughter.

With a massive effort, Anbu held back the tears. By the time his hand reached out to ring the doorbell, the calm had returned.

THIS INCREDIBLE, UNFLAPPABLE CALM WAS THE REASON HE HAD been nicknamed Captain Cool. It is possible the name would have persisted but for the fact that he got promoted and was now a mature major commanding a rifle company of his battalion. Obviously Major Captain Cool did not sound so cool and Major Cool lacked zing.

Not long after, Anbu had found himself commanding the same battalion that he had been commissioned in as one of the youngest lieutenant colonels in service. That was when the nickname evolved and he ended up being named Daddy Cool.

It was soon after this when, having finished his command, he was safely on his way to marking some time as a staff officer in the Corps headquarters that luck and calm had finally deserted him. At least, for those few critical moments, they did....

THE CORPS COMMANDER WAS CLEARLY IN A GRUMPY MOOD that morning when he strode into the Ops Room. Anbu was the first one he accosted.

'What the hell happened?'

'The final details are still trickling in, sir.' Anbu snapped to ramrod straight attention. *What's with him today? Got up on the wrong side of the bed or....* 'But it looks like the Pakistanis were trying to push through a party of infiltrators and things got a bit out of hand....'

'A bit out of hand?' the General snapped harshly. 'They fucking fired off enough ammunition to win a small war. I have the whole world and their wives screeching at me all the way from Delhi and you tell me.... What's Division saying? In fact, get me the Div Commander on the line right away.' Two minutes later, after a brief one-sided conversation, he turned back to Anbu. 'Tell them to have a bird ready. I want to leave for the Brigade HQ right away. I've told the Div Commander to meet me there.' He was walking away when he stopped and turned back to bestow a filthy look at Anbu, as though he was personally responsible for the firing going on along the LOC. 'You're coming with me.' He strode off.

Yep! He's definitely PMS-ing. Anbu sighed as he began to gather up the maps and laptop that the

Corps Commander would definitely ask for the minute they landed… *especially if he knows I am not carrying them.*

THE DISTANT THUNDER OF GUNS WAS STILL VERY MUCH IN evidence when they landed at the 71 Infantry Brigade Headquarters, two hours and forty minutes later. As is the norm for such visits, the helipad had been secured by an infantry platoon. Another platoon was engaged in securing the key features in the vicinity, primarily to ensure that the visiting VIP was safe from snipers.

All of them knew that in such rugged terrain a platoon was scarcely enough to provide any cognizable level of safety. Protection was afforded simply by the fact that the details and timings of such visits were always kept strictly under wraps. In fact, most helipads in such sensitive areas conduct the protection drill randomly so that even people staying in the nearby areas don't get to know if it is an exercise or if a VIP is actually arriving.

The General stepped out of the chopper, stooping instinctively to avoid the still whirling rotor blades, even though they were well above him. Anbu followed a couple of feet behind him. At the same time, the Division and Brigade Commanders stepped forward to receive the General.

The Division Commander was about six feet away when the red star blossomed on his chest. One moment he was walking towards them. The next he was being thrown backwards as the bullet thumped into his chest. The sound of the shot had been drowned by the slowly receding but still deafening high-pitched whine of the chopper blades. However, there was no mistaking the blood that sprayed out from his chest.

Anbu reacted on trained instinct. Lunging forward, he slammed into the Corps Commander's back. The rugby-like tackle threw the General forward and down with Anbu riding on him, literally smothering him into the ground. The side of the General's jaw shattered as he hit the ground hard, breaking more than a few teeth and ensuring his dentist would be a busy man for many weeks. Of course, a bullet in the head would have been a lot more painful, if not terminal.

Anbu was not as lucky. The bullet meant for the Corps Commander went through his left thigh.

ANBU SNAPPED OUT OF HIS REVERIE AND RETURNED TO THE moment to find his forehead slick with sweat. His hand was clutching his left thigh. And Captain Mohammed Sami was at the door looking at him curiously.

'You okay, boss?' he asked, looking more than a trifle worried, because he had never seen the unflappable Colonel thus.

'I'm fine, MS.' Anbu collected himself with a shake of his head and smiled. 'Come on in.'

'You're sure? You look quite... quite peakish to me....'

'No, it's nothing... a bad dream, I guess. I must have dozed off for a moment.' Anbu shook himself mentally, pushing away the memory of those dreadful weeks when he had been stuck in a hospital bed, slowly and painfully recovering from the bullet wound in his thigh. That was a road he did not want to walk down again, definitely not when he was awake. *The nightmares that return with unfailing regularity every night are bad enough.*

'Are you sure, sir?' Sami persisted.

'Of course I am, MS. It's nothing,' Anbu replied reassuringly. 'Anyway... where is our deadly duo?'

He had barely spoken when there was a brief knock on the door and Flight Lieutenant Ankita Bhatnagar and Captain Manoj Khare walked in. 'Ah! There you are! Both of you have a long life.' Anbu motioned them towards the chairs opposite him.

'I hope it's a happy one too, sir,' Khare smiled.

'Then we obviously need to ensure you're not around,' Ankita quipped.

'Now, now, you two,' Anbu chided gently. 'Stop behaving as though you are already married.'

'Married? To him?' Ankita's face went bright red as she replied quickly, too quickly. 'You must be joking, sir.' Her tone was caustic, but the light in her eyes was not.

The demure Ankita Bhatnagar was a flight lieutenant in the Indian Air Force. She was just over five and a half feet and built like an athlete. She made an incongruous pair with the tall, dark and burly Captain Manoj Khare. On the face of it the two appeared to have little in common. But both were capable of doing things with computers that would have made an Intel chip feel stupid. Either of them could have walked in and picked up a top job with any computer company anywhere in the world. However, both craved a life beyond the ordinary. Almost certainly, if Anbu had not found them and pulled them out of the humdrum of regular army life, they would have found their way into the arms of some willing computer corporation. Both were also physical fitness freaks, adept at a variety of martial arts and unarmed combat. The duo had been humorously nicknamed 'Beauty and the Beast' by their comrades in Force 22.

Anbu had put their special skills to good use and appointed them as the Force 22 intelligence team. Both had done cross-attachments with several of India's various intelligence agencies to hone their skills. They had even done short stints with the Delhi and Srinagar police to get their anti-terror operations up to speed. It was doubtful whether Anbu could have found a better pair to work with Rao, and help him get the NIC going.

Anbu gave them a summary of everything that had transpired and what was expected of them. An hour later, when the two of them exited his office, they went with a keen sense of anticipation... for what lay ahead.

Enter the NIC

THE HOME MINISTRY'S CENTRAL CONFERENCE HALL WAS PACKED and buzzing with a keen sense of anticipation when the PM entered. He was flanked by the Home and Defence ministers. Already present in the room were a dozen key ministers, most of whom comprised the Central Crisis Management Committee: the directors of the Research and Analysis Wing (RAW), Intelligence Bureau (IB), Defence Intelligence Agency (DIA), Joint Cipher Bureau (JCB), Joint Intelligence Committee (JIC), Signals Intelligence Directorate (SID), Satellite Intelligence Directorate (SAID), Aviation Research Centre (ARC), Directorate of Air Intelligence (AI), Directorate of Navy Intelligence (NI), Defence Image Processing and Analysis Centre (DIPAC), Central Bureau of Investigation (CBI), Anti-Terrorist Task Force (ATTF), the three Service Chiefs, and the Directors of various para-military and emergency management organizations.

The 'guest list' had been carefully scrutinized by

the PM's office to ensure that everyone who was connected with intelligence was included.

'We must ensure that every possible cog gets involved with the NIC. I want people at all levels to understand and appreciate what the NIC can do in terms of integrating efforts and maximizing resources.' That was the mandate the PM had given to his staff and that was what they were doing their best to ensure.

It took a few minutes for the pleasantries to be completed. Then silence fell as G.K. Rao walked up to the podium.

In his mid-fifties, the short portly Rao wore black, round, horn-rimmed spectacles that had faded from fashion a few decades ago. Born into a family of aristocrats, who were vaguely related to the erstwhile royalty of Hyderabad, Rao was one of the first agents to join RAW. He had to his credit several daring operations, none of which would be publically known for many years to come. Growing from strength to strength on sheer merit, Rao had also done several stints with ARC and JIC. Today he was a veteran of no mean standing and one of the few people who had an in-depth understanding of the true state of Indian Intelligence. His biggest strength was his total lack of political leanings or mentors. This, more than anything else, made him acceptable across the political spectrum.

As was his wont, Rao wasted little time in pleasantries and launched straight into the heart of the matter.

'Ladies and gentlemen, today we shall be taking a broad look at world affairs. This is essential for an understanding of the prevalent situation. The topic is vast and extremely complex and there is no way anyone can do justice to it in the brief time available to us. That is why I shall just touch upon those aspects that I think are relevant. Please feel free to question, correct or contribute whenever you feel the need to do so.'

The expressions on the faces of those assembled in the hall left no doubt in anyone's mind that they were going to do just that. However, to begin with, Rao sailed along pretty smoothly.

'A study of the history of the human race tells us that the course of most major events has been governed by the quest for power, religion, or objects of economic value such as gold, diamonds, precious metals and minerals and, in recent times, oil. These three elements have been the major cause of the emergence, resurgence or extinction of nations and peoples.

'I will not dwell on the power factor since I think it is quite self-explanatory. But let us take a closer look at religion and oil, since these two have been the root cause of most of what ails us today.'

The introduction was on the verge of acquiring pedantic overtones when Rao changed gear.

'Let us consider religion first. Much is made of which is the better faith, which god is the true god and which religion the most militant. Without getting into these debates, let us take a look at some facts. Today there are nineteen major religions and about 240 religious groups that flourish in the world.'

Rao gave a discreet nod to an unseen assistant parked in some unseen location. A computer-generated slide blazed across the giant screen behind him.

Major Religions	*Percentage of population*
Christianity	32%
Islam	19%
Hinduism	13%
Buddhism	6%
Chinese Traditional	6%
Primal Indigenous	4%
New Religions	2%
Judaism/Sikhism/Zoroastrianism/ Shinto/Confucianism/Baha'i Faith/ Taoism/Wicca	Less than 1%

Rao paused for a moment for the contents of the slide to be absorbed by his audience.

'These percentages have been taken from open sources available on the internet and what you see are averages derived from the figures available on several sites. They may not be very precise but they are more than adequate to give us an idea of the world today – in religious terms, I mean.'

The slide faded away.

'Now, while the purpose of every religion is to help us rid ourselves of sin, bring us closer to God and help promote harmony, peace and love, it is strange that since the beginning of time religion has been the root cause of bloodshed and violence. Forget about seeing eye-to-eye with other religions, most people have not even been able to co-exist peacefully with their co-religionists. That is why we have Catholics hounding Protestants and Sunnis exterminating Shias like vermin.'

A rustle of sound stirred through the room, but Rao continued without pause.

'Of all the religions mentioned above, Hinduism is possibly the oldest surviving religion. It is said to have its roots in Dravidianism, which was practiced around 6000–3000 BC and hence predates the Sumerian, Egyptian and Babylonian cultures.'

Another brief stir ruffled the room.

'Judaism finds its origins in the covenant between God and Abraham somewhere around 2000 BC, hence it is one of the older religions and its doctrines have influenced Christianity, Islam and the Baha'i faith. Despite the fact that it, like Christianity and Islam, is one of the religions of the Book, the Jews have suffered the most abuse and repression down the ages and a large part of this has been at the hands of Christians and Muslims. The Christians believe that it is Jesus Christ, the son of God, who shows us the true path to salvation whereas Islam believes

Mohammed is the true Prophet of the One God. I personally have no comments on this matter, since it is a matter of personal belief.'

The murmur of sound this time was much louder.

'However, it is undeniable that much blood has been shed over this issue and, if history is any indicator, more will continue to be spilled. The Christians always believed that the savage heathen, that is, almost everyone who is not a Christian, needs to be saved. Now we all know that saving comes at a cost. In this case the cost was borne by those unfortunate heathens who had to have their souls saved. All of us who have read about the Crusades know that many hundreds of thousands of heathen souls were dispatched to some unidentified, uncharted and unknown heaven as their earthly bodies were put to the sword.'

By now there were several red faces in the audience as blood pressures rose.

'Similarly, Muslims believe that only those who follow the tenets of Prophet Mohammed attain jannat with its seventeen virgins.' Rao paused briefly before resuming sotto voce. 'Strangely enough, it has never been specified if these virgins are male or female.'

Angry whispers and a brief, uncertain burst of laughter met these words.

'Like the Christians, for the Muslims too, everyone else is a kafir – an unbeliever – and needs to be saved. Accordingly, a large number of kafirs have been either converted or eliminated.'

Some more faces went red.

'Possibly Buddhism and Jainism are among those few religions that have no – or negligible – blood on their hands. But that could possibly be because they account for a tiny percentage of humanity and so it is safe to assume that they were too busy saving their own hides to worry about saving the souls of others.'

Somebody laughed before being glared down by his neighbours.

'To sum up, who, if any, has the moral high ground and which, if any, is the true God is largely a matter of conjecture, endless debate and possibly a lot more bloodshed. A lot of the problems caused by religion have been compounded by politicians of many hues all over the world who have unscrupulously used religion as a tool to foment division and dissent with a view to attaining their own petty goals.'

This was met with an angry and totally predictable outburst from a section of the audience. Rao raised his voice and overrode the noise that threatened to disrupt the flow of his words.

'However, what is pretty certain is that whoever the true God is, he has been hugely biased in terms of religion and the distribution of global oil reserves, which is the other major factor that we are going to talk about today. I am sure I need not reiterate which religion is in the majority in those areas where this black gold called oil is found. Whether this was reward for following the true God or whether it was merely compensation for the barren ruggedness of the terrain in which this oil is found, I leave it to you to decide.'

This time the ripple of sound that slashed through the room was loud. Rao continued unfazed, 'I trust all of you are aware that the broader Middle East-Central Asian region encompasses more than seventy per cent of the global oil and natural gas reserves. Saudi Arabia possesses twenty-five per cent, Iraq eleven per cent and Iran ranks third with ten per cent. In comparison, America possesses less than 2.8 per cent of the reserves. It is primarily because of this that, in mid-1995, the US administration released a National Security document stating that the objective of the war on Iraq was to *protect the United States' uninterrupted and secure access to oil.*'

'What?' a not-so-well-informed and very irate politician broke in. 'Can you show us this document?'

'Yes of –' Rao was interrupted before he could complete his reply.

'Why would you doubt it?' a better-informed politician cut in. 'We all know that the US economy needs oil the way a junkie needs a fix.'

'Very true, sir. America consumes about twenty-four per cent of the global oil production.' Rao took control before a discussion could develop. 'That is why Iraq, and subsequently Iran and Syria, became officially identified targets on the American road map to war. Targeting them was totally in the interests of the Anglo-American oil conglomerates, the Wall Street financial establishment and the huge military-industrial complex that has tremendous influence over the White House.'

'What business interests are you talking about? How much influence can businessmen have over the administration of a country?' a senior politician asked indignantly.

'Quite a lot, from what is now emerging,' Rao replied evenly. 'Just to give you an idea, there are several companies such as Halliburton, Bechtel, Parsons, KBR and Northstar that have made billions of dollars from the so-called reconstruction of Iraq – and this information is no secret.'

A politician seated at the back raised his voice. 'I see! So the Americans first give a new lease of life to their military-industrial complex by waging this war and now they're making money rebuilding the country they have decimated. So what? Someone has to do the rebuilding after every war.'

'I agree with you, someone does have to do it,' Rao took over again, 'but strangely enough, all the companies that landed billions of dollars worth of business were those with Republican leanings and known to be tight with the White House. And everyone knows that Dick Cheney was the CEO and Chairman of Halliburton just before he took over as the American Vice President.'

'He resigned from Halliburton before he took over public office,' someone responded defensively.

'Yes he did, but he did not give up his stock options in Halliburton. In fact, when this came to light he sold a part of these options and donated eight million US dollars to charity.'

'Well, there you are.'

'But that happened only after he was caught with his hands in the till, as it were. In the meantime the Halliburton share price went up from a dismal ten dollars before the war to a never before achieved high of forty-nine dollars.'

'Just where are you getting all this data from? How come...'

'Sir, all this data is in the public domain. It is freely available on the internet if you know where to look for it,' Rao cut in smoothly. 'Also, there has also been a very well researched program that has been run on this whole sordid matter by the BBC.'

'My God! That's daylight robb –'

'And it does not end there. Republicans own all the companies selected for these huge contracts; some had barely a few hundred dollars to their names and no prior experience in the field. Most of them defaulted or failed to deliver after milking the government of billions. In fact, a BBC investigation has established that nearly twenty-three billion dollars are yet to be accounted for.'

Twenty-three billion dollars!

The shock was clearly visible on the faces in the audience.

'This huge sum of money has simply gone missing. After the matter became public, a couple of these war profiteers are now facing legal action, but even after the passage of so many years, none of the companies involved has been indicted and no contractor of consequence has been punished.' Rao added gravely, 'I leave it to you all to imagine what is going on.'

He allowed the audience to dwell on that for a moment before he resumed.

'To enable it to wage this so-called War on Terror, the Americans needed the moral, if not physical, support of the global community. This was essential to give them the moral high ground that they always hanker for. Towards this end several other like-minded governments joined them to set up the "Coalition of the Willing". They not only helped to drown out the din of dissent on various international platforms, they even provided manpower and munitions. The Americans also needed lots of strategically sited bases in this part of the world. They found one such base in Pakistan.'

'How can the Pakistanis help anyone fight terrorism?' someone asked caustically.

'They could shoot themselves!' another retorted sarcastically.

Several people in the room laughed.

'The irony is that Pakistan proliferates nuclear technology to some of the same states that the Americans have nominated as diehard members of the Axis of Evil.'

'That's poetic justice for you.'

'I am sure all of you are right,' Rao intervened

quickly before the presentation deteriorated into a free-for-all. 'Maybe that is why it surprised no one when a classified Pentagon document, the Nuclear Posture Review, presented to the Senate in February 2002 stressed that *America must prepare for all possible contingencies, especially now when dozens of countries and even some terrorist groups are engaged in secret weapon development programs.* In this landmark decision, which was coerced by a very hawkish US administration, the US Senate granted congressional approval to the *pre-emptive use* of nuclear weapons. Now, suddenly, nuclear weapons were no longer a weapon of last resort as they had been during the cold war.'

'That's nonsense! How can anyone believe that?'

'I quite understand what you mean,' Rao said. 'Maybe you should all see this.' He gestured to the unseen aide again and a video clip came up on the silent screen behind him. It showed a segment culled from a Pentagon briefing.

'Mini-nukes – those with a yield of less than 5000 tons – are harmless to civilians because they explode underground.' A preening Pentagon spokesman was addressing a hall full of media personnel.

A stunned silence fell upon Rao's audience as the clip concluded. It lasted till the Air Chief commented, 'Mind you, in terms of potential radioactive fallout, such mini-nukes constitute a significant part of the atom bomb that was dropped on Hiroshima in 1945.'

'True, sir.' Rao took charge again. 'But the fact

remains that suddenly, in a truly fantastic piece of doublespeak, the Americans had begun to tout nuclear weapons *as a means of building peace and preventing collateral damage*. And this was only the beginning, because now the US administration actually prepared contingency plans for an offensive first strike with nuclear weapons not only against the so-called Axis of Evil – Iraq, Iran, Libya, Syria and North Korea – but also against Russia, China and India.'

'Why would they start targeting India? We're a non-aligned –'

'That's not the issue here, sir,' Rao cut in smoothly. 'The fact is that America is fully aware of the fact that these three countries have the military, economic and geo-strategic potential to counter its influence… especially if they decide to stand together. As we know, all three are already starting to make the right noises, their differences notwithstanding.'

'How much of this is conjecture and how much reality?' the Defence Minister questioned suddenly.

'All of it is real, sir. As you will note, precisely one year after this, the Americans began their march down the road to war by targeting Iraq. America used their favourite *they-have-weapons-of-mass-destruction-and-are-a-threat-to-global-peace* excuse.'

'That is rather funny when you consider that the Americans themselves have the largest collection of WMDs in the world,' someone in the audience commented.

'I thought the International Atomic Energy Agency debunked all that,' the External Affairs Minister commented.

'They did,' Rao replied. 'In fact, the IAEA Director General and the United Nations Chief Weapons Inspector went through the so-called *intelligence* presented by the Americans and the British to the United Nations Security Council and called it a load of hogwash. Neither of them found any evidence to indicate that Iraq possessed such weapons.'

'In the months following the Iraqi misadventure the forces of the "Coalition of the Willing" suffered severe losses. Despite the much-hyped initial aerial blitzkrieg, the fact was that they were being hit hard and the number of body bags flown back from Iraq to the countries that comprised the Coalition surpassed all previous records. The highest body count was of American soldiers. No, it wasn't because the Yanks were at the forefront in the battlefield, it was simply because they comprised the largest part of the Coalition and were the most favoured targets of the unseen enemy.'

'Now please observe what happened next. I'll give you the key events that help build the chain and allow you to see the grand design behind all these seemingly unrelated things.' Rao paused briefly for a sip of water.

'The bombs lobbed by both sides were exploding with meticulous regularity when, on 11 November 2004, an Israeli Defence Force delegation reached

Brussels to attend a NATO conference. They met senior military commanders from Egypt, Jordan, Algeria, Tunisia, Morocco, Algeria and Mauritania.'

'How is that relevant?'

'During this conference the Israeli delegation agreed, for the first time, to participate in military exercises and anti-terror manoeuvres with several Arab countries. The conference was part of NATO's attempt to revive the Mediterranean Dialogue program. It was also a critical step forward for the Americans. The next target was Iran. This becomes amply clear when you listen to what the American Vice President said to MSNBC in an interview on 16 January 2005.'

Yet another video clip lit up the giant screen. The American Vice President loomed large on it. He was at his prime-time best.

'There is absolutely no doubt about it,' he was saying briskly. *'Iran is right at the top of the list of rogue enemies of America and considering various ground realities there is a strong possibility that Israel would be doing the bombing for us... as and when the need arises.'* Replying to a spate of frenzied questions that erupted in the aftermath of this momentous statement, he clarified grandiosely, *'Given the fact that Iran has a stated policy that their objective is the destruction of Israel, the Israelis might well decide to act first, and let the rest of the world worry about cleaning up the diplomatic mess afterwards.'*

'Why not give Iran the same kind of nuclear deal that is being hammered out for Korea?' questioned the interviewer. *'Why don't we offer Iran an end to sanctions and free heavy oil fuel if they're ready to freeze their nuclear program?'*

'*With North Korea it is different*,' came the reply, failing, of course, to clarify why it was different. '*The Iranians won't do it. They just want to go ahead with their rogue program.*'

'*But that is exactly what the President had also said about North Korea sometime back*,' the interviewer insisted. '*So why is it different with Iran?*'

The Vice President mumbled something before he changed tack and took the conversation in a totally different direction. The clip ended.

'The answer to that last question is obvious,' Rao said. 'Unlike Iran, North Korea is not sitting on huge oil reserves. The plan to attack Iran has nothing to do with nukes. It's all about oil. Oil and money. This WMD warning was so similar to the ones the Americans had been giving as justification for their earlier invasion of Iraq that it is surprising that more people did not take note of it or protest against it.'

'Come on, Mr Rao. Nations don't just go to war....'

'That's precisely what most of us think, sir,' Rao countered. 'Most of us are not even aware of how high the stakes are. Just to give you a little idea,' Rao referred to his notes briefly, 'The value of *only* the Kurdish oil fields is somewhere in the range of five trillion US dollars at current oil prices.'

A stunned silence met these words as people struggled to work out on the number of zeroes that the figure involved.

'And do you know who has been granted the rights over this oil?' Rao paused dramatically. 'None other than Hunt Oil of Texas. Most of you may not know that the owner of Hunt Oil is a staunch Republican and a dear friend of the American President to whose election fund he has contributed very generously.'

'Damn!' someone in the front row exclaimed. 'What an investment that contribution has turned out to be.'

'Exactly! And it's only the tip of the iceberg, as the BBC investigative team concluded. That is why the Americans have been on the rampage.' Rao indicated the screen again. 'Please listen to what a former National Security Adviser had to say about the Vice President's interview a few days later.' Yet another brief video clip began to unspool.

'Yes, the Vice President wants the Israelis to do it for us,' the former National Security Advisor was saying glibly. *'In Iran the issue is certainly not tyranny – it's nuclear weapons.'*

'It is important for us to understand,' Rao resumed as the video clip faded, 'that what both the American Vice President and the NSA conveniently forgot to mention was that America was not just *encouraging* Israel in this misadventure. They were conceptualizing a full-fledged joint US-Israeli military operation to bomb Iran. For almost two years now the Neocons in the US Defence Department have been working assiduously with their Israeli military and intelligence counterparts, carefully identifying targets inside Iran.'

'Who are the Neocons?'

'Neocon is the abbreviation for the Neoconservatives,' Rao explained. 'The original neoconservatives were a band of liberal intellectuals who rebelled against the American Democratic Party's leftward drift on defence issues in the 1970s. Later they aligned themselves with the Republicans, who promised to confront Soviet expansionism. The neoconservatives, in the famous formulation of one of their leaders, Irving Kristol, are "liberals mugged by reality". A lot of American critics take issue with the Neocons' support of an aggressive foreign policy, their unilateralism and lack of concern for international consensus. Neocons have been attacked for their influence on US foreign policy, especially during the administration of President George W. Bush.'

There was a short silence as the audience absorbed this information.

Rao resumed, 'Another thing that neither of them mentioned was that for more than two years now US and British intelligence and Special Forces, working with their Israeli counterparts, have been involved in the task of stirring ethnic tensions and regime-overthrow activity in Iran. And none of this is being done very covertly. In fact, in a newspaper interview in June 2003, an unnamed British intelligence official went on record to say –'

A newspaper clipping emerged on the screen.

The campaign against Iran will not be a ground war like the one in Iraq. The Americans will use different tactics. It is getting quite scary. Their expectation is that a US-Israeli bombing raid of Iran's nuclear facilities will stir up ethnic tensions and trigger regime change in favour of the US because the Iranian opposition movement would unseat the Mullahs.

'But that's so stupid!' The RAW chief couldn't contain himself. 'It defies basic common sense and is a gross misjudgment of social forces inside Iran. Any kid on the streets will tell you that the Iranians would consistently rally behind a wartime government against foreign aggression and the entire Middle East is likely to go up in flames.'

'Whatever....' Rao returned to his sequence of events. 'A fortnight later, American, Israeli and Turkish forces began joint military exercises just off the Syrian coast. They described them as routine, but extensive aerial activity was noticed during these manoeuvres. It was obvious that considerable efforts were being expended to map all the regional air defence networks, especially the Iranian one.

'A fortnight later, in accordance with the decision taken at Brussels in November 2004, for the first time Israeli armed forces participated in military exercises with NATO. Surprisingly, these exercises also included several Arab countries. Yet again, no information was divulged about the objective of the manoeuvres, though a careful observer would have noticed that there was a concrete effort by all participants to coordinate defensive activity in case of missile strikes against any of them. Please note how the tempo of events has begun to escalate.'

'This is amazing!' the Defence Minister commented. 'How come no one took note of all this?'

'Unfortunately, not many people were observing these events or analysing them to clearly understand the horrendous implications. That is why I always refer to these as the years of unreason. And what happened next at Beirut was even more shocking.'

Beirut

14 February 2005

THE CLOCK WAS ON THE VERGE OF ANNOUNCING THE TENTH hour of another beautiful morning when the motorcade, with the imposing black car at its centre, turned onto the road surfing along the sea front. The line of vehicles had just about reached the derelict St George Hotel on the Beirut seafront when one of the several nondescript cars parked on the side of the road exploded. Over a thousand kilograms of TNT had been stuffed into it. Nine people died instantly. Over a hundred were injured.

'Among those killed was the former Lebanese Prime Minister Rafik Hariri whose motorcade had been driving past. The bomb appeared to have been directed against it,' the smart young journalist in Beirut battle fatigues told her audience. 'Hariri, a self-made billionaire and business tycoon, headed five cabinets during his decade long tenure. He had resigned as the Prime Minister and joined the Opposition on 20 October 2004 and was hoping to make a comeback in the legislative elections the following May.'

A few hours later she was back on air, reading out a statement that had been issued by a little known group called Victory and Jehad in Greater Syria, which claimed responsibility for the killing. 'The operation was carried out by one of our suicide bombers,' the statement concluded.

'However,' the reporter added, 'investigators doubt the veracity of this claim by the barely known group. Things are unclear at this stage, but both the US and the UK are pushing for and sponsoring a United Nations probe into this assassination. We promise to keep you updated about this shocking event.'

A few days later she was back with the latest.

'The UN probe sponsored by America and Britain has implicated several officials of the Syrian and Lebanese intelligence services for the Hariri killing. However,' she said emphatically, 'no one has been officially charged till now.'

'We had nothing to do with it' – Syria immediately issued strong and persistent denials.

'They definitely did!' an American spokesperson countered, without bothering to explain why or how she knew. 'Such acts cannot be allowed to go unpunished. Syria must withdraw all its troops from Lebanon immediately. Lebanon should be allowed to pursue its political future, free from violence and free from Syrian occupation.'

'You mean, just like the Iraqis are being allowed to?' a correspondent from the Middle East asked sarcastically. The question was conveniently ignored. Nor did the American spokesperson mention that the Syrian withdrawal primarily served American and Israeli interests.

Call to Action

'THE CAREFULLY ORCHESTRATED HUE AND CRY CAUSED BY THE Hariri assassination continued until sufficient pressure had been built up on Syria and her troops began withdrawing from Lebanon on 23 July 2005,' Rao said as the series of news clips came to an end. 'This automatically led to a major shift in the Middle East security situation, with the balance of power shifting firmly in favour of Israel and USA. Now America had troops and military bases in Turkey, Pakistan, Azerbaijan, Afghanistan, and of course Iraq. These countries, as well as Turkmenistan, are all members of NATO's "Partnership for Peace" program and have military cooperation agreements with NATO. In other words, by now Iran was virtually surrounded by US military bases.'

For a change, silence greeted the pause as Rao took a sip of water from the glass on the podium before he resumed.

'A few weeks after the joint NATO-Israel military exercise, the NATO Secretary General arrived in

Jerusalem for talks with the Israeli PM and the top brass of the Israeli Defence Forces.'

'The Israel-NATO protocol that came into existence now obligates NATO to align itself with the US-Israeli plan to bomb Iran, *as an act of self-defence*. It also means that NATO is clearly and closely involved in the process of military consultations related to the planned bombing of Iran. In fact, just weeks after this, American Patriot missile crews stationed in Germany arrived in Israel to participate in the joint Juniper Cobra exercise with the Israeli military. This exercise specifically pertained to the deployment of Patriot missiles and was described by a US defence spokesperson as "routine and totally unconnected to events currently underway in the Middle East". However, the fact is that Patriot missiles had seen extensive deployment and use during the first US invasion of Iraq.'

A few voices attempted to make themselves heard at this point but Rao cut them off. 'The Juniper Cobra exercise had barely concluded when there were a rash of news leaks in the Israeli media confirming that the Prime Minster had given the initial authorization for an Israeli attack on Iran's uranium enrichment plant *if diplomacy failed to stop Iran's nuclear program*. Almost simultaneously, the US Secretary of Defence embarked on official visits to Iraq, Afghanistan, Pakistan, Kyrgyzstan and Azerbaijan. At this time a Russian news editor who had been watching events far more carefully than most wrote this in his column.'

The words highlighted in a news report appeared on the screen:

Recent American military and diplomatic moves are obviously an attempt to literally encircle Iran and find the best bridgehead for a possible military operation against that country.

'This observation was not only astute, it was also a blatant warning the world should have heeded,' Rao said gravely. 'Unfortunately, these words of wisdom got submerged in the deluge of words unleashed by the American spin masters.'

'The Iranians must be very worked up about all this.'

'Of course they are… understandably so. In fact, as a direct counter to this encirclement by America and her allies, Iran has signed a military cooperation with Tajikistan, which occupies a strategic position bordering Afghanistan's northern frontier. Tajikistan is a member of the "Shanghai Five" military cooperation group, which also includes Kazakhstan, China, Kyrgyzstan, and Russia.'

'The original Shanghai Five,' this time the Army Chief took up the baton before anyone could ask the question, 'had been formed in 1996 as a forum to resolve the long-outstanding Soviet–Chinese border disputes. However, under Putin, China and Russia grew much closer, bound by their mutual distrust of America and their desire to promote a multi-polar world. Consequently, on 15 June 2001 Shanghai Five was expanded to include Uzbekistan as a member, changing the orientation of the organization. Shortly thereafter, India, Mongolia, Iran and Turkmenistan expressed interest in the organisation's activities with India and Mongolia even considering membership.'

'Precisely.' Rao stepped in smoothly. 'The obvious fact is that should India and Mongolia join up, more than half the population of Eurasia, from the Baltic to the Pacific, would soon be arrayed in a political, economic and military alliance that could pose a cognizable threat to American hegemony.'

'And this, as you said earlier, would make the Russia-China-India collaboration a reality,' the External Affairs Minister chipped in. 'America would hate to see this happen.'

'Absolutely correct, sir,' Rao concurred. 'To go back to my chronology, things were getting bad enough for the US Administration when there was yet another setback. It came in the form of Hurricane Katrina which swept the Gulf Coast of America. Katrina may have been only the sixth strongest Atlantic hurricane recorded, but it was the deadliest and most expensive one to ever wreak havoc on the American coastline. The death toll hovered in the vicinity of 1800 and the damage to property crossed eighteen billion dollars. To make things worse, the US Administration could not pin any of this on the Al Qaida or any other organization, real or imaginary.

'In fact, reeling as they were from severe criticism for lying about WMDs in Iraq and the costly military misadventure in Afghanistan, they now came in for a massive mauling. They were still struggling to cope with this when they were hit by another new crisis.'

There was another pause before Rao resumed.

'Along the Pakistan-Afghan border, a force of approximately two hundred mujahidin fighters caught two American platoons literally with their pants down. By the time the American choppers and relief force arrived on the scene, only three members of these ill-fated platoons were breathing and that too barely. The others had been chopped to pieces with unbelievable savagery.'

Rao's soft monotone did nothing to dispel the feeling of horror that gripped the room. 'It is also certain that the mujahidin fighters headed straight back towards the Pakistani border immediately after the ambush since the choppers chased them for a better part of the way. They melted away among the tribal inhabitants of that brutally rugged area and that is where the American chase came to an inconclusive end.

'The body count compelled the US administration to publicly acknowledge that Pakistan was more a part of the problem than the solution. Everyone had, of course, known this right from the beginning; however, it is never politically correct to openly discuss such blemishes in one's friends.

'The strong US reaction evoked proportionately strong reactions in Pakistan. So vociferous were the protests that the echoes of the blast which decimated seven American tourists, who were dumb enough to want to visit Pakistan in such troubled times, reverberated all the way to the White House. The blasts destroyed several buildings occupied by US diplomats and businesses in Karachi. The message was clearly audible to the Americans, all the way back home – *Get out and stay out*.'

'This is all very fascinating, Rao, but do responsible nations really behave like this?'

'Why not?' said a politician from the Left. 'Are you aware that in the last sixty years, since the end of the Second World War, America has used military force more than 220 times? They have actually threatened the security of the world and attacked nations on the pretext that they were *feeling* threatened, although most of the time it has only been about money... money and, as Rao has pointed out, oil.'

At this point, before the fracas could gain momentum, the PM indicated to Rao to announce a break for lunch and people began to trickle out, talking loudly as they went.

'I think that went pretty well, Rao,' the PM murmured as they stood back and watched people head for the banquet hall. 'It certainly got them going... and thinking.'

'I hope so, sir.'

'Oh, I am sure it did,' the PM said reassuringly. 'Though the picture you paint does not bode well for any of us.'

'I agree, sir. The world faces dark and dangerous

days ahead. I just hope somewhere, somehow, better sense prevails....'

Just then a group converged on them, seeking the Prime Minister's attention. Rao wandered away at the first opportune moment and headed for the buffet. He was halfway there when Anbu accosted him; with him were Ankita Bhatnagar and Manoj Khare.

'My compliments, Mr Rao, that was an extremely illuminating presentation.' Anbu greeted him with a smile as he extended a hand to introduce himself. 'I am....'

'Of course I know who you are, Colonel Anbu.' Rao returned the smile as the two men shook hands. 'We have never had the pleasure of meeting, but who doesn't know you? Your men have done the nation proud. I am looking forward to your support in the coming days.'

'But of course. I can assure you we shall do our best. And here are the two officers who are going to be with you for the next few weeks.' Anbu made the introductions as Rao shook hands first with Ankita and then with Khare.

'So, Captain,' Rao asked Khare, 'what do you think of all that we covered this morning?'

'Well, sir,' Khare replied thoughtfully. 'I am no authority on geopolitics and international relations, but the way I see it, humankind comprises four kinds of people: Idiots, Wimps, Bystanders and Terrorists.'

A hint of a smile appeared on Anbu's face. Rao,

too, looked amused and gestured to the young man to go on.

'One cannot say for certain whether it is the Idiots or the Terrorists who have delivered the world to the brink of disaster. However, it is certain that the Idiots could never have done it if the Wimps had not supported them. In fact, it was this support that encouraged the Terrorists to also target the Wimps and thus expand the battlefield. It is also almost certain that the march of events could have been halted if the Bystanders had shaken off their inertia and been bold enough to stand up and be counted when things were threatening to get out of hand.'

The smiles on the faces of Khare's three-person audience broadened.

'You have just started him off on his favourite hypothesis, sir,' Ankita piped up.

'That's all right,' Rao replied with a smile. 'I have never heard this stated in such simple terms.' He nodded at Khare. 'Please go on, Captain.'

'You see, sir,' Khare continued with a sheepish smile. 'The fact remains that neither the Idiots nor the Terrorists can really be blamed since basically both are idiots and one can hardly blame an idiot for behaving idiotically. Of course, the Wimps should have shown a little spine and not gone along blindly with the Idiots. But then they too were behaving in character. So, ultimately it was the Bystanders that should have stood together, come forward and confined the Idiots, the Terrorists and the Wimps to the dustbin of history instead of allowing them to write it. But then, the Bystanders were busy being bystanders. They were either so caught up in their mundane problems of daily living or they were simply not bothered with what the others were doing. Most of them did not even realize that all those seemingly trivial events taking place in those seemingly far-off places were going to affect them as sharply as if they were happening in their own backyards.'

'Very well put, young man.' Rao beamed. 'Colonel,' he turned to Anbu, 'I am really impressed with the way he has summed up the state of world affairs today.'

'The first I am hearing of it myself, Mr Rao.' Anbu smiled, but it was easy to see he was pleased with Khare's extempore speech. 'Strangely enough, the group he refers to as the Bystanders constitutes a very large part of humanity. If they were all to get together and take things in hand, they could easily whip the Idiots, Terrorists and Wimps and send them back into their kennels with their tails between their legs. Unfortunately, most of them are busy with their own petty rivalries and do not even realize the power they *could* yield if they joined hands. That is why they are either sitting on their hands or busy battling the Terrorists on their own.'

'Precisely, sir.' Khare re-entered the fray. 'The Terrorists of course are the ones who suffer the least. They don't have a conscience to appease or any rules to play the game by. They simply blame the Idiots for creating the circumstances that forced them to become what they are. They blame them for every real and/or imaginary suffering they were or are undergoing and use this as an excuse for inflicting even more suffering on everyone including their sorry masochistic selves.'

'I agree. That is how it all began and that is how it continues to be,' Rao said. 'Unfortunately, what is certain is that no matter who is at fault, all of us are going to suffer, given the way things are beginning to spiral out of control.'

The four of them continued to talk as they drifted towards the buffet table. They had no idea how rapidly the situation was escalating with every passing day. Unseen and unheard by most people, the world was moving towards the edge of chaos.

A Bundle of Straws

WASHINGTON, D.C.

WHERE THEY FOUND THE WISDOM THE PROPHET ALONE knows, but the so-called greatest democracy of the world gave a resounding thumbs-down to the Republicans. The imminent return of the Democrats to the White House was a sure harbinger of change. The new inmates of the White House, it was hoped, would review and change most of the decisions taken by the Republican administration.

THERE WERE ONLY THREE PEOPLE PRESENT AT THE MEETING that took place on the night of 16 December. Two of them had travelled several miles for the meeting, but the third had to walk only a hundred-odd feet since he lived in the large white house surrounded by sprawling gardens and protected by huge windows shielded with bulletproof glass.

The most remarkable thing about the small, rather dingy-looking room where the meeting took place was the fact that it was totally and positively free of electronic devices of all kinds, the ones that saw or listened and the ones that recorded. Though there was no formal advance agenda circulated for this meeting, the manner in which it was set up left no doubt in the minds of any of the three that the subjects under discussion would be extraordinary. No staff or security personnel was visible anywhere.

'Everything seems to be spinning out of control,' the big man began, lines of exasperation creasing his bovine features. 'None of my predecessors has ever had such a high disapproval rating. *Never!*' He spat out the last word vehemently, glaring at the other two as though they were responsible for the situation. He broke off the glare when he realized it wasn't bothering them very much. 'It's not supposed to end like this.'

'It certainly isn't,' the second man agreed.

'We were supposed to be the ones to change the map of the world,' the woman said, her voice heavy with frustration. 'We were supposed to make the world a safer place.'

'Safer my arse! Who gives a crap?' he retorted. 'We were supposed to ensure we would be remembered as the people who had made the difference.'

'Well, you can bet that we are going to be remembered, but maybe not in the way that we want to be.' The woman's tone was nasty. It was obvious she did not like the man she was talking to, despite the fact that they both worked for the President.

'Can it, both of you,' the big man sliced in sharply. 'We have enough to deal with, without you two getting your knickers in a twist.' An uneasy silence fell upon the room, until he spoke again. 'How much time do we have before the cocksuckers take over?' No one answered since they could all count. *There wasn't much time. Not for all that needed to be done.* 'We need to find a way to put an end to this... a way to ensure we go down in the history books as people who made a difference.'

The discussion spun in circles and progressed deep into the night. It was sometime after midnight that things began to take shape. The conversation became quieter and more focused. Ironically, the rays of a new sun were beginning to lighten up the darkness when they finally took the three dark decisions that would change the lives of thousands of people in different parts of the world – the three last straws that were destined to finally break the camel's back.

The First Big Straw

THREE DAYS LATER. BRUSSELS

IT WAS A WELL-KNOWN FACT THAT THE MAN WHO MADE THE call was working for the American CIA. Even if he was not on the muster roll of that honourable organization, there was no denying that he had fronted for them on a number of deals where they did not wish to appear themselves.

'We need the arms to be delivered to the Afghan army in the next three months.' Like his appearance, his tone was accent-neutral and he had that peculiar easy-to-forget personality which was ideal for the line of work he was in.

'What kind of quantities are we talking about here?' the Russian representing Rosoboronexport, the Russian defence industry giant, asked. He had dealt with the American trouble-shooter before and they shared a decent working relationship, even if there was no trace of camaraderie evident.

'To begin with, about 78 million rounds of AK-47 ammunition, 100,000 rocket-propelled grenades and 12,000 tank shells,' the CIA man replied, his tone casual.

'Wow!' The Russian gave a low whistle as he absorbed the size of the order. The quantity was roughly equal to fifteen times the British army's annual requirements. 'You guys planning to start a war out there?'

'There *is* a war going on out there, in case you haven't noticed,' the American retorted. Both men laughed. There was nothing even remotely pleasant about the laughter. 'Can we have the quote ASAP?'

'Of course you can,' the Russian replied happily, visualizing the huge bonus he would make from this deal. 'You are in a real hurry on this, aren't you?'

The other man did not bother to respond. He didn't have to. It was no secret that the present US administration was in a hurry simply because they had no clue what the incoming Democratic regime would do about Afghanistan and Iraq once they took charge. It didn't seem likely that the Democrats would pull out, but they could reduce support levels for the locals.

'Look!' the American finally said. 'You can imagine what you want to, but you need to make damn sure the deliveries begin in the next two to three weeks... if your quote is right, that is.'

Right! Arsehole! Where else do you think you can buy the stuff? At the neighbourhood 7-11? The Russian didn't speak out loud of course. *So what if he is an arsehole? His money is just as good.* 'Don't worry about it. The quote will be with you first thing tomorrow.'

'Good!' the American replied haughtily. He left the meeting satisfied that he had done his job well.

A FORTNIGHT LATER, AN ADDITIONAL 29,000 US TROOPS WERE inducted into Iraq.

On the face of it, the induction was justified by the worsening security situation in Iraq. But none of these troops was moved into any of the active theatres in Iraq. In fact, within days of their landing, the complete US contingent moved out to various locations and began induction and familiarization training. It was no coincidence that most of these training areas happened to be on the borders that Iraq shares with Iran. Slowly but surely, the noose was beginning to tighten.

The Second Big Straw

THREE WEEKS LATER. 2336 HOURS. HATZERIM AIRBASE, NEGEV DESERT, ISRAEL

THE HIDEOUS SCREAM OF ENGINES DROWNED OUT ALL SOUND. A series of thunderclaps shattered the night as the afterburners kicked in. Four fighters slashed down the runway in pairs. Lifting off in meticulous unison, the F-16Is clawed their way into the coal-black night.

Silence returned with equal suddenness as they receded into the darkness.

Codenamed Sufa (Storm) by the Israeli Air Force, the heavily modified F-16I with massive conformal fuel tanks has a combat radius of approximately 2100 km. The highly versatile aircraft is a deadly fighting machine capable of functioning in the most intensive warfare scenarios. It carries on board an amazing array of weapons that can wreak mind-numbing destruction.

That particular evening the four fighters of the 69 Squadron were carrying a highly specialized weapons load. The 69 Squadron, also known as

The Hammers, had seen more than its fair share of action since it was formed in 1948. Leading the four fighters tonight was their squadron commander, Ilan Yarkoni, a man with several combat sorties under his belt.

Tonight was not the first time that a military aircraft had taken to the skies with nuclear weapons since that fateful day in August 1945 when the nuclear bomb named Little Boy (a gun-type fission weapon with sixty kilograms of Uranium-235 that had a blast equivalent of about thirteen kilotons of TNT) had been dropped over Hiroshima from a B-29 plane piloted by Colonel Paul Tibbets of the US-509 Composite Group. Ironically, the plane had been affectionately nicknamed Enola Gay after Tibbets' mother. The bomb it dropped that day left many children motherless and many mothers childless.

However, tonight *was* the first time since then that such weapons were being carried with a firm, committed resolve to put them to use.

All four F-16s attained cruising height and levelled out. They were following a carefully plotted course. None of the men who rode in those metallic monsters had any doubts as to what awaited them as they sliced through the still, dark night. If any of them had been the betting kind they would not have put any money on their chances of returning home alive.

I just hope we are able to complete the mission. Ilan shrugged away the thought as he settled deeper into the seat. *We have to... failure is not an option.*

NINETEEN MINUTES LATER

'SIERRA TANGO STRIKE TEAM, YOU'RE NOW APPROACHING merger point. Four minutes and closing.'

The coded transmission from the unknown controller hundreds of miles away crackled into the headphones of the four flying fighters. None of them bothered to reply. Strict radio silence was in place. A few seconds later, the large, unsuspecting target appeared on their screens. With its strobe lights flashing majestically, the massive passenger aircraft was proceeding sedately along its path.

The four fighters closed ranks and came together in a tight diamond formation. As one, they angled sharply up and towards the right. Four minutes later they were in position.

'Sierra Tango, you are radar negative now. Hold steady.'

Twenty-seven minutes later, the point of no return was crossed as the four Israeli aircraft entered enemy airspace. The strike had begun.

LUFTHANSA FLIGHT LH-600 HAD TAKEN OFF FROM FRANKFURT airport at 1802 hours, two minutes behind schedule. The pilot hoped to make up the two minutes during the flight to ensure it reached Tehran at the stipulated time of 0125 hours. The flight was being managed with Teutonic efficiency and proceeding without incident. The Boeing 340 was cruising smoothly at an altitude of about 30,000 feet when it entered Iranian airspace a little after midnight.

There were exactly one hundred and eighty-seven passengers on board, including eighty-three women and sixteen children. Most of them were fast asleep, though a few were surfing the in-flight movies. In any case, none of them was aware of the Israeli F-16Is that had linked up with it a few minutes short of entering Iranian airspace and were now flying in the shadow of the huge jet. All four fighters were flying in a dense pack immediately below the jetliner. This ensured that their radar profiles merged with that of the Lufthansa craft.

Seventeen minutes into Iranian airspace.

'Sierra Tango, time to hit the deck.' The unseen controller rapped out the command.

There was a second's pause. Then, as one, the jet pack broke cover. Falling away from the jetliner, the four fighters fell into a steep dive angling away to the right.

The last leg of their journey had begun.

ON THE GROUND, THERE WAS A MOMENT OF TOTAL consternation as the four fighters suddenly erupted on a dozen radar screens of the Iranian air defence system.

However, the confusion did not last very long. Memories of the Israeli air strike of 7 June 1981 on the Osirak nuclear reactor in Iraq[2] were still sharp in the minds of the Iranians.

A few seconds later, the Iranian radars had identified the intruders and got a fix on their likely destination. Alarms began to scream as the air defence system kicked into play. Almost immediately the instrument panels of all four Israeli fighters lit up as they began tracking the inbound radar hits and missiles. Disregarding the cacophony of alarms flooding the cockpits, the four fighters dived straight towards the target lying in wait for them below. *Their lives were not important. The mission was.*

The Iranian air defence system was nowhere as sophisticated as the fighters it was up against. A legacy of the CENTO (Central Treaty Organization[3]), the Iranian early warning system was established in 1950 and had last been upgraded in 1970. It comprised a number of Chinese SA-2 missiles, Russian SA-5 and SA-6 SAMs, the highly capable

[2] Operation Opera (also known as Operation Babylon and Operation Ofra) was the code name given to the 7 June 1981 air strike on the Iraqi nuclear reactor at Osirak. A squadron of F-16A multi-role fighters used in ground assault, escorted by F-15A tactical fighters, had bombed and heavily damaged the Iraqi reactor.

[3] Iraq, Turkey, Pakistan, Iran and the UK adopted the Central Treaty Organisation, originally known as the Middle East Treaty Organisation, in 1955. The US joined the central committee in 1958. It is generally viewed as one of the least successful alliances of the Cold War.

SA-10 Grumble missile system and twenty-nine newly inducted TOR M1 systems. The areas most heavily defended were obviously Tehran, and the various R&D and production centres like Bushehr and Natanz, which were critical components of the Iranian Nuclear Biological and Chemical (NBC) weapons program. However, there was no nationwide integrated air defence network. Consequently, the Iranians relied almost entirely on point defence of key locations using SAM batteries while the SA-10 and TOR M1s posed a highly potent threat when deployed in an integrated array.

The Achilles heel of the Iranian system was its inability to generate effective real-time early warning and act as a fully integrated system. This allowed the attacker a window of opportunity. The window was only a few seconds long, but in such high speed aerial warfare scenarios, it is usually these few vital seconds that count. They are what tilt the balance between success and failure, life and death.

The scream of a dozen alarms filled the cockpits and the minds of the four fighter pilots as they raced towards their objective at supersonic speeds. Each of them tried to shut out the urgently clamouring beeps as they activated electronic countermeasures. For those few fragile seconds technologies clashed as the Israeli jet fighters sought to elude the Iranian weapons seeking them out. Jammers and active array radars glowed into action either to blind the electronic eyes seeking them out or decoy them. Chaff and flares spewed out of the aircrafts, drawing the incoming missiles away from them.

The Israelis exploited the only two factors in their favour: the slim window of opportunity that the Iranian system gave them and the shock of the tactical surprise they had managed to achieve when they had fallen out from below the Lufthansa jetliner.

Suddenly the target was right there in front of them.

'Commence home run.' Ilan's voice snapped into the headsets of Sierra Tango.

Twisting through the flak-riddled air, the four F-16Is snarled rapidly into attack profile and, splitting into pairs, began the final approach.

ILAN SAW THE TINY BALL OF FIRE FLARE OUT FROM THE DARKNESS below and arc up into the sky. Like a bolt of lightning it raced towards them with incredible speed and silently coalesced with the aircraft it had targeted. For one tiny fraction of a second the hunter and the hunted slid through the air together in perfect harmony. Then there was a blinding explosion. Bits of blood, bone and metal confettied out into the darkness.

Ilan saw the plane on his left mushroom into nothingness. One moment it was there and the next there was just an uneasy dark cloud hanging in the air. His jet tore through the night, soon leaving the flaming debris behind.

In his mind's eye, Ilan saw the missile slam into the jet. He heard Sierra Two's scream as the plane disintegrated around him. Ilan's body cringed as it waited for another missile to seek him out. His heart egged his fighter on towards the target racing towards them at twice the speed of sound.

Then a mosaic of anti-aircraft fire ripped apart the night. It seemed like a blizzard of fireflies was slashing through the skies, tearing it up into random shapes.

Suddenly he felt his mind expand and take charge. It seemed to be willing away everything that the Iranians were throwing at him. A strange icy calm settled over him. It froze everything around him, yet left him intensely aware and alive. Ilan could clearly feel each individual heartbeat as it thrummed through his body. He was acutely aware of the droplets of blood pulsing through the vein in his temple, of each icy-cold breath that swept through him. The Zen-like calm shrouding him deepened as the target loomed larger and larger on the instrument panel in front of him. His fingers flexed and stressed as they itched to trigger the bomb release. He wanted the bombs held in the belly of his aircraft to be on their way before his luck ran out.

Not yet!

His mind stilled his fingers as the target moved relentlessly into the gun sights on the electronic display glowing before him.

Not yet!

Slowly... unbelievably slowly... with each nanosecond spanning a century... the electronic cross-hairs began to settle on the target.

Almost there!

The weapons-targeting computers told him the time was right.

NOW!

The unspoken command jolted out of Ilan's mind and raced towards his waiting fingers. Simultaneously the shroud of calm enveloping him lifted away, as though its job was done.

Frantic fingers jabbed at the weapons release. There was a very slight, almost imperceptible jerk and lightening up of the aircraft as the bombs fell away. A fraction of a second later, the pair of F-16Is behind him also triggered their weapons release.

Ilan was so intent on his task that he did not see the blizzard of TOR M-1 missiles geyser out of their launchers. The second wave of Iranian missiles raced forward, converging on the Israeli jets like rapidly increasing pinpricks of light. With a hit probability of over ninety-two per cent there was little chance of the missiles missing the low flying jets as they screamed over the target area.

They didn't.

Ilan did not even realize the exact moment when his aircraft disintegrated. Nor did the pilots of the remaining two fighters, although one almost managed to get clear. He was zooming heavenwards in a perfect vertical charlie and was nearly out of range when the dying anti-aircraft missile sought him out and speeded up his journey to his maker.

They all died without knowing whether they had managed to complete their assigned task.

FALLING AWAY FROM THE F-16IS, THE B61-11 BUNKER BUSTERS righted themselves and swooped down towards their designated target.

The B61-11 is supposed to be a modification of the B61-7 bomb that was first pressed into service by the Americans in 1985. It can be fused for an air or a surface burst and has a hardened ground-penetrator nose with a retarded contact burst fusing option. It can be deployed with or without a parachute and can be configured with a variety of yields from 0.3 to 340 kilotons. The B61-11's unique earth-penetrating characteristics and its wide range of yields allow it to threaten seemingly indestructible targets from the air. In fact, this is the raison d'etre of the B61-11.

Considering the altitude at which they were to be released today, the B61-11s had been deployed without parachutes. They slid through the turbulent air and homed in effortlessly on their designated target. A few seconds later, there was a series of blinding flashes and huge balls of fire exploded above the ground. The explosions that burrowed into the ground were much more severe, but nobody remained alive to testify to this.

Though buried under seventy feet of reinforced concrete, the Natanz enrichment facility had ceased to exist by the time the dust and smoke settled. The radiation would take much, much longer to disappear.

The Final Straw

ALMOST SIMULTANEOUSLY. ISLAMABAD AIRPORT, PAKISTAN

THERE WAS A FAIRLY DECENT CROWD OF JOURNALISTS AND A whole bunch of American and Pakistani security men waiting on the tarmac when the doors of the sleek corporate jet slid open and the man emerged. The jaunty spring in his step and the energetic wave he gave them belied his age, which was clearly on the wrong side of sixty. His superbly fitted suit and general demeanour subtly but clearly bespoke the old money that he came from. He had about him the undeniable aura of a man who was not to be taken lightly, a man who it would be hard to say no to.

Richard Wentworth the Third, a true blue Boston Brahmin, touted as one of the richest men in the world, was currently on the board of one of the largest corporations of America. In his previous avtaar he had been an advisor to two successive US Presidents and he had acquitted himself quite capably, if not honourably, both times. The honour part was understandably hard for him to live up to, given that both those esteemed gentlemen and their administrations had assiduously supported a number of brutal dictators and illegitimate regimes, with arms and money. One of these august gentlemen had even been indicted for this and certain other below-the-belt activities that his electorate did not find particularly appetizing.

Wentworth's arrival in Islamabad was a much-publicized event and was touted by Pakistan's military regime as a historic achievement. Wentworth had arrived like Santa Claus, albeit a few weeks late, to announce one of the largest ever foreign investments packages for Pakistan. This gigantic investment would not only provide jobs to several thousand people but also prop up the sagging economy.

The Pakistani General currently at the helm spared no effort to let the world know that all this had been made possible only due to the support extended by his country to the global community in the fight against terror. The General also planned to use this visit to extend some measure of legitimacy to his dictatorial regime.

With news of the aerial assault on Iran just starting to trickle in, it was not surprising that a barrage of flash bulbs and questions greeted him. Adroitly side-stepping them, Wentworth strode rapidly to the awaiting limousine. Surrounded by a cordon of US Marines, the impressive motorcade took off towards the US Consulate located in Islamabad's Diplomatic Enclave, meeting an abundance of security personnel en route. And rightly so, since Pakistan's atmospheric conditions, even on the best of days, was not conducive to the health of Americans. These days, in the wake of the government's crackdown on the terror groups operating in Pakistan and the fact that US forces were operating against the Taliban from Pakistani soil, the climate was decidedly unhealthy. The Israeli air strike on Iran had simply ignited the already smouldering embers of anger.

Four hours later, at an equally impressive ceremony, Richard Wentworth the Third laid the foundation stone for the new Technology City that would soon rise in the relative wilderness west of Islamabad. The press conference held in conclusion of this ceremony lasted almost as long as the inauguration and had more than enough sound bytes for the Pakistani government to exploit over the coming months.

IT WAS ONLY NATURAL THAT A PERSON BESTOWING SUCH largesse on their economy be accorded the courtesy of breaking bread with the Pakistani Dictator. Promptly at the stroke of eight, Wentworth found himself at the General's official digs. The dinner was a sumptuous affair and a delight for Wentworth's discerning palate. Keeping in view Richard's desire, quietly communicated by his staff to the General's when they had been coordinating his schedule, the dinner was a quiet affair.

The meeting that took place just after dinner was even quieter. It was held in the room which the

General, with his literary pretensions, referred to as his library. The room had been assiduously swept and was clear of any kind of electronic surveillance device.

Wentworth was almost halfway through his cigar when he came to the point. 'The big man needs a very special favour from you, General.' His tone was quiet. The atmosphere in the room altered almost immediately.

'What kind of favour?' The General inadvertently leaned forward a little.

'You know that things are not going too well for him back home these days. There are too many body bags coming in from Afghanistan and Iraq and not enough to show for it all.'

The General nodded, his face deadpan. Only the gleam in his eyes indicated his heightened interest. 'Are you referring to the matter we spoke about last month?'

Wentworth nodded briefly. He was a wily adversary and knew when the fish was about to bite.

'Come on, Richard,' the General protested quietly. 'You know there is no way I can do that. Why is he so insistent on this?'

'You know why. Too much has been expended... too many lives have been lost. The big man is out on a limb on this one. He does not want to go down in history as the one who screwed up.' Wentworth gave him a long look. 'He wants to end his tenure in a blaze of glory.'

'Blaze of glory!' The General chuckled dryly. 'Richard, you cannot even imagine how big the blaze will be! There will be hell to pay.' He clicked his tongue impatiently. 'As it is we are having too many problems of our own and what you people have just started in Iran is not going to make things any easier.'

Wentworth drew on his cigar. 'Maybe we can help with some of those problems....' There was a question mark at the end of his statement.

'What kind of help are we talking about here?'

'You tell me, General... what do you have in mind?'

'What about a nuclear deal like the one you have offered India?'

An explosive snorting laugh erupted from Wentworth. It was clear that he had been expecting something like this. 'Get real, General. You know that's not going to happen... not with the changed equation and political climate. Ever since the election results, the present administration considers itself lucky if it can buy toilet paper without prior approval from the Democrats.'

'Then what incentive is there for us? You know there will be hell to pay... the incentive has to adequately compensate for what we'll have to deal with later.'

'There is still a lot we can do, General. I can give you many reasons for giving the big man what he wants.' There was a brief pause before Wentworth spoke again. 'I can give you a billion reasons,' he said softly.

A sudden silence stilled the room. It remained unbroken long after the sharp gleam of avarice had faded from the General's eyes. Wentworth carefully focused on stubbing out his cigar. Finally the General spoke again. 'Is that what my life is worth? And that of my family?' He seemed to be speaking more to himself than to the other man in the room.

'What is anybody's life worth, General?' the US emissary said softly. The carrot and the stick, both had been pulled out. Wentworth was now looking unblinkingly at the General.

He's taken the bait. Now we need to go through the face saving motions.

They did.

An hour later, when Richard Wentworth the Third walked out of the Pakistani President's room, he had achieved what he had come for. The man he was representing was no friend of his. In fact, deep down Wentworth detested the man as much as he did his politics and policies.

But what the hell, it's always good to have a man as powerful as the President of America indebted to you.

THE NEXT MORNING, WENTWORTH WAS ON THE PHONE bright and early. It took him just a few phone calls to ensure that the promised billion dollars were safely lodged in the four numbered accounts specified by the General. Then he picked up the phone again and dialled.

'Yes, Richard?' the General's voice answered. He had obviously been waiting for the call.

'I called to thank you for your hospitality, General, and to bid you farewell.'

'The pleasure was ours, Richard. You must come again.'

'But of course!' There was a slight pause. 'It has been a very productive visit. You can rest assured we shall deliver on all our commitments. In fact, we've already completed our part of the current transaction.'

'I know you have, Richard, I already have a confirmation from my ban....' He broke off. 'Here, I think you'd better note this down, Richard.' There was a slight rustling of paper at the other end. 'Do you have a paper and pen handy?' The General paused till there was a soft uh-huh from the other end, then he slowly read out an address.

'Thank you very much, General,' Wentworth said after he had read back the address to confirm it. 'The chief will really appreciate this.'

'Not a problem, Richard, just remind him that this stays between the three of us. It could be decidedly fata....' The General broke off in mid-sentence, searching for a more palatable word. 'Problematic,' he finally concluded.

'Don't worry, General. I will carry this to my grave.'

'I'm sure you will,' the General murmured. 'Oh yes, Richard, did I mention that the man you seek is sick?'

'You didn't, General.'

'Didn't I? Well he is sick; very, very sick. In fact, for a very long time now he has had little to do with any real operational matters. Taking him is not going to hamper their operational or organizational capability in any way.'

'That doesn't really matter, General, it's about not losing face. We cannot allow him to get away. America needs to send out a message.'

'Oh well!' the General replied. 'Whatever you do, for God's sake, don't make a martyr out of him. That would be the last straw.'

'On the contrary, General, the aim is to bring him in, make him live through the humiliation of standing trial and then punish him like the common criminal that he is.'

The two men spoke for a couple of minutes more. Richard did not put down the handset after the call was over. He dialled another number. The phone was answered immediately. The man who answered the phone did not speak much. He simply took down the address of the house in Hyderabad that Wentworth read out to him.

WENTWORTH HAD A PLEASED BUT THOUGHTFUL AIR ABOUT him as he put down the phone and finished dressing. An hour later he left his room, and after a couple of inane ceremonies, Richard Wentworth the Third departed from Islamabad in his private jet.

The sparkling jet climbed rapidly to cruising altitude. It had just cleared Pakistan's maritime limits and entered international air space when the explosion ripped through the midsection of the aircraft, slicing it in two neat halves. Both halves cartwheeled through thousands of feet before hitting the sparkling waters of the Indian Ocean below. They bobbed and lingered on the surface for a few moments before the deep claimed them.

Richard Wentworth the Third had kept his promise to the General; he had carried their deadly secret to the grave with him.

EARLY NEXT MORNING. HYDERABAD, PAKISTAN

THE ADDRESS THAT RICHARD WENTWORTH THE THIRD HAD passed on to the man during his final phone call was of a house located at the end of a quiet, but extremely expensive suburb of Hyderabad. Compared to the other houses in the area, it was not very big, but it was surrounded by huge sprawling lawns on all sides. Running all around the lawns was a high boundary wall. Beyond the walls lay vacant lots on three sides. The walls were much higher than those of other houses in the area, but this in itself was not reason enough for any questions to be asked. Nor did the occupants ever do anything to draw any special attention to the house.

At that early hour, not too many people were up and about. So nobody saw the two Toyota Hiace minibuses that drove up to the northern end of the lane. The vehicles, popularly known as the Wagon, were of a type often seen on these roads, except that these were exceptionally well-maintained and ran on smooth, almost soundless engines.

The sixteen men who emerged from the vehicles were equally quiet. The weapons they carried and the Kevlar body armour they were wearing were not entirely out of place in this part of the world. After all, security forces are known to be up and about at strange hours in the strangest of places.

In fact, the only thing that *would* have drawn attention to them was the fact that, barring one, all of them were distinctly Caucasian in appearance. *That* was definitely noteworthy, but there was no one around to notice it.

At precisely the same time, the same scenario was played out on the other three sides of the house. The only difference was that on each of the other approaches to the house from the south, east and west, there was only one vehicle with eight men.

As the vehicles approaching the house slid to a silent halt, the Kevlar-clad men within spilled out equally silently and raced towards their designated positions. The wide assortment of assault weapons carried by them would have let a discerning watcher know that a highly specialized Special Forces team was going into action.

Turning rapidly on his heels to check that everyone was in position, the man who was obviously the leader of the sixteen-man team keyed his radio set. 'North! We're ready to roll,' he whispered softly into the mouthpiece.

'South ready.'

'East clear!'

'Ditto West!'

The staccato responses came in hard and fast. Voices were terse and betrayed the battle nerves that had begun to jangle with H-hour looming large. The North man keyed his radio set again. 'Eagle, this is North leader. We're ready.'

'Roger that, North.' There was a very brief pause, as though the man at the other end was talking to someone else. Then: 'It's a go. All teams go. Best of luck.'

Tapping the transmit key of his radio set twice in acknowledgment, the North team leader turned to his group and said softly but clearly, 'We're on.'

Pivoting rapidly, the first two men took up position near the boundary wall and, using their hands, hoisted the next two men over it. The two dropped soundlessly onto the other side of the wall. There was a brief, very soft rustle of clothing. Then silence returned as the other fourteen men waited. The tension was palpable.

The assault had begun.

ON THE OTHER SIDE OF THE WALL, LANDING SOFTLY, CAT-like, the two men slung their weapons across their chests so that they could bring them into action instantly when the need arose. In their hands razor sharp serrated commando knives gleamed in the early morning light. Moving like wraiths, they raced soundlessly across to the front and rear of the house. Both gates were closed. At the front gate there were two sentries, but there was only one at the rear.

The rear gate sentry only discovered he was not alone when a hand suddenly clamped down on his mouth. By then it was too late. The knife sliced open a neat gash across his throat, from which the blood emerged initially as a thin red line but soon gushed out in a shocking downpour. The blood continued to flow long after life had ended. Lowering the man's body silently to the ground, the commando dragged it out of sight behind the bushes. Crouching behind the bushes, he hit the transmit button of his radio. 'North two clear.'

THE COMMANDO AT THE REAR GATE WAS LOWERING THE BODY to the ground when, on the other side of the house, there was a very soft, almost inaudible, metallic cough. The first sentry at the front gate gasped and slowly crumpled to the ground. His companion standing about ten feet away saw him go down, but the omnipresent early morning fog impeded visibility so he was unable to see clearly. Walking across with a puzzled look on his face, he knelt down and was reaching for the fallen man when he saw the small, neat hole in the man's forehead.

The second sentry let go of the dead man as though he himself had been shot and was opening his mouth to raise the alarm when another soft cough intruded on the silence. The sentry fell wordlessly to the ground. He was dead before his body hit the ground.

A few feet away, the commando watched impassively, waiting for any signs of life. There were none. Like his comrade at the rear gate, he too tapped the transmit button of the radio strapped to his belt. 'North one clear.'

MOVING RAPIDLY THROUGH THE SHADOWS, BOTH MEN OF the advance guard reached the rear of the house. The water spout was exactly where the satellite picture had indicated. The first man kept guard as the second one swarmed up the pipe silently. Emerging like a ghost, the commando peeped over the parapet and scanned the roof.

The sentry manning the roof was pacing across the front. His rifle was slung across his shoulder, but the man was alert, stopping every so often to scan the garden below before crisscrossing to the other side of the roof and repeating the exercise. The commando waited till the sentry was at the far end of the roof before he hauled himself over the parapet. He landed lightly on the roof, his silenced pistol reappearing in his hand.

He fired even as the sentry was turning to begin his patrol back towards him. The subdued cough of the silenced pistol was lost in the night. The tiny lead bullet met the sentry just when he was clear of the wall. It drilled a neat hole in his head, killing him almost instantly.

The commando had launched himself forward even as the bullet left the muzzle. Racing across on soundless feet, he caught the falling sentry. Lowering him to the ground, he hissed into his transmitter.

'Roof clear, North.'

AS THE THIRD TRANSMISSION ECHOED IN HIS HEADSET, THE north team leader turned and signalled to the men crouching around him. Coming alive almost as one, the fourteen fighters swarmed across the wall and raced across the garden towards the house lying still and silent before them. The night vision gear strapped around their heads lent them an eerie, outlandish appearance.

None of them could have known that one of the occupants on the first floor would choose to get up and head for the toilet just then. The man was crossing one of the windows overlooking the front garden when he spotted the dark, ghostly shapes rushing silently across the lawns. The man was no genius, but it did not take him even a second to realize that they could mean nothing but trouble.

The solitary shot rang out in the still morning air with extraordinary loudness. Hard in its wake followed the loud cry of alarm as the shooter alerted the other occupants of the house. But this was no ragtag bunch of soldiers. They were superbly trained and reacted with all the speed, skill and ferocity at their command.

North team raced ahead in sharp, irregular spurts, returning the fire with short bursts, instinctively aiming at the pinpricks of light that had begun to illuminate the dark house.

'Eagle, we're going in hot now,' the team leader hissed into his headset as they ran forward.

'Roger that, North. We're on our way.' Eagle's tinny voice was almost lost in the rapidly escalating thunder of gunfire as a continuous volley of shots followed the brief lull after the first one. Every now and then, a scream punctuated the cacophony.

The first three commandos fell almost immediately. Two of them were saved by the Kevlar jackets cocooning their torsos. They stumbled to their feet and followed their comrades who were racing towards the house. The third one was beyond caring. The two neat holes near his right eye put him beyond any help.

Pausing briefly near the window, the first commando tossed two Flash-and-Bang stun grenades through it. The strike team counted down the mandatory four seconds before they slammed against the door, blowing it open just a fraction of a second after the grenades exploded.

The team rushed in with weapons primed. Figures in various stages of undress greeted them. They were cut down almost instantly as the commandos swept through the house.

The man they had come for was on the first floor of the house. He was still in bed, trying weakly to unhook the infusion pump attached to him. The man's disease-wracked face was pale and he was breathing torturously. He seemed to be in tremendous pain, but that did nothing to diminish the hate smouldering in his eyes.

He wasn't wearing the flowing white robes that he was always photographed in, nor was his flowing beard as well-groomed as it appeared in these photographs. But there was no mistaking the sharp angular features, which for the past few years had adorned the pages of almost every newspaper and magazine in the world.

For a long moment North leader checked the face in the light of the small torch as the two others in the room kept guard at the door.

There was no doubt about it.

'It's him,' he said tersely, unable to keep the triumph out of his voice. 'Doc, he is all yours now.' He nodded at the medic as he turned and got on to his radio set. 'Eagle, we have him. Get your ass here pronto. LZ One.'

'Great job, North.' Eagle's voice crackled with excitement. 'We're already on the way. LZ One. ETA in three.'

The team leader watched as the medic rapidly checked out the man on the bed. He began with the mouth, checking for suicide pills. Then he moved on to the rest of the body. The captive watched with hatred and helpless anger glowing in his eyes.

'Hurry up, damn it, we don't have all day.'

'I'm done.' Hurriedly finishing his examination, the medic motioned to the team leader. 'Help me get him onto the stretcher.'

'What's this fucking contraption?' North grabbed at the infusion pump connected to the captive.

'Hey, careful! Gimme a moment. Let me check....'

'Fuck it! There's no time. We need to get the hell out of here.'

'Just give me a....'

'Move it, doc!' the commando grated harshly, chucking the still connected infusion pump onto the bedsheet. 'You can do all that shit on the chopper. Grab the sheet from that end and let's move him. *Now!*'

They used the sheet to pick him up and move him onto the stretcher. Grabbing opposite ends of the stretcher, they began to shuffle out with their catch, moving as rapidly as they could.

'Go! Go! Go!' North hustled as they went down the steps and out into the front garden.

In the heat of the moment the medic did not notice that the nitroglycerine drip in the infusion pump was running dry. The doctor attending to the sick man had been getting up to replenish the drip when the assault began. Now he lay just a few feet away, three bullets embedded in his chest.

By now the gunfire had almost petered out. Barring a sporadic shot here and there, an uneasy silence had fallen upon the house.

They were bringing the barely conscious captive out into the lawns when the SH-60 Sea Hawk helicopter swept out of the now lightening sky and settled noisily onto the lawn. The North team leader and the medic got into the chopper with the captive. There was a very brief delay as the body of the fallen commando was taken on board. The chopper took off immediately. The remaining commandos of North Team raced back towards their waiting vehicles.

'Eagle to Dominos. Get your butts out of here. Code Red. I say again, Code Red.'

A series of taps acknowledged the transmission as South, East and West abandoned the positions they had taken up around the house as a precaution to ensure that no one got away. Then the wagons pulled back and raced away into the gathering light. Moving out of the area rapidly, they split up and moved along predetermined routes, though all of them had the same destination to reach.

Precisely eleven minutes had elapsed since the vehicles had drawn to a halt outside the house. In a mere eleven minutes a handful of men had achieved what thousands of soldiers had been trying to do for the past few years. The man with a twenty-seven million dollar reward on his head had been taken.

'We will hunt them down and smoke 'em out,' the US President had vowed in front of the smouldering remains of the twin towers in New York. For once, he had delivered. Of course, neither he nor his advisors had any idea of the horrendous price that his countrymen would pay for it.

Meanwhile, the helicopter carrying the most wanted man on earth raced away from the house, heading straight for the US aircraft carrier hovering just off the coast of Pakistan.

'Eagle to Nest. We have him!'

'*Good job, Eagle*!' The man at the other end could not keep the delight out of his voice. 'Bring him in.'

'Roger that, Control. We're on our way.'

The man at Control was having trouble keeping the grin off his face as he reached for the phone and dialled Langley. He could visualize the huge press conference at which they would announce the news. His chest swelled with pride as the phone at the other end was picked up.

THE CHOPPER HAD BARELY CLEARED THE CITY LIMITS WHEN the nitrogylcerine being pumped into the captive by the fusion pump ran out. The man on the stretcher began to gasp for breath.

'Goddamn!' the medic exclaimed. 'His blood pressure is shooting up.' He slapped the oxygen mask on, but it did little to alleviate the situation. Soon the captive began to struggle on the stretcher.

'Hold him down!' the team leader yelled. 'What the hell is he doing?'

'He must be having problems breathing while lying down, that's why he's trying to sit up,' the medic explained breathlessly as he fought to keep the mask on his wildly thrashing patient.

Almost on cue, the captive began to cough. Blobs of sputum sprayed out of his mouth. Not much later, the frothy sputum began to bubble pink.

'Fuck! We're losing him.' The medic was frantic.

'Do something, damn you!' the commando yelled in helpless anger. 'We need the sonofabitch alive.'

'There's nothing I can do.' The medic was panting almost as hard as the patient. His forte was gunshots, knife wounds and broken bones. Nothing in his life so far had prepared him for the renal failure he was confronted with. 'He needs a doctor and a bloody hospital.'

Just then the chopper touched down and moments later, the barely alive prisoner was in the ship's hospital with a coterie of doctors and medics hovering anxiously around.

THE CHOPPER WAS ALMOST AT THE PAKISTANI COASTLINE BY the time the police, summoned by a frantic neighbourhood, reached the house. A posse of policemen stumbled through the horrifyingly large number of bodies scattered all around. It was only when they reported the matter to the local police chief that the shit hit the ceiling. The police chief knew that this was an ISI safe house, though he had no clue exactly who occupied it. He immediately called the ISI area commander.

'*What?*' The stunned ISI man who took the call couldn't believe what he was hearing. 'Are you sure? Are you absolutely sure?' he kept asking as he raced towards his car, throwing on whatever clothes he could lay his hands on. En route to the now totally unsafe safe house, he was on the phone almost constantly. By the time he pulled up outside the house, almost everybody who was anybody in the ISI had been informed of the catastrophe.

Reaching there, he raced from one body to the other like a madman.

Finally, having exhausted all possibilities, he called his boss. 'He's not here, sir.'

'Are you sure?' his boss snapped. 'Check again.'

'I have, sir. He is definitely not here… not among the dead and definitely not among the living. Three of those who are still alive confirm that he's been taken captive.'

'But who?' his flabbergasted commander asked him. 'Who could it be and how the fuck did they know where we were keeping him?'

'I have no clue, sir,' he repeated for what seemed like the hundredth time. 'I have no clue at all, but this is disastrous.'

On this count at least, the beleaguered ISI agent was right.

SOMEWHERE IN THE INDIAN OCEAN, ON BOARD USS *DWIGHT D EISENHOWER*

THERE WAS A STRAINED LOOK ON HIS FACE WHEN THE SHIP'S doctor noted the contents of the now empty infusion pump. The blue tongue and the pink frothy sputum spewing out completed the picture.

'Lasix!' he yelled urgently. '100 mg! Fast!'

It was in his hand almost instantly and he thumped it into the captive without finesse, but the Lasix didn't help much. Despite the frantic burst of activity around, they all knew they were losing the man. They could only watch him struggle, each gasping breath a litany of pain.

It surprised no one when a harsh beeping sound was heard from the monitor beside the bed. In front of their helpless eyes, the sharp green line undulating across the screen in irregular but distinct peaks and troughs flattened into a straight expressionless line. The regular beep of the monitor settled into a dreadful monotonous whine.

'Holy shit!'

'No!'

The most wanted man in the world was no more.

'THERE WAS NOTHING WE COULD HAVE DONE!' THE DOCTOR told the Captain hovering outside, then, seeing the befuddled look on his face, he added, 'Accelerated hypertension as a result of chronic renal failure. The man needed that nitroglycerine drip to keep him going. Without that they might as well have left him where he was.'

'Shit!' The Captain looked at him despairingly. The USS Eisenhower had finished a tour of duty as part of the John C. Stennis Strike Group and had been on her way home after being relieved by the USS Nimitz when they got orders to divert for this assignment. '*Shit!* Let me get on the horn and check with the brass. Let *them* decide what has to be done...

that's what they are paid for. Right?' He gave the doctor a weak, almost scared grin. 'I just hope they believe he died of natural causes.'

The Captain could hope as much as he wanted to, but no one was going to believe it. As far as the dead man's followers were concerned, the Americans had murdered him.

A COUPLE OF HOURS LATER, IN WASHINGTON, THE LARGE hall designated for press conferences was packed to overflowing with an astonishing assortment of journalists of all shapes, sizes and hues, from all corners of the globe.

The volume of sound shot up to a crescendo when the US Secretary of State entered, and a ragged volley of questions were fired at her. It took a lot of hand waving and gesticulating before some semblance of quiet settled upon the room. The Secretary of State waited till the silence deepened. When she finally spoke, her voice was carefully controlled.

'The administration has lived up to the promise that the President made to the people of America. The terrorist wanted for the horrendous 9/11 attacks has finally been captured. An American Special Forces team seized him in a pre-dawn raid and successfully extricated him to a US warship. The US government had every intention of bringing the man to trial for his horrible crimes. Unfortunately, he was suffering from severe medical problems at the time of capture and, despite the best medical facilities being made available to him, he succumbed to his condition a couple of hours ago. The body is....'

That was about as far as she managed to get before a fresh storm of questions erupted. This time there was no controlling the hysterical mob in its quest for information. The noise levels rose to unbelievable proportions until the Secretary of State realized it was futile to go on. She beat a hasty retreat, leaving the journalists at the mercy of the bland press handouts that her staff would soon start passing around.

A SHOCKWAVE OF CONFLICTING EMOTIONS SWEPT ACROSS THE globe, evoking reactions of all kinds. Coupled with the news of the Israeli strike on Iran, the emotional upsurge it caused, especially in the Middle East, was huge. Security agencies all over the world went into overdrive. Everyone knew that all stops would be pulled out this time.

Almost on cue and as though orchestrated, public outrage assumed alarming proportions. Thousands of armed people stormed the streets of cities in Pakistan, Afghanistan, Iraq, Indonesia and a host of other nations. The sheer deluge of irate humanity swamped the security forces. Entire cities and countries were shocked to a standstill.

THERE WAS FURY AT THE MEDIA BRIEFING THAT WAS CARRIED out by Adam Gadahn, the English language spokesman of the Al Qaida. There could not have been any since it was carried out through a video recording delivered to the office of the Al Jazeera news channel. At about the same time, a copy of the message appeared in the Arabian Peninsula's e-magazine, *Sawt al-Jihad* (Voice of the Holy War), which was posted on a website frequently used by the Al Qaida.

Full of vehement rhetoric, the message was simple and chilling.

The world, especially the Americans and those who support them, will pay for the murder of our beloved leader. And the retribution is about to begin.

THE RETRIBUTION CAME IN WAVES. IN BRUTAL EXPLOSIVE waves that swept the globe. Most of the attacks were knee-jerk reactions by isolated terror cells that had been activated by furious leaders without due planning, or enough thought for logistics and preparation. The majority of them either failed or failed to inflict the desired damage. But those that did succeed dealt out death and destruction to innocents across the globe. In every case the reactions they evoked were unequivocal. The state of fear was beginning to take hold.

THREE ANTI-TANK RPG-7V ROCKETS HIT THE US EMBASSY AT Islamabad precisely five hours after the US press conference. The rockets were a legacy of the Russian invasion of Afghanistan. But they were lethal enough to cause substantial damage to the building. They also decimated the two Marines who had been standing sentinel at the Embassy gates.

ON THE OUTSKIRTS OF KABUL, DUSK HAD JUST BEGUN TO settle when an old lady shuffled up to the roadblock manned by an American platoon. She had just crossed the checkpoint when she turned and threw herself at the handful of GIs on duty. They were still bringing their weapons into play when she detonated the belt bomb strapped to her waist.

IN BAGHDAD, TOO, NIGHT HAD BEGUN TO THROW DOWN its shroud of darkness when waves of armed fighters attacked seven of the smaller police stations while several others set up roadblocks at strategic junctions leading up to these stations. Simultaneously, a rash of gun battles erupted in different places, literally paralysing the already decimated town. For a change, the attacks were well coordinated and timed to precision.

Though they suffered heavy casualties, five of the police stations managed to beat back the attackers. The other two were overrun despite stiff resistance. By the time security forces managed to break through the roadblocks and push reinforcements through, both stations had been destroyed. Every security man who had the misfortune to be captured alive had been brutally hacked into pieces.

AT ABOUT THE SAME TIME, A HUNDRED ARMED FIGHTERS emerged out of the darkness and attacked the Abqaiq facility in Saudi Arabia, the world's largest oil-processing plant. Though boldly executed, the attack was badly planned and failed to do any substantial damage. But it did succeed in sending tremors of fear all over the region.

HARD IN THE WAKE OF THESE ATTACKS A NEW MESSAGE FROM the Al Qaida spokesman was broadcast on Al Jazeera.

In order to strangle the US economy we are going to hit oil interests that serve the US in all *regions, not just in the Middle East. The goal is to cut off oil supplies to the White Satan by all means.*

The threat increased the pressure on America and her allies. Almost reflexively, security in Canada – the largest exporter of oil to America, followed by Mexico, Saudi Arabia and Venezuela – was raised to wartime levels.

NEWS CHANNELS THE WORLD OVER WERE TEEMING WITH reports of horrifying violence, which seemed to escalate and spread with every passing moment. But the worst was still to come.

The Plan

MURREE, PAKISTAN

NONE OF THE EXPLOSIONS THAT KILLED AND MAIMED PEOPLE were heard in the quiet little bungalow in the remote upper reaches of Murree, the lovely hill town located a mere thirty kilometres from Islamabad and sixty-four kilometres from Rawalpindi.

Situated on the edge of a steep cliff and surrounded by tall pines that partially concealed it from the narrow, winding road below, the bungalow was equipped with a dazzling array of modern devices and conveniences that seemed totally out of place in the tiny hill resort. Its only occupants were two men and their three domestic helpers who had been living there for the better part of sixteen months.

The older of the two residents was sitting in the well-stocked library, busily browsing various news sites on the internet when the Thuraya satellite phone lying on the table began to ring. The phone was uncannily similar to the one that had been recovered from the intruder named Iqbal when he had been captured at the LOC.

The phone's ring was sharp and insistent.

The old man looked up in surprise. Not many people had this number and those who did were not the kind to waste their time and energy on social calls. He reached for the phone with a growing sense of anticipation. His excitement sharpened as he saw the calling number displayed on the screen.

No sir! General Ehsan Haque, the Director of the ISI, is definitely not the type to make social calls.

He answered the phone eagerly. 'Good morning, sir.' General Haque was one of the few people he respected and was ready to listen to. They had served together for a very long time.

'Have you been following what's happening?' the General asked without any preamble.

'Of course!' the portly old man in Murree replied indignantly. 'How the hell did things come to this?' His voice tightened. 'More importantly, how the hell did the fucking goras get to know where Sheikh sahib was....'

'We're trying to figure that out,' the General answered sharply. 'I have some ideas, but right now nothing is certain. However, we do know for sure that just two days before it happened, the big man had inquired about Sheikh sahib's health.'

'He had? Then....'

'Then nothing! That in itself proves nothing. He has done that several times in the past also.'

'I don't know when you will see the writing on the wall, sir,' the man in Murree retorted. Even at the best of times he was not the kind to mince his words. Right now he was angry. 'That bloody traitor is selling our country down the road. He has given free rein to the Americans in the Northern Frontier and even allowed those corrupt political bastards to return to Pakistan… though he knows how ruthlessly they have raped our country all these years. That *harami*!' His anger made him breathless. 'Has he forgotten how hard it was to kick them out?'

'Strangely enough, that worked out rather well for us.' There was nothing pleasant about the General's laugh. 'It didn't take much to push those perpetually conniving politicians over the edge and have them gunning for each other. One has already been blown away and the other is well on his way to hell – the PPP diehards will ensure that. The best part is that the world is busy blaming our honourable president for it.' He laughed again. 'They have become so used to blaming him for everything that they don't even stop to think that he had already cut a deal with her and had nothing to gain from her death.'

'True! That did go down rather well,' the old man in Murree replied curtly. He was clearly reluctant to relent. 'But the stupid fucker is showing absolutely no signs of letting up. Now he has even started talking peace with the bloody Indians. Before you know it, the shithead will hand over Kashmir to them on a platter. You should have allowed me….'

'*By God, man*!' The General's voice crackled with the unmistakable whiplash of command. 'When are you going to learn to keep that tongue and temper of yours in check? There has to be a time for everything.' The man in Murree tried to butt in, but the General cut him off. '*Listen to me!* I think the time has come for us to stem the rot before it gets out of control.'

'I absolutely agree. It is high time. In fact if you had listened to me at that....'

'*If, if, if*.... Damn it!' Haque broke in sharply. 'Stop living in the past and listen to me....'

'I am sir, I am.' His voice was tight with impatience. 'But where is all this talking going to get us? We will keep gassing while those fucking kafirs decimate us. Just look at the Americans! First it was Afghanistan, then Iraq, and now they have gone for Iran. When will it end? We will keep sitting on our hands and they will come for us next.'

'Will you shut up and listen?' The General sounded tired and irritable. '*Please*.'

The tone must have finally gotten through since the old man actually shut up and listened carefully as General Ehsan Haque outlined his plan in detail. Gradually, the anger abated and the hard logical thought process of a trained military mind returned. Every once in a while he would butt in and offer a suggestion, but by and large it was the General who spoke. The call lasted a long time.

For an equally long time after it had ended, the old man sat lost in thought. Suddenly his face brightened.

Turning to his computer he began to troll the internet, but this time there was a sharp focus to the information he sought and studied. The hours bled away as he systematically swept through the information and slowly began to put together an operational plan.

'You have to do better than your best!' General Haque had said. 'The strikes must be spectacular, simultaneous, and spread out all over the globe. We must ensure everyone knows that we have the capability to strike at will, when and where we choose to… and anyone who stands in the way of the One God is going to be annihilated. Everything that has been done till date must pale in comparison. Unleash the terror and let the world quiver!'

THE RAYS OF A NEW SUN WERE STRUGGLING TO PIERCE THE swirling fog of another bitterly cold Murree morning when the old man finally switched off his computer. Rubbing his tired eyes and stretching his stiff limbs, he called out to his younger companion in the house.

In his mid-thirties, the second man was tall and broad shouldered. He sported a distinctly military haircut and his grey eyes were alive with anticipation.

Sipping endless cups of coffee, the two of them sat talking for a long time. They spent even more time arguing about and refining the plan. In fact, three full days went by before they came to an agreement on the best line of action.

They spent the next two weeks mostly on their phones. On the fifteenth day the two men left the isolated bungalow in the hills of Murree. They were both on board Pakistan International Airlines flight PK-211 when it left Lahore Airport for Dubai at 1100 hours the following day. They were also on board the connecting Emirates flight that left Dubai a couple of hours later.

Male Airport, Maldives

THE MAN SQUINTED AS THE CLEAR SUNLIGHT STRUCK HIM. After the fog-laden climate of Murree, the bright sun was a shocker. Groping in the laptop bag slung on his shoulder, he pulled out a pair of dark glasses and put them on as he walked up to the edge of the ocean. The old man was watching the water lap against the low concrete wall running along the edge when his younger companion from Murree emerged from the airport building and walked up to him. He was sweating profusely.

Walking just behind him, pushing a luggage trolley, was a muscular young man with a healthy tanned complexion, in a sparkling white T-shirt with 'Sunshine Travels' emblazoned across it.

'We are ready, sirs,' the young man with the luggage trolley called out brightly. 'Please follow me. That's our boat.' He pushed the trolley around them and made his way to a speedboat that was bobbing gently alongside the wooden jetty. The trolley made a hollow trundling sound as it lumbered over the long wooden slats of the jetty. The duo from Murree waited till the luggage was on board and then jumped onto the speedboat. A few minutes later, it pulled away from the jetty and headed out into the vastness of the brilliant blue ocean. The nose of the speedboat lifted into the air as it gathered speed. A fine spray arced out in the wind, gently dousing the two men standing leewards of the tiny cockpit-like cabin. It felt pleasant and refreshing.

'Our hotel, the Blue Moon Resort, is there.' The enthusiastic young man from Sunshine Travels gestured at the distant horizon. 'It will take us about forty minutes to get there. The Blue Moon is one of the finest resorts in Maldives. I can assure you that both of you will have a wonderful time.' Though he was shouting, his voice was blown away in the wind that whipped past the speeding boat.

'What is that?' Cheema pointed at the huge gleaming golden dome sparkling in the sunlight.

'That is the Islamic Centre. You can see it no matter which direction you approach Male from. We must come down and see it one of these days. Believe me, sirs, it is really beautiful.'

The younger of the two seemed to be listening intently, but his older colleague was clearly disinterested in his surroundings. The lad's constant drone was starting to get on his nerves. Closing his mind to it, the old man turned his thoughts inwards.

Ex-Brigadier Murad Salim of the ISI was not here on a holiday jaunt. He was a man with a mission, though officially he was just a dead man, like his younger companion and aide, ex-Captain Azam

Cheema. They had both been declared dead when they had engineered their own deaths in a helicopter crash in the wake of the Delhi bomb blasts of October 2005.

Salim was impatient to reach the hotel and meet the men and women who would be gathering there from all points of the compass. They were a diverse group, from different countries and of different nationalities. But they all had one thing in common. They were gathering to plot death.

Death for a great many people....

AS THE SPEEDBOAT CLEAVED THROUGH THE SHOCKINGLY bright blue waters, Salim's thoughts whipped away from him with the wind rocketing past. Lulled by the soothing motion of the boat and the serenity of the surrounding ocean, a medley of thoughts blew him back in time; back over the tumultuous forty years that he had spent in the service of his god and his nation... or so he thought. After all, it had been a very long time since Murad Salim had sat down to think about why he did what he did... or why he had become what he was. Somehow, somewhere in the passage of years, he had lost or suspended reasoning and allowed the hate within to grow until that was all he knew – to hate... and to kill.

Like an erratically choreographed video-clip, in his mind's eye he saw the barely twenty-one year-old Second Lieutenant Murad Salim standing in silent mortification as he watched General Niazi's ignominious surrender to the hated Indian Army at Dacca on 16 December 1971.

The headlines of the *Sunday Times*, London in December 1971, flashed through his mind like a bolt of pain. *It took only twelve days for the Indian Army to smash its way to Dacca, an achievement reminiscent of the German blitzkrieg across France in 1940. The strategy was the same: speed, ferocity and flexibility.*

Etched deep in his mind was the memory of a dejected young POW with his head hung in humiliation at the knowledge that the Indian Army had taken over 93,000 Pakistani prisoners, the majority of whom had been formidably entrenched when the Indian offensive surged up and around them. Most of them had not even fired a shot.... He remembered the anger and humiliation on the faces of the people who had gathered to watch the prisoners trudge ignobly back into Pakistan after being released by the Indians following an equally humiliating peace brokered by the hateful, gloating Americans.

Tears of angry shame mingled freely with the occasional spray of ocean water each time the boat hit a big wave. Salim pushed back the tears from his eyes with an effort, but inside he seethed, and deep within the tears continued to flow, hot and red.

With an angry sigh, he propelled his mind away from those dark, dampening days and hungrily sought better times. He saw the elation on the face of the young Captain who had been selected for transfer to the ISI not long after the 1971 war. He saw the slightly greying Major and then the hardened Colonel who had first helped the Pakistani Dictator with his coup d'etat and later with the launch of ISI's fabled Operation TOPAC against India. He saw with pleasure and clarity the now well-known Brigadier who had brought about the Talibanization of Afghanistan and consolidated Pakistan's hold over that godforsaken country. He saw the silent, powerful man, perpetually moving in the shadows, who had used the jihadis to unleash terror in India and Afghanistan. He saw the Stinger missile heading for the helicopter that was supposedly taking Captain Azam Cheema and the uber powerful Brigadier Murad Salim to Islamabad....

Then suddenly, the wind whipping past died as the boat slewed sideways and slowed down. The sudden change in motion broke Salim's reverie and returned him to the moment.

THE BLUE MOON RESORT LOCATED ON THE KAAFU ATOLL IS one of the 1200-odd islands that comprise the Maldives. The resort lies on a strip of land approximately eleven hundred metres long, forty metres wide at its narrowest point and about ninety metres at the widest point. The island is so small that when the tsunami hit it a few years back, the gigantic waves had almost overlooked it. Its diminutive size had saved it from any major loss of life or damage.

If you approached the Blue Moon island resort by air, you would see a thin sliver of land surrounded by endless shoals of coral set in the brightest blue water imaginable. At the very tip of the narrow southern end of the island is a small jetty, overlooked by a huge glass hut. Heading away from the jetty, about midway to the other end of the island, is a large wooden hut-like structure reaching for the sky in a strangely birdlike manner. This hut is almost the exact centre of the resort. The eastern beach of the resort has been left untouched, probably for water sports.

Lying to the west and south and ringing the island like an ungainly cordon of wooden sentries, are cottages that rise out of the water on wooden stilts. They are all connected to the island by thin wooden bridges, which reach out across the blue water like umbilical cords. The huts are sinfully luxurious and obscenely expensive. Everything is steeped in the languid sleepiness of a high-end beach resort. It is typically the sort of place where stress, anxiety, and other ills of modern life cease to exist. In fact, after just a few hours on the island it is hard to even imagine that hunger, poverty and crime exist elsewhere on the same planet.

IT WAS ALREADY LATE AFTERNOON BY THE TIME SALIM AND Cheema finally checked into the two adjoining water villas that had been booked for them. In addition to being ultra luxurious, the suites assured total privacy, which was precisely what the two men needed.

Salim had just finished getting dressed after a long relaxing bath when there was a soft knock on the door and Cheema entered the room.

'Who's arrived?' Salim asked.

'So far only the Chinaman.' Cheema glanced at his wristwatch. 'The German and the Dutchman should be getting in any time now. The others will get in only tomorrow morning.'

'Good!' Salim was pleased that things were going as planned. 'Let's call in the Chinaman tonight and the German early tomorrow morning.'

'Why not wait till tomorrow evening, sir, and call them all in together? It will save us the bother of going over the whole thing again and again.'

'No, no Cheema, don't forget the basics. The Alpha team people will not be allowed to come in contact with Bravo team at all. In fact we will not even allow people from the same team to meet one another unless it is imperative. We don't want all the strikes getting jeopardized just because one person gets blown or is taken and decides to sing.'

'That's true, sir,' Cheema replied after a moment's thought. 'You are right… in such a massive operation someone or the other is bound to slip up and get caught.'

'Absolutely!' Salim nodded. 'That's why we have to compartmentalize everything and keep it strictly on a need-to-know basis. Even then we have to ensure that our first contact with each of these people is on a one-to-one basis. If we expect them to lay their lives on the line for us, we must understand what makes them tick and then address that particular need in them.'

'You're losing me, sir.' Cheema grinned. 'I'm a man of action, not a shrink.'

'No, no, Cheema, we're not men of action. We are the ones who make it happen... the puppeteers, as it were.' Cheema smiled again as Salim continued, 'To be a good puppeteer you must understand the basics. You must realize what makes a man a jihadi.'

'Because we are believers.' Cheema retorted sharply. 'Why else would....'

'Of course we are believers, Cheema,' Salim replied. 'Let me rephrase that statement.... We must understand fully what makes a man ready to kill with total impunity. To kill and maim men, women and children whom he does not know and who have done nothing directly to harm him in any way. *And to do all this with total disregard for his own life!*'

Salim let his words hang in the air for a moment before he continued.

'These questions have engrossed hundreds of scholars the world over... and are likely to do so for many, many more decades in the future. The fact is that the reasons behind what the world calls terrorism are as diverse as the types of people who commit these so-called terrorist acts.'

Salim got up and began to pace the floor. Cheema listened to his mentor with rapt attention.

'Until the early nineteenth century, the only

acceptable justification for such violence was religion. This was basically because religion gave its believers a socially acceptable way of recognizing evil and taking up arms against it. In Islam, the earliest form of this action was assassination, and it existed right from the time of Prophet Mohammed, peace be upon him.'

'That is true, sir.' Cheema nodded grimly. 'There is no walking away from the fact that three of his successors and nearly one-third of our caliphs were assassinated.'

'Correct. In fact, the word "assassin" itself is derived from a group called *ashishins* that was founded by Hasan Ibn al-Sabbah in the eleventh century. They spread terror throughout the Muslim world and killed Sunni Muslims in large numbers for almost three centuries till they themselves were exterminated. They sought to replace an apparently corrupt Sunni regime with a supposedly ideal Shiite one and were possibly the world's first jihadis.'

'You make it sound as though it is only Muslims who indulge in such things.'

'Oh no! Of course not!' Salim shook his head vigorously. 'The bombing of abortion clinics in America, repeated attacks by the German Red Army and the Baader-Meinhof Group, the American Weathermen, the Ku Klux Klan, the Phineas Priesthood and the Aryan Nation, the Italian Red Brigade, the Tamil Tigers of Sri Lanka and Japan's Aum Shinrikyo speak adequately of the wide-spread and universal nature of violence. But the fact remains that religious, ideological and nationalistic motives are the most common reasons why people indulge in such acts of violence.'

There was a brief pause as Salim waited for Cheema to assimilate this information. He knew that one day he would have to pass on the baton to someone, and Cheema appeared to be an ideal successor. *He is ruthless enough.* In more ways than one, Cheema was like the son Salim had never had. *It is important for him to understand and not just implement. One day he will have to take charge. Inshallah!*

'The ideological terrorist... I use the word *terrorist* loosely, of course' – Salim threw up his palms defensively when he saw Cheema start up in agitation – 'merely for the sake of this discussion.'

Salim resumed when Cheema sat back, somewhat mollified.

'Like I was saying, the ideological terrorist normally does not offer any clear view of the world he is trying to create. Generally his goal is destruction, not creation. However, the left-wing often has a well-rehearsed ideology while the right-wing is more likely to be pathological.'

'And why is that?'

'Possibly because the leftists are looking ahead at a world they hope will arrive, whereas right-wing organizations are looking backward at a world they think has been lost.'

Salim paused to take a sip of water. Then he resumed pacing the room.

'In contrast, nationalistic and religious terrorists are a different kettle of fish. They seek to implement ideas they have learnt at home and usually have a fairly clear picture of the kind of world they wish to create. More often than not, it is the world given to them by their religious or nationalistic leaders. These leaders *may*, of course, at times completely misrepresent the doctrines they espouse, but the misrepresentation normally acquires authority with the passage of time and the extent of indoctrination to which the men are exposed to.'

'Hmm!' Cheema gave this some thought. Finally he asked, 'What about economic causes?'

Salim nodded approvingly at Cheema's question, pleased that his adjutant-cum-heir-apparent was applying himself to the discussion.

'Cheema, the argument that terrorism springs from poverty and ignorance appears to be false since a study of the Middle East region found that the number of such incidents *increased* as economic conditions improved. When the intifada began in 2000, the unemployment rate among Palestinians in the West Bank and the Gaza Strip was falling and economic conditions were improving. The fact is that the jihad spread *as the economy got better*.'

For a change, Cheema did not say anything. He just sat with his head cocked slightly to one side, listening intently.

'There are also some people who use divine revelations from God as justification for racial, ethnic, or religious attacks. The Al Qaida, Hezbollah and the anti-abortionists all believe they are carrying out the will of God. Others attempt to spark a general uprising through a single, strategically placed attack designed to destroy the will of their enemies. Single-issue terrorists feel so strongly about their cause that they are willing to do almost anything to draw attention to their beliefs. Some also justify their actions by emphasizing religious duty or some kind of approaching Armageddon event. Many of them believe they are victims of political and economic oppression. They believe that because of the strength of the opposing armed forces, they have no choice but to resort to bombings and random assaults.'

A silence set in as Cheema chewed over what had been said. Salim did not speak till he was sure Cheema had dwelt on it long enough.

'Finally, Cheema, we cannot walk away from the fact that some of them are basically failures in all other walks of life and seek personal glory and fame... and, of course, the fact that some of them are simply insane.'

'How can one make out which one is which?' Cheema splayed his hand outwards, perhaps thinking of the people coming to meet them soon.

'You have to know everything about their past, especially the events and reasons that have led them to us. The key lies in the past, for we all are what we are basically because of what lies behind us.' Salim paused briefly. 'You need to watch them.' He leaned forward and jabbed a finger at Cheema's eyes to emphasize the point. 'The eyes, Cheema, the eyes... always watch the eyes. Eyes never lie. They are the windows to the soul.'

There was a long silence. Cheema seemed lost in thought. Salim watched him closely. He seemed satisfied with the way his protégé was taking it all in. Finally Salim began to speak again.

'The fact is that no matter what the motive, terrorism simply baffles people because they cannot imagine doing such things themselves. This bafflement often leads people to assume that terrorists are either mentally deranged or products of a hostile environment, especially when they indulge in acts that are grossly anti-instinct.'

'Anti-instinct?'

'The drive to keep on living, Cheema,' Salim explained. 'Anti-instinct acts are like kids blowing themselves up or....'

'Only those who have really suffered and those who truly believe are capable of such heroic acts,' Cheema interrupted disdainfully.

Salim nodded. 'That notwithstanding, the fact is that no one can ever be sure precisely what drives people who carry out such acts. Just as we will not ever know what drives the men and women who are gathering here to meet us and carry out our orders even at the cost of their lives. But, *if we are to succeed in our roles*, we need to try to find out... and *then* appeal to each individual's personal motives. That is why I suggest we go over the profiles of our lashkar and make sure nothing critical is missed out in the presentation. Come....'

The lesson was over almost as abruptly as it had begun. The two men spent the next hour going over everything with a toothcomb. The presentation was slick and put together with military precision. Salim was clearly a maestro when it came to playing with minds. He had prepared a presentation that addressed each of the visitors as specifically as if he or she were the only one it had been designed for. The two men had already thrashed out every aspect of the plan a dozen times, but both were perfectionists and could not help going over it yet again. Finally Salim was satisfied.

'I think we should call in the Chinaman now.'

Cheema made the call and ten minutes later there was a soft knock on the door.

The man from China entered.

Phase One: The Death Dealers

MAI HU STUMBLED AND ALMOST FELL INTO THE ROOM AS HE came in.

'Be careful,' Cheema pointed out, 'your shoelaces are untied. You could hurt yourself pretty badly.'

'You sound just like my mother.' Mai Hu gave a sheepish grin as he replied in fluent, but heavily accented English. Like many Muslims living in China, his original name, Mustafa Hussein, had been conveniently changed to the closest Chinese characters.

The short, wiry man with a toothy smile and a perennially fuzzy air looked exactly what he was: a geeky scientist. A loud floral beach shirt hung on him like a sack, bits of it tucked into the voluminous cotton Bermudas slung high on his waist. His outfit and demeanour spoke of a man who had almost never holidayed in his life and was now desperately trying to get into the act. The absent-minded air clinging to him gave him away as clearly as his clothes did. No one could be certain how much of the fuzziness was an act, because there was no doubt that Mai had a highly developed mind. His brilliance was the only reason why, against all odds, the youngest son of an Uighur merchant was today where he was.

Identified as a child prodigy by a vigilant teacher early in life, Mai had been put through the paces by the State. Every opportunity had been given to the special child to develop into a special asset to the State and he had not faltered even once. Mai grew from strength to strength and it surprised no one when he ended up as one of the leading lights of the Chinese Biological and Chemical Warfare program.

Given the State's keen awareness of Islamic militancy amongst the Uighurs, it was natural that Mai be subjected to the most intense security scrutiny. He cleared all these without any effort simply because he had nothing to hide. Mai was so deeply enamoured of his work that he had neither time nor energy for anything else. The only three things that held any appeal for him were biological weapons, chemical weapons and computers.

In fact, it is almost certain that Mai would have happily spent the rest of his life playing with test tubes and keyboards if he had not got married. It was Fatima, his wife, also an Uighur, who acquainted him with the hitherto unknown and unexplored pleasures of bedded bliss. This gave her almost total control over Mai. It also empowered and emboldened her to educate him about life beyond the laboratory. Fatima was a devout Muslim from a highly orthodox family. She had the same passion for religion that Mai had for chemistry.

'What do you know about our people?'

'Eh?' was Mai's erudite reply.

'Do you know anything about our people?' Fatima asked patiently.

'Of course I do,' Mai replied absent-mindedly. 'We are Uighurs, a Turkic Sunni Muslim people.'

'Good.' Fatima nodded approvingly. 'Are you aware that we have been residing in the Xinjiang area since the eighth century?'

'That long, eh?'

'Yes, that long. I'm sure you're aware that Xinjiang has a very large Muslim population.'

'Sure,' Mai replied confidently, though he was losing interest in the conversation. 'Hundreds of Kasakhs and Tajiks also live here.'

'Did you also know that in 1949 the total population of Xinjiang was 4.3 million and Uighurs constituted 75.9 per cent of this?' Fatima could be hard to shake off when she got going.

'Really?' Mai was as interested in this as he was in the weather.

'Yes. By the year 2000, the total population of Xinjiang went up to 18.5 million, but now the Uighurs only constituted 45.2 per cent of it.'

'That's most interesting.' Mai was still only half listening. Fatima reached out and shook him. 'Don't you want to understand why our people are being reduced to an oppressed minority?' she asked angrily.

'I am sure you will tell me,' Mai replied, a little more tuned in now, possibly because she was getting worked up.

'Because the Chinese government is busy moving Hans into the area in huge numbers. The Han population has gone up from 6.7 per cent in 1949 to 40.6 per cent in 2000. Can you imagine? And despite being a minority, the Hans are holding almost all the important official posts and have the best jobs.'

'Really?' The numbers had finally started getting through to Mai's scientific mind. Maybe that was why Fatima had taken the trouble to seek them out and use them. Though their marriage was young, it had not taken the astute Fatima long to understand how her husband's mind worked.

Mai's resentment at this injustice suffered by his people grew as Fatima gave him all the gory details. Even so, it took Fatima nearly two years to convert the dedicated scientist into an equally dedicated closet jihadi. That was when Salim discovered him through an East Turkestan Islamic Movement (ETIM) conduit. The recruitment process did not yield any immediate results, but then none was expected. Salim was a long-term player, fully aware of the importance of holding such an ace up his sleeve.

One never knows when such a valuable asset will come in handy.

Well, the day had finally come. And Mai was the first contact Salim had initiated.

TO PUT IT MILDLY, MAI'S BOSS HAD BEEN SHOCKED OUT OF his skin when Mai asked for a week's leave. No one could remember Mai having ever taken so much leave. Even his marriage had been a relatively rushed affair. The boss was even more shocked when he learnt that Mai was planning to spoil himself with a vacation in the Maldives. He could not imagine Mai on a beach resort. But he could hardly say no.

A couple of weeks later, Fatima and Mai were on the plane from Urumqui to Colombo via Beijing and thence onwards to the Maldives.

'IS YOUR WIFE GOING TO JOIN US OR SHOULD WE BEGIN?'

'No,' Mai replied. 'I will take notes and brief her later.'

'Take notes?' Cheema said agitatedly. 'You're not supposed to take any notes. Don't you realize what would happen if.... '

'I'm a scientist,' Mai cut in firmly. 'I always take notes.'

Cheema was about to protest when Salim restrained him with a brief gesture. 'That's okay. As long as you destroy the notes once you have briefed her.'

'Of course I will. In any case, my notes are always in my own special shorthand. Trust me, it's a lot more efficient than any code you could think of.'

They got down to it. In the beginning, it was Mai who spoke. He gave them a complete run down on the technical aspects of the weapons they were planning to use, which Salim had asked him to look into when he had first contacted him. Both Salim and Cheema interrupted him every now and then with questions. There was a long silence when he finished. Over the next hour it was mostly Salim who spoke.

'My God!' Mai exclaimed when Salim finished. 'Are you sure this will work?'

'It will! As long as everyone carries out his assigned task, it will,' Salim replied confidently.

'But most of the strikes will not be able to do much damage. Not with the small amount of material that each of them can safely carry into the target area.'

'I agree. In some cases, the actual casualty toll may not be very high,' Salim conceded. 'But do you realize the damage that we will be able to inflict on the kafir psyche? They will never know how much more we have of the weapons and where we will use them next. *That*, my dear man, is the ultimate terror.' Salim smiled triumphantly. 'The kafir will have no option but to be on guard at all times. He will be compelled to expend massive resources in trying to stay secure. To make it worse, even while he is doing so, the kafirs will know how futile it is, since we will always have the latitude to select the time, place and method of our next attack… and then the next one. The financial burden will cripple him just as the perennial state of fear will eventually wear down his will to fight.'

'I see what you mean,' Mai replied thoughtfully. 'When you put it like that, it makes perfect sense.'

'Exactly! Now, do you have any doubts or questions?'

'Not really, but I would like your suggestions on how to get the material past customs and airlines security, especially now that most countries have adopted the new European Union regulations on the type and nature of liquids and aerosols that one can carry on board commercial flights.'

'Most countries have,' Cheema concurred, 'but these are not really as stringent as they appear to be. In any case, you have to remember that most security checks at most airports focus on the passengers and their hand baggage, not on the stuff that one has checked in. That,' he emphasized, jabbing the air, 'is how we will get our material across borders.'

'Okay!' Mai replied, after musing over his notes for a long moment. 'This seems good enough for me... at least for the moment. Let me give it some more thought. I will come back to you if there's anything that comes to mind. In any case, it's not as if I can't call you even later.'

'No, you cannot,' Salim retorted sharply. 'That's one thing I want to emphasize very strongly. You must not call us once we move out from here... not for any reason whatsoever. Tracking and monitoring technology is too good to beat. Most such operations have been blown just because of one careless phone call. So whatever doubts you have, we clarify them right here, face to face.'

'Fair enough,' the man from China agreed. 'But how do we stay in touch and coordinate once we move out from here? How do you plan to exercise command and control over the strike team if you do not allow any contact?'

'I am coming to that.' Salim nodded to Cheema who juggled a web page onto the laptop screen. 'This is a matchmaking website, meetyourmatch.com. We will be using it to communicate.' Salim paused as Mai took note of the website. 'An identity has already been created for you. Your user name and password are....' Salim referred to his notes and gave them to Mai who dutifully recorded them. 'Like the others, I too have a profile created on this site under the username smurad234. You simply need to log in to your profile and then communicate with me.' While Salim was talking, Cheema had logged in using Mai's user name and password.

'Hey! That's neat,' Mai said as he saw his profile float up on the laptop screen. 'You've even put up my photo on the site. How smart is that?'

'It's basically been done to ensure your profile blends in with other users of the site since most profiles carry photos. Your identity will appear to be more genuine and our group's messages will automatically get buried among the other messages from genuine match seekers. And of course, in case you or your laptop are taken, your accessing a matchmaking site will not appear so alarming....'

'Why not? I'm already married.'

'Sure you are!' Salim grinned. 'So what? Maybe you're looking for another wife.'

'Right!' Mai laughed. 'I'm so glad you're not making these suggestions in front of my wife.' They all laughed. 'Anyway, that's very good thinking.' Mai nodded approvingly.

'That's why you must remember to write in to other people also every now and then. People who have nothing to do with our mission. It will keep things even more natural and thicken the camouflage.'

Salim watched the scientist brood over it. Then Mai grinned. 'Yeah well, what the hell.... I must say it's very neat.'

'*Precisely!*' Salim nodded with a pleased smile. 'It is simple, effective, and almost impossible for anyone to track down or monitor.'

'Why?' Mai's scientific mind could not help analysing and asking. 'I should think it is a simple enough task for anyone to break in and track our messages. It fact, I am sure the website's system-monitors will be able to do so very easily.'

'Of course they could,' Salim nodded. 'But do you realize how many millions of people communicate with each other millions of times every day? It is almost impossible for anyone to keep track of all of them... *or even want to do so*. So we should be quite safe as long as we avoid certain keywords that are bound to attract attention or raise flags. I am sure you will take care of that.'

'Of course I will,' Mai replied. 'But what do we do if there is an emergency?'

'You still don't call,' Salim answered immediately. 'Just send a text message through your mobile phone and one of us will immediately log in and check your detailed message on the site.'

'And if one is unable to access the net?' Mai seemed to be playing the Devil's advocate, or maybe he just wanted to test Salim.

'Well, if it is absolutely critical and unavoidable, then you will just have to call. Right? But I'd rather there were no calls. See, we *will* be rehearsing everything in detail over the next few days. That should take care of most contingencies that are likely to arise.'

Mai remained lost in thought. 'Neat!' he finally said as he got up. 'You have clearly thought things through in detail.' He looked at Salim earnestly. 'I'm glad. I've been slightly worried that...' He broke off. 'But you obviously know what you're doing. This detailed planning gives us a very fair chance of success.'

'I am glad you approve.' Salim smiled, genuinely pleased, and quite relieved. The Chinese scientist was a key player and Salim needed to make sure he was fully convinced. 'And now for the final part.... The username and password for your profile on the meetyourmatch website is also applicable to an account that has been opened for you in this bank.'

He handed over a slip of paper to Mai. The details of a bank, an account number and an amount were written on it.

Mai looked at the paper and gave a low whistle. 'That's a lot of money.'

'You will need it. The operation should not falter for want of something as mundane as money.'

'Like I said, you *have* thought of everything. When do I meet the others?' Pocketing the slip, Mai got up to leave.

'You will. Soon. After all, you have to brief everyone about everything – when and where they should collect the weapons from you, how they have to get them past airport security and how to use them. We will rehearse everything thoroughly.'

'Fine! When and where are we assembling?'

'No, we will not be doing any assembling. You will meet them one by one in your suite.'

'Why not all together? After all, barring one of them, there is no difference in what each has to do.'

'No! They must not be allowed to meet. The less they know about each other, the better. In fact, you are the only one who will meet all the others. *They* will only know you, Cheema and me.'

'You don't trust them?'

'I do. As much as I trust you.' A brief smile played on Salim's lips. 'We are all Allah's soldiers after all, but no one will be given any more information than they need to have. After all, what you don't know, you can't disclose even by mistake.'

'Excellent!' Mai exclaimed. 'Like I said, you have covered all the bases. Call me when you need me.'

Salim was smiling as Mai left.

Over the next few days, while his wife relaxed on the beach, Mai kept an almost constant vigil on the water villa occupied by Murad Salim. He saw the burly white man in his mid-thirties walk up to the door of Salim's suite early the next morning.

KARL GUNTHER WAS A HUGE MAN AS FAR AS HIS PHYSICAL size and his ego went. Otherwise, in every possible way, he was as small as a man could be. The wide-girthed Karl with straw blond, thinning hair and a rapidly receding hairline was the only son of a working class German family. He, too, was trying hard to blend in with the other holiday makers at the resort, but the bright shirt and even louder shorts sat on him uneasily. Trying vainly to fight the dross sweaty smell emanating from him was the cloyingly sweet deodorant that Karl had applied on himself all too liberally.

Karl's father had been a machinist and his mother a telephone operator. Both of them completed their trajectory on earth and passed on without leaving much of a mark on it. It is almost certain that Karl too would have passed through the corridors of life without leaving any trace behind if it had not been for three totally unrelated events.

The first incident occurred when Karl was twenty-three years old. While working in a small factory, he lost his left hand to a machine that suddenly went berserk. Karl was safely tucked away in a hospital bed when the owner of the factory determined that the machine had misbehaved primarily because it had not been maintained in a proper manner. Acutely aware of the huge legal liability that he was open to, the owner made a quick deal with Karl. Thus it came about that the unfortunate Karl lost a limb but was assured of a job that did not overly strain his not too considerable mental or physical faculties. Over a period of time, with the help of a reasonably well crafted prosthetic, Karl's life limped back to the monotony of mediocrity that it had been suspended in before his accident.

It would have continued on this same plane had it not been for a chance encounter with a childhood friend who had recently embraced Islam and was now busy converting as many people as possible to his new faith. The eloquence of this recent convert along with hours of research on the internet, for which Karl had all the time in the world, soon put him firmly on the path to the nearest mosque. Thus Karl Gunther was reborn and became a true believer and follower of the One God. Even then Karl would have probably left this earth unnoticed upon the expiry of his time if Murad Salim had not started looking for a factory worker.

'My requirement is quite simple,' Salim told his most trusted talent scout in Berlin. 'I need a Berlin-based factory worker not of Asian origin, who has been injured, preferably disabled. He *must* be a true believer, preferably unmarried... and it would help if he wasn't too high on intelligence.'

Fate again stepped in because the talent scout coincidentally worshipped at the same mosque as Karl and had not only seen him there on several occasions, but also struck up a passing acquaintance. It did not take long for the scout to ascertain that Karl met all the requirements stipulated by Salim.

'What about a wife or a girlfriend?' Salim had asked.

'Wait till you meet him, boss,' the scout had replied confidently. 'He is not likely to have one anytime soon.'

'Hmmm... okay, if you're sure that he fits the bill, then send him to me.'

That was how Karl came to be on the Austrian Airlines flight from Berlin to Vienna, thence onto Colombo, and finally to Male. And that was how Karl came to be walking up to Salim's suite.

There was a rare eager spring in Karl's stride as he came up to the door of the suite. This, after all, was his first – and possibly last – chance at glory. Karl would die rather than let it go by.

Mai had a good look at the seriously overweight blond haired, blue-eyed man before the door opened and Karl vanished inside. It took the scientist barely five minutes of logical thinking and twenty minutes of searching on the net to find the profile that Karl would be using on the meetyourmatch website: *'gkarl234.'* Mai muttered the name to himself as he tried, ineffectively, to climb into Karl's mind.

THE SCIENTIST WAS STILL BROODING OVER KARL'S SCANTY profile when, an hour or so later, he saw two dusky, obviously Asian girls in their early twenties walk up to Salim's suite. The diminutive and wafer-thin girls were so alike that they *had* to be sisters. From their slow, uneasy, shuffling gait they also appeared to be suffering from some serious physical deformity.

Mai had a good look at them as they waited for the door to open. They were still inside when he located the identity that had been created for one of them on meetyourmatch. com. It was the girl who had been leading the way. *kkismat234. Self-employed. Never married*, her profile proclaimed.

'Will you have the guts to roll the dice when the time comes?' Mai asked the photograph of the subdued looking girl on the screen. 'Will you two have the guts to shut your mind to the shock and the agony as death begins to scream all around? Will you be able to do it?'

The girl's photograph gazed back at him silently.

SAHIBA AND KISMAT WERE NOT JUST SISTERS, THEY WERE twins. Born into a typical middle-class family in the central Indian city of Bhopal, they had still been in their mother's womb when tragedy struck.

Their mother had been in her eighth month of pregnancy when there was a leak in the Union Carbide factory in Bhopal. Carried westwards by a brisk breeze, the cloud of poisonous fumes raced through the city. The tiny house on the third floor, which was occupied by the pregnant woman, lay directly in the flight path of the toxic gas. She called her husband who was away at work when the sense of suffocation became too strong. By the time the hapless husband rushed home and discovered his unconscious wife, the damage had been done and it was irreversible. In fact, had it not been for the fact that he himself was a doctor, it is certain his wife would have died the and there.

As things turned out, she did die, but only after an agonizing month of pain and trauma. She even managed to deliver the twin bundles of joy that she had nurtured in her womb all those months. Moments later, she died and her agony came to an end. Her God was kind enough to ensure that she was saved the final agony of not having to see the damage the savage fumes had inflicted on her precious babies.

Sahiba and Kismat were never going to lead normal lives.

'The gas has not only affected their limbs, it has also left them with a host of respiratory disorders.' The doctor's tone was not unkind but he spoke plainly, knowing that the grieving man standing before him was also a doctor. 'You have to be strong, bhai.' He placed a comradely hand on his colleague's shoulder. 'These two will need a lot of support from you.'

'I know.' Looking at the two tiny lives cocooned in the incubators, the father controlled his tears with an effort. 'It's ironic, doctor. You know we were to leave for the West Indies.'

'I know. I believe you have landed a very good job there. The superintendent was telling me about it just the other day.'

'Yes, in fact we were just waiting for the delivery and then we would have gone.' The tears began to flow.

'Don't change your plans,' the doctor counselled the grief-stricken man. 'It will be good for you to get away from all this and start afresh.'

Traumatized by the double tragedy, the distraught man left India and moved with his twin daughters to the lovely city of Kingston. To help him care for his motherless children, his aging parents accompanied him. The unfortunate twins blossomed with the love their kindly grandmother showered on them. It was their grandfather who imparted to them a basic understanding of Islam and an irrational hatred for the kafir.

'Never forget that it was a factory owned and mismanaged by the gore shaitan that blighted your lives,' he would remind them every so often. 'They only care about money. Our lives have no meaning for them.'

It was in the shadow of this hate that they grew up. Their disabilities became more and more pronounced as they grew order. So did their hatred for the white-skinned kafir.

In the end, that was what sealed their fates. Their disabilities made them the ideal weapons as far as Salim was concerned. And the hatred sheathed deep inside them made it easy for Salim's scouts to recruit them.

THE RESORT HAD ALMOST GONE TO SLEEP BY THE TIME SAHIBA and Kismat emerged from Salim's suite. Even the echoes of the orchestra that had been playing near the restaurant on the beach had subsided into silence sometime ago. Now, only the occasional laugh of a guest or a resort employee broke the relentless roar of the ocean. Otherwise, everyone slept. So did Mai. Exhausted by a day of turmoil and his constant watch, he entwined himself around his wife, and was soon snoring softly.

MAI HU WOKE ONCE IN THE EARLY HOURS OF THE MORNING. The satin warmth of his wife's supple body aroused him and, shaking her awake, he made love to her, slowly, languorously. Then, with his head buried in her breasts, he slept again. When he finally awoke, the sun was pouring into the room through the huge glass windows facing the ocean. His wife was sunbathing on the private wooden deck facing the sparkling blue-green ocean that seemed to stretch endlessly. As far as the eye could see, there was nobody in sight. And the two tall, arrogant looking men in their late twenties who had crossed the globe for their meeting were already inside Salim's suite. Dressed like typical American tourists, the men exuded an arrogance which was enhanced by the superb state of physical fitness that they were both in; not surprisingly, since both were soldiers in the United States Army.

BOTH LIAQUAT ALI AND RAHIM KHAN WERE CITIZENS OF America by birth. Their grandparents had migrated from Pakistan to the land of opportunity within a few weeks of each other. They shared a lot of other similarities. Both were born in New York in the same year, although a few months apart. Both had been brought up in the same borough in New York City and had attended the same school. Both had been decidedly mediocre students, but were blessed with impressive physiques. Both had grown up envying the big cars and bigger houses that their more fortunate classmates flaunted. Both had been subjected to the same *Fuckin' Paki* slur by the same classmates. This, more than anything else, threw them together into a bond of friendship.

But what brought them truly close was the fact that both used to accompany their parents to the same mosque. Both were recruited at the same time by the same Al Qaida scout who also doubled as a freelance ISI agent. The scout was yet another of the many devilish protégés spawned and deployed all over the world by terror maestros like Murad Salim. He had subverted dozens of young second-generation Muslim lads and then, as he had been told to do, motivated them to join a multitude of professions.

'We must infiltrate all aspects of life in the very heart of our enemies' and.' That was what Murad

Salim told all his scouts. 'Our warriors must penetrate every nook and corner of their society and be ready to strike as and when we call upon them. Then… and *only then*… can we hope to defeat these kafirs.'

'We have a special task for both of you.' The terror scout noted the physique of his recruits and guided them accordingly. 'You should join the US Army.'

'What?' The shocked expression on the face of the clean-shaven Liaquat mirrored precisely what his taller, leaner fellow jihadi Rahim was also feeling. With their unmistakable accents and slightly swarthy complexions, both men could easily pass off as native Americans.

'Of course. Can you think of a better way than to have the enemy train our army?'

'Oh! Right!' Rahim grinned wickedly. 'When you put it like that, it makes perfect sense.'

'Of course it does.'

That was how, by the time they got the call from Salim, both closet jihadis had clocked in a good three years of military service in the US Artillery and were fully conversant with the handling of all kinds of weapons. Now in their late twenties, they were perfectly suited and thoroughly trained for the task that Salim had in mind for them.

Unseen by anyone who mattered, they entered Salim's suite even as the morning sun was struggling to breach the horizon.

BARELY A HUNDRED METRES AWAY, UNEXPECTEDLY AROUSED BY the sight of his beautiful wife lounging on their private patio, Mai cajoled her back into the room and onto the huge bed. For the next twenty minutes they romped with all the enthusiasm of newly weds. They were lost in the throes of passion when the two young American soldiers emerged from Salim's suite.

And that was why Mai neither saw them enter nor leave.

HOWEVER, MAI DID SEE THE WHIPCORD-THIN MAN WITH BLUE eyes and white-blond hair who walked up to Salim's suite after breakfast.

Abraham Reis was an extremely reserved and soft-spoken man. He had been born with an innate sense of courtesy that had been nurtured and developed over the years by his father. His softness and politeness were somewhat tempered by the nature of his job as the senior maintenance manager at the new, soon to be inaugurated, BMO Field Stadium at the Exhibition Place in Toronto.

Despite this, he was known to be a pushover, one of the few managers whom his subordinates could rely on to fall for any old sob story and help them to change their shifts, or get that unplanned day off. Even people who did not report to him would often request him to speak to *their* managers. So almost anyone who worked at the new stadium was in some way or the other indebted to Reis.

Not one of them was aware of the fact that Reis,

the son of a Canadian airman and a Pakistani immigrant educationist, had been brought up as a true, practising Muslim. Not one of them knew how intense Reis's feelings were about the way America was conducting its wars on Afghanistan, Iraq and Iran. Not one of them was aware of the hatred he felt for the brutal manner in which the Israelis were persecuting the Palestinians. All this hatred and anger simmered unseen and unheard beneath the gentle, polite façade that masked the real Abraham Reis.

It had not been hard to recruit Reis and prepare him for this mission. Actually, there had been no need to do either since his mother, who had been part of the ISI's long-term global strategy, had already done both. Much like the sleeper agents of the post-World War II era, Reis's mother was one of the several hundred jihadi agent provocateurs who had been trained by the ISI, told to migrate, and then left in deep cover, to be called upon when the right time came.

Well, the time had come.

As a second generation deep-cover jihadi, Abrahim Reis was the ideal weapon. In his late thirties, Reis was older than the average terrorist. He was also ideally placed in the correct target location, had no police record of any kind and was fully integrated into the society that he was now going to wage war against.

Mai watched the gentle, unobtrusively dressed man with a slow, ambling gait walk up to Salim's suite and knock on the door. It opened immediately, and the suite swallowed him up.

MAI ALSO SPOTTED THE TALL MAN ON THE WRONG SIDE OF forty, with a wasted body and long unruly hair, who approached Salim's suite about an hour after Reis had departed. His unsure walk suggested a distinct lack of self-confidence.

There had been a time when it was almost certain that Erik Segan from New Orleans would be counted as one of the leading lights of American Jazz music and his name would be taken in the same breath as Billie Holliday, Count Basie and Benny Goodman. Erik was standing on the threshold of greatness and glory when he found drugs. Or, it would be more correct to say, when drugs began to rule him and his life. Soon, the rhythm and beauty of music was lost in a blur of detox centres and the occasional prison cell.

He finally managed to kick the habit and returned to music, only to find that the magic had deserted him. The dejected man was now eking out a miserable existence on the fringes of the music world as part of one of the several, nondescript music groups that thronged the streets of New Orleans. He would almost certainly have gone back to the cloudy safety of drugs had it not been for Azhar Mahroof.

Erik Segan had met Azhar Mahroof at one of the many rehabilitation centres that he had been in and out of. Mahroof was a devout believer of the One God and had dedicated his life to helping druggies kick the habit. In his other avtaar, he was also one of the many scouts employed by Murad Salim to dredge the back alleys of life and seek potential recruits.

It was Mahroof who kindled in Erik the burning desire to do something for the cause. Something bold that would give him the glory that he had always hankered for and which had once nearly been his. It was this quest for greatness that found Erik Segan on the long flight from New Orleans to Male. It was this quest that delivered him to Salim's doorstep today.

Like Mahroof, it did not take Salim long to recognize Erik's desperate need for recognition.

'There has never been anything so bold attempted by any of our brothers –' Salim played the man like the expert puppeteer that he was – 'They will remember you for generations to come. You shall become an everlasting beacon for millions of jihadis the world over.'

Salim's words stirred a deep sense of excitement in Erik. He could feel himself coming alive. His heart was throbbing with anticipation when, an hour later, he left Salim's suite and walked back to his own room on the other side of the tiny island resort.

HAD MAI GOT UP TO FETCH HIS COFFEE EVEN ONE MINUTE before he actually did, he would have missed the dark, not so tall, fit looking man in his mid-thirties, who came to Salim's door barely twenty minutes after Erik left. The man exuded the confidence of one who has travelled extensively and seen the world.

Yakub Khan had first worked as the representative of a buying house and then later as the owner of a small but thriving export unit located in Delhi, which specialized in exporting cotton garments to the American markets.

Yakub Khan had been in Ayodhya on work on the day the Hindutva men brought down the Babri Masjid and torched his brethren in Mumbai and Gujarat. But he was no fanatic and was careful to keep his anger to himself.

There was no doubt, however, that he was a powder keg just waiting to blow when he was recruited by a vigilant Hizbul scout.

Once again, Yakub was the ideal recruit for the mission Salim had in mind. He was a family man with two children, had no criminal record, was well established in his profession, and was older than the typical terror recruit. The man was fully conversant with the area he would be operating in and especially the area where he would execute the final strike.

'His only drawback is that he has no experience of any kind when it comes to handling weapons,' Cheema had pointed out to Salim when they were discussing the various profiles in order to shortlist the strike team.

'That's okay,' Salim assured him. 'We can fix that with some training. After all, the weapon he is going to use can be easily handled by anyone with a basic working knowledge of computers.'

MAI HAD JUST RETURNED FROM LUNCH WHEN HE SPOTTED the tall, bulky Dutchman with a prominent beer belly who walked up to Salim's door with an arrogant swagger. There was something in his walk and attitude that bespoke the military or the police and indeed, Lars Borge was an ex-cop. Not so long ago, he had walked the streets of Copen-hagen in a smart police uniform. Now Lars was employed in the security detail at Copenhagen's Kastrup Airport.

Lars had always been a good, honest cop. He had been cruising through life with the comforts and conveniences afforded to him by an affluent society that boasted one of the highest quality-of-life indices in the world when one day, without any warning everything fell apart.

It was barely half an hour after Lars left for work that the two men broke into his house. Both were very young, very stoned on some potent concoction of drugs, and looking for some money to feed their next fix. No one would ever know for sure what triggered off the orgy of violence in the house, but by the time it was over, Lars' wife, who was in the fourth month of her first pregnancy and his mother, who had been visiting them, had been completely and brutally dismembered by the two junkies. Hardened though he was by his years as a cop, Lars could not stop throwing up for hours after he saw what remained of them. The heartbreak, of course, lasted much longer.

To add insult to injury, thanks to a minor legal technicality, both killers got away with a sentence that would have made a drunk driver happy. Lars was inconsolable. And angry. His helplessness at being unable to protect his family was overshadowed by his anger at the government's inability to bring the guilty to book. Both combined to become the stepping-stone that eventually led to the birth of the completely new, cynical and embittered Lars.

'In my country they would have given them the death penalty,' the usually silent lady from the house next door said to him. She had come over to comfort her grieving neighbour. Lars barely knew her, though he knew that Helga, his wife, had spent a lot of time with her. 'Islamic law is very clear and very simple. You steal and they cut your hand off. You kill and your life is forfeit.'

Lars did not say anything to her at the time, but Lina's words festered in his head; and the more he pondered over them, the more they seemed to make sense. He began to seek out Lina and spend more time in her company.

Thirty-year-old Lina Gazzaz was a first-generation immigrant from Saudi Arabia. She had lost her husband to a hit-and-run driver barely three years after they had settled down in Copenhagen. The killer was never traced. Suddenly alone in an alien land, yet by now accustomed to the huge personal freedom she enjoyed in this liberal society, Lina refused all offers by her family to help her return to Saudi Arabia. Her decision was made simpler by the fact that her late husband had been covered by a rather handsome insurance policy. With the passage of time, the pain of his leaving began to recede, but not the anger she felt against the unknown person who had widowed her. Lina took solace in her religion, of which she was a devout follower, and her painting, for which she was wooed by the local art galleries.

Neither Lars nor Lina could ever be sure why and when the relationship between them deepened. Maybe it was just a matter of two lonely individuals leaning on each other for sustenance. Maybe it was the manner in which they had lost their spouses and the fact that the killers had walked free. Or maybe it was just karma. Barely six months after the brutal murder of his wife, Lina and Lars had become inseparable. A few months later began the unplanned but thorough indoctrination of Lars Borge by Lina Gazzaz.

By the time Salim's scouts closed in on him, Lars had been honed into the ideal terror weapon. Because of his police training and background, he knew exactly how the security network functioned. He knew what he should *not* do, to ensure that he did not feature in any criminal record or files. And, like most of the death-dealers activated by Salim for this operation, he was not of Asian origin, nor a Muslim by birth, and was fully integrated into the society he was going to attack.

Within fifteen minutes of Lars's departure from Salim's suite, Mai had located his profile on meetyourmatch.com. On an impulse, he even wrote him a message from his own profile. The message was innocuous enough and would raise no flags, yet it did link the two.

THE MAN FROM LONDON CAME IN LAST. HE WAS UNLUCKY enough to have missed his flight on the first day. But that was nothing new for Ben Ashton. Bad luck had dogged him for the better part of his life.

The only son of an Iraqi nursing professional, the stunningly beautiful Nahida Hanani, who had fallen in love with a handsome British doctor on her shift, Ben's misfortunes began with his birth, which happened six weeks prematurely. This early exit from the safety of his mother's womb into the cold, cruel world ensured that Ben's early years were fraught with repeated visits to the hospital. By the time he was ten years old, the neighbourhood joke was that he spent more time at the hospital where his parents worked than they did.

It was on Ben's sixteenth birthday that Nahida got the call from her father in Baghdad. 'Your grandfather is in bad shape; the cancer has totally wasted him. He wants to see you for the last time, before...'

'He was my constant childhood companion,' a teary Nahida told her husband David when he returned home that evening. 'I would really like to go back and meet him before he...' She burst into tears.

Dr David Ashton was as besotted with his wife now as when he first set eyes on her. He could stand everything but her tears. 'Of course you must go, darling,' he consoled her, 'but I may not be able to get away so quickly. Why don't Ben and you go ahead and I'll join you two later.'

'Thank you so much, David,' a tearful Nahida replied. 'This will also be a good opportunity for both of you to meet my family and see my country.'

That was how, two days later, Ben found himself with his mother on board an airliner headed for Baghdad. Despite the troubled times Iraq had been through in the recent past, both of them were full of excitement, one at the thought of revisiting her family and the other at the thought of the exotic journey his mother had promised him.

But Ben's ill-luck ran true to form. What was supposed to be a meet-the-family and see-the-country expedition turned out to be something else altogether.

Although several months had elapsed since that fateful day in January 1991 when the US-led air armada had pulverized Iraq and decimated its infrastructure, the effects of the 'collateral damage' caused by the 'sixty thousand tons of high explosives' dropped on Iraq in the six-week long air war were evident everywhere. Nahida had been following the march of events in her country closely through various news media and should have been better prepared for what lay ahead, but she was not.

The omnipresent scenes of death and destruction that she witnessed plunged Nahida into the depths of despair. From this despair arose a vice-like hatred that gripped her.

The Americans must be made to pay... they need to be thrown into a living hell for this... monstrosity that they have inflicted on my beloved Iraq.

It was a very subdued duo that boarded the flight back to London a few weeks later. It was an even more subdued Ben who dropped out of college a few years later, much to David's disappointment. David had always hoped that the quiet but intelligent Ben would follow him into the medical profession. But his disappointment was short-lived since his own existence was abruptly terminated by a cardiac arrest. In Ben's troubled head his father's death signalled the final break from the society that he had been born and bred in, and his mother's bitter rhetoric against the West finally held sway. A few months later, the young man officially converted to Islam, his mother's religion.

By the time the thirty-year-old Ben was elected as an office bearer in the National Union of Railwaymen, his indoctrination was complete.

Yet again, as life would have it, Ben's run of ill-luck continued and a couple of years later he was blown out of the corridors of power by the politics that flourishes in every labour union. This was the final nail in the coffin; it left him disillusioned with life in general and the country he lived in, in particular. When Salim's scout approached him, it seemed to Ben a heaven sent opportunity to make up for all the wrongs, real and perceived, that he had suffered.

Mai spotted him as he was walking up to Salim's suite. But the sun had already plunged over the horizon, and he was unable to make out anything except that he was Caucasian.

'It doesn't matter.' Mai whispered, looking at the shadowy figure entering Salim's suite. 'I will meet you soon. After all, I am the one who has to train you.'

THE SOFT, MELODIOUS RING OF THE PHONE EARLY NEXT morning put an end to Mai's vigil.

'We're planning to start the training and rehearsals at ten o'clock,' Salim said when Mai answered the phone. 'I want you to brief each of the team members in your suite, unless you prefer to do it in mine.'

'Mine would be better,' Mai replied. 'I have got some mock-ups and dummies so it will be easier to explain.'

'Good!' Salim was pleased with Mai's thoroughness. It was comforting to know that the man who was going to play a pivotal role in the operation was competent and systematic in his planning. 'Be ready at ten. I will join you shortly before that.'

SALIM WAS WAITING IN MAI'S SUITE WHEN KARL GUNTHER arrived. There was something about Karl that put Mai off immediately. *What difference does it make... you don't have to like him, just train him. In any case, he is not going to be around much longer.* With a mental shrug and an impassive face, the Chinese scientist stepped forward to greet the German jihadi.

Salim spoke up before the others could. 'For the sake of the mission, the less you two know about each other, the better. It is not that I do not trust either of you implicitly, it is just that we cannot disclose even by mistake what we do not know.'

Both men acknowledged the logic with a nod.

'Before we begin, I would like both of you to join me in a brief prayer, so that we may thank Allah for blessing us with this opportunity to strike at the kafir.'

Salim was a wily puppeteer. By the time the prayer was over, the mood had been set and he had their undivided attention.

'Once again, keeping operational security in mind, we will not be discussing the specific details of your actual target. That will be done by me later, only with you,' he told Karl. 'Today, our friend here,' he gestured towards Mai with a brief smile, 'will teach you everything you need to know about the weapon that he will hand over to you when you two meet next. He will tell you how to handle the weapon, get it past airport and airline security, how to carry it into the target area and, most importantly, how to put it to best use, so that we are able to achieve maximum....' he searched briefly for the most appropriate word, '*impact.*'

Salim paused briefly to allow the words to sink in, then focused on Karl. 'Before I hand you over to him, I would again like to stress that you must clear all your doubts and questions before you leave here. Subsequently, barring the bare minimal communication required to coordinate the strike, we will operate strictly on our own. Even this basic essential communication will only be carried out through the meetyourmatch website as you have already been briefed.' There was a slight shift in his tone as Salim moved into the motivational mode. 'Remember that what we are going to do will be truly spectacular. It will surpass anything that has ever been attempted earlier.' His voice throbbed with the conviction of the true fanatic... or the ultimate psychopath. 'You will be remembered forever.'

On that note Salim pulled back and gestured towards Mai, who stepped up eagerly to take forward the lesson. This was his moment in the sun. He had about him the eager air of a professor addressing his first student.

'Here.' Mai extended his hand towards Karl. Nestled in his palm were two marble sized glass balls. Both of them were filled with a colourless liquid. As Karl took them from Mai, one of them slipped and fell to the floor. It hit the slatted wooden floor and broke with a thin crinkling sound. 'I'd handle them carefully if I were you,' Mai cautioned. 'There was only water inside that one, otherwise....' He gave a brittle laugh. Then he told them what would have happened to all three of them if a certain chemical had been inside the vial.

The matter-of-fact tone used by Mai to describe the end they would have met chilled even the hardened Salim. Karl looked petrified. He gazed at the remaining vial in his hand with acute distaste. One thing was certain: Mai now had their undivided attention.

MAI'S SESSION WITH KARL LASTED NEARLY TWO HOURS, BUT by the end of it he was confident that Karl would be able to do what was required of him.

'Good! That's it then. Keep going over what I have told you,' Mai said as he shook hands with Karl and showed him out. 'And in case any more doubts come up, I will clarify them for you either before you leave or when we meet next.'

Salim was on the phone when Mai closed the door after Karl. Ten minutes later, there was another soft knock on the door and Kismat and Sahiba limped in.

Salim is bringing them to me in the same order that he himself briefed them, Mai thought as he watched Salim go through the same ritual that he'd been through with Karl Gunther. Then Mai began to brief the two young women. His thought was confirmed when the Canadian Reis trouped in just after the Khan twins had departed.

TO MAI'S SURPRISE, AFTER HE FINISHED BRIEFING ABRAHAM Reis, instead of Erik Segan, Yakub Khan or Lars Borge, it was Ben Ashton who hesitantly entered the suite when he opened the door.

Maybe the others will come later, he told himself as he began briefing Erik Segan, who trooped in after Ben.

The briefing given to Erik was entirely different from the earlier briefings given to the others. So was the weapon to be used. Erik's operation was going to be totally different and far more deadly.

It was almost time for dinner when Mai finished.

'I think you handled the briefings fabulously.' Salim gave Mai an approving clap on his back. 'I am sure that each of them has understood how to handle the weapons and get them past security, and they've also understood the conditions that enhance or retard the effects of the weapon.' Mai gave a pleased smile. He was about to speak when Salim continued, 'I want you to give them all some time to mull over things so that you can clarify any doubts that may come up. Okay?' Salim didn't wait for a response. 'After that you can leave. When is your return flight, by the way?'

'On the eleventh,' Mai replied, hiding the surprise he was feeling. *So who were the others who had come to meet Salim?* the perennially inquisitive scientist asked himself as Salim left. *And why am I not being allowed to meet them?*

MAI WOULD NEVER HAVE GUESSED THAT JUST FOUR SUITES away, the men he was wondering about were being given a very thorough training by Cheema. The weapon they would use called for a session with a trained military hand and for that ex-Captain Azam Cheema of the ISI was ideally suited. Of course, there was a part of the briefing that was common to both teams. For the Alpha Team personnel, this had been handled by Salim.

'From the time you receive the weapon, you must ensure that you do *not* go home, or to the home of any one you know or are related to even distantly. You must not call or contact anyone or check into any hotel under your real name. Your mobile phones must be switched off at all times. You will not even call home to check your answering machines. Nor will you use any credit, debit, ATM or loyalty cards belonging to you. I want all traces of you to dry up… you must drop off all electronic radars.'

'Why all these precautions? I thought you said the operation was secure and would be totally under wraps. Are you expecting something to go wrong?'

'I am not,' Cheema had responded firmly and reassuringly. 'But you must remember that we are going to war.' He wagged a warning finger. 'In every battle the situation is fluid, anything can go wrong at any time. So, just to be on the safe side, we will always work on the premise that our operation *has* been compromised and they are out looking for us. We shall take all precautions accordingly. This way we will ensure we're always one step ahead of those trying to hunt us down, even if they are onto us.'

The logic made sense to all the team members.

'Just keep in mind that the only way to beat them is to ensure they do not spot you. *If* they spot you, they will home in on you within no time. Once that happens, they will bring you down immediately. Do bear in mind that the technological resources available to our enemies are vast. You can be spotted if there's the slightest slip up… one single swipe of a credit card… switching on your mobile phone… one wrong phone call... and the whole operation is blown and, of course, you're as good as dead.'

'Then how does one stay out of sight?'

'The best way to beat the hi-tech resources arrayed against you is to simply revert to the basics. The key is to hide in plain sight. Once you have custody of the weapon, get as close to the target as possible as soon as you can, and go to ground. Then, having done that, *stay still*. They won't be able to lock on to you as long as you stay still.' The urgency in Cheema's tone stressed the point. 'Any movement will invariably give you away, so move only to carry out the strike and when you do, *move fast*. Don't give the enemy time to react and seize the initiative.'

'What should I do if they do manage to find me?' Most of them had asked this question in some form or the other during the briefing.

'Then you are as good as dead in any case.'

Salim had prepared Cheema well for this question. *Trust me Cheema, in such matters, harsh candour is always best appreciated and likely to get the best possible result.*

'No matter what happens, don't let them take you alive. Not only will you be subjected to the humiliation of being held like a caged animal, you can bet they will get the truth out of you and that may jeopardize the rest of the mission.' Cheema saw most of them nodding confidently. 'No!' he cautioned sternly. 'Don't even think about it. Even the best and bravest of you will not be able to stand up to the chemicals for long. These days it is not tough to get the truth out of anyone. Trust me,' he urged fervently, 'if your cover is blown your best bet is to head straight for the enemy and activate your weapon. Make sure you are in the biggest crowd and take as many of the kafirs with you as you can. Don't let your sacrifice go to waste.'

The bald, unvarnished truth was met by a long pause, but none of them had faltered. Both terror-masters had watched the eyes of the future killers carefully as they briefed them.

Eyes don't lie. They are windows to the soul, always watch them carefully, Cheema remembered Salim telling him. Now he thought admiringly, *Salim has chosen his lashkar well. They are ready to die as easily as they are prepared to kill.*

THE TECHNICAL PART OF THE BRIEFING FOR TEAM BRAVO WAS very different from that given by Mai to Team Alpha. Cheema had also ensured that barring Liaquat Ali and Rahim Khan, who would be operating together, the other team members did not run into each other. He briefed Liaquat and Rahim first, then Yakub Khan, and finally Lars Borge. Each training session lasted much longer than the ones that Team Alpha had been through, but then the complexity of the weapon that Team Bravo would be using was far greater too.

'You must remember that the timer has three settings. The first is for immediate activation, the second will cause detonation after a fifteen minute delay and the third after a thirty-minute delay. If you are activating the weapon on the target itself, then choose the second setting. However, if you're going to activate it and then carry it into the target area, you must select the third setting. Also, in this case you must ensure you are inside the target area within two or three minutes so that you have time to deploy the weapon in the best possible place and still have adequate time to get away safely.'

'What about the first setting? The one for immediate activation....'

'That's just in case they're on to you.' There was a long silence. *That's understandable,* Cheema said to himself as he silently watched the duo absorb the input. *Soldiers hate to die. They'd much rather kill.*

'Remember,' Cheema spoke softly, but firmly. 'None of us is afraid to be martyred, but it is always better if we can walk away safely and then return to strike yet another blow at the kafir at some other time and place.'

In the end, Cheema was more than satisfied with the way his deadly disciples absorbed all the information about the weapon. So focused was each person on the task that lay ahead that not one of them even spared a thought for the catastrophe they were going to unleash, for the thousands who would die or be doomed to lead a crippled existence.

SALIM AND CHEEMA WERE TOGETHER AGAIN WHEN THEY met each member of their lashkar for the last time.

Once again, they met each of them individually and clarified all their doubts. At the end of this final briefing, each person was given his or her specific target. Stunned silence descended when they heard what their target was to be. Salim had anticipated this.

'Yes,' he announced grandiosely. 'It is going to be the boldest and most spectacular strike ever... even 9/11 will pale into insignificance.' Salim allowed the thought to linger since he knew that was what would sustain them over the coming days. 'They will remember us forever.'

'Make sure you spend enough time and survey the target thoroughly. You have enough time to do so without raising any suspicion,' Cheema said. 'And remember to keep a constant check on the mailbox of your meetyourmatch profile. It's crucial that everything takes place exactly to schedule. Only then will we achieve maximum impact.'

'Also, remember to send in your arrival and departure confirmations as soon as possible,' Salim added as he bid each of them farewell.

OVER THE NEXT TWO DAYS, ONE BY ONE, THE TERROR merchants began to scatter. The time had come for the next phase of the strike to commence. The first one to leave the Maldives was Mai; the important part of his work would begin now. He was the only one who had the expertise to make the weapons and also the only one who had access to the lethal materials that would be used in the weapons.

NONE OF THEM NOTICED THE FIT LOOKING MAN IN HIS thirties enter the suite occupied by Salim. Mai's flight for Beijing had already taken off from Colombo and most of the others were in various stages of checking out, or were on their way to Male Airport. Cheema had jumped at the opportunity graciously granted to him by Salim to take a tour of the neighbouring islands on a catamaran.

Cheema took a deep breath as the wind caught the catamaran and sent it skimming away from the shores of the Blue Moon over the electric blue waters. There were several other cats surfing the waves. Perhaps that was why he did not notice the bright yellow catamaran with the name of the neighbouring island resort emblazoned on it. Nor did he notice the man who jumped off it and dragged the cat onto the beach. The man's muscular build, walk and general demeanour gave away his military background as clearly as a crew cut would have. Beaching the catamaran, the man strode confidently towards Salim's suite.

'Salaam waleikum.' A big smile wreathed Salim's face as he greeted his guest and gave him a warm, comradely hug. For a change, the smile seemed genuine. In fact, it was the first time in all these days that Salim had showed any trace of genuine emotion. 'It is good to see you again.'

'Waleikum salaam, janaab.' The man was clearly deferential. 'The honour is mine.'

The two men spoke quietly for a while. Whatever Salim had to say to him did not take long. In fact, they spent the better part of their meeting talking about old times and going over the details of a bank account in Switzerland. Finally, Salim said, 'I think it is time you left, my friend. Cheema should be back any time now. I don't want anyone to see you. And remember, there must be no further contact between us.'

'Don't worry, sir. There will be no need for any.' The man hesitated slightly. 'Please do take care of my wife and children after....' He broke off.

'Do you trust me?' Salim gave the man a deep, penetrating look.

'Of course, sir,' the man replied instantly. 'With my life.'

'Then rest assured that I will take good care of them. You have my word.' The man nodded silently. 'Just get them out of the country as soon as possible. Their travel documents and details of all the arrangements are in the packet I have given you. I will ensure the wire transfer to your bank is done before you leave the island today.' Salim clasped the man's shoulder in a reassuring grip. 'I want you to stay completely focused on the task; it is of the utmost importance. And please remember that timing is very crucial in this mission.'

'Rest assured, janaab, I will not let you down.' The man saluted as he left. 'I will await your call.'

'Khuda hafiz.' Salim watched his trump card walk out and away from his suite. He knew this was the last time he was seeing him alive.

If he succeeds in his task he will definitely die. If he doesn't, we will both be dead.

THE DAY AFTER. ISLAMABAD

THE SLEEK, UNMARKED BLACK CAR WAS WAITING OUTSIDE THE airport when the flight from Dubai landed. It took Salim and Cheema straight to the tiny but exclusive restaurant where General Ehsan Haque, the ISI Director, was waiting for them. The top floor of the restaurant had been kept vacant by the owner, an ex-ISI agent provocateur who had been unlucky during the Afghan misadventure and lost a leg when he strayed into an unmarked minefield.

Haque and Salim greeted each other with the warmth and bonhomie of old comrades. Cheema hung around on the fringes of the meeting, absorbing everything but saying little.

Two hours later, Salim left for Murree while Cheema stayed on at the safe house in the suburbs that Haque had arranged for him. Over the next few days, a variety of people streamed in to meet him. The rest of the time, Cheema was busy on the phone. When he finally left Islamabad a week later to rejoin Salim at Murree, he had about him the unmistakable air of a man who had done his duty and done it well. The manpower, money, equipment and documentation required to execute the next part of the mission were all firmly in place.

'Everything that we need is absolutely ready, sir. I just need to make one call to activate it.'

'Excellent!' Salim beamed proudly. 'You've done a fine job.'

Phase One was complete.

Phase Two: The Weapons

Urumqi Special Weapons Facility, China

CHEEMA WAS IN THE MIDST OF HIS HECTIC PARLEY AT Islamabad when Mai walked into his office. There was a noticeable spring in his step and despite the early hour, he looked fully charged.

'You are bright and early today, sir,' the security guard greeted him as he checked Mai into the secure facility, but there was no surprise in his voice since they were all quite used to the erratic and eccentric working habits of the scientists. In any case, the guard, like most of the facility staff, was quite fond of the usually cheerful Mai.

Fobbing him off with the required polite noises, Mai headed to his office. Controlling his impatience with some difficulty, he first cleared the backlog of paperwork and emails that had accumulated in his absence. Then he moved to the tiny, secluded but well-equipped personal lab that he merited as the director of the facility.

It took him a few hours to work out the precise

material requirements and place a requisition for them. He made sure he added several more items to the list to camouflage its real purpose, just in case someone was keeping tabs on him.

With a feeling of deep satisfaction, he returned to his office and went back to the grind of routine work. He knew it would take at least two days for the materials to reach him.

THE REQUIRED MATERIALS REACHED MAI ON THE MORNING of the third day. Their arrival triggered a sharp wave of impatient energy in him. In the days that followed, Mai had to struggle with himself to stay away from his lab. Despite his excitement, he did not forget Salim's warning. 'You must not say or do anything that will set off an alarm in anyone's head. Remember, this is the most critical phase of our operation; if you fail, we all fail.'

'Don't worry,' Mai had reassured him. 'I will stick to my regular routine and ensure none of my work is pending.'

Twelve days later, he was more than satisfied: he had finished making the tiny round glass vials, and redesigned the caps for the bottles of aftershave and eau de cologne, and the room-freshener spray cans. All the items required tremendous precision and taxed his skills to the fullest. Over the next two days, he carefully and repeatedly tested each one of them.

'Zero tolerance!' Mai told Fatima. 'There is simply

no room for even the minutest error. Even the tiniest leak will be fatal.'

'I can imagine,' Fatima sympathized. 'When are you going to get hold of the....' She hesitated.

'Tomorrow,' Mai cut in. 'I have to do it tomorrow. We're running out of time now.'

AS THE DIRECTOR OF THE BIOCHEM FACILITY, ONE OF MAI'S key responsibilities was to audit all controlled materials held at Urumqui every month and ensure it was all accounted for. This audit was critical since some of these materials were so lethal that even a few droplets were more than adequate to trigger off an epidemic of unimaginable proportions. The audit was supposed to be done without warning and not on any fixed or scheduled date, to ensure that no detectable (and thus breachable) pattern existed. So no eyebrows were raised when Mai began the audit early the next morning.

The audit confirmed that none of the lethal germs, viruses and chemicals that the facility dabbled in was unaccounted for. No one even missed the two tiny vials of Variola Major virus and the five larger vials of VX Gas that Mai removed from the specimen bank during the audit. And this, again, was not surprising since Mai had replaced both with similar looking vials.

It's not as though someone is going to open them and check the contents. Mai gave a wry smile as he surveyed the booty safely hidden in hermetically sealed containers in his personal mini-laboratory. Both items looked harmless and insignificant, but Mai knew just how lethal they were. He suppressed a shudder at the thought of what he had to do next.

Let me begin with the Variola, so that even if I make a mistake I will at least live long enough to complete the mission.

Stiffening his resolve, he donned his protective suit and reached for the glass vial containing the deadly virus.

VARIOLA MAJOR IS THE MOST COMMON FORM OF SMALLPOX, a contagious and sometimes fatal disease. The *pox* part of the word smallpox is derived from the Latin word for *spotted* and refers to the small raised bumps that appear on the face and hands of an infected person. There is no specific cure or treatment for smallpox, and the only prevention is vaccination. There are basically two clinical forms of smallpox and Variola Major is the severe and more common form, which causes extensive rashes and a high fever.

'The Variola virus emerged in human populations hundreds of years ago. It is unique to humans and in the twentieth century alone caused 300–500 million deaths worldwide,' Mai had told Salim and Cheema when he first met them. 'There are four types of Variola Major smallpox: Ordinary, which is the most frequent type and accounts for almost ninety per cent of the cases; Modified, the second type, which is also mild and occurs in previously vaccinated persons;

and Flat and Haemorrhagic, both of which are rare and extremely severe. In general, Variola Major has an overall fatality rate of about thirty per cent. However, the Flat and Haemorrhagic forms are extremely virulent and have a mortality rate of close to ninety-six per cent.'

'Really? But hasn't smallpox been eradicated?'

'Of course it has,' Mai replied. 'After a long but successful vaccination campaign, it was eradicated globally, and no cases have been reported since the last one in Somalia in 1977. Today the Variola virus exists only in rare and heavily guarded laboratory stockpiles in just a handful of countries.'

'That is why it is the perfect weapon.' Salim had smiled softly. 'No one will be prepared to handle it. There will be total panic and chaos. As for the death toll,' Salim shrugged, 'one cannot even imagine how many kafirs will die.'

'That's right!' Mai replied softly. 'But it is not just the kafirs who will die. Once the virus spreads, it will kill almost anyone it comes in contact with.'

'True.' Salim met Mai's gaze levelly. 'Sometimes sacrifices are necessary. We cannot win the jihad if we are going to be so squeamish.'

THE VARIOLA MAJOR VIRUS REMOVED BY MAI FROM THE URUMQI specimen bank was the type that caused Hemorrhagic smallpox, the most lethal and infectious of the lot. The virus has an incubation period of seven to twelve days and its initial symptoms of fever, muscle ache and vomiting are quite similar to influenza and the common cold. The skin does not blister; instead, bleeding occurs under the skin, making it appear charred and black. It is the bleeding and the loss of fluids and electrolytes that cause death.

'The particular strain I propose to use was stolen from Soviet stockpiles in those tumultuous days following the disintegration of the USSR. It had been developed and produced in the Siberian town of Koltsovo in 1990 when the Soviets were looking to use genetically altered strains of smallpox as a biological weapon.'

'If that's true, how come such weapons have not been used in any war so far?' Cheema had asked Mai.

'Of course they have been used,' Salim cut in with an unpleasant laugh. 'Do you think humans will ever leave any stone unturned to kill their enemies?'

'He's right!' Mai nodded vigorously. 'Almost as soon as humans had figured out how to make arrows, they were dipping them in excreta to make them poisonous.'

'In shit?' Cheema couldn't contain his surprise.

'Absolutely! In shit,' Mai replied with a grimace, not overly enthused by Cheema's choice of words. 'You have no idea how effective it was, especially in those days when there were no antibiotics.'

Cheema gave an exaggerated shudder.

'The Romans went a step further. They used to throw dead animals into wells to poison the enemy's water supply. In 184 BC, Hannibal used live snakes and in 1346 the Tartar, Khan Janibeg, had plague-infested dead bodies of his own men catapulted into Kaffa... in fact, this was also done by the Russians troops fighting the Swedes in the eighteenth century. The Spanish conquistador Pizarro gave clothing contaminated with the smallpox virus to South American natives just as Britain's Lord Jeffrey Amherst handed over blankets that had been used by smallpox patients to Native Americans during the French and Indian wars.'

Mai saw the look of revulsion on the faces of the two men sitting opposite him.

'Precisely! They are lethal beyond imagination. That's why the Biological Weapons Convention of 1972 prohibits their use. However, the primary reason that most nations hesitate to use them is simply because containing the effects of a biological agent is a nightmarish proposition... in terms of both time and space. After all, one would want to eventually occupy the ground after destroying the enemy, right?'

'Go on... tell us more about its properties,' Salim said, ignoring the question.

So Mai had.

The conversation came back to him now, as he reached for the container of Variola Major.

The deadly virus had originally been developed for delivery as an aerosol. Now Mai carefully repackaged it into the bottles of aftershave lotion and the two cans of room-freshener. Working in the heavy protective suit was hard, tedious work but there was no alternative. It took Mai six days to finish the task. Then he moved on to the next phase of the operation, and began to repackage the VX Gas he had stolen.

PRODUCED VIA THE TRANSESTER PROCESS, VX GAS IS ONE OF the most lethal chemicals created by man. Developed in England in 1952 by the Porton Down Chemical Weapons Research Centre at Wiltshire, its chemical formula is CH3CH20-P(o)(CH3)-SCH2CH2N (C3H7)2 and the unwieldy formal chemical name given to it is S-2 (diisopropylamino)ethyl O-ethyl methylphosphonothioate. Some time later, the British traded VX technology to the Americans in return for thermonuclear weapons technology. From that day onwards, the human race has expended considerable effort to make VX Gas even more lethal and virulent.

'Despite its name, VX Gas is actually an oily yellow, odourless liquid with a low volatility,' Mai Hu had briefed Salim and Cheema. 'The "V" in its name signifies its extreme persistence, unlike its cousins of the "G" variety, like GA (Tabun) and GB (Sarin). VX is an excellent adhesive. In fact, a special form has been developed that is so adhesive that it is virtually impossible to remove it from any surface it comes in contact with.'

'How exactly does it work?' Cheema had asked.

'Well, in the liquid form, VX gets absorbed into the human body through the eyes or the skin, and takes effect in about an hour. However, in the aerosol form, it has *immediate* effect. In both cases, the lethal dose for humans is a mere 10 milligrams and the end result is painful death preceded by violent tremors, incontinence and failure of the heart and lungs.'

'Damn!' Cheema raised an eyebrow in surprise. 'It takes that little, huh?'

'Yes, it's absolutely lethal.'

'Where in the past has it been weaponized?'

'Oh, in several countries. It is a well established, though little publicized fact that there are approximately 1.9 million artillery shells filled with VX Gas stored at the Shchuchye Military Base, near the Siberian city of Chelyabinsk, in South-Central Russia. Each shell is capable of delivering an instant and deeply painful death to 85,000 people. Most of them have been developed as tactical weapons....' Mai noted the questioning look on Cheema's face and clarified, 'Tactical weapons have a shorter lethality time, to ensure that one's own forces can move in safely and secure the ground once enemy troops in the target area have been destroyed.' Cheema nodded as he got the drift, and Mai resumed, 'The destruction of these shells has been put off till 2012 due to paucity of funds.'

Both the rogue intelligence officers were listening to Mai with rapt attention. They were fully aware of the awesome credentials of the man sitting before them.

'Not that America, Russia's Cold War foe, is lagging behind in the field of chemical weapons. During the 1950s, America conducted an ambitious nerve gas program during which 400,000 M-55 rockets were manufactured. Each rocket was capable of delivering a *five kilogram* load of Sarin. Many of these were found to have a serious manufacturing defect, hence in 1967 and 1968, all of them were sunk in about 2000 metres of water barely 240 kilometres off the New York coastline.'

Mai noticed the rapid exchange of glances between the two men sitting before him. 'No!' He pre-empted the thought. 'Don't even think about it. Getting them out of such deep water is simply too gigantic a task. In any case, it's hard to tell whether they would still be of any use. The entire effort is more than likely to be a sheer waste of time and money. Not to mention the fact that it would alert the Yanks for sure.'

The Brigadier had shrugged. Cheema had not bothered to respond.

As he worked, Mai's movements were deliberate and extra cautious. Unlike with the Variola virus, he would not get even a moment's reprieve if he made a mistake with the VX Gas.

Death will be instantaneous and it will be excruciatingly painful.

He suppressed the shudder that accompanied this thought as he went to work on the deadly chemical.

THE VIALS OF VX GAS MISAPPROPRIATED BY MAI CONTAINED the most virulent form of the lethal nerve gas. Handling the aerosol and avoiding detection by any of his colleagues while doing so was not easy, but the resourceful Mai proved more than equal to the task.

On the night of 18 April, when Mai returned home, he had with him several dozen glass vials, each one not bigger than a large marble. Frangible glass, three millimetres thick, had been used to make the vials. Every vial was filled with an almost clear vapour that was barely discernible to the naked eye. The glass was thick enough to withstand transportation, yet thin enough to shatter on impact against any reasonably hard surface.

Mai carefully placed the deadly vials in the huge locker in the basement of his house, along with the cans of Variola Major that were already stored there. With a sense of deep satisfaction he turned the key in the lock and went up to inform his wife that finally, he was done.

That night, before going to bed, Mai logged onto his meetyourmatch profile and sent off a message to Salim.

Thanks for the details forwarded by you. Please give me a couple of days to think over things. I will be in touch with you on the twenty-fifth or twenty-sixth of this month.

IN THE SAFE CONFINES OF THE BUNGALOW IN MURREE, SALIM laughed aloud as he read Mai's message. His face aglow with excitement, he charged out of his room. 'He's done it, Cheema. Mai has made the weapons.'

'Fantastic!' Cheema beamed broadly. 'Should I activate the others then?'

'Of course! I'll alert the strike teams. You go ahead

with your people. It's time to trigger the next phase of our mission.'

The two men went about their tasks with a surging sense of enthusiasm.

Soon a stream of messages flowed out from Salim's computer to each person on teams Alpha and Bravo. This time there was no difference in the messages sent to the two teams.

While Salim was sending the messages, Cheema was on the phone. An hour later, he left the bungalow and was on his way to Lahore.

Not too far behind him, one by one, as they received Salim's message, the members of Strike Team Alpha reached for the travel bags they had kept ready and began to move.

Strike Team Bravo also made their final preparations, but they would not be moving out of the target cities, since their weapons were being delivered to them.

The strike had now moved smoothly into its third phase and as yet, not one of the intelligence agencies in the world had the faintest idea of the calamity that was rushing towards them at breakneck speed.

Phase Three: Breaching the Barriers

KIRANA HILLS MUNITIONS DEPOT, PAKISTAN

THERE WAS NOTHING OUT OF THE ORDINARY ABOUT THE small army convoy that drove up to the gates of the Munitions Depot just after midnight. Nor was there anything out of the ordinary in the documentation carried by the young Captain commanding the rifle platoon escorting the convoy. As far as anyone could tell, it was a simple transfer of ordinances from the munitions depot to a designated military post.

What *was* a bit out of the ordinary was the nature of the consignment mentioned in the papers carried by the Captain. Keeping in view the security SOP (Standard Operating Procedure) for such special items, a call was made to the CO of the weapons depot. The CO was a man known to play by the book. As per the protocol governing the movement of such weapons, he picked up the phone and called the person who had signed off the authorizations. The authorizations checked out fine.

Two hours later, the small convoy drove out of

the munitions depot. Safely nestled in the rear of the truck in the middle of the convoy were the four pieces of cargo they had come to collect, neatly packaged and crated. Each crate contained a specially constructed mini nuclear weapon.

Also referred to as suitcase nukes, they were plutonium fuelled, gun-type atomic weapons almost identical in size and design to the Soviet RA-115 or the American MK-54 SADM (Small Atomic Demolition Munitions). Codenamed CM-911 by the Pakistan Army, they were more commonly referred to as Chote Miyan in daily parlance.

Designed for covert use by Special Forces, each nuke was barely 60x40x20 centimetres in size and almost impossible to detect. Each Chote Miyan had a yield of one kiloton (that is, the equivalent of 1000 kilotons of conventional high explosive) and was eminently capable of destroying every living thing in a small city and rendering it radioactively unfit for habitation for many, many years.

A FEW HOURS LATER, THE CONVOY DROVE INTO A SMALL warehouse on the outskirts of Lahore. The warehouse belonged to a seldom advertised, low-key freight and forwarding company headquartered in Karachi. The company was a legitimate business concern. Unknown to most people, it was also a front for the ISI and a key component in the narco-nuclear-terror trade carried out by the ISI.

There was a specialist three-man crew waiting at

the warehouse, which had been converted into a well equipped and brightly lit workshop. They took charge of the four pieces of cargo. Cheema emerged from the shadows as the convoy departed.

'I want you to check everything and let me know if there is anything else that you need,' he told the chief of the crew and then waited patiently as they went to work on the cargo.

A few hours later, the man beckoned to him. 'It's all there.'

'Good. Now make sure you guys do a thorough job.'

'Don't worry about it.' The crew went to work on the cargo even as Cheema took a last look around, and left.

BY THE END OF THE SECOND DAY, THE FIRST CHOTE MIYAN had been beautifully camouflaged and repackaged. It did not look even remotely like the suitcase it had resembled when it left the Kirana Hills Munitions Depot.

First, an additional lead lining had been placed all around it, to rule out any possibility of a radiation leak. Thereafter, a rectangular plate with four evenly spaced holes drilled into it at carefully measured distances was attached to it. Then the whole thing was neatly fitted inside an empty jeep tyre.

Cheema arrived within an hour of getting the call from the warehouse. He gave a satisfied grunt after examining the finished product. He gave a louder grunt as he ran the Electronic Dosimeter over the suitcase nuke and noted that it did not even blink.

'Just try that one there.' The chief of the crew pointed at the SynOdys Radiation Monitoring System installed in one corner of the room. 'That's the type being used at most major airports and harbours these days.'

Cheema wheeled the nuke slowly past the monitor.

Not a beep! Great! That takes care of the radiation problem.

This was essential. With the heightened security alerts prevalent these days, Radiation Monitoring Systems were deployed at almost all the main entry points of most countries.

Replacing the nuke on the rack, Cheema asked, 'What about the controller and the timer?'

'There have been no major changes. The handler has to simply strip off the outer casing that we have added on to camouflage it.' The man showed him the four key points from where the casing had to be stripped away and continued, 'And then he has to plug in the controller... that too, only for this one, since we had to detach it. This is the most time consuming part of the process and can take five to six minutes.'

'That long?'

'I assume the handler will be working under active operational conditions,' the man replied, giving Cheema a level look, 'which means he has to do it very discreetly to ensure he is not detected.' The man waited, but Cheema did not respond, so he continued, 'That's why it will take him a little more time than what we can achieve here. After that he has to key in the arming code twice to initiate the firing sequence. Finally, he has to set the timer and then key in the activation code. The whole process should not take more than fifteen to seventeen minutes max, even if external circumstances are extremely... unfavourable.'

'If I'm not wrong, the timer has only three settings.'

'That's absolutely right. The lowest is thirty minutes, the next one is forty-five minutes and the third setting is for a one hour delay.'

When Cheema spoke again, he had lowered his voice. 'Is it possible for you to alter these settings?' It was obvious he did not want the others in the room to hear.

'Right now? Here in the workshop? Yes it is, but not once Chote Miyan is out in the field.'

'Then do it. I want the first setting to be operational immediately, the second after a fifteen minute delay and the third after thirty minutes. You can do that?'

'Yes, of course I can, but that means the person who is going to deploy the weapon will have no time to get clear if he uses either of the first two settings. He will also go down....'

'Do you always ask so many questions?' There was menace in Cheema's voice. 'I want you to do it. Okay?'

'Okay.' The man was clearly cowed down. 'On all four bombs?'

'Of course. How much time do you need?'

'About an hour per device.'

'Have the first one ready right away and the others before they go out.' Cheema began to turn away when he stopped and spoke again. 'I hope you have no problems with any of these orders?' His tone was still low and even. 'And you have no problem keeping vital operational information to yourself?'

'No, no, of course not,' the man replied instantly, his tone subdued.

Cheema gave a curt you-will-bear-watching-my-friend nod.

'Get the first one ready. The one for which you have detached the controller.' Turning away, he stalked off to one corner, extracted his satellite phone and began to speak into it softly. The call lasted several minutes.

A few hours later, the carefully repackaged and reprogrammed Chote Miyan was on board a jeep headed for Karachi port.

Urumqi

WHEN MAI SAW THE MESSAGE FROM SALIM, HE KNEW THAT similar messages must have been sent out to the entire strike team. *So, finally it has begun.* He could not suppress the sharp thrill of excitement that shot through him.

It was on this high that he arrived in his office that morning. There was one final task left for him to complete before he left for the Fourth International

Workshop on Biotechnological Approaches to Chemical Weapon Destruction, scheduled to be held at New Delhi on 27–28 April. The trip would not raise any eyebrows because Mai had attended the third workshop at Saratov, Russia in August 2000.

To Mai, this final task was the least palatable. 'Must I do that?' he had argued with Salim in the Maldives.

'Yes, you must! If you want all traces of your involvement to be eliminated, you have no option,' Salim had pointed out. 'I know you are attached to the lab, but you must remember that you are a very valuable asset to the jihad. Your cover is of paramount importance.' Mai had to admit the man was right and had agreed to the plan.

Even though he was working in full view of dozens of his colleagues, Mai got away undetected simply because no one expected him to be doing anything untoward. *Cheema was right, it is always best to hide in plain sight.*

It took Mai barely an hour to slip the cans of air-freshener filled with VX Gas into the air-conditioning ducts that led into the main conference hall and the primary laboratory where the majority of the research staff worked. He had fitted highly sophisticated timer devices on the release valves and had already set the activation time before he slipped them in.

Getting the explosives into the specimen bank area was much harder, but Mai managed to get them in without being detected. Explosives were not something he was used to handling. Controlling his fear and discomfiture, he carefully followed the instructions Cheema had given him, and initiated the timer on the explosive charges. He set the same date and time that he had set on the VX Gas cans. *The poor sods will not even know what hit them.*

MAI SPENT THE EVENING WITH HIS SECOND-IN-COMMAND, briefing him on the various things to be taken care of while he was away. 'A lot of the top brass are going to be here for the quarterly research review next month,' Mai stressed. 'You must pay special attention to it.'

'Aren't they always?' The second-in-command sighed in exasperation. 'They expect us to produce results as though we're cooks trying out new recipes. Don't they realize how painstaking and time consuming research can be?'

'That's true, but it is a reality we have to live with.' Mai was used to this gripe from almost every scientist he had worked with. 'Anyway, I want you to conduct a pre-conference on the twenty-eighth and have everyone go over his or her presentations.'

'That's no problem, chief, you don't worry about it. I'll schedule it right away.'

'I've already done that. The email went out just before you came in. You just ensure everyone takes it seriously. Remember, our budget depends on it.'

'Leave it to me, boss.' On that note they parted.

AS HE DROVE OUT THAT EVENING, MAI PAUSED NEAR THE facility gates for a long time. He knew he would never see it like this again. When he returned... *if he returned*, Mai reminded himself, he would not be allowed within miles of the facility.

It would have become a devastated shell of a building. The whole facility would be flooded with the deadliest variety of viruses and chemicals known to mankind and would remain sealed off for many decades to come.

There was a twinge of regret in Mai's heart as he finally engaged gears and drove away. After all, it had been his home for many years now.

Just remember why you are doing this, he told himself. *Remember that no matter what they say or do, the Chinese State is the enemy. It has and will continue to destroy our Muslim brothers.*

Pulling himself together, Mai hardened his heart and accelerated towards the new destiny that awaited him.

A few hours later, the jet carrying Mai was airborne and heading swiftly towards Beijing, from where he would take the China Airlines flight to New Delhi. Beautifully camouflaged, the aerosolized VX Gas and Variola Major vials were safely nestled in the baggage that he had checked in.

Keeping in view the latest security stipulations, Mai had sealed the aftershave and room-freshener sprays in the See-Buy-Fly plastic security pouches with

'Open only at the Destination' printed boldly across, that all duty-free shops at all airports use these days. In each of these plastic pouches he had also neatly placed the required bill of sale from the Delhi duty-free shop that it was supposed to have been bought at. All the bills were clever forgeries, but one would have to open the packets and check them carefully to know this.

Salim had been right: *The best security precaution becomes redundant the minute it becomes routine. By now security men the world over have become so used to seeing such items in sealed pouches that they rarely give them a second glance.*

Mai had no doubts about being able to get through airport security at Beijing. His rank and status were more than adequate to ensure he sailed through all the security checks.

The airport security at Delhi will be the real challenge. Let us see if those cretins have the mental capability to see through the camouflage.

Mai smiled to himself. He was confident he would get through unscathed.

MAI'S JET WAS ACCELERATING DOWN THE RUNAWAY WHEN the first of Salim's chosen killers, Erik Segan, also took off. In the next few hours, one by one, from various points of the compass, Karl Gunther, Ben Ashton, Abrahim Reis, and Sahiba and Kismat Khan also became airborne.

The ruthless terrorist armada was starting to

converge yet again. This time the destination was New Delhi.

Karachi, Pakistan

THE MAN WHO CARRIED THE FIRST NUKE DOWN TO KARACHI delivered it to a small house on the outskirts of town. The dishevelled looking man who took it from him did not look or behave like the highly trained naval commando that he was. The man had totally submerged himself in his role, and looked perfectly at home in the fishing dhow that sailed away from Karachi harbour a little later. The three other people in the dhow with him were also similarly attired. Like him, two of them were Pakistani naval commandos.

The third was a highly talented man named Sohail Ahmed. The thirty-year-old had been employed as a postman in the Indian Postal Service for the past seven years. For four of those seven years he had also been on the payroll of the Pakistani ISI.

It was Sohail who took charge of the Chote Miyan when the dhow finally hit the Indian coastline in the dead of the night.

The Rann of Kutch, India

ALL ALONG THE COASTLINE, ON BOTH SIDES OF THE international border (IB) between India and Pakistan, there are hundreds of small channels where the Arabian Sea forays inland. Just south of the IB is one of the larger channels which runs right up to the town of Lakhpat in the Rann of Kutch.

Travelling without any lights, the dhow swept silently out of the ocean and hit land at the mouth of this channel. Waiting for them was a rugged Mahindra Bolero jeep driven by Yusuf, Sohail's younger brother. The camouflaged nuke was rapidly transferred to the rear of the Bolero. The two brothers bid a quiet farewell to the men in the dhow and quickly drove off into the darkness. Simultaneously, the dhow pulled away towards the safe anonymity of international waters.

Crossing Lakhpat in the darkness of night, the Ahmed brothers used the bypass to circle around the city of Bhuj and were at Radhanpur by morning. They stopped there for a quick, though somewhat late breakfast, and then Sohail continued onward in the Bolero while Yusuf took a bus home.

It was way past dinner time when Sohail drove off the highway onto the road that would take him to the picturesque hill town of Mount Abu. Pulling off the road, into the shadow of a large tree a couple of miles short of town, he used his mobile phone to make a call. Then he sat down to wait.

Twenty minutes later, a maroon Tata Safari SUV drove up the dark road. It pulled over about a hundred metres away. Sohail was reaching for his mobile phone when it began to ring. 'Yes. It's me in the Bolero. You're in the Tata Safari... right?'

The Tata Safari maintained a stoic watch over the

deserted road as Sohail took the Chote Miyan out of the Bolero, propped it against the tree on the side of the road, got back into his vehicle and drove away.

FROM BEHIND THE WHEEL OF THE TATA SAFARI, YAKUB KHAN watched Sohail drive away. He saw the Bolero hit the highway and accelerate. It was only after the red glow of the rear tail lamps had receded into the darkness that he started the engine and drove down to where the nuke rested.

You must ensure that none of the other operatives you come in contact with get to see you, and whatever conversation you have with them must be kept to the bare minimum. Be damn careful you don't give away anything about your identity. Cheema had drilled this into their heads during the training, and Yakub was good at following orders. He had even blacked out the number plate of his Tata Safari with mud for this brief but critical rendezvous.

Removing the large, round, hardened plastic cover placed over the Safari's spare wheel, which was fixed onto the outer side of the vehicle's rear door, he quickly loosened the four bolts that held the wheel in place. Carefully, he hefted it into the Safari. Where the spare wheel had been, a small rectangular cut had been made in the vehicle's rear door. The cut was almost in the dead centre of the four long metallic bolts which housed the wheel.

Now Yakub carefully stripped away the bomb's outer layer of camouflage and extracted the control panel from its centre. It was just slightly bigger than a television remote, though a lot heavier. It was connected to the nuke with a set of wires nearly two metres long. Typically, the control panel would have been embedded into the device. However, this was the Chote Miyan whose controller had been detached and then re-fixed with an additional length of wiring at Cheema's instructions. This was to enable Yakub to arm and trigger it from the rear seat of the Safari, without having to remove the nuke from the spare wheel bracket.

Next he placed the Chote Miyan on the four-pronged bracket, carefully passing the controller through the cut in the door till it came out on the other side, inside the vehicle. He then replaced the layer of camouflage till the Chote Miyan had once again acquired the round wheel shape that had been given to it at the Lahore warehouse. Placing it on the four bolts which had earlier carried the spare wheel, he tightened the nuts carefully, securing the bomb in the place of the spare wheel. The four holes drilled into the plate attached to the bomb fit perfectly.

Good!

Though he had sent in the precise measurements himself, Yakub had been worried. To the extent that he had even carried a small drill with him just in case he needed to make minor adjustments. Finally satisfied that the nuke was firmly fixed, he placed the huge plastic cover with Tata Safari emblazoned on it over it, completely concealing the bomb from view.

Now focusing on the inner side of the door, in the dim illumination of the Safari's rear cabin light, Yakub wrapped the remote controller in a piece of bubble wrapping and slid it into the gap between the car's body and the inner upholstery. This would ensure that it did not rattle or make any noise when the vehicle was in motion. He then fed the extra length of wiring into the gap before closing it from inside with a piece of upholstery. Now the cut was no longer visible from inside the vehicle, not to a casual observer in any case.

Having rechecked everything once, he wiped the number plate clean and drove back to the hotel in Mount Abu where he was staying.

Both the children and his wife were fast asleep when Yakub let himself into the hotel room. The excitement of the holiday and traipsing around town the whole day had exhausted them totally. They were still sleeping when he used his laptop to send the confirmatory message to Salim through his meetyourmatch profile.

Finally, before joining his wife in bed, Yakub switched off his mobile phone, snapping all identifiable links with the outside world. He had left no details of where he would be going either at his office or at his home in Delhi. At the hotel, he was registered under a false name and had paid in cash in advance to ensure there was no electronic trail.

For all practical purposes, Yakub Khan had dropped off the radar.

LATE ON THE NIGHT OF 25 APRIL, IN THE COMFORT OF HIS library in Murree, Salim read Yakub's message and smiled with satisfaction.

So far so good! Allah is definitely watching over us.

Salim rubbed his hands in glee. After all, the Delhi strike was the most important to him personally.

NEW DELHI

ALLAH MUST HAVE BEEN WATCHING OVER THEM BECAUSE neither the security man who frisked Mai, nor the man who screened his baggage were up to speed that day. Maybe it was because of the unearthly hour, for the China Airlines flight from Beijing landed at Terminal 2 of Delhi's Indira Gandhi International Airport at 0145 hours with a host of other flights. The sheer crush of passengers short-circuited the security checks considerably. Or maybe it was plain and simple luck. Either way, nothing untoward was detected and an hour later Mai found himself in the lobby of the Radisson Hotel, located on the National Highway Number 8, just a couple of miles from the airport. In fact, proximity to the airport was the primary reason Mai had opted for this hotel; it made it very convenient for the other team members to link up with him. Exhausted after the long journey and knowing he had a full day ahead of him, Mai quickly finished unpacking and retired to bed.

HE WAS STILL SLEEPING WHEN, A FEW HUNDRED MILES TO the northwest, at Mount Abu, Yakub awoke his wife and kids bright and early. An hour later, all four of them were in the huge maroon Tata Safari, speeding down the highway to Udaipur, barely 95 kilometres away. An hour and a half later, they halted at a dhaba on the outskirts of Udaipur. They had finished breakfast and were getting back into the Safari to continue their journey past Udaipur city towards Ajmer when, in Delhi, there was a tentative knock on Mai's door.

MAI HAD BARELY FINISHED DRESSING AFTER A RUSHED breakfast when Erik Segan knocked on the door. He literally flew inside when Mai opened the door.

'I'm sorry,' the musician blurted out jerkily without any preamble. 'But I've got totally confused and you'll need to explain everything to me once again.' The wasted ex-junkie had a harried, nervous air about him.

He looks like he desperately needs a fix.

'Don't worry about it,' Mai replied reassuringly. 'That's why I'm here. It's always better to be sure than to goof it up.'

He needs to calm down. If he walks into the airport like this, he will set off every possible alarm. They will stop him just because of the way he looks. At this stage, if even one person is taken, it will jeopardize the whole mission. I need to calm him….

'That's why I came early, even though my flight out is only after midnight,' Erik said, interrupting Mai's thoughts with an ingratiating smile.

Together, the two men went over everything in detail. When he finally left the hotel room a little after noon, Erik looked a lot more confident.

I might as well order lunch from room service. Mai sighed as he checked his watch. *That surly German should be here any minute now.* He'd been looking forward to stepping out of the room for a bit. *Oh well! Maybe later… there's no time now.*

Sure enough, the waiter had hardly cleared the remains of his meal when Karl Gunther arrived. He had the same doubts that Erik had, so Mai had to take him through everything from scratch. Consequently, by the time Karl left, the sun was ready to begin its descent over the horizon.

This is exhausting. Rotating his shoulders to ease the stiffness that had set in, Mai threw himself on the bed. By now the effects of the long flight and the lack of sleep had begun to take their toll on his body. *I hope the others have not forgotten everything that I drilled into them.* With a weary sigh, he closed his eyes and tried to sleep.

MAI WAS BRIEFING KARL AT THE RADISSON HOTEL WHEN YAKUB drove into Hotel Regency Ajmer. The 450 kilometre long drive from Mount Abu had sapped the energy of the whole family and it was only towards late evening that they finally stepped out of the hotel for a turn about town.

The dargah of Khwaja Moin-ud-din Chisti, the famous Sufi saint, was a scant five minute walk from their hotel. The haunting, rhythmic music emanating from the dargah tugged at them and they found themselves drawn towards it. Not once did the irony strike Yakub as he basked in the serenity of the dargah of a man who had propagated only love and peace.

The family was admiring the beautiful façade of the dargah when, in Delhi, the quiet, perennially polite Abraham Reis walked up to Mai Hu's hotel room and knocked on the door softly, snapping Mai out of his restless sleep. Still groggy, he stumbled to the door.

THE FOCUSED, SOFT-SPOKEN REIS HAD NO DOUBTS ABOUT THE weapon or how to handle it. Much to Mai's relief, Reis collected his deadly package with minimal conversation and fuss, and left. Not long after Reis had gone, the telephone rang, aggravating the migraine that had begun to balloon in the scientist's head. Mai had just finished talking and put down the phone when the housekeeping staff landed up to turn down his bed for the night. They had barely finished and left when Sahiba and Kismat arrived. Though tired by now, Mai greeted them with a smile. He had worked the hardest to put their weapon together and was inordinately proud of the result.

'It was quite a challenge, but I've managed to do them up exactly the way you two wanted it.' Mai opened two jewellery cases and held up the huge beaded necklaces he had made for the sisters. Each necklace was a strand of round, coloured glass vials. 'I've even made matching earrings and bracelets.' He gave a proud, satisfied smile as he held them out. The two sisters reached for them gingerly.

'How strong are the vials?' Sahiba asked tentatively.

'Don't worry!' Mai said reassuringly. 'You can wear them without a care. As long as you don't sit on them or drop them. See…' Opening one of the remaining jars of cream, he fished out a couple of the round glass vials. Both were covered with cream so, carefully putting down the jar, he retrieved a tissue from the box on the bedside table and wiped them clean. 'These are also made from the same material as the vials used for the necklaces. See… they're quite hard.' He handed a vial to Sahiba, who took it rather gingerly. Mai held up the other one between his thumb and index finger. 'This is how I tested them,' he said as he released the vial in his hand.

The air in the room suddenly went stiff with tension as the fragile vial fell towards the ground. It seemed to be rolling through the air in slow motion. All three of them knew what the vial contained and what would happen if it broke. Neither of them was afraid to die. They wouldn't have volunteered for this mission if they were. But none of them wanted to die just yet.

For an interminably long moment, three pairs of eyes followed the vial of VX Gas as it spun through the air, landed on the thick carpet and bounced gently a couple of times. When it finally stopped rolling and came to rest by the side of the bed, Mai spoke.

'See!' There was triumph in his voice. 'They're not as delicate as they look.' Breath hissed painfully back into their lungs as the two sisters exchanged looks and nodded.

Taking the glass vial back from Sahiba, he carefully pushed it back into the jar of cream. Mai was heading to pick up the vial he had dropped on the carpet when the phone rang. Changing direction in midstride, he went towards the phone on the study table at the far end of the room. It was Ben Ashton.

'Okay, but you're early,' Mai said to him in a low murmur, 'please give me at least two hours... yes, come up to my room. Sure... no, no problem. I'll see you then.' Putting down the phone, Mai rejoined the sisters. 'So, like I was saying, you need to ensure....'

He quickly ran through the basics of VX Gas again and explained how best to optimise the impact of the chemical. Half an hour later, the two women left with their deadly jewellery boxes tucked safely under their arms.

BEN ASHTON ARRIVED AT ALMOST THE SAME TIME THAT MAI returned to his room after a rushed dinner. His face was marred by the same anal-retentive scowl that

Mai remembered so clearly from their meeting in the Maldives.

'Are you still clear on how to handle this in transit and how to use it?' Mai asked as he handed over the family-sized jars of cream to him. There was nothing unusual about their appearance; only their weight gave away the difference. Camouflaged and cocooned in the jars of assorted cream were almost a hundred glass vials. Each of these was more than adequate to deliver a torturously agonizing death to at least three or four people and, in the worst case, inflict severe damage on twice as many.

'I'm clear,' Ben replied gruffly. He did not like the Chinaman. But then, Ben disliked almost everyone he met. 'It's simple enough. Any fool can handle it.'

'Fine then. All the best.' Mai showed him to the door, glad to see him go.

That brings my part of the job to an end. Now I just have to get through the conference and go back home.... For a moment, he idly contemplated the mayhem that would be waiting for him at Urumqi, then shut the door and went straight to his laptop. He had set it up on the study table in the far corner of the hotel room, near the huge glass windows overlooking the new, still-under-construction expressway between Delhi and Jaipur. A constant stream of traffic flowed incessantly over the flyover straddling the expressway. Mai watched it with unseeing eyes as he waited for the laptop to boot up. Soon he was logged onto the meetyourmatch website.

A moment later, he had keyed in a message to the smurad234 profile. He knew that Salim would be awaiting the message eagerly.

I have given the matter due thought and I feel we have lots in common. Don't you think we should take this matter forward?

Then, as he had been instructed to do for this particular message, Mai used his mobile phone to send a brief, innocuous text message.

MURREE

SALIM FELT HIS HEART SKIP A BEAT AS HE HEARD HIS PHONE signal the arrival of a text message. Reading it quickly, he turned towards his computer and clicked on the mouse. The screensaver vanished and Salim's profile on the meetyourmatch site appeared.

Salim was already logged in. He had been logged in almost continually ever since he had received confirmation from Mai about the weapons being ready. The mission was about to attain critical mass and this matchmaking site was the umbilical cord that tied Salim to his lashkar. When he read Mai's message in his mailbox, Salim could not hold back an exclamation of pure joy.

'What happened, sir?' Cheema looked up from the map he was poring over at the other end of the room. A heap of flight schedules of various airlines lay strewn all around him.

'That Mai is a bloody gem! He has just confirmed that everyone has collected the weapons from him in

Delhi,' Salim said, rubbing his hands gleefully as he looked up from his computer. 'I have a really good feeling about this operation, Cheema.'

'Allah be praised!' Cheema thumped the table excitedly. 'So, we're all set for the next phase?'

'Of course we are, man.' Salim pumped his arm in the air. 'Let's hope and pray that the teams reach their target areas safely. Now the security checks at the airports where they land are the only barriers that stand between them and their targets.' Turning back to his computer excitedly, Salim began to type out a reply to Mai.

NEW DELHI

MAI HU SAW SALIM'S REPLY A MOMENT LATER.

Thank you very much. I think you are heaven sent. I am sure Allah's blessings are with us.

A surge of pride went through him as he read Salim's congratulatory note. Despite the migraine now pounding in his head, Mai sat back and allowed himself to relive the past few momentous weeks. Despite the fact that he had not eaten properly for several hours, he felt no pangs of hunger. If anything, he was tired. Elated, but tired. *And no wonder,* he told himself as he checked his watch. *It's way past midnight. Where did the whole day vanish?*

He began to walk across the room towards his bed, when he stopped, returned to the study table, picked up the hotel phone and punched in a solitary key. 'Good evening, Dr Mai,' answered a cheerful voice. 'How may we help you, sir?'

'I would like to be woken up at six o'clock tomorrow morning, please.'

'Wake-up call for six tomorrow morning, sir. Will there be anything else, Dr Mai?'

'No, but listen, this wake-up call is very important. I cannot be late for my conference tomorrow morning.'

'Don't worry sir, you will be called at six sharp.'

'But that's an automated call. What if I don't respond to it? I'm really tired and may oversleep. Will you make sure I'm woken up?'

'Fine, sir. I'll ensure that personally.'

'Please don't forget. Thank you.' Mai replaced the phone and walked back towards the bed. He was just a few feet away from it when he tripped over his perennially undone shoelaces. As he tumbled forward, his hands came up instinctively to break the fall and protect his face. The left hand managed to do that successfully as he struck the floor rather hard. But his right hand landed squarely on the tiny, marble-sized glass vial loaded with VX Gas that was lying forgotten on the carpet just beside the bed. The vial was tough, but not tough enough to withstand the impact. It shattered instantly, unleashing the deadly aerosol into the air, inches from his face.

The sharp choking feeling and violent tremors came almost instantly. Death was not too far behind. It came just as he lost control over his bowels. A moment later, his heart died, Mai was screaming as he went, but no sound emerged from his starved lungs.

As life left him, he could hear his mother yelling at him from a distance. *Why can't you keep them tied properly, Mai? Those shoelaces will be the death of you....*

MAI WAS SUFFERING THE AGONY OF A PAINFUL DEATH WHEN, barely two miles away, American Airlines flight 293 lifted off from the runway of Delhi airport and began its long haul to Chicago. Seated in the middle of the aircraft was Erik Segan. Tucked away in the safety of his checked-in baggage were the aerosol cans of room-freshener with Variola Major in them. The baggage had sailed through the airport's security net without any problem. Now Eric huddled in his seat, sweating profusely. Not because his conscience was bothering him, but because he was terrified of flying. The killer cargo he was carrying only added to his discomfort.

THE WARMTH HAD BEGUN TO DESERT MAI'S BODY WHEN, AN hour and a half later, from the same runway of Delhi airport, Austrian Airlines flight 34 took off for Vienna with Karl Gunther and his lethal cargo of VX Gas on board. The second killer and his well-camouflaged cargo had also sailed unscathed through the security barrier. Luck was still with Salim's lashkar.

MAI'S BODY HAD STARTED TO STIFFEN WHEN TWO HOURS and ten minutes later, the Khan sisters departed from

Delhi on board Air France flight 147 for Paris. Thanks to Mai's ingenuity, they too breached the security barriers undetected. Their flight had almost cleared Indian airspace when, back in Delhi, there was another tentative knock on Mai's door.

IT IS ALMOST CERTAIN THAT IF MAI HAD NOT BEEN SO insistent about his wake-up call, his body would not have been found in a hurry. When he continuously failed to get any response from Mai, the conscientious operator spoke to the housekeeping supervisor.

'The guest in 517 had placed a wake-up call for six, but I'm not getting any response from him.'

'So what's new?'

'It's just that he was very insistent on being woken up for some important conference.'

'Uh huh.'

'I wonder if you could ask your person on the fourth floor to check on him and wake him up.'

'Okay, let me see what I can do,' she said and put down the phone.

Barring the electric blue stripes of the screensaver on the open laptop in the corner, Mai's room was shrouded in darkness when the housemaid who had been working on the fourth floor let herself in. She squinted in the near darkness, trying to spot the guest who was not responding to his wake-up call. Even in the dim light she could sense that the bed was empty. She was about to call out when a strange, foul smell assaulted her senses. Puzzled, but at this point still not alarmed, she clicked on the room lights. That was when she saw Mai lying on the floor. His face was contorted in a dark, hideous death mask. The mouth was still open in a pain-racked scream. Foamy flecks of vomit crusted the mouth. Visually reinforced, the stench of death, vomit and excreta surged towards her with horrifying force.

She screamed and began to back away. She was still screaming when the hotel security guard patrolling the fourth floor heard her and came rushing in. He took one look at the dead man on the floor and his stomach revolted. Controlling the rush of bile, he hustled her out of the room and slammed the door shut behind them. Even through the shock and horror that flailed him, he knew that he had to leave the room undisturbed for the police. Neither of them realized how lucky they were that the VX was a tactical variant with a short shelf life.

IT IS ALSO CERTAIN THAT THE MYSTERY OF MAI'S DEATH would have taken much longer to solve if it had not been for the fact that the hotel doctor who responded to the frantic call for help and took charge of the body had just donned civvies after a long innings in the Indian Army Medical Corps. Though lacking any practical experience of chemical attacks, he had enough theoretical knowledge to suspect that the death was due to reasons beyond the ordinary. Immediately, the National Emergency Management Authority

(NEMA) was brought into the picture. They came. They saw. They freaked.

Consequently, not even half an hour had elapsed before the Chemical Warfare Detachment (CW Det) personnel seconded for duty at the nearby airport moved in and threw a cordon sanitaire around the room. It took the two men in protective suits a little longer to ascertain the precise cause of death. The minute *that* happened, the security cordon was extended to cover the entire floor and phones began to ring with electrifying urgency. In another ten minutes, the ATTF had also moved in.

'Do we really need to do this?' the panic-stricken General Manager of the hotel asked, horrified at the public relations disaster that loomed large.

'We do,' the CW Det commander replied curtly. 'We're still in the process of evaluating the situation and will let you know soon if the hotel needs to be shut down. Right now I suggest you let us have full details of all hotel occupants, including those who checked out during the last forty-eight hours. And we want full details... and I mean *full* details of the dead man.' He gestured towards the room where Mai's body still lay undisturbed.

'But what has happened?' the perplexed GM asked in an anguished tone. The mere thought of the hotel being sealed had him reeling.

'I can say nothing more at this stage, sir,' the CW Det commander replied a little more gently. *Poor bloke! He'll mess himself if he comes to know what's really happened.*

On realizing that VX Gas was involved and the dead Chinese was a leading chemical and biological warfare expert, the CW Det commander had taken a spot decision to tamp down on all news pertaining to Mai's death. *Let the brass decide how to handle it.*

'Now, if you will excuse me, I need to take care of this. Please ensure that no one, and I mean *no one*, comes to this floor for any reason whatsoever.'

'Why? How can....'

'Just pass on the word that there has been a bomb scare and the hotel is being searched as a precaution.'

That eventually became the story for the media. After an initial short-lived spurt of enthusiasm, the news was buried under an avalanche of more gossipy, scandalous and TRP-enhancing news items. *After all, how much interest can a bomb in some hotel on the fringes of the city evoke? Unless it goes off, of course.*

Mai's death did not make it to the television news channels. Had that happened, almost certainly Salim or Cheema, who were continuously surfing the airwaves, would have picked it up.

Within minutes of the CW Det commander's confirmatory call that VX Gas was on the loose, the brass was jolted awake. So was the External Affairs Ministry (MEA), since the dead man was a foreigner. The MEA Joint Secretary was confused and upset as he picked up the phone to call the Chinese embassy.

Lahore

THE CW DET COMMANDER WAS TALKING WITH THE MANAGER of Delhi's Radisson Hotel when a truck belonging to Al-Mohsin Worldwide, one of the several packers and movers in the city of Lahore, pulled up outside the warehouse being used by Cheema's cohorts. The truck was loaded with an assortment of carefully packaged and labelled items. The men who took away two of the three remaining suitcase nukes were dressed in the off-colour khakis worn by all Al-Mohsin personnel. Before they took away the nukes, they slapped a series of stickers and packing slips on them. Both nukes now resembled suitcases that might be used by any average American household. The kiddie stickers on both suitcases clearly indicated that they belonged to a young boy or boys still struggling to throw off the influence of Pokemon, Power Rangers and Dragon Ball Z.

Half an hour later, when the truck pulled away from the warehouse, both nukes were comfortably mixed up with the rest of the luggage of the Consular Officer of the US Consulate at Lahore. He was returning home after a tumultuous two years in Pakistan. In the press of the million things to be done just before departure, the harried man had not re-counted the total number of pieces listed in the inventory of goods he was carrying back as he returned to a more staid life on home turf. Both the Chote Miyan were now part of his household baggage.

A little later, the baggage was safely tucked away in the cargo hold of PIA flight 711 which took off from Lahore. Its destination was JFK airport in New York.

THE CW DET COMMANDER WAS PUTTING DOWN THE PHONE after talking to the ATTF chief when Air India flight 187 headed for Toronto via Amritsar and Birmingham, departed from Delhi. The ever so polite Abraham Reis was on board. The fourth killer had also walked through the first lot of security barriers that he had to negotiate. Now only the security check upon arrival at Toronto and the final one at the target itself stood between him and his unsuspecting targets.

IT WAS AN OPEN SECRET THAT LIANG DESHENG, POSTED AS the Charge d'Affaires at the Embassy of the People's Republic of China in New Delhi was also a highly respected intelligence officer and a rising star in China's Ministry of State Security (MSS). A tiny, tidy, technically inclined man, Liang was an asset to the MSS. He was informed of Mai's curious death within minutes of the information being given to the embassy by the MEA Joint Secretary. Liang was fully aware of Dr Mai's critical role in the Chinese special weapons program and his presence in Delhi. In fact, the previous evening he had been alerted of Mai's arrival in Delhi – standard procedure whenever people in sensitive posts travelled out of China.

'May I request you to please keep his death under wraps,' Liang told the MEA Joint Secretary. 'At least until such time as we have a clearer picture.' The request did not meet with any resistance, especially in light of the vastly improved relationship between India and China. 'I'm sure you understand... keeping in view the suspicious manner of his death.' Despite the fact that they were talking on a secure line, both men were reluctant to say too much.

'That should not be a problem,' the MEA man replied. 'But I do hope you appreciate our grave concern about the presence of such an item on our soil. We certainly hope that we will be kept informed about whatever you people find.'

'But of course,' Liang assured him, his tone betraying the embarrassment he was suffering. No country likes to admit that its senior scientists are running around all over the globe with lethal items like VX on their person.

Liang sighed to himself as he logged onto the MSS site and accessed the secure database. It is a loosely guarded secret that the MSS maintains a dossier on almost everybody who is anybody in the People's Republic of China. Liang pulled Mai's file up on the screen. A sharp, sinking feeling assailed him as he read through it. *Shit! He's an Uighur! I just hope....* It was with a marked sense of urgency that Liang reached for the secure phone lying on the table in front of him and speed-dialled his boss in Beijing.

URUMQUI

INITIALLY, WHEN THE TWO BLACK MG TF CARS PULLED UP ON the street in front of the house, Fatima was not perturbed. Both cars were black-coloured civilian variants and not the standard type used by the local police. She recognized the cars as those used by the facility and was aware that at least five of Mai's senior colleagues also lived on the same street. It was only when she happened to look out of the kitchen window and noticed two more of them come to a halt at the rear of the house that she knew something untoward had happened. Then she saw the small knots of hard looking men with drawn handguns racing towards her house from both sides and she knew the game was up.

Somehow Mai has been blown. So be it. Inshallah.... Snatching a sharp, wicked looking knife from the fruit bowl, she ran towards the bathroom.

When the take-down teams slammed open the doors and swept through the house, they did not spot her immediately. Even the man who put his head in through the bathroom door would have missed the diminutive Fatima if it hadn't been for the blood that had sprayed onto the shower curtain.

'Bloody hell!' He recoiled in horror as he pulled back the curtain gingerly.

The knife stuck deep in her belly told the rest of the story. Fatima was still alive, but her face was contorted in agony as she struggled to keep herself from screaming.

'She is not going to make it,' the doctor who attended to her at the nearby hospital told the MSS team leader. 'In fact, I don't think she wants to live.'

'We figured that out, you moron' – the team leader threw him an irate look – 'considering that it was she who stuck the knife in her stomach. Anyway, stand aside, we need to question her.'

The doctor gave him a shocked look and then decided that it was futile to try and dissuade him. *Why the hell should I be the one to be earmarked by this MSS pig as the one who obstructed him, especially for some wacko woman who is going to die in any case?* With a resigned shrug, he stood back.

Not that it did any good to the interrogator. Fatima said nothing. There were a few snatched moments of lucidity, when she surfaced sporadically through the shroud of pain that had settled upon her. Even then, she just glared hatefully at the MSS men surrounding her like vultures. All the time, her lips moved in ceaseless prayer.

The MSS man was not able to make out much of what she was mumbling, but decided to record it anyway. Just before she went, in her final moments of pain, Fatima beseeched Allah to grant success to her husband in his strikes against the kafir.

'May the kafirs suffer as our people have suffered' were her last words to her God.

Paris

WHILE FATIMA WAS MAKING HER LAST WISH, THE AIR FRANCE flight with Sahiba and Kismat Khan on board landed uneventfully at Paris. The twins would spend a miserable, stress-filled four hours in the transit lounge before their connecting flight to St Martin in Netherlands Antilles, the second leg of their tediously long journey. However, they had far more important things to worry about than a long layover. The growing fear of the airport security check at their final destination kept them tense and silent. The suspense would have tested their nerves even more severely if they hadn't had each other for company and comfort.

Vienna

THE KILLER KHANS WERE ON THEIR WAY TO THE TRANSIT lounge at Charles de Gaulle Airport in Paris when Karl Gunther's flight landed at Vienna. He too had a stopover to suffer through before his onward connecting flight to Berlin. Luckily, the layover was only an hour long and since Karl did not have to change planes, he simply slept through the halt undisturbed. He was still fast asleep when the aircraft took off from Vienna for the final short hop to Berlin.

New Delhi

'ARE YOU SURE?' LIANG ASKED HIS BOSS AGAIN. 'ARE YOU sure she said *strikes* and not *strike*?'

'Of course I am sure,' his boss retorted irritably. 'I double-checked with the man who transcribed the tapes. There is no doubt about it. There's something very big going on down there.'

'What did we find at the Urumqi facility?'

'That bastard Hu had planted explosives all around the central storage area. If they had gone off they would have unleashed all the viruses and chemicals held there in deep storage.' His voice was near despairing. 'You have no idea what that means, Liang. Some of the stuff there is so lethal that it would have rendered the facility and the surrounding areas unfit for habitation for decades. Thousands would have died.'

Liang shuddered as his mind conjured up ill-informed images of nameless, faceless things running loose in the countryside. 'What is missing from the stores?'

'As far as we can make out, some VX Gas is definitely missing. We're still trying to work out the quantity… I should be able to tell you in a few hours. We *think* some of the Variola Major is also missing, but again' – Liang could almost visualize his helpless shrug – 'we need more time to pin down the precise details.'

'Variola Major? What the hell is that?' Liang's mouth fell open in horror as the man at the other end told him. 'Shit! And you say this Haemorrhagic type is the deadliest?' An uncomfortable silence held sway for a long moment. 'What should I do? How much should I tell the Indians?'

'The high command says we have to tell them everything.'

'Everything! They'll go crazy!'

'I know, but this is just too big a deal to hold back on. I mean, you don't screw around where VX Gas and smallpox viruses are concerned. Do you realize what the world will do to us if that stuff gets loose? In these days of free and easy travel, the smallpox will spread like wildfire. No one is even prepared for it these days. And this one is an almost certain killer.' There was another, much longer pause as both men contemplated the scenario. 'Fuck! Millions could die.'

'The Indians are going to go ape-shit!' That was all Liang could say before he finally put down the phone after a detailed briefing by his boss.

THE INDIANS DID NOT GO APE-SHIT. FOR A VERY LONG TIME, the MEA man was simply unable to understand what Liang was saying, or its implications. When Liang finally started getting through to him, he went wild. So did the others... right up the chain of command.

'Don't the fucking Chinks take care of this stuff?'

'How the bloody hell did that bastard manage to carry all that shit through airport security?'

'Exactly what did we find in his room?'

'Nothing! Barring the remains of the....'

'Nothing? So where the hell has it gone?'

The questions, most of them rhetorical and as yet unanswerable, came thick and fact. The panic was just starting to set in. Luckily, a few of the cooler heads realized what would happen if the news hit the streets, so a tight security blanket was thrown over it immediately. Only those who were already in the know and those who would be directly involved with the hunt were told.

'JUST HOW CERTAIN ARE WE?' THE INDIAN PRIME MINISTER asked when G.K. Rao finished speaking.

'It is all very hazy right now,' Rao replied reluctantly. The bespectacled Rao was almost single-handedly responsible for the new, well integrated and professional face that Indian Intelligence proudly displayed these days. 'So far the only thing the Chinese are sure of is that some VX Gas and Variola Major are missing.'

He gave the PM a very brief idea of what VX Gas and Varioal Major were and what they were capable of doing. It was enough to bring a grim look to the PM's usually serene countenance.

'These missing items coupled with the woman's dying statements leads them to believe that something big is about to go down in our part of the world. Apparently, the scientist was a closet jihadi. They're still trying to work out the details.'

'And we? What are we doing?'

'We just got the Intel an hour ago, sir. Even as we speak, our people....'

'Rao, I want you to head this investigation yourself. Bring in some top-notch people from NEMA and the ATTF. Pull out all stops and ensure you keep me posted *all* the time. And listen,' the PM added as Rao was turning away, 'I am placing Force 22 directly under your command for this mission. Keep Colonel Anbu in the loop. To my mind they're our best bet should we need to respond rapidly to any situation.'

'VX GAS? VARIOLA MAJOR?' COLONEL ANBU'S SHOCKED VOICE mirrored his disbelief. 'Do you know what you are saying? Can you even imagine....'

'I know, I know, Colonel, but that's exactly what the CW people have confirmed,' Rao interrupted him. 'The man who died is a Chinese scientist. He was in town to attend a chemical weapons destruction conference.'

'Really?'

'And the PM wants you in on this, so I suggest you get your people moving.'

'Don't worry about us, Mr Rao, most of my people are already in Manesar, close to Delhi, for a joint training with the NSG. Please consider us on high alert within the next hour.'

Anbu's instincts were working overtime as the call ended. 'I have a really bad feeling about this one....' he said to Sami who was sitting opposite him as he dialled another number. 'Ankita, I want Khare and you here,' he said when the phone was picked up at the other end. 'ASAP! Drop everything else for the moment.' While waiting for them, Anbu told Sami in detail what Rao had said. 'Alert everyone, MS. Tell the NSG that the training is off for the moment and make sure everyone is back at base, locked, loaded and ready to go.' He saw the questioning look on Sami's face and added, 'No, I don't know what the hell is going to happen but I have a feeling that we're going to hit the ground running on this one... very soon and very hard.'

A FEW MINUTES LATER, THERE WAS A SOFT KNOCK ON ANBU'S door and Ankita Bhatnagar and Manoj Khare entered.

Waving them in, Anbu went straight to the root of the matter and then gave them their tasks. 'I want both of you to go over everything – and I mean *everything*. Mr Rao, the NIA, is personally heading up the investigation and he has already spoken to the cops, the ATTF and NEMA; you'll get all the co-operation you need from them. In any case, both of you get along well with Rao.' He gave both officers a hard, level look. 'We need to find out what that crazy scientist has carried into the country. Even more importantly, we need to find out where the hell it has gone.'

They were almost at the door when he spoke again. 'And listen guys, I don't think we have much time on our hands, so pull out all the stops. We're all going to be waiting for you two to point us in the right direction.' He turned to Sami. 'Tell the others to get ready.'

Berlin

MANOJ KHARE AND ANKITA BHATNAGAR HAD JUST FINISHED going through the hotel room in which Mai Hu had died when Austrian Airlines flight 271 from Vienna touched down at Tegel airfield in Berlin. The security man who electronically scanned Karl Gunther's luggage did not find anything suspicious, and Karl walked through unscathed. The first killer had breached the final security barrier.

Lahore

KARL GUNTHER WAS EXITING TEGEL AIRPORT WHEN THE LAST repackaged and reprogrammed Chote Miyan left the warehouse in Lahore. The nuke now bore an uncanny resemblance to one of those typical black cases that almost all airline crew members carry. They are such a ubiquitous part of the airlines uniform that people barely notice them.

The Chote Miyan was delivered straight to Lahore airport by a man dressed in the uniform of the airport's ground staff. There were two hard looking men with an unmistakable air of authority waiting for him at the airport's entrance. The sinister duo had the right papers to open doors magically; they escorted the man and his precious case through all the checks and barriers, right on to the tarmac.

At 1250 hours local time, when PIA flight 771 took off from Lahore for Copenhagen via Oslo, the beautifully repackaged and camouflaged nuke was safely stowed in the aircraft's cargo hold. The man who had delivered the nuke was also on board, but now he was dressed like a member of the PIA crew. The aircraft took off and settled into the scheduled flight path for Copenhagen.

PIA FLIGHT 771 HAD BEEN LOADING UP FOR DEPARTURE WHEN the three-man crew who had camouflaged and reprogrammed the four suitcase nukes finished packing up their gear at the nondescript warehouse in Lahore that had been their home for the past few days. Loading the minivan they normally commuted in every day, they finally drove off. The minivan was well clear of the area when the timer on the bomb attached to the underside of the vehicle ran out. The bomb was small but powerful, and its location was precise. It completely decimated the van and the three men inside it.

Watching from the safe confines of his parked car, Captain Azam Cheema nodded to himself. He was not a man who liked to leave any loose ends behind.

NEW DELHI

ANKITA WAS PORING OVER A PHOTOCOPY OF MAI'S DIARY when two phone numbers scribbled on a page caught her eye. They stood out simply because there was nothing else on that page. The next four pages were full of scribbled notes, but they were in a shorthand that Mai had obviously devised for himself. Ankita was not overly surprised since her brother was a scientist and he too had a peculiar code of his own. She rapidly keyed one of the phone numbers into her laptop and began her hunt.

Thuraya satellite phones! Hey! Hello!! Those are hot favourites with terrorists operating out of Pakistan. A fresh twinge of worry ran through her. *Has this son of a bitch scientist been hand in glove with them? If he's been doling out biochems to those crazies, we're all in deep shit.* With a sinking feeling, she nudged Manoj. 'Here, take a look at this.'

The minute he saw the two phone numbers, a tiny bell began to clamour in the recesses of Manoj's mind. There was something about them that had struck a chord, but he was not sure what it was. He pushed his mind hard… harder… cajoling it to come up with an answer.

Ankita intruded upon his thoughts. 'Manoj, can you check if the chink called either of these numbers… or was called by them?'

'Sure, one sec.' Khare rapidly scanned the phone records of the room, which the ATTF had already procured from the hotel manager. A tense moment later: 'No, he made no calls from the hotel room for sure.'

Manoj picked up the dead scientist's mobile phone and scrolled through the names. 'Neither of those numbers is stored in his mobile phone memory, nor has there been any call made to or from those phones to this one… but wait… there is a text message which has been sent to one of them.' Khare clicked the 'read message' icon on Mai's mobile phone. 'It's just one word – mailbox.' Khare checked the screen again. 'The chink sent it out to the satellite phone listed on top at 2327 hours last night. That would have been just before he died.'

Khare looked up again at Ankita. 'Listen, there is something about these phone numbers that is bothering me.' He scratched his head. 'I'm not getting it right now, but I...' His voice trailed away. 'Ankita, let me track these phones down. Meanwhile, why don't you track Mai Hu's movements over the past few weeks? And we need to get into that laptop.' He gestured towards Mai's laptop. 'After all, if there is a mailbox he is referring to in the text message, then either he sent a mail or he received one.'

'First let me go over his movements in the recent past,' Ankita replied, 'then I'll take care of his laptop.'

The two got down to work and silence reigned in the room again.

BOTH FORCE 22 OFFICERS WERE DEEP INTO THEIR SEARCH when two miles away, the usually ill-tempered and ill-mannered Ben Ashton took off on board Jet Airways flight 9W122 from Delhi to London. At this moment, however, the man was in a rare good humour. Thanks to Mai's ingenuity, he had sailed through the dreaded pre-flight security checks without raising any flags.

The last killer had breached the security barrier.

PARIS

TWENTY-FIVE MINUTES LATER, HALFWAY ACROSS THE GLOBE, Air France flight 488 bound for St Martin took off from Paris. The security check for transit passengers was as cursory as it normally is. Sahiba and Kismat exchanged looks of relief as the aircraft gained altitude and settled down at cruising height. They were now into the second leg of their interminably long journey.

NEW DELHI

'CAN YOU BELIEVE THIS? THE DEAD MAN DOES NOT BUDGE out of China for months,' Ankita commented to no one in particular. 'And then suddenly he goes to the Maldives last month and now to Delhi. Do you think the two trips are related?'

Manoj looked up when Ankita spoke but he had a glazed look in his eyes. He seemed lost in whatever he was doing. Ankita smiled when she saw his expression and returned to her machine with a never-mind wave.

BERLIN

TWO HOURS AFTER THE FLIGHT LANDED IN BERLIN, KARL Gunther walked into the Park Inn Hotel and checked in. Located just off the Alexanderplatz, this was as close to the target as it was possible for him to get.

No matter what happens, you must not return home. You must not check in under your real name or use a credit card to pay for the hotel room or anything else. Cheema's warning echoed in his head as Karl wrote the name Franz Breitner in the check-in register and paid the required advance in cash for two nights.

Cloaked in vibrant blue and red colours, the newly refurbished room was warm and snug. Karl was confronted with a long wooden luggage rack with a rod and hooks above it as soon as he walked into the room.

There is no cupboard.... Damn! What will these newfangled designers come up with next? Cursing under his breath, Karl carried the suitcase nuke across to the other end of the room and placed it carefully in the shadow of the bed.

Twenty minutes later, he logged onto meetyourmatch.com and confirmed his arrival to Salim.

Remember that those of you who have a shorter travel time will have longer to wait. You have to ensure you don't get impatient or restless during this waiting period. Just keep your head down and lie low, Cheema had cautioned them. So Karl Gunther switched on the television and prepared to tide over the long wait for his tryst with Destiny.

NEW DELHI

'I KNEW IT! I KNEW THERE WAS SOMETHING FAMILIAR ABOUT these damn numbers.' Manoj Khare's voice made Ankita look up from her laptop. 'The two phone numbers that were scribbled in Mai's diary belong to a set of four Thuraya satellite phones. All four phones were purchased by the same person at the same time. The four phone numbers are contiguous and all of them are registered to a Dubai based company called Desert Apparels.' Ankita started when she heard the name, but Manoj continued excitedly, 'The company is owned by a person called S. Murad. Now here's the kicker!' He gave Ankita a pleased look. 'You remember I was telling you that something about these numbers has been bothering me? Well, now I know why. In November 2005, just after the strikes we carried out in Pakistan post the Delhi bomb blasts, a guy was captured at the LOC. He was carrying a Thuraya phone. *That* phone is one of these four.' Manoj gestured towards his laptop. 'For some reason, the old man had asked me to check out….'

'Who was this guy?' Ankita cut in impatiently.

'He was a youngster named Iqbal, from Lucknow, who'd been recruited by the Lashkar-e-Toiba and sent to POK for training.' Manoj jabbed at the page flashing on the screen of his machine. 'It's quite an interesting story. Here, I'm transferring a copy of his interrogation report to your machine. I had downloaded it from the Military Intelligence database at the time… when the old man asked me to check on it. Meanwhile, let me find out more about these phones. I have a feeling they're vital to all this.' He returned to his laptop. 'Let's see where all these phones have travelled and where they are right now.'

'Sure thing, Manoj, do that, but listen,' Ankita interjected, 'listen to this.' Manoj caught the sharp edge of excitement in her tone. 'You know that Mai spent a week in the Maldives last month. Now here's a coincidence you'll love. While he was there the guy stayed at a resort called the Blue Moon; it's a pretty exclusive high-end resort. During that week, all but twenty-seven of its 156 beach cottages, water bungalows and water villas were full. On the days that Mai was there, twelve of these water villas – which, by the way, are the most expensive of the lot – had been booked by,' she gave a dramatic pause, '*a Dubai based company called Desert Apparels.*'

'You're kidding me!' Manoj exclaimed.

'No, not at all!' Ankita leaned back and raised an eyebrow at Khare. 'Now, is that a coincidence or what?'

'Damn right it is! Now we're getting somewhere. Let me find out who was staying in the other eleven villas. I know exactly who to ask. Meanwhile, see if you can sink your hook into this S. Murad guy who owns Desert Apparels. He seems to be the key.' Khare turned to the phone in front of him with a mounting sense of urgency. The man he called was about to pack up for the day, but when he learnt who was calling and what he had to say, he got moving pretty fast.

ABDUL RASHID HEADED THE SPECIAL INVESTIGATIONS UNIT OF the Maldives Police. A year ago, he had attended a training course in counter-terror operations in India. It was during this training that Khare and he had got acquainted. Their interaction may not have been long, but they got along famously. Rashid knew and respected Khare enough to honour his request without asking too many questions. 'You are sure that none of this concerns us?' Abdul asked.

'Right now I don't know for sure,' Khare replied. 'But I promise you that if anything *does* come up, you'll be the first to know.'

'That's good enough for me.'

'And listen, right now, since we don't know exactly what is going on, I'd request you to do this yourself. Don't involve anyone else until we know more.'

'Oh!' There was a long pause as Abdul Rashid thought this over. 'I see what you mean. One never knows who may be.... Right! Don't worry about it. I'll call you back in a couple of hours.'

Chicago

WHILE ALL THIS WAS GOING ON, ERIK SEGAN'S FLIGHT LANDED at Chicago. He disembarked quickly and crossed the terminal from where his connecting flight to New Orleans was scheduled to depart after a layover of two hours and fifteen minutes. Already, thirty-five minutes of this waiting period had been consumed since his flight from Delhi had met a strong headwind and was running behind schedule. By now the ex-junkie's nerves were literally in tatters and he was almost falling apart with the stress. He sweated through the remaining hour and, despite his fear of flying, was actually relieved when they announced the boarding for his onward flight. The flight to New Orleans left on schedule and was quite uneventful.

New Orleans

DESPITE THAT, ERIK SEGAN WAS NOT PARTICULARLY HAPPY AS he left the aircraft at the Louis Armstrong International Airport in New Orleans. Most of the excitement and euphoria of his glorious role in the jihad had worn off after the incredibly long flight from Delhi. He was decidedly nervous about the lethal aerosol containers kept in his baggage and his anxiety was mounting at an alarming pace at the thought of the dreaded security check ahead of him.

These days the Homeland Security people are anything but casual. They'll tear me a new arsehole if they so much as get a whiff of what is in my bags.

'Remember, it will look rather strange for you to have room-freshener in your hand baggage, so check that in. The eau de cologne and the aftershave lotion shouldn't be a problem… so long as no one decides to try them out,' Mai had added with a laugh when he'd briefed him in Delhi, clearly enjoying the long-haired musician's discomfiture. 'What I suggest is that you check it all in. That's the best thing to do.'

That was precisely what Segan had done. But it wasn't making him feel any better as he retrieved his bags from the baggage carousel and began the long trek towards the exit.

Mopping his face and neck clean of all traces of perspiration, Erik Segan took a couple of deep breaths and forced himself to calm down as he walked up to the exit gates. Up ahead he could see a huge Amazon type Homeland Security female gesture towards one of the passengers moving in front of him. She had huge breasts, which under normal circumstances would have ensured Erik's undivided attention. Right now, the only emotion she evoked in him was dread.

'This way please, sir,' she said as she pointed towards the security enclosure where several other passengers had been stopped and were opening their bags for checking. 'Please remove all locks and stand back, sir,' Erik heard her say to the man in front of him. Her tone was sharp and stopped short of being rude.

Erik felt his breath almost wheeze to a halt as he reached the point where a couple of her equally forbidding colleagues were scrutinizing the passing crowds with eagle eyes. He felt one of them rest his gimlet gaze on him. He even felt the gaze linger for a long moment. A silent, frantic prayer shot out from him unbidden. Perhaps Allah heard it. The gaze lifted and he was through.

Gradually, his breathing picked up again. Forcing himself to retain his slow deliberate walk, he crossed the security gate. By the time he was through, his legs felt weak with stress and he had to stop himself from running to the washrooms that lay just beyond the security barrier. Throwing himself into the first empty cubicle, he collapsed on the toilet seat. It took all of fifteen minutes for his breathing to return to normal and the foul taste of fear to recede from his mouth.

Finally, leaving the safe sanctuary of the toilet, he took a cab to the Best Western French Quarter Landmark Hotel where he had booked a room, the previous month, on the very day he had returned from the Maldives. Even then it had been fairly difficult since hotel rooms were at a premium due to the Jazz Fest. Located barely a mile from his target, the hotel was perfect for his purpose. Immediately after checking in, he logged onto meetyourmatch.com and reported his arrival to Salim.

I need to know the minute you are through. Remember that. Salim's voice echoed in his memory. *A lot of things hinge on your doing things as per schedule*.

Having done that, Erik threw himself on the bed without bothering to change. He felt exhausted and suddenly unsure of everything.

COPENHAGEN

LARS BORGE HAD BEEN ON DUTY FOR ABOUT TWO HOURS when PIA flight PK 771 landed at Copenhagen's

Kastrup Airport. He had already moved all the pieces required for this part of the operation into place. Standing in the shadow of the building, he watched the passengers disembark. A short while later, the crew followed, barring the man who had placed the Chote Miyan on the aircraft at Lahore. He hung around as the baggage handlers arrived to unload the aircraft.

Lars watched patiently, allowing things to settle into the monotony of a task routinely performed every day. Then he moved in. A few minutes later, one of the baggage handlers noticed smoke pouring out from the tow vehicle standing near the bay adjacent to the one in which the PIA jet was parked.

As fire alarms began to wail, Lars raced out to the baggage handlers unloading the aircraft and began to herd them out and away from the aircraft. They all responded instinctively to a man in uniform and stepped away. In all this confusion, no one noticed the PIA crewman slip into the aircraft and emerge a few minutes later with the Chote Miyan. Nor did anyone notice him slip it to Lars in the shadow of a building a little distance away. Afterwards, the man simply joined the crowd that had gathered to watch the confusion. Lars, of course, faded away in the confusion.

Within minutes, a rash of fire fighters and security personnel had cordoned off the area and fought the flames into submission. It did not take long for the unloading to resume. The PIA crewman waited till it was over before he left to rejoin the rest of the crew at the hotel.

LONG BEFORE THE FIRE COULD BE PUT OUT, LARS WAS OUT OF the airport and halfway to the Palace Hotel at Raadhuspladsen.

With Tivoli Gardens and Ströget, the main shopping area, at its doorstep, the Palace Hotel was as close as he could get to ground zero. In fact, the balcony of Room 402, which Lars had checked into the previous day, directly overlooked the Town Hall square. He went straight to his room, secured the precious suitcase in the cupboard, placed a Do Not Disturb tag on the door, and returned to the airport. No one had even noticed his absence.

A short while later, he used a temporary lull at work to grab a coffee from the machine in one corner of the airport terminal. Just across from the coffee shop was the computer corner where four machines were available for passengers to use. It was from one of these that Lars logged onto the meetyourmatch website to send a message to Salim confirming the arrival of the Chote Miyan in Copenhagen.

LONDON

AROUND THE TIME THAT LARS STARTED THE FIRE NEAR THE PIA plane at Copenhagen airport, the Jet Airways flight from Delhi with Ben Ashton on board began its descent towards Heathrow.

Ben had no problems in going through security

either. He had to spend a few moments in line before he could get a taxi but then, getting a cab in London is always a bitch.

'The Royal Horse Guards Hotel in Whitehall Court,' he told the large black cabbie as he got in. 'It's SW1A 2EJ,' he added as he saw the driver reach for his TomTom GPS car navigation system. The driver, who was obviously not too old on the beat, patiently keyed the coordinates of the destination into the TomTom before he drove out. *Thank God he's not the talkative type.* Ben leaned back and dozed as the taxi began its long crawl to the hotel. Barring the periodic instructions from the monotonous female voice of the TomTom, silence ruled as the cab made its way towards the hotel.

At a stone's throw from Trafalgar Square and the Houses of Parliament, the Royal Horse Guards Hotel overlooks the Thames. *Damned if I can get any closer to the target than this*, Ben thought as he walked up to the reception desk.

Like the others, he signed in under a false name and paid for two nights in cash. Then, again like the others, he secured the killer cargo in the room before he logged into the matchmaking site and sent off his arrival report to Salim.

NEW DELHI

'WASN'T THE DUDE MARRIED?' ANKITA ASKED, LOOKING UP from Mai's laptop.

'Who?' Manoj asked nonplussed, eyes still fixed

on his computer screen. He was deep inside the Thuraya website.

'The dead chink. Wasn't he married?'

'He was. His wife killed herself yesterday when they went to take her in. Why?'

'Precisely. So how come he'd already started seeking a replacement some weeks ago?' Ankita saw Manoj's quizzical look and clarified, 'I'm checking his internet history and this guy has been logging onto this matchmaking site almost a dozen times every day. It's crazy....'

'Are you sure it's a matchmaking site? Not some porn site?'

'Nope! It's right here in front of me: meetyourmatch.com. Hey!' She stopped suddenly. 'Where is the copy of his diary? I had it right here.' She rummaged on the table, which was by now littered with sheaves of paper and coffee cups.

'Here!' Manoj tossed a stapled bundle to her. 'Take my copy.'

Catching it expertly, Ankita began to flip through the pages. 'I knew it! Here it is.' She jabbed her finger at the page where the two phone numbers were written. Scribbled amidst the notes on the facing page, in a small but neat hand, were the words fatima234/ fat2ima34. She silently mouthed the words as she turned back to her laptop. Clicking on the log-in option on meetyourmatch.com, she keyed in fatima234 as the user name, fat2ima34 as the password, and then hit the enter key.

'Bingo!' She smiled triumphantly as the log-in process was completed and Mai's profile began to emerge on the screen. 'I knew it!'

Working as though inspired, Ankita clicked on the mailbox icon. A long list of messages appeared on the screen. Slightly deflated by the number of messages, she gave a weary sigh and went to work on them.

It did not take her long to sift through the chaff and weed out the messages that seemed to have some meaning. Those that seemed to lead somewhere all had one thing in common – they were either written to or were from someone called smurad234. *Smurad234... S. Murad.* She sat up with a start. 'Holy cow! Manoj, you need to see this. That S. Murad bugger who owns Desert Apparels also features here.'

Manoj joined her and they began to scan through the messages one by one. A moment later, he thumped the table. 'I think you've hit the mother lode. This seems to be their primary comm channel for this op, Ankita. Look at these messages. All of them are to or from profiles that end with 234, almost as though all the profiles were created by the same person.'

'And not a very imaginative one at that,' Ankita added.

'True, but do you see the pattern?'

'Sure, it's pretty obvious.'

'Listen, you focus on this. Get into the smurad

profile and see who else is in the communication loop with him. Meanwhile, let me just finish the trace on the satellite phones and I'll help track this Murad bugger down.'

'I have a feeling we're pretty close to cracking this wide open.'

'Amen!' Manoj threw a grateful glance heavenwards. 'Let's just hope we're in time.'

They went to work again, this time with a renewed sense of energy. Ankita began the tedious job of hacking through the site's security system. Somewhere in its bowels lay the password that she sought, the password to the profile named smurad234. Across the room, Manoj Khare bored into the Thuraya website.

St Martin

AT PRECISELY THE SAME TIME AS BEN ASHTON'S PLANE WAS lining up for the landing at London, some 3,500 miles to the west, the Air France jet carrying Sahiba and Kismat was preparing to touch down at the airport in St Martin. In fact, the wheels of both aircraft touched down almost simultaneously. The Khan twins disembarked and slowly made their way towards the transit lounge. This time their layover was going to be much longer; their final flight to the target destination was due to depart in four and a half hours.

By now the stress levels were peaking rapidly for

both sisters. Their target was just a short hop away. So was the final security barrier that had to be breached. They clasped hands every so often to keep themselves going.

MALDIVE ISLANDS

THEY HAD JUST BEGUN THEIR RESTLESS WAIT AT ST MARTIN when a speedboat raced up to the Blue Moon Resort and slid to a halt at the jetty. Leaping out gracefully, Abdul Rashid jogged across to the tall, birdlike hut in the middle of the resort, which housed the reception and the offices.

'I need to see the manager.' The identity card he thumped down on the reception counter got him the undivided attention of the pretty young girl manning it.

An hour later, Rashid was back in his boat, but this time he had in his hand a thick file containing a copy of the passport of each person who had stayed at the resort during that fateful week. To be on the safe side, he'd also taken details of everyone who'd been there three days before and after. For once the scenic beauty of the ocean failed to grab Rashid's attention as he raced back towards Male.

An hour or so later, scanned copies of all the passports were crowding the mailbox of Khare's computer. Soon the printer attached to it began to spew out copies.

New York

THE KHAN SISTERS WERE ON THEIR SECOND CUP OF INSIPID airport coffee when, thousands of miles away, PIA flight 711 from Lahore landed at JKF airport in New York. The cargo on the plane went through the stringent airport security procedures that had been in vogue since 9/11. The SynOdys Radiation Monitoring System installed in the cargo area watched impassively as the assortment of items streamed past. Cheema's now dead crew had done their work well. Neither of the Chote Miyan uttered a peep as they slid past the ever alert monitors.

Despite the thoroughness of the check, everything came out clean and the diplomat's luggage was handed over to the crew from the A&M Moving Company that was waiting to collect it.

New Delhi

ANKITA LEANED BACK AND FLEXED HER SHOULDERS. 'ACCORDING to this profile, S. Murad is in communication with nearly three dozen people, but only ten of these appear to be relevant profiles.'

'What do you mean?' Khare asked.

'All ten have similar profiles... they end with 234. Also, the messages exchanged between these profiles are the same as far as timing and content go, whereas messages to other profiles are quite different in tone and content... and much more random.'

'Hmm.' Manoj came across and read through the messages. 'I see your point. They must have done it to throw up a smoke screen... anyway, go on.'

'Well, with the Chinese scientist dead, we're left with nine profiles.'

'And of course, S. Murad.'

'Of course! Thankfully we have photos on all the profiles except the smurad profile. I'm going to assume that the photos are real since the one on Mai Hu's profile definitely is.'

'True,' Khare concurred as he crossed the room to where his printer was churning out reams of paper. Picking up the pages that had come out, he glanced through them with a practiced eye. 'Hey! Rashid has delivered... this is the stuff from the Maldives, the data on all those who stayed at the resort.' He began to scrutinize each page as it came in. 'Damn! Look at this.' He waved the page in his hand, his voice taut with excitement. 'Here's Mai. And this photo tallies with the one on your screen right now.' Picking up the sheaf of pages, he returned to Ankita's computer and they began to scan through each profile in turn. Their excitement grew as more and more matches were confirmed.

'Goddamn it! So far they all tally with the people who occupied the suites booked by Desert Apparels at the Blue Moon resort.'

'Absolutely! So now we even have names and cities

to which these guys belong,' Ankita replied, controlling herself with an effort. 'I think we need to pass on this list to the ATTF and the NIA. They can push them out to Interpol and to the concerned governments so that we can at least start tracing them and confirming identities... and checking to see which of them has been visiting India. That should help us find the missing biochems.'

'True.' Manoj nodded. 'Go ahead and do that. Then take a look at what I've found.' He tapped the screen of his laptop. 'I've tracked down the billing details of all four satellite phones. You're going to love this,' he added as he gave the print command and his printer began to spit out more paper.

The trail was fast thickening.

ST MARTIN

THE US DIPLOMAT'S LUGGAGE WAS BEING LOADED ON TO the A&M truck when Air France flight WM 755 for St Kitts took off from St Martin with Sahiba and Kismat on board. The twins were now on the last leg of their long journey. They began to mentally prepare themselves for the customs and security check that lay ahead. Things were normally quite relaxed on the easygoing island, but in view of the mega event in progress these days, security was greatly heightened.

Breaching the final barrier will not be easy.

Allah will protect us.

Barbados

AIR FRANCE FLIGHT WM 755 LANDED AT ST KITTS AIRPORT AT 1833 hours local time, just three minutes behind its scheduled time of arrival. Both the customs and immigration officers who logged the two physically challenged young women took note of the exotic beaded jewellery they were wearing. The loud conspicuous pieces literally clamoured for attention. Maybe that was why they rang no alarm bells in either of their minds and they waved the two women through. A few minutes later, the twins were out of the airport.

Fighting to control their exuberance, the two sisters headed straight for the tiny bed-and-breakfast place they had managed to locate at a stone's throw from the target. An hour later, Kismat keyed in their arrival message to Salim.

Now there was only one man left to breach the security barrier.

New Delhi

THE RINGING OF THE PHONE JOLTED THEM BOTH OUT OF their seats. Khare got to it before Ankita did. He listened in silence for a long moment. 'Of course, please send it immediately. We'll dovetail it with the rest and call you. Yes, immediately,' he promised as he put the phone down and turned to Ankita. 'That was Chauhan from the ATTF. They've gotten tracks of all the people you sent them profiles of,' he said as the fax machine reeled to life. 'Those should be the details coming in now.' He headed for the fax. 'Bloody hell!' he muttered as he scanned the first page. 'This bugger was right here in Delhi... we missed him by a few hours.' He snatched up the next page, more urgently this time. 'So was she... and this one... and....'

A long silence descended. Ankita watched his face with mounting anxiety.

'Shit! Five of them were here. We missed them by a few hours.'

'Damn!' She beat back the surge of disappointment with an effort. 'But at least we now know who could have taken the VX and Variola from the dead chink.'

'My God! The biochems! We have to stop them.' Suddenly galvanized into action, Khare raced for the phone and began to talk urgently into it. 'Look, there is no time to waste. Some of them would have already landed. You *have* to alert those countries.'

Minutes later, the suits at MEA went into action again. Phone wires burnt all over the globe. Germany. Britain. West Indies. Canada. America.

VX Gas! Smallpox virus! Fucking hell!

Security levels ratcheted up as the ripples spread. Suddenly, five people who had been trudging through life barely even casting a shadow, shot onto the screens of hundreds of computers all over the world. *Who? Why? What?* And, most importantly, *where?*

Toronto

THE PHONE WIRES HAD JUST BEGUN TO BURN WHEN AIR INDIA flight AI 187 from New Delhi touched down at Toronto airport. With his quiet, dignified demeanour, Reis had no problems getting himself and his lethal cargo through airport security. Exiting the airport, he hailed the first cab he could find to Hotel Crowne Plaza Toronto. The time had come for him to go to ground.

The final killer with his deadly cargo had sailed through the security barrier. And he had got through with scarcely a moment to spare. His cab had just about cleared the airport when the security alert hit the airport computers.

'What the hell do you mean he got through?'

'We got the message only after he had cleared immigration. But we know where he lives. In fact, a team is already on its way and the local cops have been informed. Don't worry, sir, we'll find him.'

'We'd better. The bastard is carrying VX Gas and, perhaps, the virus Variola Major.'

'VX Gas… Vari… what? What's that?'

So the man at the other end told him, ruining his sleep for many nights.

Murree

'REIS IS ALSO THROUGH.' SALIM LEANED BACK IN HIS LARGE black swivel chair as he looked at the message glowing on the computer screen before him. 'He just checked in from Toronto.'

'Allah be praised!' Cheema raised his arms in supplication. 'Isn't it strange the way everything is falling into place? Surely this is a sign that Allah has blessed this operation. After all, there has not been even a single mishap so far, sir.'

Salim did not respond. He seemed lost in thought. Cheema was about to speak again when Salim replied, 'Yes, you're right. Allah is definitely pleased with us.' *The old man must be tired*, Cheema thought as he saw Salim fighting back a yawn.

'Sir, why don't we get some rest… while we can.'

'You're right. Go ahead and take a nap. I'll just follow you.'

Salim turned away and began to fiddle with some papers as Cheema got up and left the room. Salim waited for a long time after Cheema had gone. When he was sure that Cheema had turned in for the night, he picked up the satellite phone from his study table and dialled a number from memory. His call was answered almost immediately.

'We are ready,' Salim said softly. 'It is time.' There was a long silence in the room as Salim listened to the voice at the other end. 'Excellent, my friend! Then go ahead with it. Remember, you are the guardian of our faith and our country. We are all very proud of you… as is your family.' There was another long silence as Salim listened. 'Of course I will. You can bank on that. Khuda hafiz.'

With that, Salim put down the phone and turned to his computer again. It did not take him long to work out the time zones and differences. He had already done it a dozen times earlier, but he couldn't resist the urge to double-check.

It will be truly spectacular! Way beyond anything that General Haque would have thought possible. Salim chuckled silently to himself as he waited for the home page of his matchmaking profile to open. Then he typed in the last message that he would be sending to his lashkar.

For the first time since the beginning of the mission, Salim acted out of character and broke cover. Perhaps the excitement of the impending strikes was getting to him. Or maybe he was proud of the surprise he had just initiated and wanted his teams to know about it. Maybe he thought the news would motivate his lashkar. No matter what the motive, the fact remains that Salim broke his own security rules with this solitary, unnecessary act.

The message he sent out was cryptic enough. But it would be a dead giveaway for anybody monitoring the site, for it had no relevance at all to matchmaking.

The traitor's fall marks the beginning. On the morrow the world will shudder and you shall be remembered forever. Khuda hafiz.

Salim knew that if the message was intercepted, it could be dangerous. *But it doesn't really matter any more... the website has almost outlived its utility. In any case, not too long from now, none of the lashkar will be alive to access the site. What difference will it make then?*

With a wry grin, Salim logged out of the meetyourmatch website and went to bed.

The Unravelling

New Delhi

ANKITA WAS STILL LOGGED ONTO MAI'S PROFILE ON meetyourmatch.com when she saw the 'unread mail' icon begin to flash. She clicked the new message open.

'Bloody hell!' she exclaimed as she saw who had sent the message. 'It's from smurad... he is online.'

'Quick! Get a lock on him.'

Ankita's heart was thudding with excitement as she hunched forward and began the trace to hunt down the elusive man on the net. A few moments later, she slammed the table with her hand in frustration. 'Damn! Missed him.'

'He must have logged out as soon as he sent the message,' Manoj commiserated. 'Anyway, what's the message?'

'Of course! The message!' Returning to Mai's profile, she clicked open the message again. Khare saw the expression on her face change and went closer to her. One look at the message, and his mind went into high alert mode. Neither knew precisely what it meant, but the contents left no doubt that it was important.

The traitor's fall marks the beginning. On the morrow the world will shudder and you shall be remembered forever. Khuda hafiz.

'Crap! It's begun,' they both whispered at almost the same time, staring at the screen as though willing it to reveal its secrets. The tableau remained frozen for a very brief moment in time.

'True, but what?' Khare said anxiously.

'I don't know, but whatever it is will start the day after the traitor falls.'

'Who is the traitor?'

'Even more importantly, what the hell is going to happen? Where? And how?'

Ankita said decisively, 'I think we've taken this as far as we can.... We need to bring the others up to speed right away.'

'Just one second,' Khare interrupted. 'See, of all the people communicating on the site, one is dead. The second is smurad... whoever that is. The remaining five left Delhi just hours before Mai died, so we can safely assume he handed over the VX Gas and Variola virus to them when they met him.' Khare separated the relevant passport pages from the bunch in his hands and held up the rest. 'What about these four?'

'Three, not four,' Ankita cut in. 'The fourth is from Delhi itself, so we have no way of knowing whether he met Mai Hu or not.'

'Yes, okay… three… what about them?' The question seemed to hang in the air. 'Who are they? Are they part of this strike or are they….'

'Of course they are. See….' Ankita's hands flew over the keyboard, then she tapped her screen. 'Here is a message that Mai Hu wrote to one of this lot.' Glowing on the screen was the brief innocuous mail that Mai had sent to Lars when he had seen him exit Salim's suite at the Maldives resort.

'True!' Khare nodded, rubbing his chin thoughtfully. 'If they're also part of this operation, then…. '

'Either there is something we have missed or….' Ankita whispered back equally softly.

'Shit!' A sinking feeling clawed at Khare's innards.

'Whichever way you look at it, we have to work on the premise that these four are also part of the strike team. Either the weapons are being delivered to them by mules or there is something else afoot that we have not hit upon so far. Either way, we can't take a chance. We will have to track them down and take them in.'

'Damn!' This time, too, it was Khare who picked up the phone.

Minutes later, Denmark moved into high alert. America was already on the move, looking for Erik Segan. The names of Liaquat Ali and Rahim Khan were added on to the wish list. The alert for Yakub Khan hit the streets of Delhi within minutes.

Khare's next call was to Anbu. 'Let's go,' he hailed Ankita as he put down the phone. 'The boss wants us in the ATTF Ops Room. He's called in Mr Rao and the others too.'

Picking up their laptops, they headed out to the waiting car.

They were not the only ones moving with a rapidly increasing sense of urgency. Across the globe, the intelligence agencies of a dozen countries were being suddenly and rudely jolted awake.

All at once, the names and faces of Salim's terror merchants began to light up dozens of computer screens as anti-terrorist cells and task forces came alive. With every passing minute, a formidable array of high technology began to scan the air and ground waves, seeking them out. Even now, no one knew who was carrying what weapon or what the specific target was, but one thing was for sure: the key lay with these men and women; ergo, find them.

The orders went out to a veritable army of security forces.

Find them. Now!

The crux of the message was simple: *Subject is believed to be armed and very dangerous. Report sighting immediately and approach with extreme caution.*

NEW YORK

THE PANIC WAS STILL GATHERING MOMENTUM WHEN THE A&M truck carrying the baggage of the diplomat returning from Pakistan moved out from the cargo terminal of JFK and began the approximately six hour long run to the suburb in Washington where the luggage had to be delivered. Neither of the A&M men in the truck saw the dark blue Chevy suburban which was trailing them. As far as they were concerned, they were on a routine drop and had no reason to be watching out for a tail.

Two hours into the run, the truck pulled into the parking lot of Bob's Diner off the New Jersey Turnpike. There was a fair amount of activity in the diner's parking lot and the A&M crew had no qualms about leaving the truck as they went in to grab a quick bite. In any case, the truck's cab was clearly visible from inside the diner so they were not worried about its security. Unfortunately, the rear of the truck's container was not visible and that was what interested the two men who got down from the blue suburban. Both men were dressed in blue-grey overalls, the kind worn by all A&M crew members. There was nothing even slightly out of place about them as they sprang the lock of the container.

Liaquat Ali kept an eye on the entrance of the diner as Rahim Khan rapidly looked through the luggage till he came across the two suitcases. Both were easily identifiable, with their prominent brightly coloured stickers.

By the time the A&M crew returned to their truck, Rahim and Liaquat were over twenty miles away. Both suitcases were stored safely in the rear of the suburban. The fast moving car soon chewed up the distance to Washington where the two soldiers checked into the Hamilton Inns & Suites hotel on the Jefferson Davis Highway.

A little later, Liaquat Ali logged in and confirmed their arrival to Salim.

New Delhi

ANKITA GAZED WITH SIGHTLESS EYES INTO THE FAR DISTANCE as the car sped through the early morning haze. A sudden sense of despondency seized her. *Are we on the right track? Will we be able to find them in time?*

'Don't fret about it, Ankita.' As usual, her teammate read her mind. 'We did our best. What we've achieved is a miracle, considering the little time we had.' There was a long pause. 'Look at the brighter side – of the ten we have homed in on, one is dead so he can't do any harm, and we have already confirmed that eight of them are no longer on Indian soil, so whatever shit they're up to, it won't happen here.'

'There is still one man left. He is somewhere out there,' Ankita replied. 'Yakub… Yakub Khan. I wonder where he is right now. Where is he headed? What's his target?'

'Don't worry, we'll find the bastard. After all, the ATTF has huge domestic resources available to it. They'll get him.'

'Will they get him before he….' Her voice faltered. 'I have a feeling something really bad is about to happen very soon.'

AJMER

YAKUB SHOOK HIS WIFE AWAKE GENTLY BUT FIRMLY. 'I'M SORRY,' he whispered when she woke up, 'but there was a call from the office. Something urgent has come up and I need to get back.'

'The kids will be so disappointed… they're going to give you hell.' Amreen made a face, gesturing to the two children still asleep on the smaller bed beside theirs. 'You know how much they have been looking forward to this holiday. Is there no way you can manage without going back?'

'No!' Yakub looked away guiltily. 'But I'll tell you what….' He paused, as though he'd just thought of something. 'I'll just zip into Delhi, finish the work in a few hours and then we can continue the holiday in some place closer to Delhi. In fact, why don't we stop at Neemrana?' Yakub made it sound as though he'd thought up the idea on the spur of the moment. Neemrana was barely 122 kilometres from Delhi. *If I leave early I can reach Nehru Place in Delhi in about three hours, carry out my part of the mission and be back in time for a late lunch.* 'Next morning, I'll quickly drive down to Delhi, finish my work and return by late afternoon while you three relax at the hotel. Then we can spend a couple of days there.' *It's going to be a lot longer than that. Once the nuke goes off in Nehru Place, there is no way in hell that I'm going to return to Delhi with my family… not for a long, long time.*

'That sounds good to me,' Amreen replied, pacified. 'I'm sure the kids won't have a problem with it either. After all, whether it is Mount Abu or Neemrana, the two of them just want to spend time with you. They hardly get to see you when we are in Delhi.' Yakub smiled fondly at the sleeping children. *It is for you, and hundreds of others like you, that I must do what I'm going to do. Only then can we throw off the kafir yoke and be free.*

An hour later, all four of them were in the Tata Safari, speeding down the highway towards Neemrana. Five-year-old Yasmeen was busy fiddling with the car radio, flipping channels much to the annoyance of her eight-year-old brother Hameed.

'Can you *please* tell her to stop doing that, ammi, so that we can listen to any one channel peacefully?'

'Don't be so cranky, Hameed. She'll settle down soon enough, then you can listen to what you want.'

'How come she always gets what she wants?' Hameed grumbled. 'Then can I play games on abba's mobile?' he asked.

'No, you cannot,' Yakub replied before Amreen could. 'I forgot to charge it yesterday so the battery is very low. I may need it for an urgent business call. In any case, you know I don't like you messing with my phone. Why don't you play with your mother's phone?'

'But her phone doesn't have Snakes on it. That's the only game I like.'

'Tough luck, I'm not giving you my phone.' Yakub

had been warned by Cheema to keep his phone switched off.

Hameed finally settled down after a predictable bout of whining. Not long after, silence returned to the car as both kids finally dozed off, lulled by the motion of the SUV hurtling down the highway, on its way up to the beautiful Neemrana Fort Palace, India's oldest heritage resort.

ATTF OPS ROOM, NEW DELHI

THE TATA SAFARI HAD JUST CLEARED MOUNT ABU AND HIT the highway when Ankita and Khare walked into the ATTF Ops Room. Anbu and Sami were already there, conversing urgently with Rao. Chauhan, the ATTF chief, and Rawat, the Senior Liaison Officer from NEMA, were present too. Ankita hooked up her laptop to the giant screen that occupied one wall of the room. She quickly gave everyone the background and then moved on to specific details.

'The late Dr Mai Hu visited the Maldives this March and stayed there for a week. During this time the following people were also present at the resort where he stayed.' She flashed a list on the screen. 'Karl Gunther from Berlin, Lars Borge from Copenhagen, Ben Ashton from London, Liaquat Ali and Rahim Khan from New York, Erik Segan from New Orleans, Kismat and Sahiba Khan, two sisters from Barbados, Yakub Khan from Delhi, and Abrahim Reis from Toronto. All these people, including Mai Hu, stayed at suites that had been booked by a Dubai based company called Desert Apparels, which is owned by a person listed in the records as S. Murad. They are all constantly in touch with a profile titled smurad234 on the meetyourmatch.com website, which obviously appears to be the same S. Murad. From what we have seen so far, this website seems to be the primary communication channel of this group that is led by the man who calls himself S. Murad.'

'That seems to be....' Chauhan started to speak when Anbu held up his hand.

'Please let her finish, Mr Chauhan.'

'We also found two phone numbers jotted down in Mai Hu's diary. They were on the page opposite to the one where we found some notes and the username and password of Hu's profile on meetyourmatch.com. Hence, it is safe to assume that all these were noted down at the same time or are otherwise linked in some way.' Ankita flashed a scanned copy of the pages on the screen and paused briefly to allow her audience to absorb the data.

'The notes themselves seem to be in some form of shorthand that Hu had devised for himself and we will certainly need more time to make sense of it; however, both the phone numbers belong to Thuraya satellite phones that had been purchased a few years ago as a set of four by the same Dubai company, Desert Apparels.' She paused again, this time for effect.

'When we checked out the usage records of these four phones, we found that they have been functioning mostly in Pakistan from the time they were bought. In fact, three of them are still in use and all three are currently located in Pakistan... two are in Murree, a hill station just north of Lahore, and the third is in Islamabad.'

'What about the fourth one?' Rao couldn't hold himself back.

'The fourth Thuraya phone has spent most of its time in POK with occasional trips to Lahore, Multan and Islamabad. It was last in operation in Kashmir till about two years ago when it was captured by one of our patrols along the LOC. At that time it was in the possession of a man named Iqbal who'd been trying to cross the LOC and sneak into India. Since then, it's been in the custody of Military Intelligence.'

Anbu gave a visible start. Ankita paused for a moment, thinking he was going to say something, but resumed speaking when she saw that he had lapsed into a thoughtful silence.

'What is even more interesting is that both the phones that are in Murree today were also in Maldives for the full week that Hu was there. From there they moved a day later, went to Dubai, and then to Lahore the same day. This is the roaming record of both phones.' She gestured towards the giant screen as another document flashed on it. 'I have tabulated it for the entire period that the phones have been in operation. You'll note that barring short trips overseas, the third phone, the one that's in Islamabad, has remained there and in Lahore, Multan, Karachi and Peshawar.'

She was about to resume when Anbu interrupted. 'One moment, Ankita.' He turned to Sami. 'You remember that guy I told you about... who had been captured by Vinod Rai's company in the valley?'

Before Sami could say anything, Khare butted in. 'Yes, sir, he's the one they found the phone on. I've already checked him out, sir. The man is right here in Delhi, in Tihar jail.'

'Excellent work, Manoj.' Anbu gave him the thumbs up sign. 'Get hold of his interrogation file for me.' Khare nodded and turned to his laptop immediately.

Ankita resumed the briefing. 'We have tried very hard to home in on the real identity of S. Murad but have not made much headway so far. What we do have is this.' The front pages of two passports appeared on the screen. 'These are the two men who occupied the last two suites booked by Desert Apparels at the Blue Moon Resort while Mai Hu and the others were also there.' The photos were grainy and revealed nothing much beyond the approximate age of the two men. 'Both passports were issued in Lahore in December last year. This one,' she pointed at the photo of the older man, 'is made out in the name of Faiz Ali, and that one to

Mushtaq Ahmed. However, both passports have the same Murree address given on them. We believe that these are the two men who are currently using two of the remaining three Thuraya phones.'

Everyone in the room stared at the two photographs projected on the screen.

'Then, just as we were analyzing the data, this message came through on the matchmaking site. It is addressed to all ten people who have been communicating with S. Murad.'

Salim's last message to his lashkar snapped onto the screen. The silence this time was deafening.

'So where do we stand now?' Sami finally asked. 'We know that some dangerous biochems are missing and are likely to be used for a terror strike that could target several countries. We know that these people who met at Male are a part of this strike. We also know that whatever is going to happen will begin or end twenty-four hours from the time some traitor falls.'

'No, sir, it's not over just yet,' Ankita replied with a somewhat satisfied smile. 'The ATTF has confirmed that six of the people from the strike team were in Delhi. In fact, five of them left Delhi just hours before or immediately after Mai Hu died.'

'Bloody hell! That obviously means they had come to collect....'

'Precisely, sir! It is obvious that they had come to Delhi to collect something from Hu. It had to be something of high value that could not be transported through regular channels and something that Hu did not have with him when he met them in the Maldives.'

'The damn biochems, of course!' Rao breathed. 'So at least we now know who took them and where they're headed.'

'That's the logical assumption to make, sir. That is why the security agencies of all those countries have been alerted.'

'Who were the three that didn't come to Delhi?' Anbu interjected.

'They are Lars Borge of Denmark and Liaquat Ali and Rahim Khan from the US. We don't know anything about Yakub Khan since he is Delhi based and we have so far been unable to confirm if he met Dr Hu or not. However, the other three have not left their countries since they returned from the Maldives... unless they travelled on false documents,' Ankita added as the thought struck her.

'Damn!' Rao exclaimed angrily. 'So we now have highly dangerous bio-chemical weapons of unknown shape, size and lethality moving in six or seven densely populated cities in the world, including Delhi.'

'Well, sir, the surveillance tapes at the Delhi airport, where Hu landed, show that he had two large suitcases as check-in baggage and a carry bag and a laptop as cabin baggage. So whatever he carried was in those bags.'

'That means very little if we keep in mind the tiny dosage of VX Gas or smallpox virus that is required to wreak havoc.'

'True, sir,' Ankita conceded. 'We must also keep in mind the glass ampoule which killed Mai Hu. There were traces of face cream on the outer surface of the glass and a tissue was also found in the waste bin, with the same cream on it. The glass ampoule had probably been in a jar of cream and Hu must have used the tissue to wipe it clean.'

'The devilish bastard,' Rao breathed. 'The cream would have protected the ampoule and made it almost impossible for anyone to find it.'

'Very true, sir! The ampoule probably came from one of the weapons, so that does give us an idea of how the VX has been packaged. Not a very clear one, but *something*. And from what Chinese Intelligence tells us, the dead scientist had requisitioned several items a few weeks before all this began. At that time, no one gave it a second thought, but now it appears that in addition to these glass vials he may have packaged the VX, the Variola, or both, as an aerosol in some spray can.'

'This whole thing is full of too many ifs and buts,' Rawat remarked. 'We need to....'

Whatever he was going to say was lost as one of Chauhan's senior aides rushed into the room. His voice was high and he was literally shaking with excitement. 'Sir, I think you need to see this.' He turned on the television and increased the volume till the voice of the news anchor filled the room. The voice was throbbing with excitement.

Soon the room was, too.

The Traitor Falls

THE PRESIDENTIAL COMPLEX, ISLAMABAD

ACCORDING TO THE STANDARD OPERATING PROCEDURE OF the Pakistan Army special protection detail, at no point in time was the General to be guarded by less than four men. This was as much to ensure that there was no chance of anyone from the protection detail turning on him as it was to ensure that a ring of sturdy Kevlar-clad bodies always stood between him and harm's way.

The sturdy bodies that stood in the line of fire belonged to the same para-commando battalion in which the General had been commissioned as a young Lieutenant. It was the same unit where he had found his Captain's stars and his Major's pips and which he had once commanded as a young Colonel.

One of the first things he had done when he wrested control from the Prime Minister in a bloodless coup had been to move this para-commando battalion to the finest garrison in Islamabad and assign them a host of coveted duties, one of which included the protection of himself and his family.

The men assigned to the dictator's protective detail were handpicked after extensive profiling. Each one of them had been thoroughly checked and verified before being allowed anywhere near the General's august body. As an extra precaution, duty rosters were prepared in such a manner that no two men on duty in the same shift were from the same town or village.

Each man in the General's protection detail was a superb marksman, skilled with a variety of weapons and trained to kill in almost every possible way known to man. They were undoubtedly the pride of the Pakistan Army and they all took their jobs very, very seriously, which was not surprising, given the number of people who were itching to deliver the not-so-beloved General to his maker.

If there was a world record for the head of state who had survived the largest number of assassination attempts, the Pakistani dictator would have won hands-down. There had been forty-seven attempts already, of which two had nearly succeeded. More than seventy-eight people had lost their lives either in trying to get rid of the General or in trying to protect him. The list of casualties did not include the five officers who had headed the security detail over the past six years and been compelled to take premature retirement due to high blood pressure and other stress related disorders, which were very much a part of the territory as far as this particular job went.

THE GENERAL WAS IN AN EXTREMELY FOUL MOOD WHEN HE left the conference room after the morning's briefing. The *Lahore Times* and *Dawn* had outdone themselves in the nasty, sarcastic things they had written about him that day. So had most of the other papers. Each one of them sang about his sell-out to the Satanic Americans. The same rabid hardliners he had supported and fed all their lives were now clamouring for his blood.

The ungrateful Godless mongrels, the General cursed under his breath as he strode into his office. Angrily, he flung the sheaf of tightly rolled newspapers he had been clutching. The roll of papers hit the edge of the sofa with a thud and scattered across the floor.

The sound attracted an immediate response from the presidential security detail. The two men who were positioned just outside the door rushed into the room. Their weapons were drawn, and their hard gimlet eyes raked the room. They relaxed slightly when they saw what had caused the noise. There was a rapid exchange of glances and then the two men turned and made their way to the door. The one in front pulled it open and left the room. The one behind him caught hold of the door as it began to silently swing shut. However, instead of pulling it open, he softly pushed it shut and smoothly threw the latch into closed position in the same motion.

Levelling his weapon as he turned, the commando swiftly strode up to the General who was standing by a huge office table, in front of large windows with bulletproof panes. The General was pulling back his chair to sit down when the harsh snick of metal caused him to look up. He raised his eyes to throw a quizzical glance at the bodyguard, and saw the automatic pistol pointed straight at him. His mind was still trying to take this in, when the bodyguard pulled the trigger. Once, twice, thrice....

Like his comrades in the security detail, the commando was yielding a Sig Sauer P229, 357-calibre handgun. At almost point blank range, the heavy lead bullets ploughed through the frontal skull plate of the General, and lacerated the soft grey brain cells. The entry points were small neat circles, but the exit wounds were a large gory mess.

The back of the presidential head exploded. Bone, tissue and flesh sprayed through the air and spattered in a horrific mosaic across the sparkling clean bulletproof windowpanes.

The sound of the pistol shots echoed through the room with startling effect. The door of the office flew open as it was shouldered in by the Praetorians positioned outside. The three other men of the security detail flew into the room, their weapons drawn. There was a brief, almost infinitesimal pause as they took in the scene and then a crash of gunfire thundered through the building.

The bodyguard-assassin was on the point of firing

his last round into the already dead General when the first volley of bullets fired by the protective detail slammed into him. He staggered as they pounded his body, but none of them managed to penetrate the Kevlar protecting his torso. Those that encountered his head had no such problem.

The man fell in a ragged heap as more and more bullets found their mark. He felt his weapon being wrested away and then he saw the furious eyes of the team leader boring into him. Life was already fast fleeing his body so he could not hear the words, but the '*Why?*' in those eyes did not escape him.

He tried to speak, to share with him all that Salim had told him; about how the General had betrayed their Allah, their country, their....

The horrified team leader saw life drain out of the assassin's body along with the blood pulsing out of his mouth.

Fuck! Why did it have to happen on my watch? I'm dead.

New Delhi

ANBU CLICKED THE TELEVISION REMOTE, AND THE EXCITED voice of the news anchor covering the assassination of the Pakistani dictator filled the room.

'That settles one thing for sure,' Anbu said. 'Now we all know what that *traitor falls* part of the sentence means.' There were several unhappy nods in the room. 'It is also obvious that whatever is supposed to happen has already begun. We now have twenty-four hours to find out what it is and stop it.'

Instinctively, everyone looked at their watches.

Twenty-four hours!

Almost a dozen cities strung out all over the globe!

This cannot be happening!

No one in the room had any doubts about the mammoth task that lay ahead of them.

Yet again, it was Anbu who broke the silence. 'I think you'd better call the PM.' He looked at Rao. 'We need to bring him up to speed.'

Rao nodded miserably. 'I just wish we had more to tell him.'

'We will, if we get cracking right away,' Anbu replied briskly before turning to Khare in a businesslike manner. 'What about the man I'd asked you to check on? Iqbal?'

'Oh yes.' Khare jumped up with a start. 'Here is the transcript of the interrogation carried out by MI.' 'Iqbal was recruited by the Lashkar-e-Toiba and sent to Pakistan for training. He says he took the Thuraya phone off Maulana Fazlur Rehman whom he killed because the October 2005 bombs at Sarojini Nagar that had been planted by the Lashkar had also killed his mother and sister.'

'The October 2005 blasts? Wasn't that the handiwork of Brigadier Murad Salim?' Rao asked. There was an infinitesimal pause. Anbu softly mouthed the name again, as though mulling over it. 'Murad Salim....' It clicked in the minds of most of the people in the room almost simultaneously. 'S. Murad... Salim Murad... Murad Salim... *shit! It's him! It has to be him!*'

'But Salim died in a chopper crash just a few days after the Delhi blasts,' Rao interjected.

'Well, it appears he didn't,' Anbu whispered thoughtfully.

'The bloody cheek of the man! He simply inverted his name.'

'Part cheek and part ego, I would say. In any case, he must have thought his role in this strike would never surface.'

'And it wouldn't have if Mai Hu hadn't died... we would have been clueless even now.'

'It all makes sense actually, when you come to think of it.' Anbu suddenly threw off his thoughtful demeanour and turned to the others. 'Listen, if Murad Salim is behind this, we can bet the strike is going to be big. That guy is the coldest, most ruthless of them all. And you can definitely bet that India will be an important target... if not Delhi, it'll be some other major Indian city. I want you guys to get down to it right away. MS, you hold fort till I get back. I want our boys ready to go.... Keep all options open for now.' His voice crackled with urgency. 'Khare, I want you to go down to Tihar with copies of those last two passports which we have not been able to identify. Talk to Iqbal... handle it delicately. I have a feeling he will be able to confirm that they are who we think they are. Ankita, I want you to get cracking and hunt down the current location of the man using the smurad profile.' Then he turned to Chauhan. 'And could you please put more ATTF boots on the ground? We need to track down every possible lead. Yakub Khan has to be found and taken in.'

'You think we should focus on Delhi, or do we alert the other metros also?'

'I would say we focus on Delhi for now, simply because Yakub himself is from Delhi. My guess is that the strikes are going to be concentrated on the cities that the attackers are from.'

'That makes tactical sense,' Chauhan concurred.

By now, Rao had put down the phone. He threw a look at Anbu. 'Let's go. The PM wants us. *Now.*'

THEIR CAR WAS ENTERING THE PARKING LOT AT SOUTH BLOCK, having zigzagged through the heavy traffic from Delhi Cantt. when Anbu's phone rang. Khare's excited voice came through. 'Sir, that guy Iqbal says that the man in the photo is Murad Salim.'

'He is sure?'

'Yes, sir. He said he could never forget his face.'

'I thought as much.' Anbu could not hide the satisfaction in his tone. 'What about the other man?'

'Iqbal says he was Salim's aide and used to accompany him all the time. He is not sure of the name but he says it was most probably Captain Azam Cheema.'

'Good work, Khare. Get back to base now and wait for my call.'

He had barely disconnected when the phone rang again. It was Ankita.

'Sir, I have been profiling all those who were in the Maldives, and the cities they hail from. There is a pattern emerging… at least for some of the cities. In these places, it's not hard to predict the target.'

'Explain that, Ankita,' Anbu said tersely. So she did. As usual, her analysis was based on impeccable logic and meticulous research. 'Excellent! That makes perfect sense. I suggest you alert the governments involved so they can cover those targets.'

'I'll do that right away.'

'And get hold of Salim's location for me. Use the Thuraya phones and the IP address. I'm willing to bet he won't stray from his command post just yet.'

Anbu was quiet as he accompanied Rao to the PM's office. A variety of options raced through his mind. He analysed them with military precision, segregating the possible from the plausible.

PMO, South Block, New Delhi

THE STARK SILENCE IN THE ROOM WAS BROKEN ONLY WHEN the Prime Minister walked in with the Home Minister, the Defence Minister, the External Affairs Minister and the Director of RAW in tow.

'Yes, Rao?' The PM got right down to it. By now he had been given enough information to know that there was no time to waste.

'Sir, we have another terror strike coming.' Rao went straight to the heart of the matter. 'A very big one and it is coming really fast.' In a quiet level tone, Rao ran through the complete sequence of events and what they were expecting.

There was silence when he finished. Everyone in that room had more or less known what was coming since they were all in the information loop, but it was chilling to have it confirmed.

'What's the likely target in Delhi?' the PM asked.

'We don't know, sir. For Delhi we don't know for sure, but for some of the other overseas cities it's not hard to guess the target,' Anbu replied.

'Explain that, Colonel.' So he did, briefly summing up what Ankita had deduced. When he finished, the PM nodded. 'Okay, I see what you mean… it makes sense. The terrorists *will* seek out important public events and large gatherings if they want to make a statement.'

'Precisely, sir.'

'What about Delhi?'

'Sir, we have not been able to pinpoint the target, but we are pretty certain who will carry out the strike in Delhi. We have complete details of the man.'

'Then why have you not taken him in?'

'We're looking for him right now, sir. His house, factory, office and all known friends and relatives have been placed under physical and technical surveillance, but he is still not traceable. Apparently he is on holiday with his family in Rajasthan. Even his mobile phone has been switched off since the night of 24 April. Our last sighting of him is at Mount Abu, but he left his hotel there very early on twenty-fifth morning.'

'I am sure we have ways to find him.'

'We do, sir, and we will definitely find him.'

'Good!' He turned to Rao. 'What about the other countries? Who have we informed?'

'All of them, sir. The MEA did it as soon as we came to know. The ATTF and my people are working in tandem with them. The countries being targeted have been given the complete details at the highest possible level.'

'Excellent! And who did you say is responsible for all this?' the PM asked.

'Salim... Brigadier Murad Salim. He is an ex-ISI officer.'

'Sir, he is the same guy who planned the Delhi bomb blasts in October 2005. He was supposed to have died in a chopper crash the same year,' Anbu added. 'Clearly, that was a hoax. It's very clear now that the man had simply gone underground.'

'Do you think their government knows?' the PM asked thoughtfully.

'*Knows?* I wouldn't be surprised if they planned it themselves,' the Home Minister spoke before anyone could answer.

'Sir, we have a huge file on the guy,' the RAW Director said. 'He had... has always been very close to General Ehsan Haque, the present ISI Director. It wouldn't be surprising if Haque is hand in glove with him, but we can't be sure. Salim has always been a bit of a loner… a rogue.'

'Well, one thing is for certain,' Anbu said. 'The fourth Thuraya satellite phone is currently operating out of Islamabad and that is where General Haque is these days.'

'They have nukes on the loose, sir,' Rao added. 'And that cannot happen without their so-called official machinery being aware of it.'

'So let us speak to their government.'

'What is the point, sir? The civilian government hardly has any say in such matters. In any case, they will deny everything, just as they have always done.'

'Then what do you suggest? What is the solution?'

'Sir, if you ask me, the solution lies in a well-coordinated, two-pronged strategy: first, a series of prophylactic and defensive measures and second, taking the war to the enemy and fighting it on their territory rather than on our own. We have to launch a series of aggressive diplomatic and economic offensives to tie them up in knots so that they don't have the time or energy to even think of harassing us with such terror attacks.'

'I agree with Mr Rao,' Anbu said. 'We're so worried about being seen as a big bully that we've ended up playing the benign elder brother for too long. Our neighbours have always taken advantage of this.... They have mistaken our kindness for weakness.'

'That about sums it up. We should break off all contacts with Pakistan and re-negotiate all treaties, including water sharing agreements. That should wake them up so fast th....'

Nods and supportive murmurs broke out in the room. The noise subsided when the PM held up his hand. 'Do we have time for all this right now?'

'You are right, sir. We don't. The clock is ticking really fast, so....'

'So let's focus on the more immediate problem at hand. How certain are we that we can stop the strike on Delhi?'

'We *have* to,' Rao replied firmly. 'If the weapon is biological or chemical, we don't have a choice, because if it goes off, we have nothing to even limit the damage.'

His grim words were met by a very long silence.

'*This time* we can stop the strike,' Anbu finally said. He was speaking softly but his tone was firm. '*Maybe*... but the point is, how long will we keep defending ourselves? What will we defend? How many trains, how many buses, how many markets, how many malls? How many temples and mosques? How long and in how many places will we remain on guard? How long should this state of fear be allowed to rule our lives?'

'True,' Rao said. 'Sooner or later an attack is bound to get through. And then another... and another. And whenever that happens, many more will die.'

'What are you two trying to say?' the PM asked brusquely. 'We don't have time for rhetoric.'

'The time has come to hit back, sir, hard and fast,' Anbu replied. 'The time has come for us to take the battle to the enemy. To go in and hit them before they know what's happening.'

'We have to keep *them* worried and guessing.' Rao was equally firm. 'We have to keep them on the run at all times.'

'That's right, sir. This is not going to be a conventional battle that can be fought in a conventional manner.'

'The use of force is never a permanent solution to any problem,' the PM retorted.

'Very true, sir,' Anbu replied evenly, 'but neither is allowing yourself to be put under siege, waiting for the enemy to come and hit you. No war can ever be won with a strategy of permanent defence. The primary lesson that has emerged very clearly from our experiences in the Kashmir valley, Nagaland, Mizoram, Assam, Punjab and Sri Lanka is that force has to be used to bring the terrorists to heel and compel them to look at peaceful negotiations as the only way to lasting peace.'

'In any case,' the RAW Director interrupted, 'this is not a homegrown problem at all. Everyone knows that the Pakistani ISI is using these jihadis to inflict a proxy war on us. It is stupid for us to believe that Pakistan is anything but a failed state. As Mr Rao was saying, their army and the ISI have to be kept busy with their own internal problems. Only then can we hope to have some measure of peace in India.'

'Correct,' Anbu assented. 'The other thing we have all learnt the hard way is that no terrorist organization is ever going to come out and fight us in the open. They are aware of the disparity of forces and will always resort to such underhand tactics to exert pressure on us and inflict losses. So, like them, we will have to think out of the box and act accordingly.'

'True, sir,' Rao said. 'You remember in 1989 when the United Liberation Front problem began in Assam and they started extorting money from the tea plantations? The buggers were simply lining their pockets but they went around projecting themselves as saviours of the working classes, who were their major support base. There was a school of thought that advocated shutting down the tea plantations rather than giving in to ULFA's demands. But the several hundred thousand tea plantation workers who would have been rendered jobless would never have allowed it. In fact, they would have turned on ULFA the moment they realized that they were suffering because of ULFA's terror tactics.'

'Then why wasn't it done?' the External Affairs Minister enquired.

'We didn't have to. We just leaked news of this plan to the ULFA leadership. They realized what would happen and stopped pressurizing the tea plantations immediately.'

'That's all very well, Rao, but what's the co-relation here?' the PM interjected.

'It is evident, sir,' Anbu broke in. 'We need to wake up to the fact that this problem of terrorism cannot be wished away. It is here to stay and it simply cannot be handled in a conventional manner. We have to go in, infiltrate the terrorist organizations where possible and make sure we take down the people who lead them. Also, those who fund and support them.'

'Absolutely, sir!' Rao asserted vehemently. 'As soon as we cut out the heart and chop off the head, the arms will automatically atrophy.'

'And this is never going to be a one-time solution. It will have to be done again and again. Whenever and wherever the need arises.... We must not lose any opportunity to go in and hit the head.'

'Pakistan has to be made to understand that attacking India will always be an expensive proposition for them and every attack will result in a direct and proportionate counter-attack.'

A supportive murmur broke out in the room. It subsided when the PM held up his hand. 'What are you two suggesting right now?' he asked.

'Sir, we need to take strong punitive action.' Anbu spoke in his usual quiet tone but the words rang resolutely through the room. 'Salim must die.'

A hush fell upon the room.

'This is not America, Colonel.' The PM's tone was cold and inscrutable. 'The Indian government does not sanction murder.'

'With due apology, sir, this is not murder. I am talking about the need and the right to defend ourselves.'

'That, Colonel, is exactly what the Americans say when they bomb innocent villagers in their hunt for Al Qaida terrorists. That is what they say when they trample upon human rights and individual freedom in the name of Homeland Security. That is the excuse they give for holding prisoners in covert jails without due process, and for the host of unspeakable things that they have done and continue to do to nameless, faceless people who have little to do with their so-called war on terror.'

'Very true, sir,' Anbu countered, softly. 'But please remember it is America that created the Al Qaida. It is their own Frankenstein that has gone berserk and is now wreaking havoc. It is their own shortsighted policies that have rebounded on them and compelled them to act in this insane and unscrupulous manner.

'How can our situation be comparable in any way? How are we to blame? India did not create either the Al Qaida or the ISI. Nor have we done anything to have this festering wound of terrorism inflicted on us by a jealous, rabid neighbour smarting after a series of military defeats.

'As far as lunatics like Salim and his ilk are concerned, we are very much at war… in fact, we have been at war for over three decades now. I am sure I don't need to highlight the number of people, civilians and security personnel who have been sacrificed on the altar of terrorism. You may not agree, sir, but Salim and other people like him need to be hunted down… hunted down and destroyed like the mad raving dogs that they are.'

Everyone waited with bated breath for the PM's response. After a very long moment, he spoke. 'You want to send your boys into Pakistan again, Colonel? Do you think it is worth the risk?'

'What has to be done has to be done, sir. That lunatic will not stop. He will plan yet another strike and then another. We have to take him out.'

'But our first priority should be to stop the strike on Delhi,' the PM stressed.

'We're already working on that, sir. Even now our men are hunting down Yakub Khan. However, the assault on Salim must take place simultaneously, otherwise as soon as we manage to stop the strikes, we will lose him. He will know he's been blown and will simply go underground again… till the next time. And the next time we may not be so lucky.'

'I see what you mean.' Finally, the PM nodded. 'So be it, Colonel. Send in your people.'

'I will need some help, sir… including taking a man out of prison.'

'Do whatever it takes, Colonel, I trust you to do

the right thing.' Anbu saluted and turned to leave. He was at the door when the PM's voice stopped him. 'Incidentally, Colonel, I do agree with what you just said and I have no doubt in my mind that people like Salim must not be allowed to get away with such henious crimes.'

'He will not get away, sir. He will pay for his sins. So will anyone who thinks India is a soft target waiting to be hit.'

'Good! How much time did you say we have? Twenty-four hours?'

'We did, sir.' Anbu threw a quick look at his watch. 'Now we have a little less than twenty-one left.'

'Then I suggest we get moving.'

They did. Fast.

ALL OF THEM WERE ON THEIR PHONES AS THEY RAN TO THEIR waiting wheels.

'MS,' Anbu spoke quickly but calmly. 'I want the whole team in the Ops Room… this is what we're going to do.' Speaking in short staccato sentences, he rolled out a series of instructions, much like a neat bulleted list.

'What about Yakub Khan?' Sami asked when he had finished.

'Chauhan is handling that. It's the ATTF's turf and they're the best people to handle it. We will make Tiwari, Katoch, Dhankar and Vashisht available to them for any operational tasks that come up.'

'What about tactical support for the team going

in to take down Salim? Have you coördinated with RAW or do I need...?'

'No, I've already taken care of that. RAW will be providing local support for us on the ground. They should be faxing the details of their agent across the border who will work with us on this.'

The orders flew hard and fast. As they always do... just before the bullets begin to fly.

TIHAR JAIL, NEW DELHI

THE JAILOR DID NOT LIKE THE TWO HARD LOOKING MEN who strode into his office. He liked the document they placed on his table even less. But he was a seasoned sarkari mule and knew when to play ball.

'Not a problem at all... sir.' He added the 'sir' as an afterthought, deciding it was better to err on the side of caution. After all, it wasn't every day that people walked into your office with letters signed by the Home Minister that empowered them to walk off with convicted terrorists. 'You will understand that I need to clear this,' he motioned at the document on his table, 'with my superiors.'

'Of course,' Anbu replied, 'but please do it right away. We have very little time.'

'Good, good.' The jailor was the picture of cordiality as he put down the phone a moment later and turned to Anbu. 'It all checks out perfectly, sir. Sorry, but I needed to do that... duty, you know.' He gave an apologetic shrug. Then he picked up the intercom and barked out the required orders to some nameless subordinate. 'Would you like a cup of tea while we're waiting for the convict?'

'No, thank you,' Anbu replied, 'but we would appreciate being given a copy of the convict's records.'

'I have already asked for them, but they will not tell you anything. Trust me, sir, I know him well. He's a strange one. One of the strangest I have ever seen.' The jailor looked into the distance as he pulled his thoughts together. 'I have never heard him talk, unless he's asked a direct question. Though, when he does talk, he is always polite and to the point. All the man wants to do is to work out. In fact, he is much more fit than most people you'll meet. But he is a complete loner and the others give him a wide berth... especially after what happened when he was first brought here.' The jailor paused dramatically. There was that peculiar expression on his face that people have when they want to tell a juicy story, but want to be asked to tell it.

'What happened?' Anbu obliged.

'He had just been brought in here,' the jailor launched into his story eagerly, 'and you know how it is in such places... what with the weird people we get.' He pulled a disparaging face. 'One day, a gang of old timers in his block surrounded him and began to bait him. For a long time Iqbal did not react, but that only goaded them on and they began to hit him. So he hit back. By the time the guards got in and stopped the fight, Iqbal had been wounded quite badly.

One of the guys had cut him up with a surgical knife. But he did not go down without a fight. Two of the gang members were hospitalized for severe fractures and concussion.' There was a hint of pride in the jailor's tone, as though he himself had put up the fight. 'And it didn't end there, you know.' He paused again, melodramatically this time. 'A few weeks after Iqbal got out of hospital, the leader of the gang failed to turn up for the evening muster. They found him behind the toilets. His neck had been broken.'

The jailor was a bit put out at his visitors' lack of response to this sensational news. He continued with the story, nevertheless.

'And then, a few weeks later, they found the man who had used the knife on Iqbal. He too was behind the shithouse with his neck broken. We all knew who had done it but were not able to link Iqbal to either of the killings.' The jailor waved grandiosely in the air. 'But then, who cares really? It is not as if either of those guys was anything but criminal scum. The chutiyas only got what they deserved.'

The expression on Anbu's face made it clear that the last remark had not gone down well with the visitors. In fact, their deadpan expressions and silence unnerved the jailor more than a little. He continued hastily, eager to fill the silence.

'Oh yes, there is definitely something strange about this guy. The other prisoners stay clear of him. You will see what I mean....' There was a long silence as the man finally ran out of things to say. But you could see that he was wracking his brains because he spoke again suddenly, as he remembered something. 'Oh yes, another thing – till date he has not had any visitors, nor has he written to anyone or called anyone. We asked him about it once, and he said he is all alone in this world.'

Anbu exchanged a quick glance with Khare. They'd both read the Intel file on Iqbal and knew that his father and brother were still alive. Both were in Lucknow, where his father still worked at the same school; his brother was now studying at the local university.

Just then the door swung open after a hasty knock and two khaki-clad cops walked in. Sandwiched between them was a tall well-built man in his mid-twenties with a pleasant face. Had it not been for the fact that his eyes were totally bereft of any expression, he may well have been considered handsome. His body was taut and lean. Prison life had burned away every ounce of spare fat. His face lit up with curiosity momentarily when he spied Khare, but he didn't speak.

'We'd like to talk to him alone,' Anbu told the jailor.

'Are you sure?' the man asked tentatively. 'He is a dangerous terrorist.'

Anbu looked at him and gave a brief, impassive smile. The cops left reluctantly, their faces shining with curiosity. Anbu waited till they were gone and then gestured to Khare, who immediately took up position near the door, ensuring that the two men inside had the privacy Anbu desired.

Silence prevailed as the men appraised each other. Then Anbu held out two photographs. 'I believe you know both these men?'

Iqbal threw a quick glance at the photos before he nodded. 'I already told him. That one was Salim... Brigadier Murad Salim of the Pakistani ISI. He was killed in a helicopter crash in November 2005.'

'That is what they wanted us to believe,' Anbu replied softly. 'He is alive and well.'

'No!' Iqbal's face transmitted shock and disbelief.

'Yes, he is. So is the other man.'

There was a long silence. Iqbal blinked several times, as though fighting back tears. 'Maybe that is why I am still alive,' he finally whispered, more to himself than to Anbu. 'Somewhere inside, I knew my life still had a purpose.'

'We know that you went back to Pakistan to kill him... after you killed Fazlur Rehman,' Anbu continued. Iqbal nodded wordlessly, still in shock at the unexpected news. 'Would you like to take another shot at him?' Anbu asked softly.

'Who are you?' Iqbal asked. 'You're not making a fool of me, are you?'

'There is no reason why I should,' Anbu replied, ignoring the first question. 'Tell me, would you like to take another shot at Salim?'

'Yes, I would,' Iqbal replied without hesitation.

'You're sure?'

'Very sure.'

'You may not come back alive,' Anbu said bluntly.

'So?' Iqbal retorted. 'What difference would it make?' He gestured at the bleak prison surroundings. 'Who can call this living anyway?'

'Sit down.' Anbu nodded at the chair facing him. Then he introduced himself briefly and told Iqbal about the impending strike, taking care to reveal only as much as he needed to know. He gave away nothing that would hurt them in case Iqbal was taken... or double-crossed them. 'That is why we are going to go into Pakistan and take care of him.'

'But why me? I am sure there are others far more qualified for....'

'We need someone who has seen him and will recognize him.'

'I could never forget that face.'

'That is why we need you. Salim is a very smart operative. There are no photos of him, barring this one... and this is almost useless. See, our people will do the job – you just need to confirm the identity of the man,' Anbu replied. 'You help us find him and I will ensure you go free.'

'I will help you, sir.' Iqbal gave him a dark, haunted look. 'But not because I want to be free.' He looked away. 'I cannot be free.' Anbu could feel the guilt and the anger raging inside him. 'I will never ever be free. My prison is here.' Iqbal tapped his forehead. His voice was barely above a whisper. 'I am responsible for the death of my mother and my sister… and Allah knows how many more mothers, brothers and sisters. *I will never be free.*'

Anbu did not say a word. In any case, there was little that he could have said that would have made any difference.

You need to fight those demons yourself, young man.

Finally, Iqbal spoke. 'I will help you… sir, but you must promise me that I will be allowed to kill that monster. *Please*… promise me, sir.' He looked at Anbu beseechingly. 'Maybe that will finally give me some peace.'

Anbu nodded. 'Okay. Come with me.'

ATTF OPS ROOM, NEW DELHI

THE FORCE 22 OFFICERS WERE OUT IN FULL FORCE WHEN Anbu walked into the Ops Room. But the usual banter was missing.

'Have you given them the initial brief?' Anbu asked Sami.

'Yes, sir. The weapons and comm gear have also been checked and loaded. We're ready to go.'

'Good work, MS. And what about Tiwari and his team? Are they ready?'

'Yes, they are. Katoch, Vashisht and Dhankar will go with him to coordinate with the ATTF and help hunt down Yakub Khan.'

'Have we got a lock on him yet?'

'Not a blip so far, sir, but the ATTF sounds confident they will get him whenever he tries to re-enter Delhi.'

'I just hope he is not in Delhi already,' Anbu muttered under his breath. Then he pushed away the dark thought. 'Has RAW reverted with the details of their agent?'

'Yes, they have, sir.' Sami referred to his scribble pad. 'Tiwathia and Iqbal will be met by Tanaz Hassan as soon as they cross.'

'Tanaz? That sounds like a woman's name.'

'She is a woman, boss. RAW says she is highly motivated and an excellent operative.'

'Good enough. And who are you sending in with Tiwathia?'

'Myself.' Sami gave him a level look.

Anbu met it evenly. 'Excellent. I'm sure you guys will do a good job, MS. Just try and get back with both your ears this time,' he said, referring to the time when Sami had come back from the mission in Pakistan with one earlobe shot away. Everyone standing around laughed, breaking the high-wire tension momentarily. Then Anbu turned to the others. 'Guys, you are all aware of the situation and know how badly stretched we are for time.' There were terse nods. 'This is what we have to do and this is how we are going to do it.' He went over the plan in detail.

Soon the briefing was over and everyone headed

out to begin their assigned tasks. Sami, Tiwathia and Anbu stood together just outside the Ops Room, waiting for Iqbal.

'Can we trust him?' Tiwathia asked, gesturing towards Iqbal as he walked towards them. He was speaking in an undertone but Iqbal must have heard him, because his step faltered for a moment as he looked up at the three officers waiting for him.

'Can we trust you, Iqbal?' Anbu tossed the query to Iqbal blandly as he came closer.

'Yes, you can, sir,' Iqbal replied firmly, meeting and holding his gaze. 'I swear I will not let you down.'

Anbu looked back at him for a long moment. 'I trust him, Vikram,' he finally said to Tiwathia, who nodded in response.

'Thank you, sir.' Iqbal spoke softly as Anbu turned away. His voice throbbed with barely controlled emotion. 'I swear I will not let you down. Not this time and, if I do come back alive, not ever in the future.'

'I know,' Anbu replied quietly. 'And don't worry, you'll be back. He's very good at bringing his team back intact.' He gestured towards Sami with a brief smile. 'Take care, guys. Keep your transponders on, and happy hunting. I'll see you when you get back.'

With a wave, he turned back to the Ops Room. At no point did Anbu betray any sign of nerves. *This is the way it always is, whenever you send your command into action. Especially when you can do nothing but sit back and wait for them to return...*

sometimes dead, sometimes alive, and often in vain. Anbu suppressed the strong desire to turn around and watch them leave.

'Come on buddy, let's move it.' Tiwathia tapped Iqbal on the shoulder. It was a comradely touch. 'We have a long way to go.'

In unspoken tandem, the three of them turned towards the waiting vehicle and weapons. The two Special Forces professionals flanked the former terrorist as they proceeded purposefully in lockstep.

In a few hours, all three were going to sail firmly into harm's way. Each one of them knew his life depended on the men walking beside him, for it was they who would be watching his back. None of them felt any fear. The fear would come later, much later. It always did. And it would remain within them for a very long time. Long after the guns had been silenced. It would remain until it became an integral part of their existence. It was this very fear that made a warrior think and exercise caution… and thus kept him alive. After all, only fools know no fear.

However, for the present, all three men had one thought in their minds.

Salim must die.

SIMILAR CONFERENCES WERE COMING TO AN END IN SEVERAL cities all over the world. Very soon a multitude of special task forces backed by a dazzling plethora of hi-tech gadgetry would come into play.

WHILE THE HUNTERS GOT BUSY, THE HUNTED FOUGHT BACK in the simplest possible manner – by staying still. Salim, the wily campaigner, had been right when he worked out his plan based on the simple assumption that *something would go wrong*. That, after all, was inevitable. *In battle, no plan ever remains on course for very long.*

Salim knew that his lashkar could only be caught and taken down *if* they moved. That too was simple military logic. *Anything that moves can be seen. And whatever can be seen can and will be hit.*

So, for now, the killers lay dormant, biding their time. Except for those who had yet to close in on their targets. And they were moving fast and moving smart.

WASHINGTON, D.C.

ANBU WAS HEADING BACK TO THE OPS ROOM WHEN RAHIM Khan left the Hamilton Inns & Suites Hotel and caught a cab for the Ronald Regan Airport, which was barely a couple of miles away. He still had enough time for his flight, but the urge to keep moving overcame him. Maybe it was a case of nerves. Or maybe it was a keen desire to get to his target as soon as possible. Either way, it turned out to be a good thing because he clocked in before the rush built up at the check-in counters. The soldier-terrorist walked through without having to wait.

At 0715 hours, when United Airlines flight 187

took off for San Francisco, Rahim Khan, immaculately attired as a captain in the US Marines, was safely on board.

Hide in plain sight, Cheema had advised. *They will be hunting for a Corporal from the artillery, if they are looking at all… a Marine should find it easy enough to get through.*

And that was exactly what happened. Most people respond deferentially to a uniform. The security men clearing the flight were no exception. Neither the killer nor his cargo had any problem getting through security.

INDO-PAK BORDER, NORTHWEST OF AMRITSAR, PUNJAB

THE INFILTRATION ROUTE WAS ONE OF THE FEW GRIM reminders of the days when the ISI had supported the Khalistani militants as aggressively as they were supporting the Kashmiri terrorists now. The ISI never found out that Indian Intelligence had been aware of the route from the first day it had been activated since the people operating it at both ends had been taken and turned by them.

'He will take you across.' The RAW liaison officer escorting them gestured at the man skulking a few metres away, without bothering to introduce him. 'You will cross the IB after dark and cut straight across to the Lahore-Rawalpindi highway. Tanaz will be waiting for you here.' He tapped a spot on the map in his hand. 'Once he hands you guys over to her, he is going to lie low until it's time for you to return. Tanaz will take you all the way to Murree and then back to the same point.'

He makes it sound so simple! Tiwathia smiled inwardly. *As though we are going for a walk in the park.*

In the end, it did turn out to be simple. The red and white station wagon was waiting for them, parked exactly where it was supposed to be. 'I will be waiting for you here,' the escort told Tiwathia, who nodded. 'I have been told to wait for only twenty-four hours,' he added in the same bland tone. 'Khuda hafiz.' Their taciturn escort handed them over to the woman draped in a black burqa who was standing by the vehicle, and then vanished into the fields around. As the three men approached, the woman waved at them.

'Salaam waleikum! I am known as Tanaz.' Her voice was surprisingly young and well modulated.

'Waleikum asalaam,' the men responded automatically.

'I was asked to give you this.' A slim hand emerged from beneath the burqa, holding out a sleek Motorola smart phone. 'The GPS Navigator you need has already been loaded on it. I was told you would configure the email account yourself.'

'Great! Thanks.' Sami took it from her. The smart phone's screen lit up as he thumbed the Start key and began to type out a text message. *For such below-*

the-radar missions, it is much better to use easily available commercial technology rather than a military radio set that will definitely give away the fact that something is in the offing.

A moment later, Sami hit the send key and the text message he had typed out swirled away into the ether.

NEW DELHI

'WHERE'S THE PARTY TONIGHT?' ANKITA LAUGHED AS SHE read Sami's text message on her mobile phone. 'Sami and Tiwathia are through,' she called out to Anbu and Khare, who were huddled over a map at the other end of the control room.

'That's great,' Anbu replied, throwing an inadvertent glance at the giant electronic battle board that straddled the longer wall of the room. Sure enough, the two large green dots representing the GPS locators carried by all Force 22 officers on every mission glowed on it. Both were on the Pakistani side of the line that marked the IB.

'Party address is on the way,' Ankita replied to Sami's text message. Then she turned to the computer in front of her. Glowing on the screen was the interlock of the two Thuraya phones operating from Murree. Both phones were grid-locked at the same address that had been mentioned on the passports being used by Salim and Cheema.

On the second screen beside her was the display

from the feed being sent in live by Cartosat-2. The Cartosat series of satellites are the worthy successors to the 1008 kg Technology Experimental Satellite (TES) that had been launched into space by ISRO (Indian Space Research Organization) in October 2001, making it the only civilian agency in the world other than the privately owned US Ikonos to possess this technology. Fitted with high resolution one-metre cameras that had the capability to detect objects as small as one metre, the Cartosat-2 was presently beaming down a clear panoramic view of the isolated bungalow in Murree.

Damn! They're fantastic! Despite having seen such images from the Cartosat earlier, Ankita could not help admiring the crystal-clear satellite feed. She could clearly see the sloping red-tiled roof of the bungalow peeping out from the pine trees.

Breaking away from the scene on the screen before her, she began to compose an email to Sami.

'Click on the link to download real-time map.' Inserting the link, Ankita clicked the send mail icon.

Then she keyed in another text message from her mobile phone. 'Check your mail. Am maintaining live watch. Will message in case of change in venue. God speed.'

With that done, she went back to keeping an eye on both Thuraya phones as well as waiting for the smurad profile to log in again.

Not that it's required. It's pretty obvious that Salim

is at his operational base and likely to remain there until the mission ends. Either way.... She shrugged and went back to her vigil. *It is the hunter's job to stay the course till the quarry is down.*

INDO-PAK BORDER, NORTHWEST OF AMRITSAR, PUNJAB

SAMI SMILED AS HE READ ANKITA'S SUCCESSIVE MESSAGES. 'She's good!' he murmured to Tiwathia as he showed him the message. Then he rapidly configured his email settings on the phone. A minute later, the email from Ankita was glowing on the phone's 2.4 inch LCD screen. He scrolled to the download icon and pressed it.

A few restless minutes later, the required map had downloaded and mated with the GPS Navigator that Tanaz had pre-loaded on the phone. The tiny glowing red dot on the top right corner of the screen that marked their objective in Murree beckoned to them. Running down from it was a thin blue line depicting the route that eventually merged with the bright green dot in the lower corner of the screen which marked their current position near the IB.

'We're ready to go now.' Sami looked up at the others with a triumphant smile.

'That's good,' Tanaz replied. 'But we will wait here for a while to allow the traffic on the roads to build up a bit. It will be safer. Right now the roads will be almost deserted and we will stick out like sore thumbs.'

'Okay.' The two commandos exchanged a glance. 'That sounds reasonable.'

Tanaz nodded. 'Why don't you three get some rest? I am sure you could do with some after that long walk.' She saw the look on the faces of the two Force 22 officers. *Special Forces!* she told herself. *They're not used to letting their guards down.* 'Don't worry, I'll keep watch while you three catch a nap.' Stepping forward, she threw back the burqa's veil and stepped across to the station wagon parked between them.

Perhaps she was used to the effect she had on people, for a faint, slightly amused smile briefly lit up her face as she saw the jaws of the three men drop. Her finely chiselled features and flawless complexion were absurdly out of place in the present surroundings.

The Uzi machine pistol she took out from the station wagon was even more incongruous. 'Please rest assured that I am more than capable of putting this to good use,' she said as she cocked it expertly. The Uzi disappeared into the voluminous folds of her burqa and the veil fell back in place. 'Don't worry, I will not let you down. I joined your RAW of my own free will....'

'*Your* RAW?' Tiwathia asked, slightly taken aback. 'You are not an Indian?'

'No! I'm from Pakistan.'

'Then why are you helping us?' Iqbal asked, almost petulantly.

'Because I, like many others here, believe that the

Pakistani leadership is wrong. The rabid power-hungry Generals and some mad mullahs have betrayed our country by giving free rein to these fundamentalist jihadis... for their own shortsighted and selfish gains. Do you realize where Pakistan would be today if we had concentrated our energies on our economy instead of frittering away our frugal resources on this futile, endless war with India?'

There was a long pause. The anger in her was palpable. So was the sadness.

'Don't you think we Pakistanis also want to live peacefully?'

None of the three men responded. In any case, no response was required.

'You think we are not aware of how different things are there?' Tanaz jabbed a finger across the border towards India. 'Where is India and where is Pakistan today? This so-called religious war has drained us of every inch of life and left us bleeding. Today we have to fight for basic things like food, clothing, shelter, healthcare... and basic education for our children.' Her voice rose in anger. 'For these so-called basics we are today at the mercy of bullies like America, who want to interfere in our country and use us for their own petty gains. And, mind you, we share the same culture, the same land as your people... no matter which way you look at it, we are the same people... separated by religion and by an artificial line drawn on a map.'

'True!' Mohammed Sami said softly. 'What

difference does it make which God we worship... or don't worship?'

'Absolutely! Religion should unite, not divide. It should foster peace and love, not hatred or violence.'

There was a longer silence this time, as they pondered the futility of it all.

Sami regained his composure first. 'Hello Tanaz, I am Humayun.' He gave the cover name allotted to him for this operation. 'This is Akbar,' Sami pointed at Tiwathi, 'and that's....'

'Jahangir,' Tanaz finished his sentence. 'And I, Jahanpanah,' she added dramatically, 'am Anarkali.' They all laughed and the gray mood that had fallen upon them dissipated slightly. 'They really come up with some strange cover names, don't they?'

'They sure do,' Vikram Tiwathia replied with a smile. 'Where did you learn to handle that?' He gestured to the Uzi now concealed in the folds of her burqa.

'Where else?' Tanaz gave a grim laugh. 'I joined the jihadis. They were more than happy to teach me whatever I needed to know. Of course, your RAW helped close whatever gaps remained in my trade and field craft.'

'How did you get into this... this... line of work?' Iqbal broke in suddenly.

Without warning, the gray mood returned. For a long time Tanaz did not reply. 'We all have our reasons,' she finally said. Since the veil was back in place, her expression remained hidden, but her tone was flat and did not encourage any further communication.

'I'm sorry,' Iqbal replied red-faced, realizing he had overstepped some unseen line. 'I did not mean to pry. It's just....' He broke off lamely.

'I think you're right.' Sami broke the awkward silence that threatened to settle upon them. 'We will get some rest.' He got into the station wagon. Tiwathia was right behind him.

'My name is Iqbal.' Iqbal spoke up suddenly, as he started to follow them. 'My real one, I mean.' He paused. 'I don't really need a cover name, you see,' he added lamely. Tanaz merely nodded. Perhaps her controller had briefed her. Perhaps she didn't really care. Either way, silence returned.

A COUPLE OF HOURS LATER, TANAZ SHOOK THEM AWAKE. 'It's time,' she said as she got into the rear seat of the station wagon with Iqbal.

Tiwathia was already in the driver's seat, with Sami seated beside him. The engine leaped to life immediately, its powerful hum contrasting with the battered exterior of the vehicle.

'Just head for that highway.' Tanaz pointed from the rear seat as Tiwathia engaged gears. 'Turn north and keep going.'

The station wagon powered its way through the early morning traffic, its powerful engine eating up the miles effortlessly. Barring the wind rushing past, the occasional cacophony of horns from the traffic around, and the deep-throated thrum of the engine, there was silence.

On the tiny screen of the mobile phone in Sami's hand, the tiny green dot representing them could be seen moving steadily along the glowing blue line that snaked towards the glowing red dot beckoning in the far north.

All of a sudden, Iqbal broke the silence. 'I'm here because they killed my mother and my sister. Both of them died because of the bombs planted on Salim's orders in Delhi's Sarojini Nagar market.' His voice was soft. It barely overrode the thrumming of the engine and the whoosh of tyres on the road. 'Can you imagine I have actually been trained by these... these....'

No one in the vehicle responded as Iqbal spoke; yet he continued, almost as though he were unburdening his soul. Or maybe he was not sure if he would return alive and felt the need to let someone else know the ugly truth he had nursed within for all these years.

It was a very long time after Iqbal's cathartic monologue had trailed into an awkward silence that Tanaz spoke equally suddenly.

'I'm here because of my brothers. They were subverted by the Jaish-e-Mohammed and before anyone in the family even realized it, both of them had been pumped into the Kashmir valley. The Jaish sent both of them to carry out a suicide attack on the Jammu Police Lines.' She paused. 'One was twenty. The other was only eighteen. Neither came back alive.'

The silence this time was oppressive.

'They were both good, caring boys. I cannot even imagine them doing any harm to anyone. Neither of our parents survived the blow.'

Her voice broke. When she spoke again, the words came like an angry torrent of molten lava.

'All our lives we supported them… the mullahs who exhorted us and appealed to us to donate to the cause from our meagre earnings. We need to help our Muslim brothers in Kashmir to overthrow the kafir yoke, they told us… and we gave…. It is for Allah, they told us… and we often went hungry, but we gave… we were so stupid….'

Iqbal leaned forward slightly and touched her lightly on the arm. The gesture was curiously formal, yet intensely intimate. 'I'm sorry', he said. Tanaz did not respond but she did not draw away from him either.

Twin souls! With their own terrible crosses to carry. Tiwathia watched them in the rear-view mirror. *Maybe they can help each other sort out the demons that torment them.*

SAN FRANCISCO

THE AVENGERS HAD BEGUN THEIR JOURNEY TOWARDS MURREE when Rahim Khan strolled into the lobby of the San

Francisco Marriott hotel. Fifteen minutes later, he and his precious briefcase were safely ensconced in a room on the fifth floor.

Five has always been my lucky number. Rahim gave a satisfied smile as he used his laptop to report his arrival to Salim's meetyourmatch profile. That was also when he read Salim's last message.

The traitor's fall marks the beginning. On the morrow the world will shudder and you shall be remembered forever. Khuda hafiz.

He was pondering over the message as he settled into the huge armchair facing the television and flicked it on. News of the Pakistani dictator's assassination filled the room. He jerked forward in surprise as the contents of the message clicked into place. Then he laughed aloud. *That Salim is a cool bastard.*

RAHIM KHAN WOULD HAVE BEEN A LOT LESS HAPPY HAD HE known that Ankita had read his arrival message to Salim at almost the same time as Salim had. So had the FBI counter-terror specialist who was by now firmly in the loop. If Rahim Khan had remained online for a little more time, the Feds would have been able to locate him and bring him down immediately.

By now the hunters were very awake and very alert. The only problem was that none of their quarry had as yet surfaced on any of the radars which were desperately searching for them.

But in battle that is the way it often is. Just as it is true that in no battle do things remain static for very long. Dynamics change. People move. People attack and people defend. In both cases, people die.

Strike One

New Orleans

DESPITE THE LATE HOUR AT WHICH THE LOCAL FBI OFFICE got the alert, it reacted quickly. Which was not surprising, considering the alarming brief they had just received.

The subject Erik Segan is a white male in his mid-thirties. He is alleged to be in possession of a highly virulent chemical or biological weapon. The weapon is most probably packaged and ready for use as an aerosol. Subject is likely to be armed and dangerous. Approach with extreme caution. No chances are to be taken.

The resultant APB (All Points Bulletin) that went out conveyed nothing of the acute anxiety being experienced by the officer who had been given charge of the situation.

In a matter of hours, hundreds of boots hit the ground. Telephone wires and airwaves burned as every possible source was contacted and activated. Hundreds of electronic sentries stood alert with raised antennae as they began a relentless vigil over Erik Segan's home, car, the warehouse where his band usually hung out, the restaurants they played at, the rehab centres he had been to, the church he used to frequent, the mosque he had prayed at more recently, his credit cards, bank accounts, police files, telephone bills, mobile phone… anything and everything that could help find him. Photographs were shown to hotel receptionists and cab drivers, to the hookers and dealers in his neighbourhood. The tapes from surveillance cameras at airports, railway stations and all major traffic junctions in the city were placed under 24x7 surveillance.

Nothing! Nada! Ziltch!

The man seemed to have completely vanished once he got off the flight from Chicago.

'Listen, it doesn't matter. At this time of the year, in this city, we certainly don't need Einstein to tell us what the target is going to be.' The Head Fed was trying to keep his morale up and sound as upbeat as possible. 'I want every possible entry point to the fairgrounds locked down… as tight as a goddamn virgin. Get every pair of eyes, ears and boots out there. If that psycho gets into the fest grounds, we're screwed.'

Tirelessly, the vigil continued.

ALL THIS TIME, THEIR QUARRY LAY SLEEPLESS ON HIS HOTEL bed, tossing and turning restlessly. Finally, Erik couldn't take it any more.

You are the only one who does not have to worry about keeping to a precise schedule. Salim's voice echoed in his mind. *The weapon you are going to deploy will have no immediate effect. In fact, no one will even know you have released the weapon until ten or eleven days have passed. Of course, once it starts working, it will spread like wildfire. Millions of kafir will die.*

Hauling himself out of bed, Erik took out the cans of Variola virus and arrayed them on the bedside table, like a child marshalling his army of toys. One by one, he picked them up and went over the operating mechanism to reassure himself that he had not forgotten what he had to do.

The timer is a very simple one that can be set for five, ten, fifteen or twenty minutes. Erik replayed Mai's briefing in his head for the nth time. *All four settings are more than adequate to allow you to deploy the weapon and get away safely. Use the highest time setting on the first one you deploy and then come down progressively as you go along. Immediately after deploying the last one, head for the airport and get out.*

What if the timer gets spoilt or jammed? Or if I need to release the virus manually?

That's simple. In both cases, just unscrew the timer and depress the knob that is exposed. Mai had removed the tiny timing device carefully and shown it to him.

Finally satisfied that he had it all under control,

Erik put the cans back into their small knapsack and placed it next to his guitar case.

The guitar was an exclusive, top of the line, handmade Heins, the sole surviving souvenir of Erik Segan's brief brush with stardom. Erik treated it with the same love and affection with which he would have treated his child, if he'd had one. At that moment, his prized possession was safely ensconced in its beautiful black case, with the name of the maker proudly emblazoned on it.

The bath he took was long and leisurely. Rather like the last meal of a man on death row. Then, having cleansed his body, he surrendered his soul to the One God. Silently repeating the niyyah in his heart, as he unfurled his prayer mat, Erik faced the Qiblah, the direction of the Holy City of Mecca, raised his hands to his ears with his palms facing outwards and, adopting the Qiyam posture, began to chant the Salat Al-Fajr, the dawn prayer.

Like the bath, the prayer too was long and unhurried. When he finally arose he was seized by a strange calm. Erik Segan was ready to take on the world.

Slinging the knapsack over one shoulder and his precious Heins guitar case over the other, he left the hotel room and descended to the lobby.

IT IS ALMOST CERTAIN THAT IN 1970, WHEN GEORGE WEIN started the New Orleans Jazz Festival, he had great expectations from it. However, it is doubtful that even he would have imagined that thirty years later

650,000 people of all colours, nationalities and religions, from all walks of life, from all over the world, would flock to attend the Jazz Fest, as it had come to be popularly called. It had already grown beyond just a music festival and was now a well-established tourist attraction rivalled only by the Mardi Gras. Signalling the resurgence of New Orleans after the devastation wrought by Hurricane Katrina, the Jazz Fest this year was heralded to be one of the biggest in recent times. New Orleans had begun to bustle with crowds several days before the fest was due to begin. By now the crowds had surpassed all expectations. A riot of colours and a medley of music merged to make the city unbelievably vibrant.

Pushing his way through the crowd, Erik had just exited the French Quarter and was crossing the road to head for the Fairgrounds Racing Track, the venue of the Jazz Fest, when he was spotted.

ALICE DESTIN LOVED MUSIC WITH A PASSION THAT BORDERED on the fanatic. She had devoted a better part of her youth to music and had been the lead guitarist at one of the local bands before an early marriage to her childhood sweetheart, the pressures of domestic life, and the need to balance the home budget drove her to take up the relatively sedate life of a city cop. On that day, she had been pulled out of her routine shift to man the surveillance cameras that stood sentinel on the roads leading in and out of the French Quarter.

Taped to the top of the small bank of monitors that she was watching was the photograph of a man that she, like the eighteen other men and women in her shift, had been given. She had no idea who he was or what he had done.

Keep an eye open for him. If you spot him, call it in immediately. Right?

That had been the mandate given to all of them.

The exercise of watching cameras transmitting live feed of city traffic to spot a single person is quite akin to looking for a needle in a haystack, or water in the Sahara desert. More than anything else, it betrayed the frustration and desperation of the people hunting down the fugitive. It is almost certain that the exercise would have proved fruitless if it had not been for one of those quirks of fate which occur once in a rare while and get termed as miraculous.

Alice Destin was staring at the monitors gleaming in front of her, diligently but desolately, when the beautiful black guitar case with Heins painted all over it in startling white floated into her field of vision. The fabled name drew her envious eyes like a magnet. She was fondling it with her eyes, trying to visualize the beautiful instrument in the case, when her gaze happened to fall on the man on whose shoulder the guitar rode. It took a moment for the face to register. When it did, Alice sat up straight. Her gaze flicked between the face on the screen in front of her and the photograph tagged on above the monitor.

Goddamn! That's him alright!

Electrified, Alice reached for the phone and called the number she had been given. The Federal agent manning the control desk who took her call leaped out of his chair as though he'd been touched with a hot cattle prod in a tender part of his anatomy.

Almost immediately, the ball began to roll.

'All units! We have a confirmed sighting of the subject Erik Segan. The man is at the crossing of....'

FBI AGENTS MURRAY AND LANGER WERE CRUISING DOWN Columbus Street towards the point where Bayou Road turns on to Gentilly Boulevard when the call came in. 'We're right there, Control,' Langer snapped into the radio immediately. 'Give us more details.'

'Subject has just crossed the Columbus intersection and is heading down Gentilly. Likely destination is the Gentilly Pedestrian entrance to fairgrounds. He is wearing a white tee with *I Love Rod* on the front and has a guitar case slung on his right shoulder. He also has a black knapsack on the other shoulder. We're losing him now, till he comes up to the next camera on the Paul Morphy intersection.' Control's voice crackled with tension.

Murray, the younger and more enthusiastic of the two agents, who was at the wheel, was about to floor the accelerator when Langer preempted him. 'Easy now! We don't want to spook him by blazing in. Go slow and keep your eyes peeled. Don't pull up in mid-traffic when you spot him. That would definitely give us away.'

Murray nodded.

The Fed car flowed along with the traffic.

'There!' Langer prompted. 'That should be him... the one going past those two drag queens there.' Murray followed Langer's pointing finger. He nodded as he confirmed the sighting.

'Now pull over to the side and let's take him on foot.'

Murray slowly eased out of the traffic and pulled up along the kerb, drawing the ire of the cars behind. One of them tooted its horn angrily.

'Shit!' Murray hissed. 'Don't do that, arsehole. You'll have the whole world looking at us.' He cursed, willing the other man to stop honking, as Erik Segan strode past them, barely fifteen feet away.

The minute the car had slowed down adequately, Langer jumped out. 'Park somewhere and catch up soon,' he hissed at Murray as he turned to follow Segan.

'Control, we have him now,' Murray barked into the radio. 'Langer is onto him. I'm just going to ground the wheels and go after them.'

'Be very careful,' Control replied sharply.

Murray did not bother to reply. No longer restrained by Langer's calming presence, the young, excitable agent threw the car in front of the No Parking sign a few feet further down the road and, getting out, raced behind the two men striding away from him. *What the hell! City Hall can live with the ticket.*

It took Murray barely a minute to catch up with Langer. Now the two agents were just twenty feet behind Segan and closing in fast.

'I'm going to grab him from the back. You take the right flank, just in case,' Langer hissed at Murray.

'No.' Murray pulled at his arm, 'Let me tackle him, you back me up.'

The older man assimilated this before he nodded. 'Okay! Go ahead.'

By now they had more than halved the gap between them and the man they were hunting. Both agents reached for their handguns and separated laterally from each other as they stepped up the pace. Another five or six strides and they would have brought Segan down.

That was when fate interceded.

'HEY! YOU! SIR!' THE TRAFFIC COP WAS ANGRY. HE HAD SEEN Murray literally throw his car in front of the No Parking sign and walk away. That irked him no end. *No sir! Not on my watch!* Stepping forward, he hailed Murray loudly. Both Federal agents turned instinctively. So did almost everyone within earshot. Erik Segan was one of them.

The cop saw the guns in the hands of the two Feds when they turned. Nothing in their dress or demeanour gave away their profession. In any case, people rarely tend to notice dress or demeanour when confronted with guns. Instantly, the cop's survival instincts soared and he, as most armed men are wont to do in such circumstances, went for the gun at his belt reflexively.

When Segan turned, he saw two men brandishing handguns a few feet behind him. A little further away from them, he saw a cop frantically grabbing for his gun.

They've found me. Erik automatically assumed the worst. Every fibre of his guilty mind and body shook in panic. *How? How the hell....* For a moment, the shock froze him.

Most of the other people around also turned to see who the cop was yelling at. Many of them saw the guns in the hands of the two men apparently confronting the cop. Some saw the cop snatch his gun out of the holster. The panicked screams that erupted differed in tone, content and duration, just as the directions the suddenly galvanized crowd scattered in also varied. However, the panic was widespread and it was instantaneous. It added to the confusion enveloping the minds of the four men involved in the high drama.

Murray saw the cop reach for his gun and, working on the same survival instincts as the cop, threw up his hand in the air as he shouted a warning. 'It's okay! We're Feder....' That was about as far as he got. In the heat of the moment, he had forgotten about the gun in his hand.

Murray's words were lost in the cacophony of sound emanating from the panicked crowd. The traffic cop saw the gun hand of the excited man come up. He presumed it was coming up at him. By now his own weapon had cleared the holster and was halfway up. Without wasting any more time or thought, he fired.

At the ten feet distance separating the two men, it is extremely doubtful that anyone with even a rudimentary knowledge of firearms would have missed. The traffic cop's knowledge was a little better than that in any case. His bullet clipped Murray neatly in the right shoulder, tossing him around in a half circle before felling him. And there he lay screaming, adding to the confusion all around.

Langer watched in horror as Murray collapsed to the ground. He gave an equally horrified look at the cop who had fired and then instinctively turned to see where his quarry was.

Erik Segan was watching the whole sequence open-mouthed. He saw Langer turn and look at him. Their glances locked for one infinitesimally small nano-moment. That was enough. Segan knew that Langer had been coming for him.

The glance seemed to trigger some release valve inside Segan's head, snapping him out of his shocked reverie. He turned abruptly, and began to run. Weaving through the crowd, he headed straight towards the Fairgrounds Racing Track. The blood in his veins began to pound harshly and the distance between him and Langer increased as his stride lengthened. As Erik ran, his beloved guitar fell away and his free right hand reached into the knapsack slung over his other shoulder. Grabbing the largest can he could lay his hands on, he drew it out of the knapsack. As he ran, he began to unscrew the timer cap so that he could release the virus manually.

Langer and the cop, who was by now totally shaken and confused, saw Segan break into a run. The tableau was still frozen in their minds when a frantic woman darted between them. Using that momentary distraction, Langer decided on his immediate priority and, bolting into the thick of the crowd, began to race after the fleeing fugitive who was fast receding into the crowd. The time for finesse was long gone.

By the time Segan reached the Gentilly Pedestrian entrance to the Jazz Fest, he had managed to arm the first can and was trying to arm a second one. Freeing it from the knapsack, he finished unscrewing the timer. Then he stopped to face the man chasing him. Chanting his final prayer, Segan waited for his enemy to come within striking range.

O Allah, you are my Lord. There is none worthy of worship except You. I rely upon You. You are the Great Lord of the Throne. Whatever God wills happens and whatever He does not will does not happen. There is no power or strength....

There was no longer any fear on his face or in his heart.

The hunted had become the hunter.

All around him, a frenzied crowd swirled.

Sprinting up the road, Langer suddenly shuddered to a stop, his chest heaving from the exercise. Open-mouthed with amazement, he saw that the subject had stopped and was calmly waiting for him.

Karl stood Christ-like with both his hands extended outwards and slightly upwards. The sound of his harsh chanting rose above the hullabaloo of the crowd and filled the air. In both hands he held long metallic spray cans. Both cans pointed towards the sky.

Remember! Mai Hu's instruction came back to Erik Segan as his fingers closed on the release knobs. *The aerosol is heavier than air, so if you spray it upwards, it will be better dispersed by the breeze and will cover a larger spread on the ground.*

Langer had no clue what the subject was holding in his hands, or what he was trying to do. He just knew that he had been repeatedly warned to approach with extreme caution. He had just seen his partner fall, albeit to friendly fire. His mind was already too cluttered to absorb any more. The weird man with the weird cans in his hands and chanting a weird, prayer-like chant drove him beyond the purview of cohesive thought. Closing up to Erik Segan, he drew his gun, aimed straight at his head and fired.

The heavy, leaden slug covered the remaining few feet between the two adversaries and smashed the contented expression off Segan's face. As the death dealer fell, the release buttons of both cans remained firmly pressed.

Unknown to Langer and unseen by anyone, the deadly Variola Major virus from both aerosol cans slid silently out into the atmosphere. It wafted away in the lively breeze, and settled amongst the panicked maze of people milling around. Some of it settled on Langer as he walked up to the fallen terrorist and began to check him for weapons and any sign of life. The deadly Variola virus wormed its way into his nostrils and entered his body. He did not know it then, of course. Just as he did not know that twelve days later, he would be one of the first people to die. So would his wife and the teenage daughter he doted on, who would pick up the dreaded disease from him.

But that would happen later. Much later. Before that, many more people were destined to die. Salim's killing spree had just begun.

Strike Two

URUMQI SPECIAL WEAPONS FACILITY, CHINA

THE GRIM, UNIFORMLY GRAY COMPLEX COMPRISED OVER THIRTY large buildings. A sixteen-foot high double fence of barbed wire stood sentinel between the complex and the surrounding areas. The complex itself appeared like an ungainly duckling in the midst of a Macbethean heath, starkly devoid of any growth or vegetation. On all four points of the compass were tall towers manned by grim looking guards. Machine guns stared ominously from the shaded tops.

Most of the buildings in the inner cordon were linked by a series of tunnel like paths, quite like the tentacles of an octopus. A large part of the inner complex lay almost a hundred feet below the ground, safe from prying eyes and almost any kind of bomb that a potential adversary might throw at it. And rightly so, since the chemicals and viruses stored there were dangerous beyond belief. If they ever got free, the havoc they unleashed would outdo any damage that any bomb could do. On the surface, at the edge of the inner compound, was situated the main conference hall, which was used for all large facility meetings and presentations.

The conference that had been scheduled by Mai before his departure for Delhi, was due to begin. However, in the wake of Mai's death, the conference had little to do with the agenda that had been set by him; it was about Mai himself. Maybe that was why people started trickling into the conference hall well before the stipulated time. The hubbub of unsubstantiated rumours and mindless chatter filled the long rectangular room. Most of them were still trying to fully understand what had happened. Despite the discovery of explosives in the primary lab and the specimen storage areas, and the totally shocking end to Mai's wife, no one was quite clear exactly what had transpired, mainly because of the MSS-ordered clampdown on all information. The only thing they knew for sure was that new and far more suffocating security procedures had been inflicted on the facility since then.

'LADIES AND GENTLEMEN, SETTLE DOWN PLEASE.' MAI'S erstwhile deputy, who was now officiating as the Facility Director, finally called the meeting to order. It took several loud and very unscientific yells for people to take their seats. By then the conference was already twenty minutes behind schedule.

However, the electronic timers on the large aerosol cans came alive exactly on schedule. Mai had taped these cans inside the air-conditioning ducts that led into the conference hall.

Activated by the timers, the release valves of both cans opened with a silent snap and the thick oily vapour began to trickle out. The VX Gas ventured out of the aerosol containers into the ducts. Swept along by the conditioned air, it was delivered into the room through a vent located at the upper end of the wall running along the left side of the conference hall.

The result was almost instantaneous and absolutely spectacular.

The seven men and two women occupying the seats along the wall were senior researchers and key players in the Chinese chemical weapons development program. In fact, some of them had been actively involved in the design and development of the timer-activated aerosol cans lying in the air-conditioning duct just seven feet above them.

All nine of them began to gag and choke almost simultaneously. Faces contorted in agony and muffled shrieks erupted as, one by one, they toppled like ninepins. Blood and faeces spewed out as their bowels went out of control.

The panic exploded through the room as those seated in close proximity to the afflicted moved forward to help. All of them died in a similar fashion, within minutes.

Then the fear hit like one gigantic screaming wave and people rushed wildly towards the exit. Not many made it out alive.

By the time some semblance of sanity was restored, and the room was sealed and the air-conditioning system shut down, the deadly VX released in the central conference hall and the primary laboratory had taken out most of the senior scientists and administrators of the facility.

An hour later, a total lock down of the facility was firmly in place.

Nothing moves in or out. Not till the containment people have scoured the place from top to bottom.

Given the secrecy that afflicted the Chinese regime, not even a hint of the disaster that had struck down their top-secret biochem facility reached the media, domestic or international. But the truth was that, in one fell swoop, Mai's strike had eliminated over fifty-three people, and had set the Chinese biochem program back by at least a decade.

Strike Three

NEEMRANA FORT PALACE

BARRING HAMEED WHO, LIKE MOST KIDS HIS AGE, WOKE UP early on Sundays and school holidays, the holiday makers at Neemrana were all fast asleep when Yakub Khan awoke. For the first time in many years he came awake instantly and sprang out of bed with alacrity. His head was clear and, despite the pangs of anxiety starting up inside him, he was eagerly looking forward to the next few hours.

'Good morning, abbu!' Hameed greeted his father with a big smile and a bigger hug. 'Can I watch television?' he asked with the innocent guile of the young.

'No, Hameed!' Yakub replied softly with a laugh. 'Not so early in the morning.'

'Then what should I do? I'm bored.'

'Come.' Yakub beckoned. 'I'll give you a bath and get you ready. Then you can go out and play.'

'No, thanks.' Hameed shrugged, an exasperated, exaggerated gesture. 'I'd rather sleep.' He shoved his head back under the covers. Yakub gave a fond laugh. *Kids! All the same.* Shaking his head, he headed into the bathroom. *The faster I go, the faster I can get back.*

Hameed waited till he heard his father lock the bathroom door from inside. Then, reaching over to the bedside table, he picked up his father's mobile phone, switched it on, muted the volume and happily began to play Snake. He was still at it when he heard Yakub at the bathroom door. Quickly flipping the lid closed, Hameed put the phone back on the table and put his head back under the bedcover as his father emerged from the toilet.

The phone was still powered on. And it was sending a steady, continuous signal towards the cellular phone tower two kilometres away.

ATTF OPS ROOM, NEW DELHI

CHAUHAN WAS CONFERRING WITH A DOZEN LIEUTENANTS on a dozen phones when the SIGINT (Signals Intelligence) man exploded into the room.

'We have a lead on him,' he yelled excitedly.

'Who?' Chauhan asked irritably.

'Yakub Khan, sir,' the man replied, a little more calmly.

'Yakub Khan. What!' Chauhan's irritation vapourised into excitement. 'Where....'

'His mobile phone just came on, sir. It has been tracked to a hotel in Neemrana. We have a live track running on it.'

'Fantastic!' Chauhan reached for the nearest phone. 'What are the closest resources we have to Neemrana?'

'Only the local cops. Otherwise our closest dedicated assets are either at Jaipur or closer home at Gurgaon.'

'Okay, get me the Neemrana SHO. *Now!*'

'Let me get him on the line and call you back, sir.' Seven minutes later. 'Sir, Inspector Meena is on the line. He is located just two kilometres from the Neemrana Fort Palace hotel.'

The inspector was still groggy with sleep when Chauhan began to speak. It took Chauhan's first two sentences to jolt him awake rudely and fully.

Eleven minutes later, Inspector Meena was on his way to the hotel with the two cops he had hauled out of the police chowki closest to his house.

Despite the early hour, and the fact that all three cops had been unceremoniously pulled out of bed minutes ago, they were all armed. And they had just been given the license to kill. Chauhan had been clear about that.

Find him! Take him down! Dead or alive, I really don't care. Though if you do manage to take him alive, I will personally ensure you get the President's medal and at least one out-of-turn promotion.

That was why all the three cops were not only armed, they were motivated and raring to go. And such men are dangerous.

YAKUB THREW A GLANCE AT THE CLOCK ON THE WALL AS HE exited the bathroom. *It's already six-fifty. I need to move fast, otherwise I'll be hitting the rush hour traffic all the way from the Gurgaon border to Nehru Place.* Throwing on his clothes, he grabbed the car keys and his mobile phone from the bedside table, and hurried out. A few minutes later, he was on his way. The Tata Safari had barely left the resort and turned towards the Jaipur-Delhi highway when the posse led by Inspector Meena hurtled up to the hotel entrance and screeched to a halt. Getting hold of the receptionist and prying the required information out of him took up a few more valuable minutes.

'WHAT THE HELL DO YOU MEAN YOU MISSED HIM?' CHAUHAN was beside himself with rage when the call came in. Then, controlling his anger and frustration, he took a deep breath. 'Can you at least give me the details of his vehicle?' He noted the colour and registration number that Inspector Meena had gleaned from the hotel staff. 'Did you meet his family or go to his room?'

'No, sir,' Meena replied. 'I didn't want to alert them that anything was amiss. They would have called him on his cell otherwise.'

'Good thinking!' Chauhan heaved a sigh of relief as he cut the call and turned to the SIGINT man. 'Where is he now?'

'We have him on the highway, sir. He is heading for Delhi. Should I get the Gurgaon people to send a team out for him? They can intercept him on the highway.'

'No! Wait....' Chauhan turned back. 'Where are the Force 22 officers right now?' he asked the second aide.

'They're operating out of the NSG base at Manesar, so I guess they should be there now. Should I check?' He got on the phone when Chauhan nodded. 'All four of them are there,' the man said, a moment later. 'The call is being transferred to them.'

'Great! Let me handle it now.' Chauhan took the phone, and when Squadron Leader Rajesh Tiwari of Force 22 came on the line, he briefed him.

'Don't worry about it, Mr Chauhan. All four of us are right here, and we're ready to move immediately. Just hook us up into your comm network and tell SIGINT to keep us updated at all times.'

'Don't worry about that,' Chauhan assured him. 'It will be done immediately. But tell me, where do you plan to intercept him?'

'I was thinking of the toll barrier ahead of Manesar. In any case, all vehicles have to halt there, and there are always people milling around, so Yakub Khan will not have any reason to be suspicious. We don't know for sure what he is carrying and how he can trigger it, so we definitely don't want to spook the son-of-a-bitch.'

'That's an excellent idea!' Chauhan replied after a moment's thought. *These guys are good. Thank God! We need all the luck and all the men we can come up with. Who knows what that crazy bastard is carrying into Delhi and where he plans to use it?*

The man at the receiving end of Chauhan's not-so-happy thoughts was at that very moment cruising along the highway towards Delhi. He did not hear the automated text message alerts his telephone company sent him as he sped along the highway since Hameed had put the phone on silent. The road was good and the traffic was light. Soon, Yakub Khan had crossed the Bawal Industrial area. By the time he reached Daruhera, the four Force 22 officers with an NSG rifle section had moved into position.

THE TOLL BARRIER ON THE DELHI-JAIPUR HIGHWAY LIES AT the Bilaspur-Pataudi Chowk about eight kilometres ahead of Manesar, which is not only a huge industrial hub, but also home to the elite National Security Guard. The massive toll barrier straddling the highway has a total of twelve traffic lanes, six on either side. The two outermost lanes on both sides of the highway are for vehicles that are exempt from paying toll – those equipped with a monthly permit or a return ticket purchased earlier that day. The four inner lanes on both sides are for vehicles that have to stop and pay toll. All the lanes have small glass cubicles located in a row in the middle. These cubicles house the toll-collection counters. No matter which lane you use to cross the barrier, it is certain that you have to stop at the toll counter and either pay toll or show your pass or ticket.

By the time Yakub Khan came up to the toll barrier, Squadron Leaders Rajesh Tiwari and Gautam Vashisht of the Indian Air Force, Captain Pradeep Katoch of the Indian Army and Lieutenant Commander Ranjit Dhankar of the Indian Navy, all presently seconded to Force 22, were spread out, one to cover each of the four inner lanes on the side of the highway that led to Delhi. The outermost lanes were covered by two of the NSG men. All six men were wearing gray-green dungarees, like those worn by the other security guards and toll collectors manning the barrier. The 9mm Beretta pistols they carried were carefully concealed in their clothing.

They should be more than enough, Tiwari had reasoned. *After all, we are not here to fight a war. We just need to take one arsehole down.*

The other eight NSG men had taken up position a hundred metres behind the toll barrier. These eight had no weapon concealment problems to worry about and so were loaded for bear. Of course, their weapons were in their vehicles, safely out of public view. They were the back up, in case Yakub Khan somehow managed to break out and get past the toll barrier. On Rao's insistence, two more ATTF teams were moving rapidly to take up positions at various strategic points further down the road, on the stretch between Manesar and Gurgaon.

'He is coming up now,' Tiwari cautioned the others as the tiny earpiece of his radio crackled into life. 'That maroon Tata Safari,' he hissed to Vashisht who was on his left. He nodded unobtrusively at the large SUV about two hundred metres away that was nosing its way towards the toll barrier. Vashisht signalled to the others on his left.

Then their quarry was upon them.

YAKUB KHAN SAW THE TOLL BARRIER COMING UP IN THE WAY most people see things that exist but are not germane or relevant to them at that point in time. Toll barriers are now so much a part of most metropolises that people scarcely notice them. Easing the pressure on the accelerator, Yakub reached for his wallet as his vehicle cruised up to the tollbooth. Automatically throwing a glance into the rear-view mirror, he swerved a bit and selected the centre lane, which happened to have the least number of vehicles in it. It was the lane where Pradeep Katoch was positioned.

By the time the vehicles in front had cleared out and Yakub's turn came to pay the toll, he had a hundred rupee note in his hand. He rolled down the window and stuck out his hand. He did not notice Vashisht on the left abandon his lane and start moving towards the Safari. Nor did he notice Tiwari from the lane on the right moving towards the front of the SUV.

As the Safari came to a halt near the toll collection window, Yakub held out the currency note towards Katoch, who was standing just outside the toll booth's cash window.

Katoch stretched out his hand, but instead of taking the proffered note, he caught hold of Yakub Khan's hand in a steely grip.

'What the....'

'Switch off the engine and step out.' Katoch's tone was curt.

There was one brief moment of consternation and then Yakub Khan saw the gleaming pistol in the other hand of the man who had caught him. Yakub felt his heart lurch at the suddenness of the assault. He instinctively looked towards the opposite side, only to see another pistol-borne man coming up to the door.

VASHISHT CLOSED IN ON THE CO-DRIVER'S DOOR OF THE safari and, pointing the pistol at Yakub Khan's head, tried to open the door. It was locked from inside. *Shit!* Meanwhile, Katoch had tightened his grip on Yakub's right hand and was ordering him to get out. Tiwari was coming up to the vehicle from the front. By now his weapon too was out and pointed straight at the man behind the wheel. The vehicles coming up behind the Safari in the lane had ensured that the quarry was thoroughly boxed in. Logically, Yakub Khan had no option but to comply. The problem is that logic seldom comes into play in the heat of battle, especially when an amateur is involved.

Yakub Khan suddenly floored the accelerator of the Safari. The powerful SUV lunged forward like a startled antelope. It swatted Tiwari down like a mosquito, pulverizing him under its massive front tyre. The sudden shock as the vehicle leaped forward forced Katoch to release Yakub's hand as he was jerked forward without warning. The shock snapped Yakub's hand neatly at the elbow. He yelled in pain as the Safari thudded over Tiwari and snarled down the road, out of control.

Vashisht had fired instinctively, almost in tandem with Yakub's flooring of the accelerator. As the vehicle lurched forward, the bullet passed neatly through the air behind Yakub Khan's head. Shattering the window glass, it cleaved through the computer inside the tollbooth and embedded itself in the chest of the guard in the next lane. The man began to screech, adding to the confusion.

Vashisht's second bullet, however, made no such mistake. Coming up from the rear left, it thudded into the back of Yakub's head, propelling him forward and slightly to the right as he slumped onto the steering wheel. The horn began to blare as the Safari careened out of control towards the right. It ploughed into a small Maruti 800 that had emerged from the next lane. The tiny car toppled and both vehicles came to an ungainly halt a few metres away. The screech of metal grating on the road resounded in the air a long time after the dust settled.

Yakub Khan was dead by the time the Force 22 commandos reached the toppled Safari. So was Tiwari, the security guard at the counter who had been unfortunate enough to take Vashisht's first bullet, and the two men in the sedan Yakub Khan had slammed into.

'WE GOT HIM, SIR,' KATOCH TOLD ANBU. 'BUT TIWARI DIDN'T make it.' At the other end of the phone, Anbu flinched and closed his eyes momentarily.

So, they have finally drawn blood.

It had to happen sometime.

For a very brief moment, he allowed himself the luxury of grief. Then, from the back of his mind, he dredged up the words that never failed to gave him sustenance.

You grieve over those who should not be grieved for.... Arise O son of Kunti, determined to fight. Treating alike pleasure and pain, gain and loss, victory and defeat....

Lord Krishna's immortal advice to the warrior Arjun snapped him back to the present.

Tiwari fell doing his duty... you must do yours...

The soldier in him knew that he had to stay focused on the task at hand.

'What happened?' he asked.

Katoch told him.

'Did you find the biochems?'

'There weren't any, sir,' Katoch replied. 'The weapon was a suitcase nuke.'

'*What?*' Anbu could not keep the shock out of his voice. 'How the hell did they put one together?'

'This is no makeshift device, sir. It's a highly

sophisticated one.' Katoch described the weapon in detail. 'This whole operation reeks of a sanctioned strike, backed and supported by a government.'

'Bloody hell!'

The call ended on a sombre note.

Strike Four

Berlin

A DEEP SENSE OF UNEASE PLAGUED KARL WHEN HE WOKE UP that morning. A long hot shower did nothing to dissipate the feeling. Nor did the exercise of taking out all the glass vials from the jars of cream, cleaning them with tissue paper and packing them into the specially crafted prosthetic that he extracted from his suitcase.

The prosthetic looked exactly like the one he normally wore, except that it was thicker and had been hollowed out, leaving a rather large cavity inside. Karl packed the glass vials of VX into this cavity and then carefully tried it on. It was certainly heavier and quite uncomfortable, but he was certain it would not look out of place or draw attention to him. He removed it carefully and emptied out the vials, then practiced taking off the prosthetic and bringing it into action a few times. Finally satisfied, he re-filled it and put it on.

The sun was still a long way from breaching the

horizon when he finished his preparations for the strike and began to pace the room restlessly. The deep-seated sense of unease would simply not go away. Finally, he surrendered himself to the glory of prayer.

Bismillaah ar-Rahman ar-Raheem. Al hamdu lillaahi rabbil....

Time and the turmoil within, both stood still as the serenity of the Fatiha, the first surah of the Holy Koran, enveloped him. When he finally rose, Karl could feel the calm coursing through him like a rising tide. Powered by it, he watched the clock inch forward till it was finally time to move. His target was waiting for him. From all over Berlin and the outlying suburbs, hundreds of people were on their way to the venue. Most of them would not be going back alive. Karl was going to make sure of that. He pulled the door shut behind him and walked towards the elevator that was waiting to take him down. Towards the people who were coming to die.

THE INTERNATIONAL COMMEMORATION DAY FOR DEAD and injured workers is celebrated (if that word can do justice to such an event) with much gusto by a host of trade unions all over the world on 28 April every year. This being the tenth celebration, the excitement surrounding the event was greater than in the past. A series of massive rallies were being organized in capitals and major cities all over the world.

The one in Berlin was to start from the Alexanderplatz. The rally was scheduled to proceed down Alexanderstrasse, turning left and going down the Karl-Liebknecht Strasse before. From there, it would head towards the Telespargel where it would end with the usual speeches by some local politicians and trade union leaders.

The first batch of people who arrived at the starting point comprised mostly those who were part of the organizing committee, but the others were not far behind. They started trickling in soon after, in threes and fours. About three hundred people had already gathered when Karl exited the Park Inn Hotel and began to walk briskly towards the starting point.

Karl saw the small, loose knot of cops watching the crowd that was slowly beginning to build up. But the crowd was quiet and orderly and there was no hint of trouble emanating from them. In fact, the cops did not even seem to be keeping an eye on them. They appeared to be scanning the people converging on the starting point.

Who are they looking for?

The first hint of alarm grazed Karl's mind.

To reach the venue of the rally, he would have to cut through the cluster of cops on this side of the road.

Damn!

The very thought made him acutely uneasy. He looked around, trying to seek an alternate route that would allow him to bypass the cops. That was when he noticed the other cops scattered all around the venue. Almost all of them were carrying what looked like a photograph in their hands.

Shit!

They know!

Without thinking, he reached for the prosthetic, releasing it from his body as he walked. By the time he was twenty feet from the nearest cop, he had almost freed it. By now a couple of the cops and some of the passersby had begun to take note of the strange sight of a man removing his prosthetic in public. However, there were still no alarms ringing in anyone's mind. Then, suddenly, one of the cops recognized him from the photograph in his hand.

'That's him!' he yelled. Reaching for his gun, he started towards Karl. *'You! Stop! Raise your hands in the air!'*

The minute he shouted, most of the other cops around began to reach for their weapons.

By now, Karl had finished removing the prosthetic. Seizing the fingers of the false limb firmly in his good hand, he raised it above his head and began to whirl it around, yelling like a madman.

As the hollowed out limb arced through the air, the tiny vials of VX Gas placed in its cavity began to stream out. They sparkled in the early morning air as they whirled out and away from Karl, landing at random.

As each deadly vial hit the road, it broke open with a faint tinkle. The sound was lost in the rising cacophony of pain and terror that erupted all around.

Even as the bewildered cops reached for their guns and targeted the terror merchant, the fatal VX gas continued to rise in tiny spurts whenever a vial landed and broke. Each spurt of gas condemned the people in the immediate vicinity to an instant and horrible death.

The cavity in Karl's prosthetic was empty by the time the first cop's bullets slammed into him.

The television cameras standing by to cover the rally for dead and injured workers covered this vicious dance of death as efficiently as they would have covered the rally. Not long thereafter, images of the gory, bone-chilling strike began to beam into a million homes the world over.

MURREE

'JUST LOOK AT THAT!' SALIM EXULTED AS HE SAW THE television footage of Karl going down amidst a welter of bodies. 'Goddamn! Can you imagine the shock those bastards must be in?'

'Yes, sir! We have whacked them right in the heart.' Cheema was delirious with joy. 'How many people do you think Karl managed to get?'

'It doesn't matter, Cheema. What's more important is that the television cameras managed to capture the hit. They will ensure it stays starkly alive in the minds of the enemy by showing it again and again. That will automatically ensure that the morale of our fellow jihadis grows from day to day.'

'I never thought of it like that.'

'You should, Cheema. It is as important to applaud each strike as it is to kill the kafir. Our perennial battle is to strengthen the hearts of our jihadis and strike terror into the minds of the kafir. In fact, the key is to use the basic strength and freedom of Western society against them.' Salim saw the bewilderment on Cheema's face and elaborated. 'See, every time there is an attack, the so-called free press shows it again and again in complete detail. Don't you see how images of the 9/11 strike have been firmly implanted in the minds of everyone everywhere? Well, whenever that happens, they are doing the jihad a huge favour... it is free publicity for us, and each time, it spurs on yet another brother jihadi somewhere or the other.'

'That makes perfect sense, sir.'

'Of course.' There was a brief lull before Salim spoke again. 'Let's hope the others are doing equally well. I'm a little worried that we haven't heard anything about the strike on Delhi yet.' He threw a quick glance at his wristwatch. 'Yakub should have struck by now, yet there's nothing in the news....'

'Maybe he got held up somewhere,' Cheema said optimistically. 'Don't worry, sir, he will do a good job.'

'Inshallah!'

'Ameen!'

Both men went back to surfing cyber space and the air waves for news of their lashkar.

Strike Five

COPENHAGEN

LARS HAD ALSO WOKEN UP EARLY. NOT BECAUSE HE WAS ANY more nervous than the others, but simply because he wanted to prepare the bomb at leisure. Before that, he purified his body with a bath, his soul with prayer, and his stomach with a hearty breakfast.

I wish I could talk to Lina. Lars yearned to hear her voice, but he knew it was not to be. He was an experienced cop and knew just how the hunters would be looking for him. *If they are on to us by now*, he mused. *They should be. After all, in such a massive operation someone somewhere is bound to fuck up... and it takes just one loose end to unravel the whole ball.* Shrugging off thoughts of Lina, he got down to the task of prepping the bomb.

To begin with, he got rid of all the add-ons and the lead shield that had been placed by Cheema's team at Lahore to camouflage the bomb and make it immune to detection. Cleaning it up and restoring it to its original form took the most time. Now the

Chote Miyan was a lot lighter and more manageable. Then, exposing the control panel, Lars carefully punched in the arming code twice. The control panel glowed to life.

Once the control panel lights up, you have to set the timer and then key in the activation code. Cheema's instructions echoed in his memory.

Lars carefully closed the case, so that it looked exactly the way it would when he actually carried it into the target area. Then, timing himself to the second, he began to practice opening the case, setting the timer and punching in the activation code. He did it a dozen times before he was confident he had it down pat. By now he was doing the whole thing in less than a minute. *Good! Even if I set the timer on the second setting, I should be well clear of the area in time. Fifteen minutes is good enough for me to get to Central station and take the first train out.... Hopefully it will be heading north....* He played out the various possible scenarios in his mind as he shut down the suitcase nuke for the last time.

Lars pulled a chair up to the balcony and sat down to wait. His hotel room was on the edge of the Town Hall Square that sprawled to the right. This was his ground zero.

With the big square in the Italian town of Sienna as its inspiration, Copenhagen's Raadhuspladsen was originally built in the shape of a shell. Standing sentinel around it are the Town Hall, the house of Politiken, the Bus Terminus and a host of outdoor restaurants, radio booths, and hotdog and newspaper stands.

On his left, he could clearly see the huge golden clock on the exquisite Town Hall building with the shining wind vane above it. Large buildings peppered with countless billboards and hoardings rose up on the other side of the square and to his extreme right.

Carlsberg – probably the best beer in town, shouted the huge white letters painted across a red building on the other end of the square.

Lars grinned wryly, trying to imagine what it would be like after the bomb....

JUST AS IN BERLIN, THE RALLY FOR THE TENTH INTERNATIONAL Commemoration Day for dead and injured workers was a major feature in the day's schedule of events in Copenhagen. However, unlike in Berlin, it was not going to be a single march. Instead, small groups of people had gathered at about twenty points all over Copenhagen and were now beginning to converge at the Town Hall square. The rally would terminate with the usual round of speeches that are inevitable at such events.

From the balcony of his carefully chosen hotel room, Lars Borge watched as people began to arrive at the square. Along with the people participating in the rally came the tourists who are an omnipresent part of the Copenhagen landscape.

No matter how many manage to escape, this part of Copenhagen is going to be really quiet for a long,

long time. The radiation will ensure that. Lars smiled to himself.

By the time Lars got up from his vantage point, the square was teeming with people. A marked tone of excitement and gaiety, not at all in consonance with such a sombre event, pervaded the square. There were several television news crew and tourist cameras faithfully recording every nuance of the rally.

When he was certain that the crowd had built up sufficiently, the terrorist exited his hotel room and headed for the solitary elevator to his right.

The time to kill was nigh. Adrenaline pumped through his system and his breathing quickened as the elevator jerked to a halt on the ground floor and the doors began to slide open.

THE HUGE, BURLY COP HAD ENTERED THROUGH THE GLASS doors and was walking across the lobby up to the solitary elevator when it opened and Lars Borge emerged from it. Lars had barely taken two steps out of the elevator when the two men saw each other. Recognition was immediate. The effect was electric.

The two men went back a long way. The cop had been Lars's immediate supervisor at the time when Lars lost his wife and quit the force. He had retired only a week ago, and was on his way up to meet an old friend passing through town who was staying at the Palace Hotel. The retired cop had no idea of the APB that had been issued for Lars. He simply recognized the man coming out of the elevator and automatically raised his hand to greet him.

Lars had served under the man but the two of them had never been close. He had no idea that the man was no longer in service. He saw the cop coming towards him, noted the sharp flare of recognition in his eyes and then he saw the cop raise his hand. In the excited, guilty, hyped-up-for-combat state that he was in, Lars completely missed the amiable smile that was starting to appear on his ex-colleague's face.

Without pausing for thought, he pulled out the gun stuck in his waistband with his free right hand and fired twice in quick succession.

At pointblank range, the round-nosed slugs went clean through the retired cop and dropped him dead instantly. The smile of recognition and welcome was still visible on his bloodied face. His body was sinking to the blue carpeted floor when the door immediately to the left of the elevator opened and a bellhop emerged. The sudden movement startled the already nervous Lars. He swivelled and fired again. The unfortunate bellhop took the bullet in his chest and collapsed with an agonized scream.

The hollow scream echoed in the hotel lobby. It shattered all semblance of control in Lars. He broke away and raced mindlessly towards the exit, as total pandemonium seized the room.

There were over a dozen people in the hotel lobby at the time, including three men manning the reception desk just a few feet to Lars' right. They dived for cover as soon as the shots rang out. The others scrambled out of the way of the armed man as he ran through the lobby. Most of them instinctively made for the main entrance.

The two cops walking up along the Vester Voldgade towards the square noticed the sudden commotion. Among other things, they saw a man with a pistol in his hand and a suitcase in the other heading straight for them.

Lars saw the cops when he had barely taken half a dozen strides down the road. Turning rapidly, he fled in the opposite direction. The cops automatically went for their weapons as they started to give chase to the man with the gun. However, neither cop fired because there were too many people milling around in the square.

Lars darted past Ripley's Museum and the Burger King to his right, instinctively seeking the safety of the crowd that he knew he would find on the Stroget. Then he saw another cop coming down Frederiksberggade towards him. Lars had no way of knowing that this cop had neither heard the shots nor had any idea of the drama unfolding in front of him. He again changed direction and ran towards the people crowding around the two hotdog stands in the square.

I can do it. I know I can do it. Fifty seconds... that's all I need.

The thought ran through him like an endless litany.

I need a place where I can stop for just one moment and activate the bomb.

And then he found it.

BEYOND THE HOTDOG STAND IN FRONT OF LARS WAS A BLUE and white Radio 100 booth. Weaving through the tables and chairs in the two food stalls on his right, Lars crossed the booth and dropped to the ground. Now he was safe from the two cops chasing him. Not for long, but they would certainly take a moment to spot him in the crowd.

That's all the time I need.

Crouching on the ground, Lars opened the case. He selected the first setting of the timer, the one that triggered the bomb immediately, and began to punch in the 12-digit activation code.

He was already on the third digit when the two pursuing cops spotted him.

'What the fuck is he doing?'

'How the hell do I know? It can't be anything good for sure....'

The guns in their hands came up.

Lars had keyed in the fifth digit when the cop in front skirted clear of the Radio 100 booth and settled into the shooter's classic extended arm stance. The seventh digit had been keyed in when, taking careful aim, the cop fired.

The eighth digit of the bomb's activation code had been entered when the first bullet found Lars's chest. His fingers were keying in the ninth digit when the second bullet smashed into his head. But the brain had already passed the next command to his fingers. As the dying killer toppled over the open bomb case, his fingers depressed the tenth digit and began to reach for the eleventh. They found the correct key and pressed it just as the second cop reached him and kicked the suitcase out from under him.

Stay with me! Lars's dying brain urged the suitcase nuke soundlessly as he extended his hand towards it. *Just one more key... one more....*

Then the cop fired once more and the darkness of death settled upon Lars. His extended hand twitched once before it fell lifeless, inches from the deadly suitcase.

A few metres away, an intrepid television cameraman watched the whole sequence. His mouth was open in horrified fascination as his silently whirring camera recorded everything diligently. The camera was a high power professional model and noted the solitary dark space on the glowing control panel of the suitcase nuke. No one watching the footage could fail to notice that the hundreds of people in and around the square had been just one digit away from a horrifying death.

Minutes later, the camera was relaying the event to countless television screens the world over.

MURREE

'BLOODY HELL!' CHEEMA WHISPERED, OVERWHELMED AS HE watched the scene play out on the giant plasma screen before them. 'Just a second more. One tiny fraction of a second and....'

'Look at it this way, Cheema,' the calmer and more pragmatic Salim said, masking his own disappointment. 'Even now the kafirs will tremble in fear. Now they know we can reach them and strike whenever we want to... be it with nukes, or with biological or chemical weapons. They now know for sure that they're not safe anywhere, and they will live in perennial dread of when and where we are going to strike next.'

Strike Six

LONDON

THEY SAY THE BRITISH ALWAYS LIKE TO DO THINGS ARSE WAYS. Maybe that was why, unlike the rallies in the other European cities, the one in London that was scheduled to start at Trafalgar Square, could only be flagged off after a series of motivating and inspiring speeches in support of dead and injured workers. The rally was to proceed from Trafalgar through the Admiralty Arch, down Whitehall Street, passing Horse Guards Parade and Downing Street. Thereafter, it would go down Parliament Street and onto Parliament Square, where the Houses of Parliament are situated. Here the rally would end after the usual submission of petitions.

Ben joined the rally at the point at which it passed closest to the Royal Horse Guards Hotel.

Leaving the hotel well before the rally reached it, he stood on the sidewalk for several minutes and watched the procession move past. There were several others doing the same, so he didn't stand out.

When he found a gap in the stream of cops riding shotgun on both sides of the road, Ben merged with the thick mass of people flowing down the road. His killer cargo was safely tucked inside the large plastic water bottle slung from his shoulder. The vials of VX Gas had been thoroughly cleansed of cream and were ready to deliver death to the slogan-shouters around him. But Ben was not yet ready to kill.

'*The best place to strike is when the rally reaches the Houses of Parliament,*' Salim had told him. '*Strike when they're handing over the petitions. You may get lucky and take out a couple of politicians. Also, you can be certain that the television crews are going to be around in abundance.*'

So Ben bided his time, though his breathing had begun to quicken with every passing moment, and he could feel an uneasy coil of stress knotting up in the pit of his stomach. He steeled himself. A silent prayer began to build up in his head as he flowed with the others towards the finish.

FORTUNATELY OR UNFORTUNATELY, THERE WERE NO IMPORTANT politicians around when the rally reached the Houses of Parliament. There were a couple of minor fry, who had nothing better to do that day and needed the media exposure rather desperately.

The chosen posse of leaders banded together as the rally trickled into Parliament Square. A few tense moments elapsed. Ben could feel the pulse in his forhead throbbing. Every fibre in his body was alert and on edge as he willed the men to finish their speeches. Time seemed to pass as slowly as the giant London Eye wheel turning against the skyline in the distance.

Finally, the speeches were done and the rally leaders stepped forward to hand in their petitions. Simultaneously, Ben reached for his water bottle and began to unscrew the cap. He drew no attention since almost everyone there had some kind of beverage to fortify himself with.

Everyone's attention was more or less on the small knot of people walking forward. A few shouted slogans fell unheeded on Ben's ears. Now the open water bottle was out of the sling and in his right hand. He gripped it at the base, in much the same way as Karl had held the prosthetic in Berlin. Ensuring that he had the bottle firmly in his grasp, Ben stepped away from the crowd.

Suddenly the prayer that had been thrumming silently in his head burst out of him. He raised the open bottle and began to whirl it over his head.

Like brilliantly coloured marbles, the vials of VX Gas sparkled through the air, catching the dull London sunlight as they sped away on their mission of death. They scattered to the ground, some simply pulled down by gravity, others after a collision with a head or a shoulder, and still others crashing into each other in mid-flight.

No matter how they fell, when they fell or where they landed, the result was the same: the sound of breaking glass before the lethal gas sprang free with tiny, barely discernible puffs.

Strike Seven

Barbados

BARBADOS LOOKED LIKE A CITY CELEBRATING THE DANCE OF life. Everything was lit up and psychedelically vibrant with colour. It's not every day that a nation hosts the ICC World Cup. For the cricket crazy West Indians, few things could match the fervour of this event.

Although a series of shocking defeats and upsets had thrown the cricketing world into turmoil, with giants like India and Pakistan falling to the minnows, cricket was cricket and the excitement hadn't abated one bit. The long awaited finals were to be played today, with the mighty Australians taking on the Sri Lankan challengers. It was certain that the crowds would hit the stadium bright and early.

Whether it was by design or just plain luck, Sahiba and Kismat timed their arrival at the Kensington Oval well. When they pulled up outside the stadium, there was a huge crowd gathered there, slowly winding its way in through the stringent three-tier security cordon that had been thrown around the stadium.

They were about to get out of the tiny nondescript car when Sahiba tugged urgently at Kismat's arm, stopping her. 'Wait, Kismat. Look at that.' She pointed at the string of cops threading their way through the parking lot, carefully scanning each parked vehicle. Two of the cops were led by huge dogs, which sniffed assiduously at everything in their path. The Khan twins had spent too much time at the stadium – they had both been employed at the customer relations desk for almost two years – not to notice that something out of the ordinary was afoot.

'I've never seen them do that before,' Sahiba said, after watching them for a moment. 'Certainly not checking the parking lot with sniffer dogs.'

'We've never seen a World Cup final before, either,' her sister commented evenly, but she too watched the cops with a growing sense of unease.

'No, this is different. Look!' Sahiba pointed out the various locations where groups of cops were clearly visible. 'I haven't seen so many of them at any of the matches.'

'You think they know?'

'I don't know. Let's just wait and watch for some more time.' The sisters sat in silence, scanning the area carefully. It did not take long for the pattern to become evident even to their untrained eyes.

'They know for sure.'

'I think so too.'

'I wonder how they know.'

'Does it make a difference?'

A heavy silence met the question.

'Now what?'

'Now nothing,' Sahiba replied firmly. 'We have not come so far to be foiled by some dumb cops.'

Another long silence.

'Can you think of any other way to get in?' Kismat finally asked. The two of them were still giving the question due thought when fate stepped in.

THE BUSES CARRYING THE TWO TEAMS PLAYING THE FINAL match pulled up in front of the stadium at almost the same time.

'Isn't that the Australian team getting down from that yellow and green bus?' Sahiba pointed with a half raised finger. Both sisters watched closely for a moment. 'Yes, it is,' Sahiba answered herself.

'And that's the Sri Lankan team getting down from the second one.' Kismat gestured at the blue and white bus that was parked behind the first one.

They watched in silence as the Australian team disembarked and began to offload their gear. In the other bus, the Sri Lankan players began to follow suit.

The twins exchanged glances. Harmonized as they were to each other's thoughts, both came to the same conclusion almost instantly.

We may not be able to get inside the stadium, but could we hope for a better target outside?

Not likely!

In fact, this is even better. Imagine the publicity!

'You take the Australian team,' Sahiba whispered. 'I'll go for the Sri Lankans.' Kismat acknowledged this with a nod.

By now most of the players had gathered in two tight, talkative knots and were waiting for the stragglers to join them. Surrounding them on all four sides was a cordon of security personnel. Each man was armed to the hilt and each grim face displayed firm resolve to put the weapons to use should the occasion so demand.

In tandem, the twins opened the doors of the vehicle and got off. Both reached for the huge beaded necklaces around their necks as they emerged from the car. Like ungainly prayer beads, the necklaces were in their hands as they turned and began to shuffle towards the lively young men in cricketing colours.

IT WAS PROBABLY THEIR INFIRMITY THAT ATTRACTED THE attention of the security officers herding the teams towards the stadium. The two guards nearest to them gave them a closer and more thorough look as the sisters shuffled closer. The security detail had been on special protection duty with the Australian team since the start of the tour. Due to some Dilbertian faux pas, they had not received the APB which had been issued for the Khan sisters. However, in these days of heightened security threats, all of them functioned at optimal alert.

'Hey! Excuse me, miss!' It was a security guard in the outermost cordon of the Sri Lankan team who stepped up and placed a restraining hand on Sahiba's right shoulder. 'Where do you think you're going?'

The shock of being suddenly accosted just when she was preparing to throw the necklace in her right hand at the Sri Lankan team froze Sahiba.

'Where do you think you're going, miss?' the guard repeated, not so politely this time, his hand on her shoulder tightening. Sahiba snapped back to reality.

'I just wanted to gift this to him,' she blurted out without thinking, holding up the necklace in her right hand and gesturing to one of the Sri Lankan cricketers.

'That?' The security guard took note of the large, and what he thought ugly, beaded necklace she was holding. *It takes all sorts, I suppose.* 'Okay!' He shrugged. 'I'll give it to him on your behalf, but you cannot go any closer.' Taking the necklace from her numb fingers, he turned to see where his protectees were. By now both teams had crossed the last security barrier and were disappearing inside the stadium.

'Right, miss. I'll personally ensure that he gets it.' Twirling the lethal necklace casually in the air, the security guard briskly rejoined his mates and vanished inside the stadium.

Sahiba stood rooted to the spot, her mind having totally shut down on her.

'What happened?' Kismat's voice nudged her back to the present.

'I... I... he stopped me... just when....' Sahiba mumbled, feeling embarrassed and deeply ashamed. 'I have let them all down.' She was unable to meet Kismat's eyes.

'Don't worry.' Her twin could feel Sahiba's agony. She reached out and patted her back. 'You couldn't help it.' For a moment they stood in silence.

'Why didn't you....' Sahiba asked tentatively.

'I saw him stop you and didn't know what had happened, so I....' Kismat hesitated. 'I was worried about you getting caught in the middle of....' She gestured at the necklace in her hand.

'Salim will be very upset with us,' said Sahiba.

'Let him.' Kismat's chin went up defiantly. 'We couldn't help it.'

'And we still have these.' Sahiba gestured at the necklace in Kismat's hand. 'Maybe we'll get an even better opportunity to use it.'

The two sisters began to slowly walk back towards their car.

'I wonder what the guard has done with the necklace he took from me.'

They mulled over that for a moment.

'I hope he sits on it.'

That made Sahiba giggle; a neighing, high-pitched giggle. The giggle became a laugh and by the time the twins got into their car, they were in splits. They were still laughing as they drove out of the parking lot and headed home.

INSIDE THE STADIUM, THE SECURITY GUARD WAITED TILL THE players had vanished inside the dressing rooms and he was placed on standby by the leader of the security detail. Then he sauntered off to the area reserved for them. Just at the entrance was a coke vending machine. He pumped in the required change and watched a can clang out.

Just beside the vending machine stood the mandatory garbage can. For a moment, the guard looked at the ugly beads still in his hand, and without a second thought, he tossed the necklace into the garbage can.

The necklace landed with a soft plop on the clutter of paper cups and assorted items that were stuffed inside. And there it lay, waiting.

HALFWAY ACROSS THE WORLD, THE TWO PUPPET MASTERS anxiously awaited news of the Barbados strike.

'It should have happened by now.' Salim checked the array of clocks on the wall; each of them displayed the local time in the city where the action was taking place.

'Maybe they got caught.'

'Maybe they lost their nerve.'

'Maybe they were not able to do it at the designated time.'

While they surfed the airwaves, the red and white station wagon carrying the Indian commandos crested the final slope and began to nose its way through the dense, slow moving Murree traffic.

Strike Eight

TORONTO

ABRAHAM REIS WAS SO CONFIDENT THAT HE WOULD BE ABLE to sail through the security barrier at the new BMO Field Stadium that he did not bother to take any major precautions. After cleaning all traces of cream from the vials of VX Gas, he simply placed them in his lunch box on a cotton pad. Before closing the box, he placed another large wad of cotton over them to cushion the vials and prevent them from knocking against each other.

Most of the security personnel know me well. He could visualize himself smiling at them and nodding at their how're-you-doing-todays as he went past.

To be on the safe side, Reis ensured that he reached the stadium a little after the match had started. *People are always more antsy and alert at the start of any event. Hopefully things have settled down by now and the security will be engrossed in, or at least distracted by, the game.*

When Abraham Reis reached the parking lot, nearly thirty minutes had elapsed since the kick-off.

Toronto FC, Canada's first professional soccer team, was playing its first home match against the Kansas City Wizards. It also happened to be the inaugural match being played at the newly completed BMO Field, an open-air stadium with a seating capacity of over twenty thousand. It was primarily because of this that the stadium was filled to capacity.

A festive air permeated the atmosphere and the raucous chant of fans boomed through the stadium in rhythmic waves. Reis could feel the excitement pounding through the stadium even as he approached the entrance. Coupled with the adrenaline rushing through him, it unleashed a huge surge of energy that threatened to swamp him. Controlling himself with an effort, he kept his pace even and the pleasant Reis smile plastered on his face as he headed for the entrance.

Situated in the northwest corner of the spanking new stadium is the reception area that has the ticketing offices and the offices of the bus operators, team coaches, sales managers, communications personnel and the various BMO officials. Down the hall lies the vast VIP area that serves food and beverages to the privileged clients who can then move directly to the VIP lounge that comfortably seats three hundred people. Off to one side are stairs that descend to the ground floor and lead to the eight community dressing rooms, each of which can be used to access the field directly.

To the southwest of the stadium is the four-thousand capacity supporters' section. Sandwiched between the first and second decks is a huge concession area that serves everything from fish and chips to samosas. To cater to those too lazy to move out of their seats, there are seven authorized portable carts that move through the decks dispensing food, drinks and souvenirs.

REIS PLANNED TO GET IN AND CROSS THE HALL TO REACH the VIP area.

That's the best place for me to transfer the VX vials from the lunch box to my pockets.

Having done that, he planned to walk straight to the VIP lounge. As it was the inaugural day, there were bound to be more VIPs than usual.

Let some of them die today. Commoners die every day in any case. Reis gave a wry smile as he walked up to the main entrance.

Reis had been right. All the security personnel there knew him well. But not one of them smiled when they saw him.

That's understandable. It's the first game and a big one at that. They must be stressed, Reis told himself as cognitive dissonance kicked in; he needed to know that everything was fine.

Reis nodded to them half-smilingly as he came closer. That was when he saw the second tier of security personnel and knew he had miscalculated.

None of the second tier of security men knew him and none of them was smiling. They *did* know *of* him. In fact, it was suddenly clear that they had been waiting for him. He could tell from the expressions on their faces and the way they moved towards him.

'What should I do if they do manage to find me?'

'Then you are as good as dead in any case. No matter what happens, don't let them take you alive. Your best bet is to head straight for the enemy and activate your weapon. Make sure you are in the thickest part of the crowd and take as many of the kafirs with you as you can. Don't let your sacrifice go to waste.'

Without further thought, he began to grope at the lunch box in his hand, but even as he did that he knew it was too late. Four burly cops closed in on him rapidly and boxed him in. Unforgiving hands gripped him from both sides. Even rougher hands relieved him of his deadly meal box.

'Take it easy, pal,' the man on his right growled. 'Don't make us hurt you.' His tone was taunting and harsh, almost as though he was daring Reis to try something.

They marched him off to the small side exit and towards the patrol car waiting outside.

They can't take me alive. Damned if I am going to spend the rest of my life in jail.

As they frog-marched him out, Reis allowed his shoulders to slump and his body to go slack, as though in defeat and despair. With every step, he felt the grip of his escort loosen; not much, by just a tiny fraction. It was not enough for him to break free and make a run for it. However, it was enough for him to jerk his hand free and grab at the holstered weapon of the man on his right. The attempt was as amateurish as it was ill-advised.

'You stupid fuck!'

The butt of the pistol in the hands of the cop behind him slammed down remorselessly on Reis's head. He lost consciousness instantly and slumped to the ground.

FAR AWAY IN MURREE, THE TWO TERROR MASTERS WAITED impatiently for news of the terror spectacular to beam in from Toronto.

'Do you think something has gone wrong?' Cheema asked for the umpteenth time.

'Let's wait and see.' Salim's tone and expression were noncommittal. 'The game lasts a long time. Perhaps Reis is waiting for the best possible time to strike.'

And so they waited, unaware that retribution was at hand.

Not too far away, Tiwathia pulled over to the side as Sami took a moment to get their bearings right.

'That's the ridge.' Sami pointed. 'That's where the house should be. Take that turn ahead.'

Tiwathia engaged gears and headed for the turn Sami had indicated.

Strike Nine

WASHINGTON, D.C.

THE PATROL CAR CARRYING REIS HAD BARELY REACHED THE maximum security detention centre he was being taken to for interrogation when Liaquat Ali entered the Washington Convention Centre. The Experimental Biology Conference was due to start this morning. The innocuous looking Chote Miyan was in Ali's hand. It had already been primed and armed by him in the hotel room earlier that morning; now only the activation code had to be keyed in. In his other hand was the cardboard carton he had procured some time ago. The carton had the words 'Alpan Packaging' printed prominently on all sides. The same words were also printed in red alongside the company logo on the identity tag pinned to Ali's coat label. If somebody had bothered to look closely at the photograph on the identity tag, he would have noticed that it bore only a cursory resemblance to the man wearing it. The real owner of that particular identity tag lay dead in a toilet cubicle not far away from the conference registration desk. Ali had killed him barely five minutes ago.

Ali had then walked up to the venue layout map displayed near the registration desk and checked out the location. His destination, Booth No. 730, was a tiny box located in the inner circle of Hall B of the convention centre. Alpan Packaging, a laboratory and miscellaneous equipment manufacturer, had booked it and the adjacent booth, to display its wares. Hall B lay on the level immediately below the street level of the lovely five-storied building that housed the convention centre. Two of these five levels lay below the street level and two above it.

Hefting the Chote Miyan in one hand and the cardboard carton in the other, Liaquat Ali forced himself to look purposeful as he headed for the booth on the lower level. Between the booth and him lay the final security barrier that he had to breach.

There were four men manning the entrance to Hall B, two on either side of the gate. Squaring his shoulders, Liaquat Ali stepped off the escalator and headed towards them.

THE SECURITY GUARD AT THE ENTRANCE OF HALL B DID NOT recognize the face of the wanted man walking up to him. He had received the APB issued for Rahim Khan and Liaquat Ali. However, the photographs used in the APB had been of two men in uniform. That proved to be a mistake. *Men in uniform always look different.*

But the guard was a diligent man and adhered strictly to the basics that had been drilled into him. The basics dictated that one must always tally the photograph on the identity card with the person wearing it. That was precisely what he did each time someone came up to him.

That was how he noticed that the man who had now halted in front of him did not match the photograph on the Alpan Packaging identity tag pinned to his lapel.

Bloody cheapskate! Why don't these companies just pay the entry fees for all their people instead of switching tags all the time? The bastards earn enough.

Raising his eyes, the guard gestured to his shift supervisor and the other security man standing across, on the other side of the entrance, behind Ali. It was a very slight gesture, a tiny, barely discernible shake of his head.

If he had not been so pumped up, Ali would not have caught the gesture. But he was and he did. He automatically assumed the worst.

They're onto me! The soldier-terrorist reacted on highly honed reflexes. *I must get away from here. Find a place where I can be alone for a moment. That's all the time I need.*

Dropping the cardboard carton, he whirled around and started to run. The security personnel stared in disbelief at the sudden commotion. As Ali turned, he collided with the two men who were coming up just behind him. They were so close that he had no chance of avoiding them. Suddenly they were a tangle of arms and legs. The Chote Miyan fell out of his hand and away from him as his hands automatically came up to try and break his fall.

By the time Ali regained his balance, his precious suitcase had been picked up by one of the security guards, who was quite taken aback by its weight. Ali made a run for it, but they had surrounded him. Seconds later, they had him dead to rights. A short while later, they recognized him.

Another man had been taken alive.

Murree

TIWATHIA PARKED THE STATION WAGON ON THE NARROW, winding road at the base of the ridge on which the bungalow was sited. The road straddled the outermost periphery of the town and there was very little traffic, barring the occasional pedestrian and the even more occasional vehicle. The red-roofed, low-slung target building was barely visible through the shroud of pine trees all around.

They waited till there was no one in sight on either side. Then, retrieving their weapons, the four of them raced through the trees and up the hill. Moving cautiously and ensuring that they made no noise, they began to close in on the man they had come to kill.

Strike Ten

San Francisco

THE INTERNATIONAL PERFORMANCE IMPROVEMENT conference being held at the San Francisco Marriott Convention Centre was just about to kick off that morning. Rahim Khan did not anticipate any problems in reaching the venue since he was already staying at the Marriott.

Like his comrade-in-arms, Rahim Khan had woken up early and prepped the bomb and himself. Then, impatiently pacing the hotel room, he had waited for zero hour to arrive.

Timing! The timing is important. We want the maximum strikes to take place at the same time... or as close to each other as possible.

The two soldiers had coordinated their clocks before they parted ways at Washington. Rahim Khan took one final look at his watch.

Liaquat should be entering the target area about now. I wonder how he is faring. He tuned out the random thoughts cluttering his head and forced his attention back to the task at hand.

Picking up the armed and ticking Chote Miyan, he left his room and descended to the Conference Centre level. Rahim tried to still the battle nerves beginning to clamour for attention inside him by focusing hard on what he had to do over the next few minutes. In his mind's eye, he could see himself striding in, getting into an appropriate corner, keying in the digits of the activation code, putting down the case, exiting the hall, and making his way out to the first cab that he could find. Then a little while later... *BOOM!*

Preoccupied though he was, the minute he emerged from the elevator, Rahim Khan noticed the beefed-up security arrangements at the entrance.

Shit! Either they know about me or they're being extra cautious.

The death dealer stopped and pondered for a moment.

We will assume at all times that the mission is blown and act with total caution. That way we can be sure.... Cheema's advice came back to him. Making up his mind, he turned swiftly on his heel and headed straight back towards the hotel lobby.

There were groups of people crowding the lobby when he entered. Rahim Khan spotted an empty couch somewhere in the centre of the lobby. There was a group of people standing beside it, talking excitedly.

Good! This should do very well.

But can I leave the bomb behind, unattended?

No!

He paused momentarily.

So be it!

He altered direction slightly and headed straight for the couch. He sat down, placed the Chote Miyan on his lap and opened it. Raising the lid just a bit, he put his hand into the case and set the timer for immediate detonation. Then, slowly and cautiously, he began to key in the 12-digit activation code.

... they fight in Allah's way, so they slay and are slain; a promise which is binding on Him in the Taurat and the Injeel and the Koran....

The glorious verse from the Holy Koran reverberated in his mind as his fingers punched in the fatal digits one by one.

Fourteen seconds later, the last digit of the activation code silently glowed into place. A nanosecond later, with a thunderous roar, the plutonium fuelled atomic bomb cradled on Rahim Khan's lap exploded. It vapourised him into nothingness, along with the others around him.

No one would ever know for certain how many people were annihilated by the bomb that day. Very little of anything or anyone was left behind. No one who had been present in or around the hotel survived the explosion. The few who survived the initial blast succumbed to the huge ball of fire that raced out and away from the epicentre of the explosion. As for the number of people whose lives would be blighted by the radiation... only time would tell.

MURREE

AS NEWS OF THE HORRENDOUS EXPLOSION SPANNED THE globe, several hundred miles away, the terror maestros gloated.

'Bring out the champagne,' Salim yelled at their elderly servant.

Standing in front of the giant plasma television screen, which was beaming scenes of bloodshed and mayhem, Salim and Cheema were hugging each other, delirious with joy, when there was a loud crash followed by a dull thump.

Before either of them realized what was happening, the XM-84 Flash-and-Bang grenade that had blown in through the glass window, landed in the centre of the room and exploded. There was a roar and a blaze of bright, blinding light filled the room.

Salim Must Die

TIWATHIA, SAMI AND IQBAL BURST INTO THE ROOM HARD on the heels of the stun grenade. Their drawn guns sought out the befuddled figures in the room, reeling from the sudden, intense explosion of sound and light. Tiwathia was almost halfway into the room when a door to his right opened with a crash. He turned and saw an elderly man running into the room. The man had a bewildered look on his face and a pistol in his hand. He took in the chaos prevailing in the room at a glance and, automatically, his gun hand started to rise.

Tiwathia noted the gun in the man's hand and saw it coming up. Driven by adrenaline-powered nerves, the silenced weapon in Tiwathia's hand stuttered to life. Hastily aimed though they were, his bullets zipped through the air and stitched tiny holes in the neck of Salim's helper-cum-bodyguard. The man was dead even before his body crashed to the ground.

'Watch out!' Iqbal's sudden shout alerted Tiwathia. 'Behind you!'

Cheema had used the momentary distraction to regain his bearings and grab the pistol from his waistband. By the time Tiwathia turned to see what Iqbal was trying to warn him about, Cheema's pistol had cleared the belt and was almost level. It was pointed straight at him. The two men were barely seven feet apart. At that distance, there was no way that Cheema would miss.

Too late! Tiwathia's mind raged at him as he swung his own weapon around.

Too late!

He knew he would not be able to bring his weapon into play in time.

There was a flat, sharp thump as Cheema fired. Tiwathia heard it echo through him even as he returned fire, but he knew he was too late. The bullet had already cleared the barrel of Cheema's pistol and was rushing towards him.

Neither man had seen Iqbal launch himself forward a split second after his warning shout to Tiwathia. He met Cheema's bullet in mid-air, just a foot before it was due to strike Tiwathia's head. Iqbal was hurtling through the air when he ate the bullet. It slammed into his body, spinning him around. He hit the ground hard as he fell between the two men.

By now, Tiwathia's bullet had also completed its short journey. It thudded into Cheema's chest, pushing him back a step, but the fight was not yet over. Though in pain, Cheema was aligning his weapon to fire again when, from across the room, Sami fired. All three of his bullets pin-cushioned Cheema's head and sent him toppling backwards.

Salim gave an anguished cry as he saw his trusted lieutenant fall.

Iqbal heard Salim's shrill cry through the fog of pain clamping down on him. He was trying to sit up when his eyes fell upon its source. A huge shard of anger skewered through him, driving him to his feet.

'You!' His voice was a harsh guttural whisper. 'It's you… you bastard.' He tossed a look at the Force 22 officers whose guns were trained on the man. 'This is Salim. The harami who caused me… my….' The intensity of Iqbal's anger choked his throat and words dried up.

Just then there was a sharp burst of gunfire from outside, interspersed with the soft, muted spit of a silenced weapon.

'Tanaz!' Both commandos spoke simultaneously. Tanaz literally flew into the room. Her chador and hijab were gone, revealing the black salwar-kameez she was clad in.

'There were three more of them, two men and a woman,' she said breathlessly. 'They were headed this way and both were armed. I took care of them.' She saw the look on Sami's face. 'That's what you left me outside for… right?' At that moment, her eyes fell upon Iqbal, who had slumped to the ground again and was trying hard to staunch the flow of blood from his arm. 'Iqbal!' Her cry reverberated with a touch of something that was more than just concern for an injured comrade. 'What happened?'

'Tanaz!' Sami's sharp command reined her in. 'Get a field dressing from my pack and dress that wound.'

The professional in her regained control and she raced forward to comply. Taking out the field dressing, she began to expose Iqbal's wound so that she could dress it.

Finally, Salim spoke. 'Who are you?' His voice was controlled again.

'Your death!' Sami's ice-cold voice cut him off. 'You have killed enough people, old man. Now it's time for you to die.'

Whatever else he was, Salim was no fool. His mind had begun to tick as soon as the effects of the Flash-and-Bang grenade wore off. He had gauged the threat confronting him and was rapidly clicking through the various possibilities available to extricate himself from this situation.

'You're Indian commandos, aren't you?' The question in his voice was very slight, almost non-existent.

Neither of the Force 22 officers bothered to reply. Instead, Sami threw a sharp command at Tiwathia. 'Search the house. We need the phone, diaries, PDAs, pen drives, computers... if there's a desktop, just get the hard disk.' He added as Tiwathia began to move, 'Hurry up! The grenade and gunfire would certainly have attracted attention, even on this lonely stretch.'

'Tanaz? Iqbal?' Salim turned on them as Tiwathia strode out of the room. 'Both of you are Muslims?' The wily old man began to look for a way out of this conundrum. 'Then why are you helping these kafirs? We true believers must....'

'*You* call yourself a true believer?' The anger in Iqbal overrode the pain pulsing through him. 'You fucking psycho! You are a disgrace to Islam. Sub-human monsters like you....'

'The jihad calls for us to make sacrifices,' Salim retorted proudly.

'Jihad? Jihad only calls for us to bring purity and peace to society... by ridding it of maniacs like you....'

'The people of Pakistan will not rest till we wrest our dues from India.'

'The people of Pakistan? When have you ever stopped to ask them anything? Your mad Generals and corrupt politicians have played the India card and the Islamic card at the drop of a hat to keep this madness going....'

'Don't waste your breath, Iqbal,' Sami cut in. 'These bastards have no nationality and no religion. He will not understand anything you have to say. In any case, it doesn't matter, since he doesn't have much longer to live.'

'Go ahead.' Salim glared at him arrogantly. 'It

does not matter whether I live or die. Every time a Salim dies, a hundred more will rise to take his place. No matter what you do, the jihad will go on.'

'So be it!' Sami replied evenly as he raised the silenced pistol in his hand and levelled it straight at Salim's head. His finger had begun to tighten on the trigger when Iqbal cried out.

'No! He's mine. The Colonel promised….' Sami slackened the pressure on the trigger and lowered his weapon slightly as Iqbal broke free from Tanaz, who was trying to finish the dressing on his wound, and began to rise. He swayed slightly as he came to his feet. The high velocity impact of the bullet and the loss of blood had weakened him much more than he cared to admit. Tanaz reached out to support him but he shrugged off her hands and, stooping slightly, propped himself against the ornate centre table in front him. Decorating the table was an equally ornate, jewel-studded scimitar that had once adorned the waist of a Mughal king, its sharp blade gleaming brighter then the bevelled glass it lay upon. 'This man,' Iqbal pointed a finger quivering with anger and pain at Salim, 'is responsible for the death of my mother and my sister.'

'And both my brothers.' Tanaz turned to Iqbal, giving him a long, questioning look. He saw the hard, flat glint in the eyes of the extraordinarily beautiful woman before him and knew that she needed this closure as much as he did… if she was ever to come to terms with the death of her brothers.

Watching them frozen in their strangely intimate tableau, Sami got the feeling that they were totally unaware of everything and everyone else in the room.

Neither of them even noticed Tiwathia return. He was about to speak when he took in the atmosphere in the room and subsided, indicating the laptop bag on his shoulder with a brief nod to Sami. Sami's attention was momentarily diverted as he acknowledged Tiwathia's gesture.

Maybe that was why none of them noticed Salim when he suddenly bent down to grab the weapon Cheema had dropped. By the time Sami and Iqbal took in the blur of motion, Salim had stooped down, snatched up the pistol, and was coming up with it. Despite his age, he was moving incredibly fast, spurred on by his instinct and the need to survive. The pistol was coming to level as he started to straighten up.

Once again, Sami was the first to react. He levelled his weapon and fired. Tanaz fired a moment later. The bullets drove into Salim's chest and belly, throwing him back again. However, his gun hand continued its relentless journey upwards. It was coming up straight at Tanaz who was standing right in front of him, a few scant feet away.

Tanaz pulled the trigger again. There was a dull click as her weapon jammed.

Damn!

Trying to swivel out of the way of Salim's weapon,

Tanaz strayed into the line of fire between Sami and Salim, forcing Sami to stay his hand.

Iqbal noted the threat immediately. He instinctively snatched up the shining scimitar from the table in front of him and lashed out with it. The gleaming blade was as sharp as it had been on the day it left the royal forge a hundred years ago. It sliced smoothly through the flesh and bone of Salim's hand. A horrible cry erupted from Salim as he watched his hand holding the pistol fall with an ugly thud onto the floor. A fountain of bright red blood sprayed out from his severed wrist.

By now all signs of sanity had fled the room. A fearsome battle cry thundered out from Iqbal as he leaped across the table and whirled the blood-soaked scimitar. It cleaved through the air in a wide, powerful arc, not even pausing momentarily when it met Salim's neck and emerged red from the other end. A fraction of a second later, Salim's neatly severed head toppled free of his torso, abruptly cutting off his cry of pain.

In the shocked silence that fell upon the room, the severed head thudded dully on to the floor and rolled away... once... twice... thrice... till it finally came to a stop.

The silence persisted as the portly terror master's headless body slumped to the ground in slow motion. There was a final twitch before the stillness of death settled upon him.

Then it was over.

THE FOUR AVENGERS WATCHED THE TERRORIST'S HEADLESS body slowly settle down in the grimace of death. As he looked at the dead man lying before him, Iqbal felt the heavy slug of hate that he'd carried in the pit of his heart all this while dissipate. Then he noticed Tanaz watching him. An incredible warmth flooded through him as their eyes met and held.

The sensation was strange, perhaps because he had never experienced it before.

I love her!

The realization was sudden... and acute. He felt a strange new feeling sweep through him. It rushed into the void that the cancerous hate for Salim had vacated.

Tanaz's eyes were inexplicable. Iqbal thought he saw his feelings mirrored in them, but he couldn't be sure.

SAMI MOVED FIRST AND BROKE THE TABLEAU. 'THAT'S IT, guys. Let's get a move on. This place is going to be mighty unhealthy very soon.'

They hurried out of the bungalow and began to move down the hill towards the station wagon waiting for them. Sami, his weapon at the ready, was in the vanguard while Tanaz brought up the rear. Moving between them, Tiwathia half carried, half supported Iqbal as they went. The first few steps were difficult as both men struggled to find a common rhythm, but soon they had synchronized their movements, the former terrorist and the Force 22 commando.

'Thank you,' Iqbal said as they went towards the waiting vehicle.

'None required. That's what buddies are for,' Tiwathia replied simply. 'In any case, the bullet you took was meant for me. I owe you, buddy.'

His words triggered a sudden moistness in Iqbal's eyes. Even he was not sure whether it was the sudden warmth of camaraderie or the resurgent pain of the bullet wound.

'Where will you go now?' Tiwathia asked, more to distract his attention from the moment than anything else.

Iqbal looked at him quizzically. 'You mean I don't have to go back to prison?'

'No! Isn't that what the Colonel promised you?'

'Yes, but....'

'There are never any buts with the Colonel, Iqbal.'

By now they had reached the station wagon. Tanaz helped Tiwathia put Iqbal into the rear seat before she got in next to him and began to fuss over the wound again. Sami jumped in behind the wheel and steered the vehicle back the way they had come.

They were almost a hundred metres away when Iqbal noticed the scimitar still clutched in his hand. He looked at it, bewildered.

'I didn't even realize I still had it,' he said to no one in particular.

Turning back to see what he was talking about, Tiwathia gave a brief smile. 'Looks good to me.' He took it from Iqbal and, wiping the blade clean, gave it a closer look. 'It's definitely an antique.' He handed it back to Iqbal. 'Must be priceless.'

'It is!' Tanaz said simply. 'It rid you of the hate within. Just keep it. Maybe it will continue to bring you luck.'

Rebirth

BARRING THE ESCALATING PAIN THAT HELD IQBAL IN ITS talons, the return journey was so uneventful that it was almost an anti-climax. The pressure of the field dressing that Tanaz had tied on him had staunched the bleeding quite a bit, but the pain intermittently lanced through the fog of painkillers she had fed him. The tremendous loss of blood had drained his energy. Whenever he floated out of the state of semi-consciousness, he saw Tanaz watching over him.

The sun had begun to recede into the shadows of another night when they reached the turn off for the border crossing that would take them back to India.

'Turn off the road on the dirt track near that tree,' Tanaz said. 'That will take us straight to the hut where we met. Rehmat, your guide, should be waiting there.'

He was. Sami brought the station wagon to a halt near the solitary hut. 'Give us a few minutes to rig up a stretcher for Iqbal,' he told Tanaz as he leapt out of the vehicle.

'I don't think it's a good idea for you to try and attempt the border crossing with him in this state.' Tanaz's tone was troubled, her anxiety evident. 'What if his situation worsens on the way? He will not only slow you two down, he may even inadvertently give you away.'

'We can't leave a buddy behind, Tanaz,' Tiwathia replied immediately. 'Don't worry, we will get him across. In any case, how will he manage alone?'

'He's not alone,' she retorted sharply. 'Not unless he wants to be.'

For a very long moment only the crackling, ticking sound of the cooling engine broke the silence. Sami and Tiwathia watched Iqbal exchange a glance with Tanaz. She looked away immediately, her face devoid of expression.

Smart girl! She's going to let him make his own call. That's the way it should always be. Tiwathia watched with envious admiration. *Everyone should find a soul mate.* He suddenly realized he was holding his breath.

'No, I am not alone.' Iqbal finally spoke. 'In any case, if I stay on this side I can help with the task we have begun,' he rationalized, more to himself than to them. 'After all, there will be many more Salims and Cheemas to take the place of the ones we have killed.'

'True,' Sami concurred softly. 'This is going to be a long battle... long and bloody. But it is not just your problem....'

'It is everybody's problem,' Iqbal interrupted him. 'All of us have to act and I, having been through it all, am relatively better poised to contribute something to this fight. In any case, I have much to atone for...' He looked up. His breath was running short and he was in obvious pain, but there was a firm resolve in his gaze. 'I will stay here.'

'He needs a doctor,' Tiwathia said. 'And he needs one fast.'

'I can get him to one,' Tanaz replied. 'One who will not ask any questions... one of us. He is less than half an hour away from here.'

'Where do you guys plan to go?' Tiwathia asked.

'To the desert.' Tanaz pointed to the far distance. 'I was born and brought up in the desert. I know it well. The sands will hide us.'

The two commandos exchanged a glance. Sami gave a brief, almost imperceptible nod. 'Okay. Take care, then. Tanaz, I suggest you move fast. You have to get him to a doctor before... he is losing a lot of blood.'

'Don't worry,' Tanaz reassured them. 'We only have a few miles to go.'

The two commandos helped to shift Iqbal into the co-driver's seat.

They were walking towards their waiting guide when Iqbal called out weakly, 'Please tell the Colonel that I'm sorry for what I....'

'Don't worry about the past, Iqbal.' Sami turned to face the young man. The haunted expression that had returned to Iqbal's face reached out to him. 'All of us make mistakes. Very few have the courage to try and redeem themselves. I think you have already atoned for whatever wrongs you may have done. Now it is time for you to put away the past and set yourself free. Go man, your destiny awaits you... wherever you go, whatever you do, may Allah watch over you.'

'Thank you... thank you very much.' There was a sharp glint of tears in Iqbal's eyes and his voice broke as he spoke. 'Tell the Colonel that he can always call on me whenever the need arises. I will not fail him.' There was an awkward pause as he looked at the Force 22 commandos. 'In fact, it would be an honour.' Then he threw an equally awkward salute at them.

The salute was sloppy, but the emotions that came with it were not.

Fighting back the waves of pain, Iqbal turned wordlessly towards Tanaz. She reached out and touched him ever so briefly on his chin. The promise of love and togetherness was nestled warmly in that touch. Then she powered the engine and gunned the vehicle.

The two commandos watched the station wagon race away into the gradually gathering darkness, towards the waiting desert sands.

'COME ON! LET'S GO!' REHMAT GESTURED URGENTLY. 'WE have to get across before first light.'

He strode ahead, and Sami and Tiwathia followed. As he walked, Sami pulled out the Motorola mobile phone Tanaz had given him. He quickly keyed in a text message and pressed the send key. He had barely taken five strides when the message-delivered confirmation glowed on the screen.

That's that. The Old Man must have been waiting for this.

Rehmat saw Sami return the phone to his pocket and immediately picked up the pace. Wordlessly, the three men raced through the night towards the safety of the Indian border.

ATTF OPS ROOM, NEW DELHI

ANKITA LOOKED UP FROM HER LAPTOP AS THE TEXT MESSAGE alert chimed on her phone. Snatching the phone off the table, she clicked open the new, unread message.

'The party is over. The chief guest has departed. Rehmat is dropping us home in a few hours.'

She felt a wave of relief go through her.

'What is it?' Anbu asked, looking at her expectantly, trying to keep the concern off his face, but not quite succeeding. Seated beside him, Rao and Khare looked equally anxious.

'It's done!' Ankita couldn't keep the triumph out of her voice, or the smile off her face. 'They've taken Salim down and are on their way back. They have already linked up with Rehmat at the Extraction Point.'

'Yes!' Khare punched the air with his fist. The infinitely more composed Anbu and Rao exchanged smiles, though neither could mask his delight.

'I think you should let the PM know. I am sure he is....'

'No, Colonel,' Rao intervened firmly. 'This is a call that only you can make. It's your boys who have done it... again.'

Anbu gave a brief nod, acknowledging the praise. He reached out and picked up the phone.

'I am sorry for calling you at this late hour, sir, but I thought you would like to know,' he said when the PM finally came on the line.'

'Salim?'

'Salim is dead, sir.'

'And your men?'

'They're on their way out now, sir.'

'Excellent!' The PM's voice rang with pleasure. 'Congratulations, Colonel. Your team has done it again. India is proud of you.'

'We're just doing our job, sir,' Anbu murmured.

'You're very modest, Colonel,' the PM replied. 'But the fact remains that this country owes all of you a huge debt of honour. As long as there are people like you to guard our borders, India's enemies will need to beware.'

'We will always be there, sir.'

There was no doubting the resolve or the quiet assurance in the voice of the Colonel.

Acknowledgements

THIS BOOK WOULD NOT HAVE BEEN POSSIBLE WITHOUT THE tremendous support that I have received from my family over the years.

I must thank my comrades-in-arms in the Indian Armed Forces who were kind enough to ensure that I did not make any major blunders while writing about tactics, weapons and weapon systems. However, I must stress that all technical data used in this book is freely and easily available on the internet and has not been provided to me by any person or persons.

A very special vote of thanks to Karthika V.K. and Nandita Aggarwal for believing in me, keeping me on track, and for giving final shape to this book. And to Neelini Sarkar, Shuka Jain, Amit Sharma and the others at Harper Collins India who helped to make this book possible.

I would also like to thank Dr Chitralekha Khatti and Dr Rajni Saxena for helping me find my way through the jungle of medical jargon and for ensuring that I did not stray too far from the truth in matters medical.

Any errors, factual or technical, that still exist in this book are solely my fault or have been deliberately left in there by me to prevent any misuse of a technology or an idea.